Someone's Still Watching
(Return of the Stourbridge Serial Killer)

Steve Barnbrook

Acknowledgements

Karen Taylor

CONTENTS

1

ALLDAHOPE

The imposing Victorian building resembled something that would not look out of place either in an old black and white hammer house of horror film or a setting for a Victorian Dickensian workhouse. It was spread over several floors and stood in its own spacious but overrun grounds; bramble bushes, overgrown trees and foliage covered every available space. The crumbling red brickwork, the misshapen roof and the leaking and broken waterspouts were showing the effects of years of neglect and the extremely poor and infrequent shoddy maintenance added to the overall foreboding presence of something not right something eerie and sinister.

On this particular night the stormy weather added an extra uneasy spine-chilling dimension to the atmosphere. The relentless freezing cold bone chilling rain whipped up by high gusting winds constantly pounded the building with a deafening tumultuous roar. The only other sounds to be heard was the rattling of the ill-fitting and worn out window frames that seemed to be in danger of being ripped clean out from their mooring. This was interspersed with the odd rumble of distant thunder and the sudden violent crack of lightening that lit up the night sky.

Inside the decaying building in a small attic room situated at the extreme top of the dilapidated structure a young girl was lying in bed with the covers pulled up around her. The only thing visible of her was her long blonde curly locks falling onto her forehead and sandwiched between this and the sheets a pair of bulging staring frightened eyes that flickered from side to side scanning the sparsely furnished bedroom. The room was in almost total darkness, the moon providing only the faintest glimmer of light as it fought to break through the storm clouds. This created grotesque shadows in the corners and recesses only becoming visible when the occasional burst of sheet lightning illuminated everything for a few brief seconds.

Eight-year-old Barbara Guthy who was more commonly known as Babs was a hard nut, a product of her upbringing. From a very young age she had witnessed the incredible violence inflicted upon her mother by her father Stan Guthy who was known locally as an enforcer for a number of criminal gangs who recruited him to carry out contract beatings. The reasons for the contracts would vary immensely from hospitalising a drug dealer who had strayed off their turf or slashing the face of a housewife who had fallen behind or missed a payment on their never ending overinflated high interest loan from the local back street money lender. His violence however wasn't just reserved for his work and the bruises and broken bones of his long-suffering wife were testament to that.

Babs had never known any different and for her it had become the normality. She had over time become hardened to the violence and she had progressed from cowering in the corner shaking and crying listening to her mother's screams to burying her head in her hands and simply waiting for it all to stop. If she was able, she would run upstairs and hide under the bedsheets with her fingers in her ears and pretend it wasn't happening. It had all culminated when after a particularly prolonged intense onslaught late one-night Babs crawled out from under the bedsheets when it had all became quiet and made her way downstairs where she found the still, lifeless body of her mother. Her head had been smashed to pieces against the living room wall and her brains had spilled out onto the carpet from her broken skull, one of her eyeballs had come out of its socket and whilst still attached to the optic nerve was resting on her cheek and was staring hypnotically at the traumatised now motherless Babs. Not knowing what to do she had simply returned to the safety and comfort offered by crawling back under her bedsheets and remained there until the arrival of the police the next day who had responded to concerns by the neighbours. That was when Babs was handed over to social services who subsequently arranged for her to be placed in the custody of the hell hole of a children's home called Alldahope. Even for one as hardened to life as Babs this was an imposing scary place full of dark secrets and unmentionable acts of human depravity. In the corner of the room she could hear the gentle whimpering of her roommate Tipe Moor.

Tipe was a couple of years older than Babs and had been in care at Alldahope for some time. She had told her about some of the scary things that happened here especially during the night hours. Tipe had told her about the crazy looking monsters that appear in the middle of the night and take you away to what they call the punishment room, she didn't know exactly where it was because they put a bag over your head and take you downstairs and when the bag is removed you are inside the dark windowless room. The night monsters who had taken you there told you that you were being punished for being naughty and that you were never to tell anyone about it and if you did you would be punished even more. Babs had believed everything Tipe said because she could see how frightened she was, but Babs was a tough cookie and she was determined not to show any fear and would try and fight the monsters off if they came for her, that is why she was tightly clutching onto the small bar of soap that she had stolen from the toilet, along with the razor blade taken from the staff bathroom which she had embedded within the soap leaving a bladed edge sticking out, she had learnt how to make this vicious weapon when she overheard her father speaking to one of his ex-prison compatriots.

Babs' senses were on edge and she could hear every creak, squeak and groan from the ramshackle building whereas Tipe seemed to be slowly drifting into a daze like semi consciousness. This was her second week here and she had not seen any of the so-called night monsters so she thought that they may not come tonight and she also began to relax albeit ever so slightly. It had been a long night and she wanted it to end. Another sudden burst of lighting sent an almost blinding flash of light into the room and Barbara turned over in her bed to shield her eyes. Then she saw them, the night monsters. They were in the room, two of them standing next to her roommate's bed. Bab's heart jumped into her mouth and she grasped the bar of soap even tighter, she stared at the two figures one of them had a dark coloured bag with them and whilst one of them lifted up Tipe's head the other one slid it over her head and tightened it around her neck with two chords hanging from the bottom of the bag. Strangely Tipe seemed unusually calm and was offering no resistance to what they were doing.

Babs wouldn't simply accept it she knew exactly what she would do when they came for her, Babs was a fighter she would use her homemade weapon and try and slice their eyes, this was better than just letting them do what they wanted and meekly accepting her fate. She would pretend to be asleep and when they were close enough and trying to take her out of her bed she would strike. The night monsters had now taken Tipe out from under the bed clothes and laid her on top of the bed where she lay still and motionless.

One of the monsters then turned their attention towards Babs; they were looking straight at her. Babs pretended to be asleep with her eyes shut but she was managing to squint very slightly so she could just about see. The monster walked over to her bed and bent over towards her their face was now only a few inches from hers and was looking intensely at her, they appeared to be studying her for some reason. Bab's heart was now pounding faster and faster, she knew she would only have one chance. She would wait until the monster was lifting her out of bed and with his arms underneath her, they would leave themselves unprotected that is when she would strike, she would slash him across the eyes. She had gotten this idea from a TV programme about old time gangsters in Birmingham called Peaky Blinders; they would use razor blades hidden in the peaks of their flat caps and swipe them across the eyes of their victims. She would then run as fast as she could for the door, if she was quick enough and caught them by surprise then there was a chance of getting past the second one by Tipes bed.

Through squinted eyes Babs kept gazing at the face of the monster it was so close it was almost touching her face, near enough so she could smell him it was disgusting was this the smell of the devil she thought was this in fact the devil himself. The bar of soap that was grasped so tightly in her hand was now beginning to get slippery with the heat from her hand she could feel it beginning to melt and her hand becoming sticky she began to worry if she would be able to grip it tightly enough when she needed to. The monster put his face even closer to Babs and she tried to look at his eyes the eyes that she would try and slice open, but she couldn't see anything there at all there just two dark holes. The monster then turned his gaze to the other one who had now picked Tipe up in his arms and was carrying her towards the door he took one last look at Babs and then turned towards the door.

When they left the room closing the door behind them Babs took a few deep breaths and tried to calm herself she thought about the strange eyeless face that had been so close to hers it was not only terrifying but oddly weird and she was sure she had seen something similar before but she couldn't remember where. She could now hear the stairs creaking as the monsters made their way down them carrying poor little frightened Tipe. Her mind flashed back to all the beatings her mom had been subjected to at the hands of her father who was also a kind of monster there had been no one to help her she had been all alone and had to endure beating after beating.

Babs felt guilty at not being able to help her mother especially with the last extremely violent and relentless pummelling that resulted in her death, Babs had become hardened to life and didn't display emotion very often but when she thought about her mum a tear rolled down her cheek. She sat bolt upright in bed adrenalin pumping through her veins the fear beginning to leave her and was being replaced with rage she jumped out of bed and began to get dressed she was going to help she wasn't going to let Tipe be on her own she was determined to do something but she needed to be quick

She opened her door quietly and peered out onto the stairs, there was no one there but she could still hear the footsteps on the stairs some floors below. She began to tiptoe as quietly and as fast as she dared until she neared the ground floor. The monsters carrying Tipe were just below her and they had reached the hallway that ran most of the length of the building so she had to stay still until they made their way along the hallway and out of view. Once they were out of sight Babs made her way to the hallway just in time to see Tipe being taken through a side door at the far end of the hallway. Once the door was shut Babs inched her way down the corridor and placed her ear against the door she could hear more creaking sounds as if they walking down some more stairs. When she guessed they were far enough away not to be able to hear her she began to open the door the rusting hinges made a horrible squeaking noise that seemed to reverberate throughout the building, her heart began to pound and she held her breath worried that the noise would wake everyone and alert the monsters so she held the door still and waited listening for any sign that anyone had heard the door opening.

After a short while when no sound could be heard Babs not wishing to open the door further squeezed through the small gap between the door and doorframe. She found herself at the top of another set of stairs that seemed to descend deep into the depths of the building and she gingerly and carefully started on downwards, the walls were bare brick and everything seemed to be a bit damp it resembled a prison or some sort of dungeon. The only light illuminating her way was coming from under a doorway at the bottom of the stairs. She began to feel frightened and stopped on the stairs a short distance from the doorway that was exuding the light and she thought for a moment that she ought to go back, her breathing had become rapid and fear gripped her stomach.

She turned around and slowly began to make her way back up the stairs feeling a little ashamed of herself for deserting her poor friend and leaving her alone with the monsters who Babs knew would do horrific things to her helpless frightened little friend. Her mind went back to thoughts of her mother and she paused on the stairs and ran through some of the constant beatings she had witnessed and how little she had done to help. Anger and frustration now took over and she turned around with a renewed vigour and a sense of the need for her to do something and not just stand by and do nothing as she had with her poor mother. She was determined to do whatever she could to help her defenceless friend and not let whatever terrible things were in store for her to happen.

She quickly went back down the flight of stairs and was now standing outside the door with her ear pressed hard against it; she could hear her friend crying and pleading with somebody begging for them to stop. Babs took hold of the door handle with her left hand and began to turn it slowly and deliberately. In her right hand she clutched the bar of soap, she had made sure the razor blade was sticking out far enough to inflict maximum damage her plan was to burst in the room as quickly as possible and start slashing the monsters faces and in the ensuing panic she and Tipe may be able to run off. The handle was now fully turned and she put a little pressure on the door but it didn't budge, she pushed harder but again there was no movement.   It was useless, the door was locked from the inside; she slowly turned the handle back hoping that no one inside the room had noticed. Babs was racking her brains what could she do, it would be impossible for her to break the door open and anyway she would lose the element of surprise and wouldn't stand a chance against the monsters.

Then it hit her she thought of something that might work. She ran up the stairs as quickly as she could do without making a noise and into the darkened hallway, she began to scan the walls but the light was poor and it was difficult to see but she knew it was there somewhere but where? Think, think she said to herself. She kept hearing in her mind the pleas of her friend begging for them to stop whatever it was they were doing to her. She was becoming frantic she knew it was here somewhere she remembered it was at her eye level so she began to run her hand along the wall at what she remembered would be the right height. There it was she felt it she had found what she had been looking for it was the fire alarm. If she broke it everyone would have to get up and begin evacuating the building and the fire service and police would also turn up. She smashed her elbow against the glass but it didn't break so she tried it again and again but was unable to smash it she wasn't strong enough, she looked around for something to use conscious now that she needed to find something quick because the noise she had made may have been heard by the monsters. She saw a plastic chair at the end of the corridor with metal tubular legs, she sprinted with all her might and retrieved the chair turned it upside down and aimed one of the metal legs at the glass but she missed and succeeded to put a dent in the plaster she tried again and this time it worked the glass smashed. Immediately deafening sirens began to screech, lights began to flash, she had done it, now she had to get out of the hallway quickly. She began to run back up the stairs but it was too late her room was at the top and people had already begun to come out of their rooms everyone shouting

"Fire, fire, everyone out." She wouldn't be able to explain why she was already dressed and had made it downstairs so quickly so she went back down the stairs into the hallway and hid under the stairs. After a short while there were people everywhere the hallway was packed with people running for the exit. When no one was looking in her direction she slipped from under the stairs and mingled in with the crowd and together with them made her way outside where the distant sound of emergency services sirens could already be heard.

Babs was now concerned for Tipe. Everyone had assembled on the overgrown grassy area at the front of the building and she was frantically searching for her. In the dark with so many people huddled together it was difficult to see much but eventually she saw her. Tipe was standing near the driveway; she appeared to be in a bit of a trance as opposed to everyone else who were in a state of excitement caused by the fire alarm and the freezing cold weather, they were stood out in. Babs put her arm around her friend and guided her away from the driveway where the fire engines and police cars would soon be dashing down.

"Are you ok?" Babs whispered in her ear.

"I'm feeling a bit better now but I am not sure exactly what happened." came the reply.

"It was the night monsters; they came for you." said Babs.
Tipe seemed to be coming to her senses more as she rubbed her eyes.

"I vaguely remember that and being taken into the same room again. The room where they do horrible things to you. I asked them to stop but they wouldn't. They were half undressed when everything suddenly began to get loud and they were shouting and running about. They grabbed me put something on my head so I couldn't see and the next I know I am outside on my own. I don't really know what happened."

Babs whispered in her ear again "Keep quiet for now and I will tell you when we are back in our room."

Tipe didn't say anything but instinctively knew that it was thanks to Babs that she was ok and they held each other tight taking comfort from each other.

By now the whole area was full of firemen, police and even ambulance staff and it wasn't long before the fire service announced that there wasn't a fire and the building was declared safe to go back in. The staff had already made a head count of the children and were now counting them back in. When Babs and Tipe returned to their room it was freezing cold as were they, so they climbed into the same bed for warmth and comfort. Babs told Tipe who now seemed to be completely different she was somehow more alert and wider awake everything that had happened right from when the night monsters came into the room and took her away to setting off the fire alarm and importantly, she now knew where the punishment room was.

Babs asked what happened in the punishment room and Tipe went quiet and mournful obviously deep in thought and greatly affected when she recalled what had happened to her. There was silence for a long time and then slowly Tipe began to tell Babs what had happened to her, tonight had been okay because the fire alarm went off before too much could happen but, in the past, she recounted everything that she had been subject to.

Both girls were silently weeping with tears falling from their cheeks as the full horror of what the night monsters did, Babs in her short lifetime was used to and had seen more violence than was imaginable but this was something else, something completely different to pure violence and she didn't fully understand it all but she knew it was vile and disgusting and that no one should ever have to go through that treatment let alone young frightened and helpless children.

When she had finished speaking neither girl said anything, they lay there silently the trickle of tears still rolling down their cheeks. Babs broke the silence and said ,

"You need to tell somebody, not the police though, they are useless and they won't believe you anyway but somebody who can help."

"My mom is coming to see me tomorrow," said Tipe "but if I tell her the monsters will make it worse and they will come for me again in the night."

Babs reached under the pillow and took out the bar of soap with the razor blade embedded and said,

"If they do come for you or me, I will be ready for them, I will take out their eyes. I will look after you so you must tell your mom."

Tipe thought for a while, looked at Babs and the razor blade and said

"Okay, I'm going to tell her, she will be here sometime in the afternoon."

The girls slowly drifted off into an exhausted sleep clinging on to the reassuring knowledge that they weren't alone they had each other.

The following morning the girls were in the dining area eating breakfast when they overheard the staff talking amongst themselves about last night's fire alarm being activated and how they were trying to find out who had done it. Babs wasn't worried though, she knew no one had seen her and no one would suspect her because her room was at the top of the building. They were chatting with another girl over breakfast, her name was Marion. She was always very talkative and would always speak to everyone, some considered her a bit nosey; others thought of her as being nice and showing an interest. She was the kind of person you could open up to because she seemed genuinely concerned.

Tipe was excited because in a few hours her mom would be here and she would tell her all about the night monsters. She would know what to do, she would make things better. She wanted to tell everyone about what she was going to do but thought it best to keep it a secret with only Babs and Marion knowing what was going to happen.

Today was Saturday which meant it was a free day they could all do what they wanted. The three of them sat in the games room and chatted Babs and Marion played the occasional board game from the odd job collection of second-hand toys and games that had been donated to the home over the years. Most of them were missing some pieces and hardly any of them were complete but they just made the best of it. Tipe didn't join in she was too excited to concentrate. She just kept thinking about seeing her Mother whom she had not seen for a long time, she would have given anything in the world to have her Mom take her back home with her and to get out of this god forsaken place. Tipe had ended up in this place because her Father had abandoned them and her mom had turned to drink which she couldn't handle very well and was being constantly arrested for being drunk and incapable and often spent a night in the police cells leaving Tipe home alone. When some nosey albeit concerned neighbours found out that she was home alone then it wasn't long before social services stepped in and placed her in this home. Tipe knew about her Moms drink problems but she also knew that she was trying to do something about it and she had promised her that she would eventually get her back home.

Tipe's mom looked at her watch; it was ten thirty in the morning and her head felt like shit, her stomach was tied up in knots and she was sweating profusely. She was working out what time she needed to catch the bus to get to Alldahope for one o'clock. It wasn't far from Brierley Hill and the buses ran frequently, she checked her change and put the bus fare in her jeans pocket.

She had quite some time before she needed to leave so she shouted

"Another pint here mate." to the barman who was sat behind the bar reading the paper trying to pick out the horses he would back later in the day. Another pint of strong cider was placed in front of her and she handed over the exact money, there was not so much as a please or thank you from either party; this wasn't that type of pub, it was full of winos and dropouts and poor wretches who couldn't get through or even start the day without a bellyful of booze.

Back at Alldahope Babs and Marion were playing draughts, not all the pieces were there so they were improvising with buttons and other odd bits when Matron stormed in and shouted Fern, I want to see you in my office. She was referring to Marion, the staff always called the children by their last names it was there way of letting the children know who was in charge.

"She sounded angry, you had better go straight away." said Babs.

Marion just looked back at Babs with a frightened expression and with head cowed down she reluctantly stood up and began to walk with obvious trepidation towards matron's office. Babs watched as Marion slowly followed Matron down the corridor and into her office. Marion stood in the centre of the room whilst Matron stared at her from behind a huge desk her face was stern and cold totally devoid of any show of emotion. The order to 'sit down' was shouted in a bullying tone and Marion gingerly took a seat at the desk opposite this imposing brute of a woman. No words were spoken between them for some time and there was an uneasy atmosphere. Matron then looked over towards the door to ensure it was fully closed her gaze then returned back to Marion and then simultaneously they both began to smile and sat back in their chairs. Physically relaxed Marion even let out a little giggle. Matron quietly asked.

"What have you found out; do you know who set the fire alarm of yet?"

Marion shook her head and replied in a hushed voice

"I don't know who set the alarm off yet but I have found out something else you need to know about."

"Go on." came the reply and the two moved a little closer so they could speak quietly

"It's about Tipe, her mom is coming this afternoon and she is going to tell her about the night monsters. She said they came for her last night but let her go when the alarm went off."

Matron took a deep breath "Are you sure?"

Marion replied, "I'm positive; she has just told me in the games room."

Matron thought for a while.

"Ok leave it with me, don't say anything else about it to anyone and keep trying to find out who set the alarm off. Remember it's important that no one knows about our little arrangements so if anyone asks what we have spoken about then tell them I have told you off for leaving your room untidy do you understand?"

Marion nodded adopted her serious face again and got up to leave the room. She even summoned up a fake tear as she went back into the games room and began chatting with Babs and Tipe telling them how horrible Matron had been.

In the rundown booze-soaked carpet hovel of the ramshackle pub, another pint of cider had been ordered by Marion's mom. She was sitting on a shabby bar stool with one arm sprawled across the counter. The flat cloudy looking drink was placed on the bar in front of her and the barman stuck out his hand for the money, clumsy fingers awkwardly began fumbling in the purse that had been placed on the bar when she began her drinking session. Eventually turning the purse upside down but nothing fell out as the purse was empty. The barman stretched out his arm to retrieve the unpaid for pint but some drunken mumbling and a raised hand stopped him and after a frantic search through her pockets enough coinage was scraped together to pay for the pint. She took several deep swigs and looked at her watch realising that she would need to leave soon to get her bus to Alldahope. She gulped the last few dregs of the pint down and got up of the stool to leave almost falling over in the process, the several pints of strong cider beginning to take effect. She put her hands in her jean pockets then it suddenly dawned on her that her pockets were empty she had just paid for the last pint with the money she was saving for the bus fare. Oh god she thought as she realised what she needed to do to get some quick cash something she had done many times before but it made her feel physically sick at the prospect of having to prostitute herself again. She scanned the bar for possible punters with whom she could flog her trade someone who would give her a few quid for a hand job in the gent's toilet.

Tipe looked up excitedly at the clock in the games room, there was only an hour to wait for her mom's visit. She was sure her mom would know what to do when she found out about the night monsters, she would make it all better. Then loudly and suddenly from out of nowhere she heard

"Moor come with me."

Matron was shouting as she stormed into the games room. Tipe stood up startled she was frozen to the spot and her heart began to beat fast but she immediately calmed down when Matron bawled at her again

"C'mon hurry up your moms here to see you."

A huge smile spread across her face and she willingly followed Matron to the interview room at the extreme end of the building. Matron opened the door and ushered Tipe in, the room was sparsely furnished and badly decorated. In the centre was a table with two chairs, it was used for meetings normally with either family or probation workers the walls were bare and drab but this didn't bother Tipe she would be seeing her mom soon. Matron guided her to a seat and told her to sit down and wait, Tipe did what she was told. She sat down with her back to the door and she heard Matron leave slamming the door behind her. On the wall facing her she began to study a picture that had been crudely hung using string and a nail hammered into the wall it looked a bit like Alldahope but if it was it must have been a long time ago because it appeared to be in immaculate condition. She was that fascinated by the picture that she failed to hear the door open behind her. Tipe saw a reflection in the picture and realised that someone had entered the room and as she turned around shouted

"Mom."

But the face she was now staring into wasn't that of her loving mom it was her worst nightmare it was the night monsters.

Before she could scream a hand had been placed over her mouth and she was forced back into the corner of the room. She tried to struggle and cry out but she could do neither the hand that was clamped over her mouth was not only preventing her from making a noise but it was also pressing her body so hard that both her shoulders were wedged against the walls holding her in a vice like grip. She recognised the faces of the monsters from last night when they took her out of her room, but this time they were dressed differently they were covered head to toe in strange looking white overalls. Tipe instantly recalled what Babs had said to her today about what they would do if the night monsters came back, we would fight as hard as we could. Tipe fully stretched her left arm above her head and took a deep breath, intending to summon up all her strength and bring her fist crashing down on the monster, but as she tried to force her arm down it wouldn't move at all she tilted her head upwards and saw that another hand had taken hold of her wrist and was pressing it against the wall. Then she saw it and her entire body became filled with the most extreme terror that she had ever felt. She wanted to cry, scream, run away or just do something anything but she was unable even to turn her head away as she watched the bright shiny coloured knife being drawn across her wrist. The razor-sharp blade was slicing into flesh and cutting through blood vessels with surprising ease. Blood initially spurted out like a fountain and splashed against the wall until the gushing gave way to a steady crimson coloured tide cascading down her still raised arm. After a few minutes that seemed to last a lifetime the blood flow slowed to a trickle and them stopped completely. One of the monsters stared into Tipe's eyes; she knew exactly what the monster was looking for they were waiting for her to die. The Monster turned his gaze away from Tipe and towards the other one and shook his head. They let their grip go on her and Tipe crumpled slowly to the floor, they are letting me go she thought it's all over my mom will be here soon and make it all better. But she was wrong it was far from over she now felt herself being raised up by her ankles until she was completely upside down with her arms dangling down, then she felt her wrist being taken hold of and violently and forcibly bent backwards exposing and opening up the wound and the blood began to gush once more. She realised that they were never going to let her go and she now began to feel extremely cold and shivery and everything was beginning to go dark she wasn't in pain anymore her body felt numb and limp but she knew something was wrong. She summoned up in her mind an image of her mom in happier times before she had started drinking, they were walking through Stourbridge Park with ice creams in their hands then the image disappeared and she was alone in the darkness. In desperation she managed with a weakened muffled voice utter the words "Mommy I want my Mommy."

Then there was silence.

2

I'VE GOT YOU

Tipes mom almost fell out of the taxi in the driveway of Alldahope. Realising that the alcohol was having quite an effect on her she paid the driver, stood up straight and took a few deep lungful's of the chilly afternoon air and composed herself as best she could before strolling towards the main door. She stood in the enclosed entranceway gathering her thoughts and running through some of the things she would say to Tipe whom she missed terribly. She was also anxious not to appear the worse for drink in front of her because she knew she would be disappointed especially as she had promised Tipe that she had stopped drinking. Another deep breath and she rang the doorbell, after some time the door was opened by a surly looking woman who brusquely announced

"I'm the matron how I can help you?"

"I've come to see Tipe. I'm her mom." came the sheepish response.

"Follow me, she is already in the meeting room so I'll take you there."

Matron made her way along to the extreme end of the hallway and stood outside the interview room door.

"She's waiting for you in here. You have thirty minutes; I will come back when the times up."

Tipes mom stood outside the door for a while and once again composed herself, it had been some time since she had been sober enough to visit her daughter and she wanted to look her very best for her beautiful little girl. Another deep breath and she pushed the door open and strode in.

When she entered the room, she was surprised that Tipe wasn't sitting at the table, she was nowhere to be seen. She wasn't in the room at all so she needed to go and tell someone and find out where her daughter was. As she turned back towards the door to go and find matron out the corner of her eye, she spied something on the floor in the corner of the room, it looked like a pile of old rags. Curiosity aroused so she walked slowly round the table to get a closer look at the mess, whatever it was it was covered and sitting in a large pool of liquid.

As she neared the crumpled pile of rags in the corner, she realised what she was looking at. She stood there in a state of shock frozen to the spot unable to move or even cry out it. It wasn't a pile of old rags piled up in the corner it was her poor sweet little girl. The only reason for her existence her inspiration to carrying on living and now it was gone she lying in a heap and the liquid was a pool of her own blood. She felt her knees buckle and she collapsed to the floor next to Tipe putting her arms around the cold lifeless body of her little angel and hugged her tightly. There was a strange silence as she gently rocked back and forth with her daughter still held tight to her chest. Then she began to cry and scream uncontrollably the sounds reverberating throughout the corridors and walls of Alldahope filling the entire building with the saddest sounding heart rendering wails.

Babs was in the games room with Marion when she heard the screams and she instinctively knew that something had happened to her friend. Without showing any emotion she promised herself that her best friend would be avenged someone would have to pay.

Detective Constable Latifeo was sitting in the CID office at Brierley Hill Police Station with his feet up on the desk when he received the radio message. Latifeo was infamous for being the office layabout everyone knew full well that he was incredibly idle and would do anything to avoid work. This particular day he was the weekend CID cover for the area.   He   was technically based at Stourbridge Police Station but due to financial cutbacks Stourbridge station had been closed and all the staff relocated to Brierley Hill, a move that had incensed the Stourbridge residents at being left without any local police in the town. He had been looking forward to spending the day in the office with his feet up drinking tea and thinking about the return of his girlfriend Sam. She was on holiday in Benidorm with her friend Shirley Wallows who also happened to be a Detective Sergeant and his supervisor. He hadn't wanted her to go but Sam was her own woman a free spirit and in their strange relationship she was the one who wore the trousers. He put her out of his mind for a while and picked up the local free newspaper. The 'Stourbridge News' had been in circulation for about thirty years and its readership had grown considerably in that time. One of the reporters for the paper was well known to him and over the years Latifeo and Martin had become sort of friends. Martin as his job required was particularly inquisitive and this had landed him in a few tight spots over the years but equally his prying nature had resulted in some journalistic scoops. In reality he would have made a far better detective than the lacklustre disinterested Latifeo. The main headlines in the paper revolved around a recent spate of carjacking's and burglaries that had been perpetrated in order to get the keys of the householder's car.   Apart from the carjacking's it had been reasonably quiet on the serious crime front which suited Latifeo, it meant that there was not a lot for him to investigate. The violent car jacking's were being dealt with by a specialist squad that had been set up in response to a surge of such crimes so he had been left with little to do which fitted in with his overall general lack of enthusiasm and laid-back attitude to anything work related. The police radio lying on his desk next to his cup of tea cackled into life with the request for the on-duty CID. Latifeo sighed as he took his feet off the table and reluctantly answered the radio call. He was informed that there had been a suicide at Alldahope children's home and the uniform officer at the scene was requesting CID attendance. As he was the only CID officer on duty, he realised he couldn't palm it off on anyone else, so he unenthusiastically answered that he was responding and on his way. After finishing his cup of tea he slowly gathered together the appropriate bundle of papers and documents that he would need and casually strolled into the vehicle compound to allocate the CID vehicle. He parked the vehicle in the driveway of Alldahope and when he alighted, he took a good look round the building and thought to himself how run down the place was. He had been there several times before to deal with various incidents and on each visit the place appeared to him to be more and more dilapidated.

Matron met him at the door and ushered him along the corridor towards the interview room. Latifeo wasn't very good at dealing with violent or grisly scenes and he was known to be tickle- stomached especially where blood was concerned so he took a dep breath and entered the room. Inside was a very young and inexperienced officer PC Ainslo, she had only just finished her initial Police training and this was one of the first scenes she had been sent to deal with so she was much relieved to see a CID Officer.

Tipes mom was still in the room quietly sobbing to herself and repeating the phrase over and over again

"It's all my fault because I was late."

"Right what have we got?" Latifeo said to the young officer.

"That's the young girl's mother she was the one that found the body it was a prearranged family welfare meeting in this room."

"What has she said about it?" enquired Latifeo.

"When I came in this room and spoke to her all she could utter was that her little girl was dead and she pointed to the body."

PC Ainslo moved to one side so that Latifeo could see the little girl's dead body which had been directly behind her. Latifeo almost instantaneously wretched and put his hand across his mouth to prevent him from throwing up. He had not been prepared for the sight of so much blood. He left the room immediately and beckoned the PC Ainslo to follow him. As he always did, he was now thinking of ways to pass on as much work as possible so he asked the young officer

"Are there any other witnesses?"

"The only other witness is matron who took the girl into the room earlier to wait for her mom." Ainslo replied.

"What is your gut feeling about this?"

PC Ainslo was a little surprised at being asked her opinion. She had assumed that CID would take over and deal with everything, but she was new and did not know about Latifeo and his propensity to pass the buck to other people to deal wherever he could.

She replied "It seems to me that she was put in this room awaiting her mother whom she had not seen for a long time and because her mom was late she perhaps thought that she wasn't coming so in desperation she slit her wrist with the knife that's on the floor next to her body."

"So you think it's a straightforward suicide, nothing suspicious about it then?"

"Well I don't know if she meant to kill herself or if it was just a cry for attention gone wrong but I can't see anything suspicious about it."

Latifeo thought to himself. Great if she declares it non-suspicious then the responsibility is all on her head and also it means she can deal with it.

"Right here's what you need to do, take her mother home and take a statement from her then take a statement from the matron here. Ask for scenes of crime to examine the scene and inform the coroner's officer can you remember all that?"

"Yes," she replied, "but I have already asked for SOCO and they have said they will be here in three to four hours they are busy examining the scene of a carjacking."

Latifeo gave this some thought. If SOCO were to examine the scene someone would have to wait here and keep the scene secure and he didn't want to hang about for any longer than necessary.

"Cancel SOCO, tell them it's non-suspicious and take a few pics with your camera phone. Put the knife in an evidence bag and submit that to SOCO for fingerprinting and arrange for the body to go to the mortuary. Have you got all that?"

Once again PC Ainslo was surprised at how much she had been left to do and how little CID were doing but she was young in service so she just got on with it. Satisfied that he had managed to offload all the work onto the shoulders of the young officer he went in search of matron to update her with what was happening. He found Matron in her office and explained to her that it seemed to be a straightforward suicide the tipping point probably being the fact that her mother had arrived late. He further outlined that as a straightforward suicide there would only be a minimal police investigation. Matron seemed relieved to hear this and thanked him for his actions.

Latifeo went back to his vehicle parked on the driveway but before getting in he lit a cigarette and cast a further eye over this grotesque building. He saw a young child staring vacantly out of one of the downstairs windows the girl was staring right at him unblinkingly. Her stare was strangely intense and he thought he recognised her from somewhere but couldn't think exactly where he quickly dismissed it from his mind and looked up to the sky wondering whether it was going to rain or not. The girl staring at him was Babs Guthy, Latifeo hadn't recognised her but she knew him as she knew a lot of the officers from Stourbridge. Most of them had been to her house at one time or another, either to arrest her dad or to stop her mum being beaten up.

Babs realised that whatever had happened to her friend would not be taken seriously even she knew about his reluctance to work; she had overheard other officer talking about him several times in the past. She was even more determined now to do something herself in response to whatever had happened to Tipe. Latifeo made a radio call to the control room stating that he had dealt with the incident at Alldahope and that he was leaving a uniform officer there just to finish things off. The log would then be endorsed with this information giving the false impression that Latifeo had actually done something.Satisfied that he had absolved himself of all responsibility and work related to the incident he returned to the police station and resumed the arduous task of putting his feet up and idly browsing the newspaper and thinking about the return of Sam whilst waiting for his shift to finish. After numerous more cups of tea he looked at his watch yet again, it showed an hour left to go before the end of his shift so he decided it was time to call it a day. He was just about to leave the office when in walked Martin the local news reporter. Latifeo knew he was here concerning the suicide at Alldahope and he wondered how he always seemed to find out what was happening so quickly. He also knew that Martin would not disclose his sources so there was no point in asking him. After a brief exchange of pleasantries the reporter was briefed with the current state of the Alldahope enquiry. Latifeo sensed that Martin was displaying an unusual level of interest in what was a straightforward suicide, but as was his nature he couldn't be bothered to ask why. A few questions later Martin left the office having thanked Latifeo for the information. The uniform police car was winding its way through the myriad of high-rise tower blocks that overlooked an area of Brierley Hill known as the Delph. The area was showing the signs of a prolonged recession, it used to be renowned for its number of pubs was popular with weekend drinkers and stag parties doing the Delph run pub crawl. Most of the pubs had either been knocked down boarded up or converted to other uses. The Cottage Spring was now a veterinarian's, the Dock and Iron had been demolished, the Crown boarded up and the Rock Tavern was now a convenience store. The entire area was suffering from a lack of investment and it showed. Everything looked tired and outdated. It had been a few hours since Tipe had been found dead and her mother had now stopped crying and shaking and seemed to have regressed into a world of her own she looked to be in a trance completely out of touch with reality. Ainslo was pleased with her own progress into the investigation so far, she had taken what she thought were all the relevant photographs on her phone and sent them to Latifeo. To save time she had taken a statement from Matron meaning she wouldn't have to go back to Alldahope. The bloodstained knife had been packaged in an evidence box and now all that was left to do was to take a statement from Tipes mom. This was something she was not looking forward to even though she had appeared to have calmed down a lot the police car had stopped outside one of the taller of the tower blocks and the officer had to try and wake Tipes mom from her catatonic like state to get her out of the vehicle. No words were exchanged as they made their way in the much-graffitied lift to the top floor of the building. The landing was a complete mess and was also heavily graffitied with litter strewn everywhere. They both stood outside the door to the flat and whilst Tipes mom searched for the keys in her handbag Ainslo studied the door, the paint was almost non-existent the letter box was almost falling off and the spyhole was an actual hole about one inch in diameter. It seemed to be an age before the keys were eventually produced and they went inside, Ainslo having seen the state of the front door expected the place to be something of a tip but even she was shocked when they entered.

The young officer looked around at the filthy state of the place there was rubbish strewn everywhere empty cans and bottles of cider piled up on every available surface and it stunk of stale cigarettes and booze. There was also a much stronger more pungent overwhelming odour that she couldn't put her finger on but she knew it was making her feel sick to her stomach. She found what looked like the cleanest place to sit and opened her folder of papers and produced a blank statement form and some spare paper to make notes on. She had not taken many statements so she was anxious to make sure that everything was correct. Whilst running through in her head what she needed to include in the statement she felt a cold breeze and she shuddered slightly and looked to see where it was coming from.

"Oh my God." she screamed when she saw where the cold wind was blowing from. It was coming from the open balcony door where Tipe's mom was standing. She was the other side of the balcony safety rail and teetering precariously on the edge and they were on the sixteenth floor.

The officer gently put her folder of papers on the seat next to her and stood up slowly and began to inch her way towards the balcony. Her mind was thinking back to her recent police training and she remembered that whatever she did it must be done calmly with no sudden moves. Her heart was racing and she had an awful gut-wrenching feeling in her stomach when she stepped onto the balcony.

"This is not the answer; this isn't what Tipe would have wanted." the officer said gently.

"It's all my fault she only did it because I was late. If only I hadn't had that extra drink, she would still be alive."

"It's not your fault you must understand that." the officer said sympathetically.

"But it is my fault everything has been my fault I'm the reason she was in care in the first place."

"There was nothing you could have done and you can't blame yourself."

Ainslo edged closer and closer, she could now see the ground below and was instantly gripped with fear. It hit home to her how incredibly high up they were, there was a children's playground immediately beneath them but they were so high up the playground apparatus the swings, slides and climbing frames looked tiny as if they were miniature toy replicas. She tried to block this out of her mind and concentrate on talking this suicidal woman off the ledge. She continued with repeated pleas for not to jump and that her daughter would not have wanted this. She continued in a slow calm manner remembering from her training that it was important to maintain a constant dialogue and not to apportion blame to anyone and to give them some glimmer of hope for the future. This is going well so far, she thought I'm gaining her trust and developing an empathy with her just as I remembered from training school. She opened her arms wide in a welcoming gesture as she edged nearer the pathetic creature that was hovering between life and death. Tipes mom screamed and Ainslo stood stock still her and lowered her arms her heart was thumping in her chest as she was frantically thinking what to do next. She was now almost within touching distance, should she risk it and make a grab for her or play it cool and calm. If she tried to grab her, she could miss and it might force her to let go. But if she did nothing she could jump anyway; thoughts and ideas were racing through her mind. Play it cool she kept repeating to herself play it cool. But she was so close she was sure she could grab her and drag her back over the safety rail and back on the balcony to safety. Despite feeling terrified inside she managed to keep her cool and kept a broad welcoming smile on her face. This smile was now being returned and Tipe's mom was looking more relaxed. Ainslo wanted to call her by her first name but realised that ridiculously she didn't know what her name was, she had only been referred to as Tipes mom and it seemed to be the wrong thing to do to ask her name when she is balancing on a tiny ledge hundreds of feet up in the air. They were now standing face to face the only thing separating them was the wrought iron safety rail. Once again, she opened up her arms in a welcoming gesture and this time Tipes mom didn't scream or react. Inching forward ever closer and closer with her arms open the young officer decided that when she was close enough, she would put her arms around the pathetic creature.

Slowly Ainslo put her arms around Tipe's mom and began to hug her tighter and tighter. Eventually the hug was reciprocated and the two of them were locked in an emotional embrace. Thank god for that Ainslo thought she could now relax slightly it was over the crisis had passed. They remained in this comforting embrace for some time until Ainslo said.

"It's okay I've got you." with a broad beaming smile across her face.

Tipe's mom smiled back and looked gently into the eyes of her saviour and said quietly and softly.

"You haven't got me I've got you" then she grasped the officer even tighter and suddenly with an almighty pull yanked Ainslo clean over the safety rail and launched the two of them into mid-air hundreds of feet up whilst laughing hysterically.

The pair of them were still locked in an embrace but now they were hurtling towards the ground at breakneck speed towards certain death. It was Ainslo who was now frantically screaming and crying in absolute terror while Tipe's mom was smiling from ear to ear whilst all the time staring into the eyes of her terrified victim as they fell faster and faster towards the concrete below.

"I'm going to see my Tipe now; I'm coming darling" she shouted "I'm coming."

The last thing either of them heard was the screams of the children and their parents in the playground below them. They had been watching events unfold most of them stunned when they saw the police officer dragged off the balcony towards certain death. They landed with such force that both bodies appeared to explode causing bits of brain, bone and body tissue to scatter over a wide area. They initially crashed into a wooden climbing frame which was almost demolished with the force of the impact, this then catapulted them across the playground and the entwined broken bodies landed square on top of a metal framed roundabout. It was Saturday afternoon and the playground was full of children and young moms with their toddlers.

Everyone began to scream and shout youngsters were running around hysterically splattered in blood and covered in fragments of body parts that they were frantically trying to wipe off. The child's roundabout was rotating slowly as if in some sort of macabre display with the corpse's blood dripping and forming patterns on the ground. The stomach of Pc Ainslo had been completely ripped open with the force of the collision with the climbing frame and her intestines were dragging on the floor going around and round as the roundabout continued with its slow grotesque display.

.

3

SUN AND SANGRIA

Shirley Wallows and Sam Gail were sitting on the terrace of the White Lion in Benidorm overlooking the beautiful sun-drenched Levante beach. A large pitcher of iced Sangria adorned the table together with two glasses.

"This is the life" said Sam as she poured herself and Shirley another glass of Sangria. They were on the last day of their holiday and both were feeling relaxed albeit a little tired. The pair of them had a few too many late nights followed by long hectic days interspersed with bouts of drinking.

Several nights had been spent trawling the back streets of Benidorm on the look-out for down and outs or for drunken revellers who were so out of it they had passed out or were on the verge of passing out. They had met last year during a Police investigation into a serial killer that had been slaughtering couples engaging in the act of dogging in Stourbridge. As part of the investigation the then Detective Constable Wallows spoke with Sam as a potential witness as she lived opposite the park where the first murders had taken place. Sam had instantly recognised Wallows and knew of a potentially life changing secret of hers but had decided to keep it to herself. She only revealed to Wallows their previous knowledge of each other when it had become necessary to protect her. Both girls had been brought up from a young age in a children's home where they were both subject to the most awful atrocities. This had helped them form an unbreakable bond with each other this had then been further strengthened buy their joint actions since.

They were both now aware of each other's innermost and darkest secrets and the reasons behind them they were not only best friends but allies for life.   "When are you back at work Shirley?"

"The day after we get back, I am the duty CID supervisor so I have to go in its going to be a real pain not only do I have to work from Brierley Hill police station but I also have to supervise that idle git Latifeo."

Sam laughed "He is a bit of a dipstick he still thinks I'm his girlfriend he definitely thinks with his dick."

"We need to forget about home and all that crap lets concentrate on enjoying the rest of our holiday, what shall we do tonight Sam?"

"Why don't we go to the Pig and Whistle in the old town, those two guys might be there the ones that keep giving us the eye."

Shirley smiled. She was under no illusion about her own attractiveness to the opposite sex. She knew she was fairly attractive with dark hair and eyes and a curvy but slightly fuller figure. Sam on the other hand was an absolute stunner. She had long blonde hair with a gorgeous face and the brightest of electric blue eyes. Her figure whilst quite petite was to die for with curves in all the right places. She also had a presence about her an allure that most men found irresistible they simply adored her and she was able to twist most men round her little finger.

"You mean the guys that keep giving you the eye" Shirley retorted with a cheeky grin.

"Stop putting yourself down I'm sure one of them has got the hots for you, anyway it doesn't matter it's our last night so we will never see them again, let's just have some fun."

"Ok if you want it'll make a change from Neptunes I suppose, wouldn't it be great if we could stay another week."

"I'd love to stay another week" said Sam "Only problem is I have a customer that I need to attend to."

"Surely you could rearrange it, I might be able to get some time off if I ring my Chief Inspector and he happens to be in a good mood".

Sam shook her head "Afraid not, I can't re-arrange it he's my best customer an extreme submissive masochist. I've got him chained up in the cellar; if I don't go back the poor sod will probably snuff it, that's if he hasn't done so already."

"Good god Sam you know some real perverts. Why on earth would anyone want to be locked up in a cellar for a week?"

"He gets some weird kick out of it but he's a clever bloke. He used to have his own steel business and is rolling in money and also very generous with it. I have a feeling from what he has said that he is punishing himself for something he has done or thought about doing in the past. I am going to try and find out what his secret is, it will give me an extra hold over him that I can use."

Their conversation was broken when another pitcher of Sangria was placed on their table with an announcement from the waiter that as such good customers this was on the house. They poured themselves another drink sat back in their chairs and soaked up the afternoon sun. Thoughts of home and the return to normality were pushed to the back of their minds.

The newsroom of the local Stourbridge newspaper was buzzing with activity; everyone was busy editing stories and features to meet the weekly deadline. It had been a fairly ordinary routine week up until now but in the space of a few hours there had been a number of breaking headline stories. A recent spate of car-jackings had intensified with three occurring in broad daylight within the space of a few hours including breaking into houses and threatening the occupants with a machete in order to steal their car keys. There was also the suicide at Alldahope, but the one that eclipsed them all was the horrific murder of a young female police officer. The senseless slaughter of PC Ainslo who had mercilessly been yanked off a sixteen-storey balcony by a drunken mentally unbalanced mother had gripped the public's attention. The previous year Stourbridge had attracted worldwide attention when a number of serial killings had taken place. And now Stourbridge was once again back in the spotlight and making national and even international headlines. Some of the foreign newspapers had shown the story and included graphic pictures of Ainslo and her broken and almost disembowelled body. Some of the young mothers who had witnessed the incident had snapped away with their mobile phones. The subsequent images of the police officers body impaled on the children's roundabout had been sold to the highest bidder.

The Stourbridge news however had taken a different approach. Their reporter Martin had done an in-depth interview with the young officers family. Her parents had described her as a kind and caring person whose biggest ambition was to join the police force. They had been immensely proud of their daughter who had attained the position of top student in her recent graduation from police training school.

Martin also made enquiries at Alldahope to try and establish a link between the deaths of Tipe and her mother. He had spoken with the Matron and several of the young residents especially ones that knew Tipe. Something was giving him a nagging doubt in the back of his mind concerning Alldahope, he couldn't put his finger on it but he knew that everything was not as it should be. His natural inquisitiveness as a reporter told him that he needed to look deeper, there was a story to be uncovered he was sure of it and he was determined to find out. However for now he needed to prepare his copy for publishing his enquiries would have to wait. After a long day and with the paper put to bed Martin sat back in his chair put his feet up on his desk. He sipped at his coffee whilst staring out of the window across Stourbridge ring road. They had recently moved offices and were now directly opposite the towns Police Station. It would have been the easiest of tasks for him to simply stroll over the road and speak with the CID to start his enquiries into Alldahope. That was of course before the cutbacks that had forced the Station to close and all the staff relocated to Brierley Hill Police Station. He looked at his watch it was getting late and it a bit of a journey to Brierley Hill just on the off chance that he might be able to speak with the late turn CID. Should he risk it or not they may not even be in the nick they could be out on a job or more likely in the pub he thought. That was it, his mind was made up the thought of the pub and a couple of beers swung it he would go back home and finish the day off with a couple of pints of Bathams. After shutting off his laptop and locking his papers away in his desk he wearily donned his coat and tried to put recent events out of his mind, for a short time anyway.   The journey to Alicante airport had been long and tedious. The distance between Benidorm and the airport wasn't too far but they had made a great number of stops to pick up passengers including a couple of noisy stag parties. The heat and humidity were intense and the air-conditioning on the coach hadn't been working and both Shirley and Sam were suffering with hangovers from their previous night's drinking in the pig and whistle. However they had now arrived, checked their bags in, passed through customs and were enjoying hair of the dog drinks in the Carlsberg bar. They had a few hours to wait before their flight and they wanted to make the best of their last few hours of the holiday. The alcohol had suppressed their hangovers they were beginning to feel a lot better and were chatting excitedly about their week in the Spanish sun.

"I can't believe how many drinks you got those two guys to buy us last night; it must have cost them an absolute fortune. How on earth did you smooth talk them into spending all that money?"

Sam giggled "I just promised them what they wanted that's all."

"I assume you are talking about sex" Shirley replied with a curious expression.

"Of course I am I told them they would have the time of their lives when we meet up with them tonight, they were like putty in my hands especially when I promised them some real dirty stuff."

"But we're on the plane home in a few hours' time and we'll never see them again."

With a shrug of her shoulders and a devil may care look spread across her face Sam replied "Of course we will never see them again, but they don't know that? They will be waiting for us in the pub tonight while we are thirty thousand feet in the air on our way home. They won't even realise how lucky they have been, or how close they came to seeing what we can do."

Both of them burst into fits of hysterical laughter and celebratory touched their glasses together with a joint shout of "Cheers boys." With one eye on the departure screen they continued to enjoy the last bit of their vacation by drinking as much as they possibly could before boarding the plane for home.   Stourbridge CID were busy making enquiries into the murder of their colleague and no one noticed the reporter Martin walk in the office. He looked around the room for a face he recognised and, in the corner, he saw Latifeo. He was the only one in the office not working but was casually flicking through that weeks edition of the Stourbridge news. He looked up as he saw Martin approaching.

"I'm just reading your story on the murder of Ainslo, it comes across well you make her sound like a hero and not an idiot who stupidly got too close to a maniac jumper."

"That's a bit harsh she was trying to save the womans life."

"Well she shouldn't have. She should have let her jump then we wouldn't have all this paperwork to do" he moaned. "Anyway take a seat, how can I help you?"

Martin sat down. "I'm making enquiries into the death of the young girl at Alldahope. There's something not quite right about it but I can't figure out exactly what."

Latifeo folded his paper and indignantly threw it on the desk. "Look I've investigated it and it's a straightforward suicide, simple as that. There is nothing suspicious about it at all. There is no story there and the matter is now closed."   "What about the scene of crime examination. What are their conclusions?"

"Scenes of crime were busy dealing with car-jackings so they didn't make an examination, but as I've already said it was non-suspicious therefore, they don't technically have to examine it. They have examined the knife and matched a fingerprint in blood on the handle as hers so it's an open and shut case."   Martin was aware of Latifeos lack of enthusiasm and realised as did his CID colleagues that he was famed for not wanting to anything that involved working. Realising that he was getting nowhere fast with Latifeo and was unlikely to get any assistance from the idle good for nothing he decided to wait for the return of Detective Sergeant Wallows from her holiday. He had been told that she was back on duty tomorrow on late shift. He and Wallows got on well together, they had spoken several times before mainly during last year's investigation into the infamous Stourbridge serial killer and he knew that she would be a far greater help. He thanked Latifeo and left the office. In the games room at Alldahope Babs and Marion were passing the time away by playing board games. They were both in a sombre mood and had been since the death of their friend poor little Tipe. Bab's violent family background and upbringing had not only hardened her outlook on life and made her almost impervious to fear and given her a maturity way beyond her years it had also given her an extraordinary insightfulness. She could read into situations and people and could sense things that most people never could even in adulthood. When she had heard Tipe's mom screaming she had instinctively known that something sinister had happened. Everyone else automatically assumed it was suicide but Babs new otherwise, there were bad things happening at Alldahope that were being covered up and not everyone was who they seemed. She was positive that Tipe had been murdered because she had intended to expose what was happening here to her mom. It was no coincidence that Tipe died before she could do it. If Babs had the opportunity, she would also have told her parents. However, her mom was dead having been murdered by her dad and he was now in prison for her murder, so she would have to do something herself. She had thought long and hard about the circumstances of Tipes death and deduced that someone must have revealed what Tipe was about to do. The only ones who were aware of Tipe's intentions were herself Tipe and Marion. She had decided to keep an eye on Marion and her suspicions became further aroused when she noticed how many times Marion had been summoned to Matrons office on the pretext of receiving some form of admonishment. It simply didn't make sense there was something happening between them and she devised a plan to find out. But she had to wait for the next time Marion would be called to Matrons office. She didn't have to wait too long Marion was just about to take her turn and throw the dice in their game Ludo when Matron stormed in and shouted at Marion telling her to go to her office immediately. Babs was now convinced more than ever that this was a show, it was a put-on Babs had been ready for this and observed both their actions and expressions, she knew they were acting.

As soon as they were both out of sight Babs left the games room and sneaked out of the rear entrance into the garden into the early evening darkness. Then carefully and quietly she made her way through the overgrown bushes until she was outside one of the windows to Matrons office. Earlier in the day she had gone into Matrons office and opened one of the sash windows by easing it up very slightly so that it was unnoticeable but enough to be able to listen to any conversation. She had a clear view as Marion came into the office, Matron had a face like thunder and Marion head bowed looking slightly nervous. Then amazingly almost instantaneously as soon as the door was shut behind her both of them looked relaxed and were smiling at each other and Marion made herself comfortable on one of the easy chairs in the office. It was dark enough outside so that Babs could not be seen through the window but she had a good clear view of the both of them and could easily make out what they were saying. "What have you found out; do you know who set the fire alarm off yet?"   "No one seems to know I've asked around but no one is admitting to it or who they think might have done it."

"Well someone set it off and I need to know who and I need to know quickly do you understand?" Matron said sternly.

"Perhaps if I had something to offer, a bribe or anything to give them" "Do that then tell the older ones you've got some drugs or cigarettes with the younger ones bribe them with chocolates or sweets. I will give you what you need but do it quickly. Above all make sure you don't get found out I want our little arrangement to keep going I need you to keep telling me what everyone is doing." It was her; it was that bitch Marion who had told on Tipe she was the reason that she was now dead. Bab's blood began to boil she was so angry listening to the pair of them plotting against them all. She had known something was wrong and now she knew who was behind it. They had a traitor in their midst a sneak a squealer.

Her gangster father the legendary Stan Guthy was renowned for dealing with squealers. Amongst the criminal underworld the worst crime of all was to be
an informer it was the lowest of the low, completely taboo. Her father would regularly beat up people on demand, break arms and legs and so on, but for grasses he had a special way of dealing with them. He did something that would put the fear of god into anyone thinking of becoming an informer. It would send out clear and gruesome message that would make squealers think twice about snitching. His trademark punishment for a lowlife grass would be to cut out their tongue. But her father was in prison so it was now up to Babs she would have to deal with it.

The pair of them would be made to pay for her friend's death she needed to exact revenge in whatever way she could. She wanted to cry out, to shout and scream at the two horrible scheming bastards. She felt as if she could burst into the office and attack them with her homemade weapon her razor blade embedded in a bar of soap, another of the things she had learned from her father. But she knew she needed to be coy she had to keep her temper and rage under control and calmly and coolly plot her revenge. Matron and Marion's conversation was coming to an end and Marion had stood up in readiness to leave the office. Babs decided it was time for her to go back to the games to avoid arousing any suspicion but as she prepared to move the door to the office opened. And as Marion was leaving the room a tall man carrying a bag entered and passed by her as if she didn't exist. He breezed in and without any invitation he put his bag on the table and sat down and made himself comfortable in one of the luxury armchairs. Babs stayed where she was. This new person intrigued her, he had a presence and an air of authority about him, and she needed to find out more about him and why he was there.

"Good afternoon doctor I've been expecting you." Matron said with a smile as she got up and walked across the office and locked the door.

Babs was confused, what was a doctor doing here. He wasn't here to treat anyone because that was a different doctor. Whenever anyone was sick at Alldahope they were always treated by the same doctor and this wasn't him. Babs looked around her surroundings she had been outside the window for some time. She knew that she couldn't be seen in the undergrowth or through the window but she didn't want anyone to come looking for her, so she listened hard for any sound or noise that might signal some else's approach. Satisfied that she was alone she returned her attention to what was going on in the office. The doctor had now opened his bag and had emptied what looked to be hundreds of foil blister packs of drugs onto Matrons desk. "These should keep you going for a couple of months, remember they are very strong. If you give them the right amount, they will just become tired and drowsy and not fully aware of what's happening but if you give them too much they will go into a deep sleep and be good for nothing. You can't tell by taste or smell because they are completely tasteless and odourless. So you have to make sure that you measure the dosage out carefully." Matron began to put the drugs into her desk drawer "What happens if someone has too much?"

"You just make sure that doesn't happen, an overdose could easily kill one of them and we don't want the police here again so soon. Fortunately for us it was that useless idiot Latifeo who turned up last time and he couldn't detect his own arse. But we may not be so lucky in future, so just be careful when you put it in the milk make sure it is stirred well to evenly distribute it."

This was all making sense to Babs this was why her friend would always be sleepy and seemed to be a bit out of it at bedtime. The bastards were drugging us with the bedtime drink of milk that everyone was forced to have. The only reason it hadn't affected Babs was because she hated milk and she would just pretend to drink hers. But when no-one was looking, she used to pour it away, normally in one of the plant pots in the games room where the milk was usually served. The tall man reached inside his jacket pocket and pulled out a brown envelope which he handed to Matron "there is a little extra in there for you. We have some very special clients who wish to pay a visit soon, so I want them treated to the very best if you understand my meaning."

Babs was amazed when she saw Matron begin to thumb through the contents of the brown envelope. It was money but not just a bit there appeared to be thousands and thousands of pounds. There was more money than she had ever seen in her life. Matron's eyes lit up as she flicked through the wad of notes.

"Don't worry I'll make sure they get everything they want their every need will be catered for." The money was then placed in the same desk drawer as the pile of drugs.

"Make sure it is and keep those brats of yours under control. We don't want a repeat of last time when that fuckin alarm went off".

"That's all under control don't concern yourself"

"Ok I'm going now you can walk me to my car I got some more things for you."

After they had both left the office Babs could hear the door being locked from outside and a turn of the handle and a rattle of the door confirmed it was locked. It's now or never thought Babs if I'm going in, I need to do it straight away. Her heart was pounding as she slowly inched up the sash window just wide enough for her to clamber through. She brushed aside the thin net curtain covering the window and pulled herself onto the windowsill. Half in and half out of the room whilst balancing awkwardly on the ledge, she listened for the sound of anyone returning. When nothing could be heard she dug the toes of her trainers into the wall and levered herself through the window and landed in a ball on the floor. Once inside she quickly made her way to the door and checked to make sure it was locked. That way if someone came back, she would have an extra few seconds to escape while they unlocked it. She put her ear to the door and listened for the faintest sounds of anyone coming back along the corridor. There was nothing or anyone making any sound at all, just an absolute empty silence. Babs tiptoed over to Matrons desk and slowly opened the drawer where she had seen the drugs and money being placed. The drawer was almost full to the brim with silver blister packets of pills and resting on top of them was the bulging brown envelope bursting at the seams with wads of banknotes. She began to grab handfuls of packets of pills and started to stuff them into her knickers. There were so many in the drawer that even though she had taken lots and lots it didn't even seem to make the slightest difference to the pile. When she had taken as many as she dared Babs made her way back to the window and carefully looked outside. Everything appeared quiet and still and she was sure no one was about. She felt she had stayed in the office long enough and she didn't want to push her luck so she began to climb out of the window. Before she was fully through the window her mind turned to the money she had seen in the envelope. There were so many notes there and it hadn't been counted so a few would not have been missed she now regretted not taking a few of them. Babs was now back outside safe in the undergrowth she was cursing herself for not taking some money when she had the chance. Then suddenly with a mad rush of blood to the head she recklessly began to climb back inside fully aware that Matron could return at any time. This time she didn't waste time listening for anything she went straight to the desk drawer and opened it quickly. Picking up the brown envelope she plucked a number of notes from the middle of the pile and then lifted her skirt to try and stuff the money in her knickers that were already crammed with the packets of pills. In her haste she had not been as careful and methodical as she would normally be otherwise, she would have heard the movement of the door handle earlier. Oh god she thought as the door began to open, how she could have been so stupid not to pay attention. There was no time to get to the window that was certain she was going to be caught. Voices could be heard in the corridor and the door that was now half open had stopped moving. Matron was speaking to somebody; okay this is my only chance thought Babs. She shut the desk drawer and ran across the room. She was about to launch herself through the open window when she noticed a bright glow coming from outside. It was a member of staff who had gone around the back of the building to have a sneaky fag. She was stuck in limbo she couldn't stay and she couldn't get out. Think she kept screaming to herself silently think. Her eyes scanned the room for a hiding place but there was nothing; the office didn't afford any hidey holes what could she do. She was regretting her stupid decision to go back for the money she was now going to get caught. What on earth would they do to her what atrocities would they inflict on her? Babs was resigned to her fate when she noticed that the faint glow outside the window had disappeared whoever it was who had been having a smoke had finished and they were gone. She wasted no time and escaped through the window as quickly as she could. As she gently pulled the sash window down to its closed position, she saw Matron enter the room and take a seat at her desk. It had been too close for comfort and Babs vowed to herself she would be more careful in future. She had been lucky this time but she might not be so fortunate next time. She remained in the undergrowth for a while and saw Matron count the money in the brown envelope; she was obviously completely unaware that some had been taken out or that any pills were missing.

Babs made her way back to the games room and subsequently resumed the board game she had been playing with Marion. The conversation between Babs and Marion had mostly been idle chitchat until the topic turned to something more sinister.

"I don't know about you Babs but I'm getting a bit bored I want something exciting to happen." Bab's acute insight and armed with the knowledge that Marion was a squealer she knew that this comment was a lead up to something.

"I'm okay" Babs replied indifferently. "I want to do something exciting; we haven't had any fun since someone set the fire alarm off that was great. The fire engines flashing lights and everything I would love to know who did it I bet they are really fun to be with."

Babs was filled with rage inside; she would have loved to tell Marion that she knew all about her being a snitch and then introduce her to her special bar of soap. But somehow, she managed to remain completely calm and composed. She had been expecting this from Marion and had her answer prepared.

"I think I know who set it off" Babs replied casually. Trying not to sound too excited Marion asked who it was. Babs deliberately pretended she hadn't heard the question and rolled the dice to continue their board game.

"I've rolled a six, that's my last counter on the board" Babs said excitedly. Marion couldn't control herself and asked once again with more urgency.

"Who was it that set the fire alarm off?"

Babs was enjoying stringing Marion along; she knew that the snitch was desperate for the information and she had decided to use it for her own ends. There was another girl that Babs didn't like; she was much older than her probably about twelve or thirteen. When Babs first came to Alldahope she had been teased by the older girl concerning her father. She had said some terrible things about him being a gangster and a murderer. Her comments came from newspaper articles and most of the things she said were actually true. But that didn't matter to Babs, it was a matter of pride so Babs had started a fight with her. Although the older much bigger girl had managed to get the better of Babs, she had not come out of the fight unscathed. There was a bald patch where she had lost a large clump of hair and still had the teeth marks on her face where Babs had bitten a chunk out of her. The fight had been vicious enough to frighten the older girl into silence and nothing else was said about Bab's father. But this still wasn't enough for Babs, she needed to be punished further; this would be a warning to all the other girls to not mess with her. "If you tell me, I can get you some sweets or chocolates."

"I don't want any sweets have you got anything else?"

"How about some cigarettes? I can get you as many as you want."

Babs pretended to think about it and replied "Ok I'll have some ciggys. The one who set the alarm off was Patty I heard her telling her friends she smashed it with a chair leg. She wanted to see some firemen I think."

Marion made an excuse about being tired and said she wanted to have a rest as she left, she told Babs that she would get her the cigarettes later. Babs had deliberately chosen cigarettes over chocolates for two reasons the first and most important was that cigarettes were hard to come by and Marion would only be able to get them through Matron. So if the ciggys turned up this would mean that the message had been delivered. Also in here as in prison, cigarettes were almost as good as currency and could be traded. Babs still had the pills and the money stuffed inside her knickers and it was becoming uncomfortable.

She needed to find a safe hiding place for them and get prepared for the next stage of her plan to exact revenge. Babs didn't have long to wait to find out that the message had been delivered.

Whilst they were eating their evening meal Marion whispered in her ear "I've got your ciggys I'll give them to you in the games room when we have our milk." This was fitting nicely into Bab's plan this would work out perfectly she thought. As the cigarettes were surreptitiously passed to Babs she stood up with her glass of milk and walked over as she always did to the main window. She did this deliberately because there was a large plant pot with an overgrown monstrosity of an indoor palm tree which meant that she couldn't be seen. What she normally did now was to pour her milk in the plant pot but tonight was different. She carefully undid the fold of paper she had made and the powder contained within was poured into her milk. The powder had been crushed from a large number of the pills stolen from Matrons office and she hoped she had judged the right amount. She swirled the milk around with her finger until she was sure it was all mixed in. Babs looked around to make certain she could still not be seen and when she was sure she lifted up her skirt and put the ciggys into her knickers. Returning casually from the window she sat next to Marion and placed her contaminated milk next to Marion's.

This was the one time of day when they were allowed to watch television and everyone's attention was given over to one of the popular soap operas. With all the girls glued to the telly Babs picked up Marion's drink of milk having left her own in its place and walked back over to the window. When out of sight behind the palm tree she poured the milk away and then returned to her seat. Once the girls had drunk their milk and only when they had drunk it they were allowed to go to their bedrooms, no one had a choice you were all told you had to drink your evening milk. Babs remained with Marion until she witnessed her drink all the drugged milk. Then with the telly switched off one by one the room began to empty as they all made their way to bed. Bab's room was next to Marion's and they made their way upstairs together. As they said goodnight Babs could see that the drink was beginning to take effect and she already looked drowsy and was beginning to stifle a yawn.

Babs lay awake on top of her bed her thoughts reminiscing about her friend Tipe who she missed so much. She was such an innocent and fragile but lovely young girl. She had been Bab's best friend and now she was dead and the bastard in the next room had something to do with it. Babs had not been able to protect her and she regretted that enormously but she knew one thing she would avenge her friend and soon. In the dead of the night when everything was still and quiet and no-one or anything could be heard stirring Babs decided to make her move. She put her ear to the door and listened for a while, not a sound could be heard so she slowly turned her door handle and gently opened the door. She took the few short steps to Marion's room and again slowly and gently turned the handle and entered the room. Marion was fast asleep lying on her back lightly snoring. Babs walked across the room and sat on the edge of the bed staring into the face of the squealer. The cowardly snitch that had caused the death of her best friend.   "Wake up, wake up." Babs shouted as loud as she dare and began to shake Marion violently.

Marion's eyes opened and she weakly uttered "Help me, help me. I'm not well I can barely move I am so tired."   Babs continued to stare into directly into her eyes and a satisfied broad smile appeared as she saw how incapacitated Marion was.   "Please get me a doctor I think I'm dying, please why aren't you doing anything to help me?" Marion pleaded.   Bab's expression changed. She now had an evil aggressive scowl and she began to speak venomously. "You fuckin grass, I know what you did you backstabbing piece of shit. I've seen you and that cunt Matron scheming behind our backs."

"I'm sorry she made me do it. I didn't mean to hurt Tipe."   "But you fucking did and now she's dead and it's your fault."   Marion was to too tired and weak to cry properly but the tears were streaming down her face. She was beginning to drift back into semi- consciousness and feebly managed to utter in a hushed tone.   "I'm so sorry please help me I'll do anything please get a doctor help me."   "I'll fucking help you bitch; I'll help you go to fucking hell."

Marion looked terrified when she saw what was in Bab's hand.   "Oh please no, please no dear god no." Marion wanted to scream to get help but she was now couldn't move at all, even the muscles controlling her mouth didn't seem to be working it was like everything was shutting down. The lack of control over her muscles meant that she was now beginning to drool and she could feel the saliva cascading down her chin onto the pillow. She could see what Babs was about to do and was absolutely terrified. One by one Babs pushed out tablet after tablet from their blister packets until she had a complete handful. With one hand she stretched open Marion's mouth whilst the other poured the pile of tablets into her mouth. Once they were all in Marion's mouth Babs forcibly closed it and clasped her hand over her mouth and pinched her nose. Marion was unable to resist and she knew that as soon as she was forced to take a breath then she would have to swallow the tablets and that would be the end of her.

"Swallow you bastard, swallow."

Babs took her hand away from Marion's mouth and used her fingers to force the tablets further in. Marion was involuntarily gagging as tablet after tablet was pushed down the back of her throat with Bab's fingers pressing them deeper and deeper. Babs took out a small bottle of water from her pocket and began to pour it down Marion's throat to ensure all the tablets were fully swallowed. Marion had now become completely still and lifeless there was no movement at all even her eyes though wide open were unblinking and cold.

"Die you fucking squealer, die."

Babs turned her head up and looked towards the heavens.

"It's done now Tipe it's done I've got the bastard for you."

Babs wiped the surfaces of the bottle and the packets of tablets with the bedsheet to remove any trace of her prints. She carefully wrapped Marion's hand around the bottle and some of the wrappers and placed them on the floor. Babs stood up "That's you done, now for that fucking Matron"

4

UPSTAIRS DOWNSTAIRS

The flight from Spain had been delayed and didn't land at Birmingham until the early hours of the morning. Shirley and Sam had spent most of the delay trying their very best to drink the Carlsberg bar in Alicante airport dry, because of the late hour and the girls being a little drunk and extremely tired they decided it would be easier for both of them to stay at Sam's.

Sam lived in a big Victorian three storey detached house opposite Stourbridge park. It was all bought and paid for. She had managed to pay off the mortgage and the substantial property had been fully modernised and brought up to date. She had been able to do this because of her very successful business that rewarded her extremely well. Men were more than ready to pay her large sums of money for her unique services. She was also able to satisfy her own dark needs and desires. After having had a few hours drunken sleep they were both now sitting at the breakfast table nursing cups of black coffee reminiscing about their holiday. As Shirley sipped at her steaming hot drink she asked.

"I wonder how long those guys stopped in the Pig and Whistle when they realised that we weren't going to show."

Sam laughed "Who cares, they served their purpose a free night of drinks and a good time to boot. But they're typical blokes they think with their cocks instead of their head so they deserve everything they get."

"I've seen you do it before but I'm still amazed by the way you can twist men round your little finger"

"Let's just forget about them they weren't the first and they won't be the last anyway what time are you on duty today?"

"I start at 2 o'clock, I always hate the first day back it takes ages to get back up to speed with everything that's happened. Especially supervising Latifeo he avoids and passes over so much work it's unbelievable. I'll spend most of today tidying up the mess he will have inevitably left. How about you what are your plans for the day?"

Sam suddenly sat bolt upright and blurted out.

"Oh Christ my punter in the cellar I'd forgotten all about him the poor bastard he's been down there eight days. I hope he hasn't snuffed it I earn a small fortune from him".

Shirley looked in disbelief "I thought you were joking, are you seriously telling me that you've got someone tied up in the cellar and they've been there over a week."

"He's an ultra-extreme submissive masochist he wanted to be tied up for a week. I get paid a lot of money to abuse him, in fact if he's still alive I will charge him for an extra day. Come downstairs if you don't believe me."

They both left the kitchen and walked along the hallway towards the large dark wooden door that gave access to the cellar. Shirley thought how foreboding it looked. It reminded her of something you would see in a Frankenstein horror film. She could imagine the door creaking slowly open as it was opened by some scary figure. Sam tilted a large plant pot adjacent to one side of the door and slid her and underneath and produced a large old-fashioned key.

"Good grief you don't lock him in do you, what happens if there's a fire?" Shirley asked incredulously.

"It wouldn't make any difference to him would it; he's already chained up so if there was a fire, he'd be dead meat anyway".

With a shrug of her shoulders Shirley nodded in agreement. When Sam began to open the door the first thing that hit Shirley was the smell. It was difficult to describe but it was like a mixture of a dank musty smell tinged with a stagnant body odour. The cellar was dimly lit and as they made their way down the stone steps it was taking some time for their eyes to adjust. Once at the bottom and with her eyes now accustomed to the light Shirley looked around and took in the surroundings. She had never been down here before and it was not as she was expecting. The walls consisted of dark painted bricks and the floor was made up of some sort of old cobblestones. It didn't match the rest of the house whereas the upstairs had been fully modernised and was bright and airy, the cellar had been left untouched. It resembled a prison cell something you could envisage in an old Dickensian. It was an impressively large area and Shirley followed Sam to the far end. Their eyes were now fully used to the dim light they were now looking at some poor wretch dressed in black leather suit with a full-face mask. A portion of the suit had been cut away around the genital area and the backside showing an expanse of white almost anaemic flesh. This had obviously been removed to enable the tethered captive to use the toilet. The toilet was in fact nothing more than a bucket and it was nearing its capacity it was almost full to the brim with foul smelling urine and faeces. Shirley began to wretch when she saw and at the same time smelt the disgusting filth. The only other thing this pathetic creature had access to was a hosepipe connected to a water standpipe projecting up from the cobbled floor. The leather clad figure was shackled with a metal chain and manacle attached to his arm; the other end of the chain was secured firmly to the wall at a height of approximately three feet. There was no sound or any sign of movement coming from the poor creature.

Sam and Shirley looked at each other their faces showing grave concern both obviously fearing that what they were looking at was dead.

Sam gingerly approached the foul-smelling body and stooped down.

"Victor" she continually repeated as she shook the apparently lifeless body by the shoulder. There was no response not even a murmur or the faintest of movements. In desperation the shaking increased in intensity the body being shook so violently that the head continually banged against the wall. "Wake up you fucking pervert wake up." She screamed.

Shirley took hold of Sam and pulled her friend away from the body

"it's no good he's obviously dead."

Sam shook her head and then began to shout at the lifeless body "You selfish bastard how dare you peg it, you worthless piece of shit" as she repeatedly and violently kicked out at the corpse before stamping on his head. When she had finished venting her anger she spat on the body and asked Shirley "What shall we do with him now?"

Shirley started to think methodically using her police training and forensic knowledge

"Right first things first, what was his name and does anyone know that he is here?"

"His name is Victor S Petersham and no one knows he's here. He lives on his own, never been married and he doesn't have any kids".

"That's a strange name why the S in the middle?"

"He's a well to do businessman from a wealthy background he told me his parents put the S in the middle just to sound impressive. He has his own factory adjacent to the Stourbridge canal. It's shut down now but it was some form of foundry or steel mill he must be worth an absolute fortune he gave me five grand to chain him up."

"So we haven't got to worry about anyone looking for him that's a good start. What we have to do now is to get rid of the body and remove all the forensic trace evidence. So firstly don't spit on him again and clean the blood of your shoes where you stamped on his head"

Sam went upstairs and did as she was told and began cleaning her shoes with bleach, leaving Shirley downstairs with the body. When she re-joined Shirley in the cellar, she was standing over the body and assessing the scene.

"Right this is the plan" Shirley announced.

"He is quite a big guy so we would have trouble humping him about so we will chop him into pieces in the cellar and burn him. Your back garden is not overlooked so we will use that big old oil drum. Then we will hose this place down and bleach it everywhere. I need you to go and get something to chop him up with. I'll use the hosepipe and start to wash things down.

Sam went into the back garden and searched through the shed collecting as many things as she see that they could use to dissect the body. Together with some knives from the kitchen Sam made her way back down the cellar. Shirley looked at the array of knives and tools and picked up a large rusty saw.

"This should do nicely I think we'll start with his head, if you grab hold of his hair Sam and keep his head still, I'll saw through his neck."

Sam grabbed hold of Victors hair and pulled him away from the wall a short distance so that Shirley had room to use the saw. Shirley put the rusty blade against the pale fleshy part of his neck and instructed Sam to take a firm hold. Shirley pulled the saw blade across the neck in a practise swing and as she did so the body let out a huge scream. Both Shirley and Sam jumped up began to scream hysterically in shock. Victor had now gotten to his feet and was holding his hand against the wound on his neck.

"My god we thought you were dead Victor" Sam shrieked.

Victor began to speak in muffled tones. He was obviously extremely weak and feeling the effects of spending a week in a cold damp cellar with nothing more than water from the hose pipe as sustenance. Victor managed to explain that for the last couple of days he had been slipping in and out of consciousness.   "Let's get you upstairs and get you sorted out" said Sam.

With help from Shirley and Sam the leather clad incredibly weak poor wretch made it up the cellar steps into the warmth and comfort of the house. After a couple of hours warmth a hot shower, clean clothes and some high protein food and drink inside him Victor though still weak as a kitten was much improved from the near-death state the girls had found him in.

The three of them were sitting round the kitchen table drinking tea and chatting. From their conversation it was clear that Victor was obviously a well-educated guy. He was extremely well spoken and very knowledgeable. Shirley was perplexed something was bugging her She couldn't help thinking, how does a nice intellectual guy who comes across as very warm and amiable get his kicks from being tied up and abused. Shirley could hold her tongue no longer she just had to know.

"Victor can I ask you a somewhat personal question?"

Victor instinctively knew what the question was going to be and why she wanted to ask it so he simply nodded his head.

"Of course ask away."

"Well I'm intrigued as to why someone such as you gets some sort of pleasure or kick out of being chained up in a cellar for a week. Why do you do it and what do you get out of it."

Victor was quiet for a while he was obviously mulling over his response. Eventually he took a deep breath and began to speak.

"I have an illness, a perversion but it's a sick horrible one it's a depraved and abhorrent sexual perversion. I am so ashamed of it that I have contemplated suicide on several occasions. Before I tell you what it is you must understand that although I have these feelings, I have never given way to them and I have never indulged in them. I realise that it would be wholly wrong for me to practise my perversion. I have tried several things to cure me of this perversion including joining a self-help group. That didn't work because I found out that the members weren't interesting in curing or controlling their perversion. In actual fact the group wanted to do the opposite their purpose was to participate in it and to actively recruit new members so I left. I then looked into chemical castration but that could have long term serious side effects. Then I came up with the idea of self-humiliation and submissive masochism, this process gives me a feeling of satisfaction. It's as if I'm being punished for being a pervert. This reminds me of how bad my perversion is and how sick it would be of me to partake and prevents me from wanting to indulge."   Both girls were fascinated by Victors account and were desperately eager to find out what this so-called sick perversion was.

Sam was the first to speak.   "Go on then Victor tells us more we've got to know what is so bad that you have to subject yourself to this kind of treatment."   "Remember I have never and will never indulge in it I will do everything in my power to prevent it. My perversion is that I get sexually excited by kids I have paedophiliac feelings. But that is as far as it will ever go just feeling nothing else, I will never allow myself to take them further."

Shirley and Sam were stunned they stared at each other in shock and disbelief. Unknown to Victor both girls were brought up in a children's home and the pair of them had been subjected to the vilest and sickest sexual practises imaginable at the hands of predatory paedophiles.

They both loathed and detested paedophiles and they had spent a lot of their adulthood exacting revenge on the beasts who had robbed them of their childhoods. They turned their attention towards Victor who was now sitting head bowed in disgrace and gently weeping. He managed to quietly utter through his tears.

"Please don't think badly of me you must believe me when I say I will never succumb to my fetish."

Neither girl knew what to think. Should they regard him as the lowest of the low disgusting pervert or admire him for his resolve and determination in combating and fighting against his depraved feelings. Shirley and Sam had an incredible almost telepathic empathy with each other and they both knew that they were experiencing the same feelings and mixed emotions. They realised they would need to speak with each other in some depth when Victor had gone in order to try and make sense of what they had just been told.

After an uneasy hiatus in the conversation Sam and Victor began to discuss and arrange times and dates for his next session which was to be in four days' time. Normally Victor would avail himself of Sam's services every couple of days but because he felt so weak after his mammoth session, he needed a longer recovery time.

Victor lived in a houseboat moored in Stourbridge canal basin near a well-known local building called the bonded warehouse. It was a short walk from Sam's house opposite Stourbridge Park and Victor would usually take a casual stroll home via a few hostelries where he indulged in his other passion of drinking real ale. However on this occasion due to his physical state he had arranged for a taxi. Victor knew he had taken a huge risk in confiding in Sam and Shirley concerning his fetish and he hoped they would understand. He realised it had caused an atmosphere around the kitchen table between them all. But he had desperately needed for some time someone with whom he could unburden his guilty secret. The taxi arrived and sounded its horn a few times, Victor stood up from the table and looked towards the girls in a humbled almost cuckold manner. In a low and quiet voice he pleaded with the girls.   "Please don't think badly of me, my sick perverted feelings are something I didn't choose. Believe me when I say I will always do everything in my power to keep them in check."   As he left, he put a bundle of notes into Sam's hand.

"Thanks for everything, there's an extra couple of thousand for you".

Sam and Shirley sat back down round the kitchen table and stared at each other in utter disbelief and bewilderment. It was Sam who eventually spoke.   "Wow I did not see that coming, I've been doing business with a paedo for all this time a dirty rotten kiddy fiddler. "

"He's got paedo feelings" Sam said, "But if he is to be believed he doesn't act on them and he doesn't interfere with kids".

Sam thought for a moment "If what he says is true that he hasn't and will never succumb to his perverted feelings then he is to be applauded but how can we be sure of that. He's incredibly generous and I want to milk him of as much money that I can. But if I continue to do business with him, I need to be one hundred positive."

"Don't do anything rash for the moment Sam; just keep on doing what you have for him as normal, I've got an idea."

5

THESE BOOTS AREN'T MADE FOR WALKING

Detective Sergeant Shirley Wallows strolled into her office at Brierley Hill Police Station and sat down behind her desk. The office was quite small, nowhere near as big as her previous office at the now closed Stourbridge Station.

She was grateful however for the fact that she still retained an office to herself, most of the staff who had been relocated from Stourbridge had been forced to office share often in quite cramped conditions. She had only been on holiday for a week. Her area of responsibility was to supervise the detective officers responsible for investigating crime in Stourbridge only yet her desk was overflowing with files and reports for her attention. First day back bloody hate it thought Wallows as she picked up the first file. It related to a number of burglaries in the Oldswinford area which is a small village on the outskirts of Stourbridge. The crimes had been investigated without success by two of her Detective Constables, Frank Fergas and Robert Peeves.

The pair of them habitually worked together as if they were joined at the hip and as such, they had been given various nicknames by the other officers including Laurel and Hardy. But the name that they were invariably referred to most often was dumb and dumber. Due to cutbacks in police numbers Shirley only had five staff to supervise and two of those had been seconded to a specialist unit investigating a large number of violent carjacking in the Stourbridge area.

They were also investigating house burglaries where violence was used in order to take vehicles by stealing the keys. In a lot of these crimes various weapons had been used including quite frighteningly iron bars and a machete. Shirley had no choice or say in the matter concerning her staff being seconded and she simply had to struggle through with only three staff. They were the idle good for nothing Latifeo together with dumb and dumber. This meant that most crimes were now only given lip service in terms of investigations by her staff. Her detectives were never going to set the world alight and certainly wouldn't overwork themselves and Shirley was well aware of this. But they were easy to supervise as they all liked to keep their heads down and not make waves, that way they could indulge themselves in their own particular interests whilst supposed to be working. Latifeo liked to sneak away from work and see whom he thought was his girlfriend the stunning Sam Gail, he was too stupid and besotted with Sam to realise that he was simply another customer who Sam was using to make money.

Dumb and dumber on the other hand were well known as what was commonly referred to as chubby chasers. They could often be seen frequenting pubs and clubs that hosted grab a granny nights especially when they were working the late shift as area CID cover.

Detective Constable Trevor Peeves had a fetish bordering on an obsession for the larger ladies whilst DC Frank Fergas wasn't choosy, he would make a play for anything that moved. Also one had to be wary of Frank Fergas he was known to be a backstabber and it was widely accepted that he was a snitch for the bosses. He would appear to be friendly to your face but in reality, he would always be looking for an opportunity to stitch someone up in order to enhance his own reputation with senior officers. In the same way that it was common knowledge within the Police station that Latifeo was bone idle, the same applied to the sexual exploits of Dumb and Dumber. After a couple of hours of signing off investigations as no further enquiries required she sat back in her chair and rubbed her eyes and stifled a large yawn. This is not why I joined the police force for this is not what police work is supposed to be about she thought. She knew that there were still plenty of lines of inquiry that could be pursued into each case but from a practical standpoint it was simply impossible from both a time perspective and grossly inadequate staffing levels. Shirley was very much a hands-on type of police officer and she enjoyed working hard and investigating real and serious crime. She hated with a passion the endless and ever-increasing paperwork and red tape. She was about to pick up another file when her line manager walked into the office.

Detective Inspector Grant Courtan breezed in and made himself comfortable on a chair opposite Shirley at her desk.

"Welcome back Shirley, how was Benidorm?"

"The usual, lots to eat and drink plenty of sun I had a great time thanks."

"I bet you're glad to be back" Grant said mockingly with a huge grin spread across his face in an equally mocking fashion Shirley replied.

"Yes, I'm having a great time sifting through this mountain of paperwork I assume you are going to bring me up to date with what's been happening."

"You got it; it won't take too long though it's been fairly quiet crime wise for us. The same can't be said for your two detectives attached to the carjacking unit though it's reached almost epidemic proportions. The attacks have also become more violent and more frequent. So it looks like you won't be getting them back for considerable time." Grant then ran through the previous week's events and the more significant crimes that she needed to be aware of. Apart from the tragic demise of the young police officer who had been dragged to her death over the balcony there wasn't anything that greatly interested Shirley. Most of it was mundane and routine that was until Grant outlined the suicides at Alldahope. Shirley's ears pricked up at hearing the name of the childrens home where she had been bought up.

Shirley had not told anyone about her upbringing and it was her intention to never let it be known that she had spent all of her childhood in care. She especially didn't want anyone to be aware of her association with Alldahope. The place held a lot of bad memories for her; she together with Sam Gail had been subject to the most appalling abuse. When Grant had finished his briefing Shirley asked.

"Can you tell me a bit more about the suicides at Alldahope?"

"There's not a lot more I can tell you they were quite straightforward as far as I know but if you want more info then ask Latifeo he was the investigating officer on both of them."   At that Grant stood up welcomed Shirley back once again and left the office.   Shirley looked at the pile of papers on her desk that still required her attention but she couldn't concentrate her mind was racing with thoughts of the events at Alldahope. She picked up her phone and dialled the detective constables office. The phone rang and rang until it was eventually answered by Latifeo.

"Ah just the person can you come to my office please Oli?"   "Welcome back boss I'll be right there".

Shirley sat back in her chair her thoughts still with the events at Alldahope, if she had been here at the time, she would have allocated a different officer to investigate the suicides. She knew Latifeo would only have conducted the minimum amount of investigation needed and if there were more to them than straight forward suicides then he would be unlikely to find out.   "Did you have a nice holiday boss" Latifeo asked chirpily as he entered Shirley's office.

"Yes, it was great thanks weather was good I had a great time, but it's back to work now. The reason I want to speak to you is concerning the suicides at Alldahope. What can you tell me about them?"   "Well there's not a lot to tell they were both tragic but simple suicides the first one was Tipe Moor she was in care because her alcoholic mother couldn't look after her. She slit her wrist on the day that her mother was coming to see her. She was apparently really excited to see her and was looking forward to her visit she had been telling everyone that her mom was going to take her home. But because her mother was late Tipe assumed she wasn't going to turn up again. Her mom had failed to turn up to lots of previously prearranged visits. Mostly down to her alcoholism she would either be found in the street paralytic drunk or sometimes in the lock up here. I suppose it was the final straw she must have felt as if she was on her own and killed herself in despair. Or possibly it was a cry for help that went wrong but either way the poor mite ended her own life."

"Was it witnessed by anyone or did anybody hear anything?"

Latifeo shook his head "No, Tipe was waiting for her mother in the interview room on her own she was shown in there by the matron. She was later discovered dead by her mother who was the next person in the room."

"And how about scenes of crime what did their examination reveal"

"There was no SOCO examination. I asked for them but they said they were too busy as they were dealing with a couple of carjacking's. But I did submit the blade for examination it was like a small craft knife."

"Have you had the results back yet?"

"Yes boss, fingerprints in blood on the handle of the knife were found that matched with the girls and they were the only prints on there. PC Ainslo also took some photographs of the scene on her phone which I've had developed." Shirley shook her head at the mention of the name of the brutally murdered young officer.

I've been wondering about that she was only a probationer so why did she go to the flat on her own why didn't anyone go with her?"

"I offered to go with her but she was adamant that she wanted to be independent and go alone" Latifeo lied.

Shirley mulled this information through in her mind, something didn't seem quite right with that statement but she pushed it to the back of her mind for the time being before asking.

"What did the photographs show?"

"Not a lot to be honest" Latifeo said with a shrug of his shoulders "They just show a load of blood where she was found in the corner of the room"

"And how about the post-mortem what was the pathologists conclusion?"   Latifeo shook his head "There was no post-mortem the chief inspector deemed it not necessary because it was a straightforward suicide, and it didn't justify the expense." Shirley was becoming increasingly agitated at the total lack of investigation into what see saw as a tragic and needless death of a vulnerable young girl. She didn't want Latifeo to see her frustration so she kept her thoughts to herself and decided to move on.

"Ok now how about the second death tell me the circumstances".   "the second one was a young girl called Marion Fern she was a close friend of Tipe and its assumed that her friends death tipped her over the edge and it drove her to take her own life".

"How did she do it did she slit her wrists also?"

"No she took an overdose she managed to get

hold of some strong sedatives the empty blister packets were found next to her body" "Did scenes of crime find anything out of the ordinary?" "No scene examination or post-mortem because like the first one it was deemed non-suspicious"

"Where did she get the tablets from has that been established?" "No that's not been established they were prescription only so I she most likely got them from a drug dealer. But as you know yourself there are so many dealers in Stourbridge it's like looking for a needle in a haystack." "Please tell me that a toxicology exam has been done" Shirley uttered in an exasperated tone.

"Afraid not boss again it was deemed not necessary" Shirley shook her head in despair she was not happy with what she considered to be an apathetic approach to the deaths of two young girls. Their deaths needed to be fully investigated and not merely given lip service and swept under the carpet.

Their conversation was interrupted by a knock on the office door and a young officer walked in "Sorry to disturb you sarge but there is a reporter here who wants to speak with you".

"Ok could you show him in please, Oli I think that's all for now". Latifeo stood up and made his way to the door as he did so he turned and remarked "Good luck with the reporter I'll bet it's that nosey busybody Martin from the Stourbridge news, he never takes no for an answer Latifeo then went bright red in embarrassment as he turned his head back and saw Martin standing right in front of him obviously well within earshot. "Hello Martin" he spluttered awkwardly as he quickly made his way out of the office.

Shirley looked Martin square in the eye as he walked over to her desk barely able to contain herself trying her hardest not to laugh. When they were sure that Latifeo was out of earshot they both began chuckle. "Did you see the look on his face when he turned around and saw me, I thought he was going to die of embarrassment" Martin blurted out in between fits of laughter.

Shirley and Martin knew each other well and they held each other in high esteem the reason behind their respect for each other was their single-mindedness and they both shared a passion and dedication for their respective jobs. They were staunch believers in justice and both had a dogged determination to see that it carried out even if it meant stepping on peoples toes or bending a few rules.

"Where did you go on your holiday Shirley?" Martin enquired "Nowhere special I just had a week away with my friend in Benidorm it was good fun though just the thing to re-charge the batteries if you know what I mean".

"Yes, I do know what you mean I could do with a break but right now I feel like I'm banging my head against the wall. There were a couple of things happened while you were away that I can't shake off my mind they just don't seem right."

"Are you talking about the suicides at Alldahope?" "Yes, you have obviously been made aware of them there are a few things I'm not happy with but I've tried talking to Latifeo and your Chief inspector but they don't seem interested".

"Ok what's giving you cause for concern?"

"Well as far as I can work out the first girl was found by her mother when she walked into the interview room. But as you know her mother was an alcoholic who couldn't cope very well so the policy at Alldahope as in other similar places is that the girl wouldn't have been left alone with her mother she would have been accompanied or supervised at all times."

"Are you implying the mother had something to do with it "Shirley asked in surprise?"

"No that's not it at all I just can't understand the lack of supervision and how the girl managed to sneak a knife into the room because again as you know they are subject to constant and frequent random searches. They even use those hand-held metal detectors so even if it was well concealed it would have been picked up. I spoke to Matron about this and she couldn't give any explanation and to be honest she didn't seem overly concerned even though she's the one responsible for safety procedures."

Shirley listened to what Martin had to say and was quietly considering to herself the implications and possible scenarios for the security lapse. Having spent nearly all of her childhood at Alldahope she was fully aware of the couldn't care less attitude of the staff. But this was her secret no one knew she was brought up in care at Alldahope she had never told anyone about her upbringing and vowed never to divulge it to anyone. "I can understand that their procedures are slipshod but that is not much to go on is it."

"No I agree but there have been suicides at Alldahope before in the not-too-distant past, probably before the start of your police career but I can remember them well and they also didn't feel right."

"What methods were used in the previous suicides Martin can you remember?"

"I didn't deal with them myself but as far as I can recollect the two previous ones cut their wrists but the unusual thing about them for me was, they both used the same type of knife and it was never established where they got the identical knives from."

"What type of knife was it? "Shirley asked curiously

"The knife used was a craft knife the sort one would use in model making"

Shirley sat bolt upright at this news and Martin knew he had struck a nerve.

"What is it what have I said that has got you so interested"

unsure as to whether she should divulge the information to a reporter she instinctively felt as if she could trust Martin.

"Well I shouldn't really tell you this but Tipe also slit her wrists with a craft knife can you remember exactly what they looked like?"

"My recollection is a bit vague but as far as the knife is concerned, I can remember what it looked like as if it were yesterday."

Shirley opened up the envelope that Latifeo had left on her desk containing the photographs of the scene of Tipes death including the bloodstained knife. The photograph was put to Martin with the words
"Did they look anything like that?"

Martin studied the photograph and then lifted his head up and looked straight at Shirley, the expression on his face was like he had seen a ghost. In a sombre tone Martin said in astonishment "They are absolutely identical."

Shirley knew immediately that something was dreadfully amiss with the recent and historical suicides. For an identical knife to be used three times on separate occasions. Compounded by the fact that extensive enquiries had been made and it had not been established where the knives had come from. This was far more than an incredible co-incidence and this should cast enough doubt on the suicides to justify a full investigation.

"I think you have a point Martin there is something not right about all this I will speak with the Chief Inspector and see if he will authorise further and more detailed investigations."

"Good luck with that I've already spoken to Trevor Cappoten and he basically didn't want to know I've also spoken with Latifeo and he's adamant that they are not suspicious."

"I know he's under considerable financial constraints in terms of allocating resources and he does tend to side-line a lot of enquiries but even he must take this anomaly with the knives seriously. I will speak with him this afternoon and let you know what he says. Regards Latifeo he just wants an easy life he's what I call a coaster so just leave it with me."

Feeling satisfied that the deaths were now going to be treated seriously Martin stood up and firmly shook hands with Shirley.

"If you do get any news perhaps, we could meet up later in the pub?"

Martin suggested.

"Ok that sounds fine I'll probably ring you later."

Pleasantries concluded Martin left the office and headed back to Copthall house the new location of the Stourbridge News.

Shirley sat back in her chair and considered the implications of what she had just learned. Whatever the truth was there were grounds for further and much deeper investigation. Her biggest problem now would be to convince the Chief Inspector and win him over in order to allocate resources. She knew it would be hard work given the extremely sparse resources. If she revealed details of her upbringing at Alldahope and the abuse she had suffered she knew that swing the balance but she was determined to keep the dark secrets of her past firmly hidden away. The only person she could talk with about the abuse was her best friend Sam Gail and that was simply because they had both been through and experienced the same horrific acts of depravity. She decided to give it some thought and get her rationale prepared before speaking with the Chief.

Patty Stola was crying her eyes out floods of tears were seeping through her fingers that were forlornly trying to stem them from cascading down her face. In between the uncontrollable sobbing she managed to repeatedly blurt out the words "I didn't do it I swear I never touched the fire alarm.

" She was sitting on a chair in the middle of Matrons office her head bowed towards the floor her body shaking like a leaf in fear. Matron took a deep breath and stared at the pathetic bundle of nerves before her wondering what to do next. If her informant Marion Fern had been correct then this gibbering wreck was responsible for setting off the fire alarm. Which meant she knew more about what went on at Alldahope than was good for her and she needed to be dealt with. But surely, she would have confessed by now. Even the most hardened of Alldahopes residents would have cracked by now. She was beginning to have nagging doubts, could her snitch have been wrong, but of course annoyingly she couldn't ask her because the selfish little girl had killed herself. Either way she knew she couldn't afford to take chances with what Patty knew or may know she needed to be silenced. Convinced that she would get nowhere with her continued harsh interrogation Matron decided to adopt a different approach.

"I had such high hopes for you as well Patty, I had earmarked a special project for you but you've spoilt it all now." Matron said in a sympathetic tone of voice designed to stimulate Pattys attention.

Sensing a change in tone and a possible way out from this constant barrage of threats and the seemingly endless intimidating questions Patty asked meekly and subserviently.

"What was it I can still do it whatever it is I promise I'll be a good girl honest".

Patty looked at Matron hoping for some crumb of comfort some sign of hope that there was a way out of this mess, this nightmare situation that she was in and didn't even why or where it had come from. She had no idea why Matron was repeatedly accusing her of setting off a fire alarm but she did know that despite all her pleading Matron didn't and would never believe her. Whatever this other thing she was talking about had to be better than this. Matron knew that she had Patty on the hook and that she would comply with anything she was asked to do. She could see the fear and desperation in the young defenceless girls eyes. Patty pleaded again this time almost begging "Please tell me what it is I know I can do it honest".

Matron took a deep breath and replied, "Ok but you must promise me something first"

"Anything you want anything at all" Patty said with obvious relief.

"Well then I want you together with Sue Birther to organise a field trip for the rest of the girls. I need the pair of you to go and identify as many wild species of flowers shrubs and plants as you can. You can then set everyone else the task of searching for and identifying as many of them as possible. Do you think you could manage that?" Pattys heart rose immediately not only did this mean that this situation was over she was actually going to be doing something she would enjoy. It would also get her away from this place which was an added bonus. The only downside to it was working with Sue Birther who was known to be an extremely nasty bullying type. She was a huge girl for her age and very intimidating everyone was scared of her and what she said you did without question. But even working with that horrible bully was preferable to sitting in Matrons office being accused of something she hadn't done.

"I can do that please let me do it please."

"Ok but remember Patty this is meant to be a nice surprise for the rest of the girls, so must not tell anyone that you are doing it do you understand?"   Patty who was now overjoyed simply nodded her head in agreement   "Sue has all the details and the appropriate reference books to help you I have identified an ideal place not far away by the river Stour where it passes under the viaduct. You should because of the river be able to find plenty of different species of flora. And remember when I said tell no-one I mean absolutely no-one is that clear?"

Breathing a lot less heavily now Patty once again nodded and said with a sigh of relief "Yes."

Patty was told to go and wait in the games room for Sue and once again reminded to say nothing about it to anyone.

Babs Guthy saw Patty walk into the games room and watched as she took a seat near the pool table where two older girls were trying to have a game. But given the state of the cloth and the battered equipment it was almost impossible. Babs was very astute for her age and she had seen Patty go into Matrons office. She had been in there a long time and given the redness of her eyes had obviously been crying. Babs didn't like Patty she was too stuck up to prim and proper for her liking and she wondered if she had been questioned about setting the fire alarm off. Babs had deliberately and falsely told Tipe that Patty was the one who had set the alarm off as a test. She wanted to see if the information would get back to Matron and she was now pretty sure it had been. It wasn't long before big Sue walked in and gruffly told Patty to come with her. Without replying Patty subserviently obeyed and both the girls left the room. Babs immediately went to the window and saw both the girls walk down the driveway and out the main gate. Babs instinctively knew something was up but what on earth could it be. She decided she would keep a close eye on the pair of them when they get back.

The river Stour seemed more like a brook Patty thought, its waters quietly lapped against the banks as it flowed almost silently and effortlessly through the meadow and under the huge Stourbridge viaduct. It was very peaceful where they were the only other sounds to be heard apart from the distant rumble of cars using the Stourbridge to Halesowen road were the birds who tweeted away merrily.

Big Sue had seemed to Patty to be totally uninterested in their task of identifying wildflowers and the like and she was obviously preoccupied with something else. This didn't bother Patty though she was just happy to be outside in the sunshine and the fresh air. Sue had barely spoken the whole time the girls had been there. When eventually she did speak she turned the air blue with her tirade.

"This is fucking useless I can't find anything down here it's a load of shit c'mon let's go up there and get a better look."

Not wishing to get on the wrong side of Sue, Patty simply followed along obediently without saying anything. When Sue began hacking her way through the undergrowth on the embankment adjacent to the viaduct Patty dared to speak.

"Where exactly are we going?"

"Up there to the top" Sue replied whilst pointing with her outstretched arm to the railway track that ran along what seemed to be the sky-high structure. Nervously Patty replied, "I don't think we are supposed to go up there were not allowed."

"Don't be such a wimp c'mon follow me" and undeterred Sue continued her climb up the embankment. Closely followed by the ever more nervous Patty who was too scared to defy the orders being meted out by this overbearing bully. When they had at long last reached the top both gasping for breath Patty once again uttered her concerns about being there.

"We shouldn't be here what do we do if a train comes along?"

"Don't be so stupid there's no bleeding trains run along here if we walk along here, we can see better we might see some stupid flowers or something now keep up."

Patty was more scared of Sue than she was of the viaduct so she decided to follow and together they awkwardly made their way to the centre of the bridge. The track was full of ballast which made it awkward to move quickly and the stones hurt the soles of Pattys feet her old ill-fitting boots only had a thin lining and didn't offer much protection. A brick wall lined the sides of the bridge which made Patty feel a little more secure but she was still scared of what would happen if a train were to come.

"I don't like this can we go back down now" Patty pleaded.

"We haven't looked for any flowers yet," said Sue.

"It's too high up to see anything let alone tiny little flowers lets go back down" Patty pleaded.

"I'll tell you what if you just have one look over the edge to see if you can see any crappy plants or anything and then we will go back down".

Sue pointed towards the wall and said,

"Go on then get a move on."

Desperate to get back down to the ground Patty thought that if she had a quick peep over the edge of the wall knowing that it was far too high up to see anything then that would satisfy the bully. She was renowned for always having to get her own way so this would be the only option

"I'll have a quick look and then we can go straight back down ok".

Patty slowly and with great trepidation inched her way to the wall taking one small step at a time. On reaching the parapet she gingerly poked her head over the edge and was immediately filled with dread. The drop to the floor was phenomenal it was even further down than she had imagined. She had never been so high up in her life.

"Have a proper look lean over a bit you'll be alright" Sue said from behind.   Even more anxious to get it over and done with Patty did as she was told and leant over the brick parapet. It was impossible to see anything as small as flowers or shrubs even the river Stour looked like a tiny trickle. I've done it now Patty thought that should shut her up now. But before she could pull herself away from the edge, she suddenly found herself being lifted up into the air and in a split second she was over the edge of the wall and dangling by her feet suspendered in mid-air hundreds of feet up in the sky.

Patty began to scream there was nothing between her and the ground.   "Oh god what's happening help me Sue help me for god's sake"   "Stop your fucking screaming you stupid bitch and listen to me" Sue laughed.

Patty turned her head around to see Sue with arms outstretched over the edge of the wall grasping hold of Pattys boots one in each hand with a huge smile on her face.

"Now listen to me I don't know how long I can hold you here without dropping you so answer me quickly understand?"

Patty shrieked in terror "Pull me up pull me up please I'll tell you anything please pull me up."

"I'll pull you up when you answer my questions now tell me did you set off the fire alarm?"

"No it wasn't me honestly please get me up" Patty begged

"How do I know you are not lying to me remember I can only hold you for so long?"

"Honestly it wasn't me I told Matron that it wasn't me please get me up"

"If it wasn't you then who was it tell me quickly or you are going for a little flying lesson"

Between the terrified tears Patty managed to blurt out repeatedly that it wasn't her and she didn't know who had done it she didn't even know where the fire alarm was.

Sue was quite sure that Patty was telling the truth anyone being dangled hundreds of feet in the air would have owned up by now. As strong as she was, she could also feel her arms beginning to ache.

"Ok I'll pull you back up now but if I find out you've been lying and making a fool out of me, I will bring you back up here and throw you over do you understand.

"Yes, yes please lift me back up" Patty begged once more.

Patty felt herself rising back up towards the safety of the parapet, almost there now. Sue had underestimated how hard it would be to lift Patty back up. It was one thing to hold something still at arm's length but to raise it up was harder than she had imagined and she began to struggle. She decided the best thing to do would be instead of lifting her slowly it would be easier to try and yank her back up in one swift movement. So she held Patty steady for a second to regain her strength took a deep breath counted one two three in her head and jerked her arms up as quickly as she could.

"Oh shit" Sue stood there adjacent to the parapet with mouth agog and her arms stretched out in the air firmly grasping a pair of shabby girls boots and that was all. In her attempt to lift Patty back up with a quick movement she had only succeeded in pulling off her boots. Poor screaming Patty was now hurtling down headlong towards the ground and certain death.

6

THE GANG OF FOUR

Detective Sergeant Shirley Wallows was fuming mad she felt like she had spent the last thirty minutes banging her head against the wall. She was in the office of detective Chief Inspector Trevor Cappoten and had meticulously outlined her reasoning for further investigations to be made into the deaths at Alldahope and getting nowhere fast.

Reluctantly Shirley decided to give it one more go otherwise the morning will have been a complete waste of her time.

"All I'm saying is that there has been two recent suicides and if you consider there have been other suicides in the past then we need to look more deeply into them. We are talking about the loss of young girls lives they shouldn't be brushed under the carpet because of financial constraints."

Detective Chief Inspector was equally fuming mad,

"What do you mean previous deaths at Alldahope they happened some time ago and long before you joined the force you shouldn't be aware of them. I know what's happened here. You've been talking to that nosey reporter Martin from the Stourbridge News he's been filling your head with all sorts of nonsense."

"Yes he did mention them to me but it's a bit much to say he's filled my head with nonsense" Shirley replied a little indignantly.

The DCI stood up put his hands on his desk and in an attempt to intimidate her leant forward towards Shirley looking her straight in the eye and said forcefully.

"Look I'm going to tell you the same as I've told him the suicides at Alldahope whilst regrettable and tragic are just straight forward suicides. The deaths have been fully investigated including the actions of the staff at the home. Ideally supervision of the girls could be better but the staff are very thin on the ground and there is no evidence of blame or culpability on their part and I consider the matter to be closed."

"So that's it you are not going to look into them further" Shirley said in a dejected tone.

"No I am not going to look further into them and what's more neither are you or any of your staff and that is a direct order. Let me leave you in no doubt Detective Sergeant if I find out that you have disobeyed this order your feet won't touch the ground and you will be subject to a reg 15 discipline notice do you understand?"

Shirley left out a sigh of obvious frustration and with teeth clenched replied

"Yes Sir."

Now that the Chief had imposed his authority and Shirley albeit reluctantly was compliant, he softened his stance a little, and in a softer slightly more compassionate manner said.

"Shirley, I know your intentions are genuine and I appreciate your concern but I have to look at the bigger picture. I only have so many resources to deal with an ever-increasing workload. In the Stourbridge area alone we've got an epidemic of armed carjacking's and related burglaries We can't afford the luxury to go looking for and creating extra work purely on a hunch. Just because there have been three recent suicides it doesn't make them suspicious. You need to understand that the girls in these homes are there for a reason they are already vulnerable. They invariably come from broken homes and therefore more likely to do themselves harm. That's just the way life is unfortunately." A surprised and puzzled look came across Shirleys face. "Three recent suicides at Alldahope don't you mean two Sir?" "No I mean three there was another one came in overnight; I was the on-call duty officer and I arranged for Latifeo to go and deal with it. Before you say anything, it is not suspicious and it doesn't change things, you are not to interfere."

"What exactly happened Sir?"

"The body of a young girl was found in the river Stour at Stambermill where the river passes under the train viaduct. There were no signs of a fight or struggle the girl was just a mass of broken bones it seems she jumped from the top of the viaduct. She had been reported missing from the home by the Matron. A search of the girls room revealed that she had left a handwritten suicide note. It didn't give any specific reason why she did what she did just that she wanted to kill herself. So as far as I am concerned the matter is closed and that applies to you as well."

Due to the pressure and threats excerpted by the Chief, Shirley had almost resigned herself to let the two suicides go. But now there was a third one this was a different matter altogether. She was not prepared to let them be ignored she was determined to find out what was happening. She realised that she would need to tread carefully though or risk the threat of discipline procedures. This needed some thoughtful planning. She knew she had to be a little cute about it and needed to appease the Chief so she simply replied.

"Well you're the boss it's your call"

"Yes I am the boss and I'm glad that you respect that. Now I'm sure that you still have plenty to catch up from after your holiday so if there's nothing else I'll bid you good day Shirley."

Shirley nodded in acknowledgement and left the office in a calm relaxed manner. But all the time she was fighting an inner gut-wrenching desire to scream and shout at the stubborn pig of a senior officer. The idiot who hadn't a clue what he was doing and couldn't detect a crime even if it happened under his nose.

Back in her office Shirley re read the files on the first two suicides she needed to make a connection but what was it, she knew must be missing something. In frustration she threw the paperwork down onto her desk when she noticed another file nestling in amongst her mountain of paperwork. The file had not been on her desk the previous evening so someone must have put it there first thing this morning and she hadn't noticed it.

She picked it up and realised why she had missed it before the file only consisted of a couple of pages. Inside the plain buff folder there was a one-page copy of a coroner's report and a short statement from the Matron at Alldahope. She closed the file and reads the front cover it simply stated Patty Stola suicide investigating officer DC Latifeo.

Shirley had been fuming before but now she was completely incensed this report into a young girls death was the scantiest and most incomplete she had ever seen. Her resolve to get to the bottom of these deaths had intensified and she began formulating a plan and ran through a few ideas to facilitate an investigation without alerting the Chief Inspector. She knew that she needed to be very careful in choosing with who to confide in and whose help to enlist. Her best friend and confidante Sam Gail was the first one person she thought of. They both shared the same values and attitudes towards life and more importantly they had both suffered unspeakable abuse and atrocities during their upbringing at Alldahope children's home. Neither of them had known their parents and their only memories of childhood centred around feelings of fear and hopelessness with no one to turn to for help. This had given them a common bond and they were as close and as loyal to each other as was humanly possible. The next person she thought of was Martin the local newspaper reporter.

She was not sure how far he could be trusted not knowing him that well, but she was aware of his doggedness to get to the bottom of things. He would also probably have some useful contacts that wouldn't normally be available to police officers. The next obstacle to overcome was access to forensic investigation and information. She had someone in mind and the more she thought about him the more she realised that they would be perfect. It was someone she had worked with before it was Steve the crime scene manager. What made him ideal was his knowledge of and access to forensic services and even more vital was his attitude. He was well known for his lack of respect for a lot of senior officers, especially the ones who didn't know what they were doing so Steve wouldn't have a problem working behind their backs. Especially when he realises it's Chief inspector Cappoten as the pair had crossed swords on previous occasions, mostly over the Chief interfering with and occasionally overruling Steve's decisions on forensic strategies.

Shirley sat back on her chair and sighed as she scanned the meaningless pile of crime files that lay on her desk. Each one of them should be worthy of further investigation but instead she was required to endorse them as no further action required. They would then be confined to the archives and become another forgotten statistic. She was determined that the same would not happen to the Alldahope girls. The girls were foremost thoughts in her mind when she screwed up her mouth and silently but grittily said "I'm not going to forget you."

With renewed vigour she picked up the phone and began to set about getting her team together.

Sue Birtcher was waiting for Matron to return she was sitting in her office and had been put on a chair in the middle of the room. Sue was known as a very hard girl she was big and strong and had a violent nasty streak. But even though she had a well-earned reputation as being as hard as nails she was feeling very uneasy. There were only two people at Alldahope that scared her one of them was Babs Guthy. Even though Babs was much younger and considerably smaller than her, Babs could not be intimidated there appeared to be something strangely missing from her. She had no sense of fear and whatever you threatened or did to her she wouldn't back down or succumb and she would always fight back with all her might no matter how big you were.

Everyone assumed that this was a trait that she had inherited from her father Stan Guthy who was a renown gangland enforcer. He was a huge brute of a man who was now on remand in Birmingham prison for killing his wife and a young Police Officer. The other equally frightening character was Matron she ruled Alldahope with a rod of iron and it wasn't just the young girls resident there that she scared, even the male members of staff would visibly cower in her presence and none of them were ever seen to challenge or stand up to her. And right now Sue had to face the wrath of Matron over the death of Patty Stola. Sue was used by Matron not only as an informer but as a bully to keep the rest of the girls in line. Sues orders had been to frighten Patty to find out if it was her that had set the fire alarm.

Sue sat up straight with alarm as the door suddenly opened and shut with a bang and Matron entered the room and marched past Sue.

She took her seat behind her desk whilst eyeing Sue with an icy stare and remaining silent. After what seemed like an eternity to Sue, Matron eventually spoke.

"What the fuck happened; you were only supposed to frighten her not throw her off a fucking great bridge."

"I didn't throw her off I just dangled her over the edge. I was holding her upside down by her boots but they slipped off. I never meant to kill her it was just an accident."

"Why didn't you do what I suggested and just hold her head under water.
That's why I sent you pair down there the bloody river runs through it and you are not overlooked from any nearby houses or passers-by. "

Sue didn't reply just sat there with her head bowed.

"Don't you dare ignore me answer the question" Matron screamed through clenched teeth.

Sheepishly and with head still bowed Sue muttered under her breath

"I couldn't I'm afraid of water."

Matron sat there in silence for a few seconds mulling over what Sue had just revealed to her, then from nowhere she suddenly burst into a fit of uncontrollable laughter.

Sues feeling of trepidation began to give way to deep humiliation.
She had never told anyone about her fear of water and it had always been her secret embarrassment and her face became as red as a beetroot as she squirmed in her seat.

"A great big nasty girl like you who can beat the shit out of anyone I tell you to without blinking an eye. Yet you're scared of a little bit of water it's the river Stour for god's sake it's not exactly a raging torrent it's more like a tiny babbling brook and probably only a couple of feet deep at very most."

Sue continued sitting there soaking up Matron's taunt's and shameful jibes until the laughter subsided. A slightly more subdued atmosphere returned and Sue was continually asked if she had found out about the fire alarm. Sue detailed the conversation between her and Patty in which she had denied all knowledge of it. She also added that she thought that if Patty had known anything, she had been so terrified she would have said something.

After further questioning a grateful but red-faced Sue was eventually told that she could leave the office whilst Matron appeared to be on the brink of breaking out into another fit of laughing. Perhaps if Matron hadn't been so distracted, she may have noticed that her window that overlooked the overgrown brambles and weeds in the garden was ever so slightly ajar. And with a bit more attention she may have even seen the diminutive shadow of Babs Guthy secreted amongst the undergrowth. Babs had seen and heard everything; the entire conversation was imprinted into her remarkable memory banks. The anger and vengeance that was stored inside her was now greatly intensified. Her determination to seek retribution had increased tenfold and deep inside she knew that somehow; she would find a way to exact her rage on them. She thought about her father who was locked up behind bars he would now how to sort them out easily but for now she was completely and utterly alone.

Babs remained motionless and quiet until she thought it was safe to abandon her vantage point. She would return later to close the window she would not risk it now in case it alerted Matron.

Shirley Wallows was sitting in the Cross public house sports bar in Oldswinford a small village on the outskirts of Stourbridge. She had assembled her team there as opposed to anywhere in central Stourbridge so as not to be seen by anyone who could interfere with her plans.

The only patrons of this pub were the local residents and sports fans whenever a sporting event was being shown on the big screen. As there were no sporting events taking place at this time the only other customers were a handful of locals. A couple of them playing pool and a small group monopolising the dartboard. Big Dave the landlord was keeping a beady eye on the only other customer in the bar who was relentlessly ploughing tens of pounds into the gambling machine. Shirley felt secure that she was able to speak with her small band of what she was hoping to be dogged and intrepid investigators without the danger of being anyone hearing or seeing them. First, she went around the table introducing everyone to each other.

The team comprised of Martin the local newspaper reporter, Steve a crime scene manager and her best and closet friend Sam.

She opened the meeting with a sombre word of caution to everyone,

"The first thing I want to say is that I believe that a travesty of justice may or indeed may have not happened but that there is sufficient evidence to warrant further investigation. For various reasons including financial cutbacks and restraints this matter is not receiving the attention it deserves from any authority including social services and the police. I think that between the four of us we have sufficient knowledge, experience, expertise and last but most importantly the social conscious to do the right thing. However I must warn you all that this is totally unofficial, although we aren't or will not be doing anything illegal it is not sanctioned or backed by the police. In fact quite the opposite I have been specifically ordered by senior Police officers to close the case file and not to devote any time or resources whatsoever to it.

As a consequence of this we must all agree to keep whatever we do completely secret. No one outside us four can be party to what we are doing until we have uncovered sufficient evidence to either support a prosecution or have established that nothing untoward has happened.

So to that end I want everyone to give some thought to what we may be about to do and agree that we all have to and will keep it a complete secret otherwise it is a nonstarter and we forget the whole thing.

There was silence around the table for a while as the group cogitated the implications and consequences of their possible forthcoming endeavours.   It was Martin who broke the stony silence saying,

"You haven't yet said what it is about, I have a good idea but I assume that you will not reveal any details until we are all in agreement. But I think it will help if you can assure us that we will not be doing anything that will be breaking the law." The rest of the group looked towards Shirley for her response this obviously concerned all of them and they were eager to hear her reply.

"As I've already said we are not and will not be doing anything illegal or even unethical but we will be acting on our own volition without any formal sanction or authorisation. The only persons here that could face any form of recrimination would be me and Steve as we are serving police officers and have been ordered to not deploy any time or resources into it. We could therefore face possible internal discipline and that is one of the reasons why we all need to agree to keep our investigation completely covert and to ourselves.

Steve chirped up and said, "Well you can count me in".

The other two with heads nodding and affirmative responses almost simultaneously agreed.

Before Shirley could begin to outline what, they would be investigating the reasonably quiet and relaxed atmosphere was interrupted by an extremely loud string of expletives filling the air. Their attention was drawn to the gaming machine where big Dave the landlord was inspecting the gaming machine.

The person who had been piling notes after notes into it had now left the pub.

Dave shouted to no one in particular

"The fucking jammy bastard has taken another hundred bloody quid out of the machine again" he banged the machine with his fist so hard he almost broke the screen and then stormed back to his position back behind the bar.

He pulled himself a pint of Strongbow cider and in between gulps continued to utter expletives.

This suited Shirley and the rest of the group as most people's attention was focused on big Dave's rantings and no one was paying any attention to their little gathering. Shirley outlined to the newly formed band of clandestine sleuths how they were going to go about investigating the Alldahope deaths.

Steve the crime scene manager was tasked with looking into the forensic examinations of the three suicides. He needed to interpret the results and conclusions of each individual death and explore the possibility of further forensic laboratory submissions. Steve explained that getting access to the scene examination reports was for him a simple matter. However to submit or re-submit any further samples it technically needed the authorisation of a Chief Inspector i.e. Trevor Cappoten. He further said he would be able to circumvent this standard procedure by calling in a couple of favours at the forensic lab.

The next problem to overcome was how to find a way to speak with the children residents of Alldahope. They would be the most likely source of useful information but neither Steve nor Shirley could go anywhere near the home. Should either of them be found out then they would risk the wrath and possible disciplinary procedures instigated by DCI Cappoten.

Martin chipped in with a suggestion to get around this problem. He could approach the home under the pretext that he was doing a human-interest story for the local paper about the trials and tribulations of a child brought up in care as seen through their eyes. This would give him unfettered access to all the children.

Shirley also as were the rest of the small group were greatly impressed with this idea. They were beginning to realise that as a reporter he would have been used to finding out ways to gain information using methods not normally available to the Police. They agreed on a time and date for their next meeting in the Cross, finished their drinks and left. No one noticed their departure as all attention was still focused on big Dave who was still continuing with his rantings and ravings concerning the gambling machine.

7

PERSONAL DELIVERY

Stan Guthy stood in the dock of court number 1 at Birmingham crown court, smiling from ear to ear. He was a massive brute of a man with arms as big as most people's legs. With his shaven head and several days growth of stubble on his face he looked every inch the brutal gangland enforcer he was famed for.

He listened with smug satisfaction as his legal aid team fronted by a legal aid funded barrister outlined the grounds of his appeal against conviction for murdering his wife and a young police officer. The grounds of his appeal surrounded the now disgraced former Detective Chief Inspector Frank Twead.

The ex-cop had been in charge of the CID team that investigated what became known as the Stourbridge killer in addition to the two murders attributed to Stan Guthy.

The first being the beating to death of his wife whilst the second was that of a young police officer committed during his arrest. Frank Twead who was now deceased had come crashing down to earth at an alarming rate. His demise from a high ranking and well-respected Senior Investigating Officer to a scapegoat for every possible miscarriage of justice and any and all allegations of police misconduct had been swift. It had been greatly hastened by his chronic alcoholism and nearly all of his previous cases had been challenged and appealed against through the judiciary. Such was his slipshod approach it had been a simple process for any defence lawyer worth their salt to expose loopholes and mistakes in his investigations.

With Twead now dead and buried and every other senior police officer steering well clear of any previous involvement with him there was little or no opposition to getting all of his guilty verdicts overturned. Today would be no different and it would be a forgone certainty that the brutal thug Stan Guthy will be walking out of court a free man.

Having heard all the evidence in support of the appeal against conviction the judge looked towards the much beleaguered and overworked Crown Prosecution Service representative. With a look of resignation they wearily stood up and addressed the court. No one paid much attention to what he was about to say because everyone knew that without any support from the police who had been conspicuous by their absence there was little, he could do to rebut the grounds for appeal.

They cleared their throat and with a voice that displayed obvious acceptance of defeat said,

"We will not be challenging the evidence put before the court."

A sickly smirk appeared on the face of Stan Guthy and he let out a derisory stifled laugh as he waited for the judge to formally uphold the appeal. The judge looked Guthy square in the eye as he gave his verdict. In a big booming voice the judge with obvious displeasure said "Mr Guthy I'm satisfied that you are an extremely violent and dangerous man and the public expect and quite rightly deserve protection from your acts of Barbarity. However in view of the evidence put before me I have no choice but to uphold the appeal. But I am also satisfied that you have a long history of violent domestic abuse and to this end I am imposing restrictions on your release.

Because of your previous violent domestic behaviour the law allows me to impose restrictions on your access to your child. This court denies you any and all contact with your daughter. This includes physical contact and all verbal and written contact whatsoever. Should you breach this order it is within the power of the court to recall you immediately back to prison. Do you understand Mr Guthy?"

Guthy nodded his head and simply replied

"Yes."

"In that case you are free to go."

Guthy with a derisory laugh strolled cockily out of court eyeing the judge the court officials and security staff with a menacing look. He had studied the face of the judge intently so that he could recognise him again. Because sometime in the not-too-distant future Guthy would make sure that their paths would cross again. Only this time it would be on Guthys territory and the pompous bastard of a judge who would not let him see his daughter would be made to suffer. But all that could wait for a short time Guthy thought. The most important thing to do now was to get pissed and with a bit of luck pick a fight with someone and vent his frustrations by kicking the living daylights out of him.   Babs Guthy gazed intently out of her bedroom window; she had a clear view of the driveway leading out to the main road. Her insightfulness had alerted her to something not being quite right. She along with all the other girls at Alldahope had been spoken to at length by a reporter from the local newspaper. Allegedly it was for a human-interest story but why would anyone be interested in them.

No one gave a shit about the girls here we are the forgotten ones. We and our problems just get brushed under the carpet no one gives a damn about us and the story of our pathetic existences certainly wouldn't sell any newspapers.

Even more interesting was why the reporter had been dropped off from a car driven by a police officer. This car had remained parked on the main road a few yards from the front gate.

Babs recognised the female officer even though she was in plain clothes because it was the same one that had turned up at her house when her dad was beating her mom up. Babs had a hatred of police officers but this one was different she was nice she had helped Babs as well as her mom, but why on eat would she give a lift to a local reporter. She heard the big heavy downstairs entrance door slam shut and then she saw the reporter leaving. He walked along the driveway out of the main gate turned left and got in the police officers car. Babs watched as the car drive off in the distance until it eventually went out of view. "What did you find out?" Shirley asked eagerly as soon as Martin got into the passenger seat.

"Not a lot to be honest"

he replied a little with obvious disappointment in his voice "But I'll tell you more when we get to the pub." They drove in silence for the rest of journey to the pub they have now made their regular haunt, the Cross at Oldswinford.

The others were already there they had taken a table in the corner out of the way. Steve and Sam were just finishing their drinks so Shirley got a round in for everyone and took them over. It was a lunchtime and there was the usual spattering of locals and one stranger who was drinking alone at the far end of the bar away from everyone else.

One of the locals was entertaining the other regulars with his grandiose tales of big business interspersed with

"So I gave him one and then his mate started so I knocked him out with one punch."

With everyone hanging on his every word and in eager anticipation of what new escapade he would expound the group felt safe to start their meeting.

Nobody was within earshot and everyone could update the rest with what they had found out about Alldahope in relative safety.

Martin went first from the outset by his very demeanour it was obvious it would not be good news. "I've just come from Alldahope where I interviewed all the kids there. I did it under the pretence that I was doing a human-interest story. Unfortunately I wasn't allowed free access to the kids.

All the interviews took place in the presence of the Matron. So I not only couldn't ask the full range of questions that I had planned to, but also the responses I got were obviously rehearsed and quite muted. All the kids are clearly terrified of her and scared to say anything out of order in front of her. But I did get the feeling that they were concealing something and that they wanted to tell me all about it but because of Matron they couldn't. So we need to find some way of being able to speak with them when they feel free to talk perhaps away from the confines of the home, I will need to think of some way to achieve that."

"Thanks for that" said Shirley "Steve have you got any updates re the examination of the forensic evidence." Steve pulled out a few sheets of handwritten notes from his jacket pocket and looked around to check again that no one outside their group was within earshot.

The guy who had been entertaining the regulars with his exploits was now telling them all about his luxury yacht moored in the south of France. The big guy at the other end of the bar was busy throwing pint after pint down his neck and no one was paying any attention to their little group.

"Firstly because of the secretive nature of this enquiry I have not committed anything to any electronic records. There are no emails nothing on any computer or hard drive, not even any phone calls that can be recorded. I have done everything by word of mouth to close personal friends and contacts. I have only dealt with people that I trust they in turn will not record anything anywhere. Any forensic examinations and tests together with any subsequent results will be conveyed to me by word of mouth in fact I am expecting a call on my mobile any time now. The call will be made on a pay as you go mobile so not only the call will be private but also the identity of the caller. I will destroy these handwritten notes that I have made when I have updated you all. The downside of this is that we would not be able to use them in any future possible prosecution or criminal proceedings. With regard to the death of Tipe Moor I have found out that the knife is one normally used by model aircraft enthusiasts. The scene referred to scenes of crime so there are no results there. However I have examined the photographs taken on a mobile phone and I have made a blood pattern analysis. This has revealed several anomalies. Firstly Tipe's arm was raised outstretched above her head when the initial cut was made and extraordinarily it remained there for some time. There are a number of areas near the body where you would expect to see blood but there is none. In addition there is visible bruising on Tipe's wrist and lower forearm. The next major area of bloodstaining is at a much lower level very close to the floor. The only way she could have inflicted this on herself would be to hold her left arm up high slit her wrist and leave her arm outstretched until the bleeding stopped due to congealing or the elevation of her arm.

Then she would have had to put her wounded arm near the floor and reopen the wound until she bled out." Shirley as did the rest of them looked really confused and puzzled "But that doesn't sound like normal behaviour does it." Everyone in the group agreed. "But didn't they find her fingerprints on the

knife" Shirley asked." Yes, they did and I am waiting further information on that very soon"
Steve replied.

"As for the death of Marion Fern once again no scene of crime examination was requested however I have obtained a sample of her hair and submitted this for analysis."
The reporter Martin said, "Why have you submitted a hair sample what could that tell us Steve."

"Because the cause of death was given as a self-inflicted drug overdose and as no bloods were submitted for toxicology at the time, we don't know what drug and how much was involved. It's too late to submit bloods now but hair retains evidence of drug abuse for a much longer period of time sometimes up to six months. Again I am waiting for those results that I am expecting shortly. I can't see any other line of forensic evidence we can chase up on her death." "Do you have anything on the death of Patty Stola?" asked Shirley.   "The only line of enquiry there is her boots for some reason they were found on the viaduct and not with the body. I cannot see any reason why she would take them off so I have sent them for fingerprint examination. Hopefully I will have all the results before we finish this meeting."

The group then looked towards Shirley and Sam in anticipation of any updates from them. It was Shirley who answered for them.
"Unfortunately we haven't managed to uncover anything I have been trying to find out details of previous deaths there that I know from Martin have happened but I can't find any police records relating to them."   In reality Shirley and Sam were hoping for results from their submissive self-confessed paedophile Victor S Petersham. Sam had complete and utter control over him. His absolute obedience to her was part of his perversion and he would comply with whatever he was told to do. She had made him apply for a handyman's post at Alldahope which he had secured and he was already in post. His brief was to infiltrate any possible Paedophile connection which because of his perversion and underworld sexual deviant contacts he should be able to achieve. But this was something that Shirley and Sam were keeping and would always keep to themselves.

"I'll get another round in" said Martin as he stood up and reached inside his coat pocket for his wallet. As he did so an envelope fell out landing on the floor next to Shirley who picked it up and was about to hand it back to Martin when she became enthralled with what was written on the outside.   Sam picked up on this straight away and remarked "What's the matter?"   Shirley looked at the group and turned the envelope towards them so that they could all read it. On the cover in an untidy handwritten scrawl were the words "This is for Shirley the woman copper in the car." Martin studied the envelope saying, "That wasn't in my pocket before I went to Alldahope someone must have put it in there when it was hanging up on the coat rack."

Shirley gingerly and carefully opened the envelope to find a single sheet of paper inside folded in half, she unfolded it to see the same untidy handwritten scrawl in blue biro. Martin sat back down; the drinks can wait a while he thought as he together with the others were intrigued to find out the contents of the mystery letter.

"Before you tell us the results give me a minute to get a round in" said Martin as he stood up make his way to the bar. Big Dave was busy arguing with the huge guy at the end of the bar who was obviously intent on getting blind drunk. In the meantime Dave's wife Sharon had stepped in behind the bar to serve. "What's the matter with him," said Martin.

Sharon shook her head in despair

"It's just another drunken arsehole who wants to cause trouble I'm fed up to the back teeth with this". Martin eyed the loudmouth drunk who was now calling Dave all the names under the sun. He was also threatening to drag him over the bar and throw him through the window which given the size of big Dave would take some doing. Some of the regulars began to close ranks in a bid to support Dave. Some of them were known to be handy in a fight and one of them locally referred to as Brummie because of his broad accent used to have a reputation as a bit of a scrapper. Martin looked the group up and down and then looked back at the huge mouthy drunk. As intimidating as the locals tried to appear it was obvious that they would have no chance against this giant of a man. Martin quickly took the drinks back to the table; he didn't want them to be knocked over or smashed in any possible fight

"What's all the commotion at the bar" queried Sam as Martin put everyone's drink on the table.

"It's some huge drunken guy at the bar looking for trouble but it looks like the locals might gang up on him, but they wouldn't stand a chance look at him he's enormous." Their views were obstructed a little by the bar but Shirley managed to get a glimpse of the troublemaker.

"It looks a bit like the guy we locked up for murdering his wife who then murdered that young probationer. It obviously can't be him because he is serving life for murder but he looks about the same size. But anyway let's forget that and let's hear what news Steve has for us regarding the forensic results."

"Right guys the fingerprint results on the craft knife that was used to cut Tipe's wrist confirm that the only fingerprints on the knife are hers."

Shirley shook her head "I really thought that we would find something that would help us but that doesn't take us anywhere."

"I've not finished yet"

Steve replied with an air of expectation.

"The one and only set of prints on the knife were matched to Tipe's left hand."

Steve paused for a while to let the information sink in but no one seemed to grasp the significance and they all waited in hushed silence.

"The wound that sliced open Tipe's ulnar artery and caused her death was on her left wrist. Obviously, the only way she could have inflicted the injury herself she would have needed to hold the knife in her right hand. In other words guys it looks very much like a third party is involved. If you put this together with the anomalies with the blood pattern analysis then something is clearly wrong.   The sound of heavy objects crashing into the wall and glasses and bottles smashing as they hit the floor interrupted their conversation. This was closely followed by loud excited shouting and swearing coming from the other end of the bar. Dave was flat out on the floor behind the bar, he had lost his balance when he had to duck down in double quick time in order to avoid the barstool that had been hurled at his head by the obnoxious drunken giant. The next earth-shattering sound was the exit door being slammed so hard by the drunken giant as he left the pub that it nearly came off its hinges.   Some of the regular punters rushed to the window to and saw the huge drunkard making his way down the hill away from the pub. The carnage behind the bar was considerable. The stool had flown over Dave's head and missed causing him any injury. But the damage to the bar looked like a bomb had gone off. Several of the optics had smashed together with dozens of free-standing bottles of spirits. All of them spilling their contents either over the prostrate Dave or the floor which was swimming in sticky strong-smelling alcohol. The fridge door was broken as was the wall clock and some photo frames were smashed to pieces.   With the perpetrator well clear of the pub some way off in the distance one of the regulars, who had previously been entertaining the regulars with the stories of his exploits on his yacht in the south of France emerged from the other end of the bar.

                   "He was fucking lucky it's a good job he's fucked off I was just going to start." Someone else shouted.

"And just what was it you was going to do?"

"I was going to batter the cunt and he knew it that why he pissed off if he had hurt anybody then I'd have no choice but to twat him."

There was however one person injured, as Big Dave had ducked and lost his balance when avoiding the bar stool he had unfortunately knocked over and landed on top of poor hapless Sharon. She was now firmly pinned to the floor and squashed underneath Dave. And as anyone in the pub would testify if anyone was to fall on top of you then Dave would not be your first choice. He wasn't called big Dave for nothing. Sharon whilst gasping for breath shouted, "Well don't just stand there you numpties come and lift him off me."

With the excitement over and the clean-up beginning Steve continued his update on forensic results. They all listened with renewed concentration as Steve explained that the drugs found in the hair sample of the second victim Marion had contained some sort of tranquiliser. They became even more intrigued when he explained that traces of the same drug had been evident in her system for a period of at least six months. The biggest surprise was still yet to come when Steve detailed the fingerprint examination of the boots in the third death relating to Patty Stola.

"Because of the material that the boots were made from it allows for various chemical treatments that can detect fingerprints by reacting with amino -acids and as such can give excellent results. Various fingerprints have been recovered belonging to Patty in the positions you would normally expect to see them i.e. around the top edge of the boots as you pull them up onto your legs. However two full sets of finger and palm marks not relating to her have been recovered in a location you would not normally expect to find them. They have been recovered from near and just above where the ankle would be. More importantly they are upside down as if someone was holding on to her boots whilst Patty was upside down wearing them. This as with the evidence from the other deaths relating to the girls at Alldahope shed a completely new light on things. Remember though we are working outside our authority and none of this is legally admissible. So all this new evidence is for our information and use only."

The group were silent for a while whilst everyone digested this new information and what it meant.

One thing that were all sure of was that the deaths at Alldahope were not straight forward suicides and they needed to delve much deeper. Shirley thanked Steve for his input and briefed the group on their next actions. They scheduled their next meeting in the pub after Shirley had met with the anonymous author of the note left in Martins pocket.

As they left the pub and whilst getting into their vehicles Steve said to Shirley

"Did you see that big drunken guy in the bar throwing his weight about he reminded me of that guy who killed his wife and that young PC I wonder where he's gone?"

"I couldn't see him very well from where I was sitting but I did get a glimpse of him I agree he did look similar but as I said before it can't be him, he's serving a life sentence anyway I'll see you tomorrow hopefully with some information."

"You be careful tomorrow you don't know who you are meeting it might be wise to take some back-up." Farewells said they all left the carpark each thinking how to complete their allotted tasks.

8

WRONG PLACE, WRONG TIME

Stan Guthy stomped down the road like a man possessed he had wanted to smash everyone's head in in the pub give them a beating they would never forget and he knew he was well capable of doing it. He had changed his mind though when he had seen Detective Sergeant Wallows sitting in the corner of the pub with a group of people. The last thing he wanted for now was to be seen by the police to be doing anything wrong because that would mean his immediate recall to prison. And it was that bastard woman who had arrested him up for beating up his wife some months earlier. His anger was intensified by the amount of alcohol he had drunk, having spent the last few months in prison he wasn't used to it and it was affecting him badly. The incredible violent nature intrinsic to the huge thug was boiling away like a cauldron ready to explode. His rage was so intense that he barely knew where he was walking and was oblivious of his surroundings.

He had unwittingly found himself walking along the canal towpath. The Stourbridge canal only ran for a short distance starting at the bonded warehouse adjacent to the town centre.

Historically it had been quite important to the area supporting the now long-gone glass making industry. It meandered its way through the mass of now derelict buildings and empty factories until it joined the Staffordshire and Worcester canal at Stourton. The once busy waterway was now only used by the occasional cyclist and dog walker. Stan Guthy continued in his ill-tempered drunken stomp not paying any attention to his surroundings and didn't see the cyclist heading towards him along the narrow towpath. Even the frantic sounding of the cyclists bell and their warning shouts went unheeded. Then suddenly with an almighty crash they both collided with the cyclist going headfirst over the handlebars. Stan Guthy was such a huge man that the force of the impact barely affected him physically it did however further incite his Herculean rage. He looked down at the crumpled heap on the floor, the blooded rider and bike lying entangled in a crumpled heap on the towpath.

"I'm sorry" stuttered the injured rider looking up at the giant standing over him menacingly with a face that looked like thunder.

Stan Guthy bent over with an outstretched hand; the injured rider offered a hand in return expecting assistance to get to his feet.

The hand however was not one offering help and it bypassed the riders expectant hand and grabbed him forcefully round the throat. Within the blink of an eye the rider was now being held aloft with his feet dangling in mid-air.

Such was the strength of this huge drunken bruiser that he was suspending the terrified cyclist by his neck using only one hand. In a blind panic amidst repeated shouts of

"I'm sorry" and

"Please let me go"

the cyclist was struggling and kicking his feet in an effort to escape. But such was the mismatch in size and sheer brute strength between the two it had no effect whatsoever.

The poor frightened wretch realising escape was impossible resorted to more and more repeated pleas and begs to be released.

Stan Guthy was revelling in the obvious terror and suffering of his pathetic defenceless victim who was now sobbing uncontrollably. The more fear and trepidation exhibited by his victim the greater the pleasure it gave him. Whilst still suspending the poor innocent in mid-air he with his other hand began to punch him ferociously in the head. A loud crack ripped through the air as his nose snapped clean in half and blood began gushing out from the resulting gaping hole in his face.

Next to break, again with a resounding crack was his jaw, the lower mandible becoming completely detached with teeth flying everywhere. His face soon became un unrecognisable mound of pulp and a steady stream of thick gooey blood was cascading down the victim drenching his bright yellow reflective cycling jacket.

 The pounding was relentless with blow after blow from the huge fists of Guthy smashing time and time again squarely into the defenceless victims face. With little left of the now totally destroyed face he concentrated on the poor guys eyes. Forming a v shape with one of his knuckles he repeatedly aimed blows at first one eye then another wondering which one he would drive into the man's skull first. This was a technique he had used several times before in his role as a paid enforcer for various criminal gangs. It had become somewhat of a trademark for him and it wasn't long before the first eyeball disappeared into the bloody recess of the socket no longer to be seen. The next eyeball however didn't retreat into the socket but somehow bizarrely popped clean out of the socket and was dangling in the air still connected to a membrane.

The grotesque sight of this eyeball swinging about in mid-air combined with the vacant space in the adjacent socket amused Guthy and he began to laugh uncontrollably letting his victim fall to the floor. This was what he had needed this outburst of extreme violence inflicted on some totally random and defenceless stranger had helped assuage his inner anger and rage and he was feeling quite satisfied with the carnage he had inflicted.

To his surprise what he thought would be a lifeless corpse began moaning gently and was making a feeble effort to crawl away. He bent down and stared curiously into the mush that had shortly before been a human face wondering how he could still be alive having sustained such catastrophic damage. In a last twist of utter evilness and sadistic savagery he took hold of the eyeball that although still attached by a membrane was resting on the towpath. He placed it in such a position that if the eye was still functioning then the victim could witness the final act of brutality that would end his life. He picked up the bent and twisted bike and raised it above his head holding it here for some time in the hope that his victim was able to see what was about to befall him and subject him to even more terror right up to the moment of his death. Then with a loud grunt he bought the metal frame of the bike crashing down onto the body of his victim.

He continued remorselessly pounding his victims body until it was a horrific mangled mess of broken bones. The last few blows were aimed at the already grossly disfigured head until with his anger satisfied and breathing heavily, he stooped. Such had been the severity of the beating that the mashed-up head had almost become detached from the body.

Stan Guthy was feeling pleased with himself nothing gave him such rewarding pleasure as inflicting extreme violence and misery upon other human beings and the terror in his victims eyes had been intense and this had given him an instant buzz pandering his need to feel all powerful and totally in charge.

He had also revelled in the repeated cries and pleas for help from his victim this had satisfied his sadistic tendencies. Having recovered his breath he looked around to make sure no one was watching, something he hadn't thought to do before such was the overpowering passion of his all-engulfing rage. He picked up the lifeless body and casually threw the corpse into the murky waters of the canal.

Then he picked up the battered and bloodstained bike and threw that in aiming to land on top of the body to prevent it resurfacing. Looking at his fists that although uninjured were covered in his victims blood so kneeling by the side of the canal, he washed his hands in the filthy water.   He stood up inspecting his hands for any remaining signs of blood and when satisfied there was no longer any sign of the bloody carnage, he had inflicted he strolled off unremorsefully intent on finding a pub to have a celebratory drink.

He was completely devoid of any emotion or the slightest feeling of guilt for having so brutally and rapidly extinguished the life of an innocent human being whose only mistake was to be in the wrong place at the wrong time. The rest of Guthys day was now to be filled with consuming as much alcohol as humanly possible in order to get blind drunk.

Shirley sat at her desk cradling her morning coffee and began to half-heartedly log onto her computer terminal. She hated this office it felt as if she were in a goldfish bowl.

Since Stourbridge police station had been shut down in a ridiculous cost cutting exercise and the subsequent relocation of the staff to Brierly hill police station there had been a public outcry from local residents complaining about the lack of police presence. In an attempt to appease the publics dissatisfaction with their local police they had resorted to using and occupying empty disused shops in the town centre shopping precinct.

The vacated stores invariably had large, fronted glass windows so every Tom Dick and Harry could stare in and gawp with impunity at their local police, similar to what they would do if they were having a day out at Dudley zoo. This combined with her mind focusing on her mysterious meeting under Stourbridge clock in a few hours' time meant she couldn't concentrate fully.

She began to peruse the daily crime and incident bulletin but it was filled with the same old stuff there was nothing that particularly stood out. There had been the now almost daily carjacking in Stourbridge, theses being perpetrated by outside gangs coming into the area due to the availability of expensive vehicles and the complete absence of any police presence. There were a few other minor incidents and one missing person report.

The missing person report related to a sixteen-year-old student who was last seen cycling to college but that looked fairly routine as it wasn't unusual for teenagers to go missing, he had most likely bumped into friends and ended up getting drunk or high on drugs at a party.

Shirley spent the rest of the morning reading through completed crime enquiry folders and then endorsing her signature to them so that they could be written off as no further investigation required. The majority had emanated from that idle good for nothing Oli Latifeo he had made it his speciality to do the minimum amount of work necessary to complete an individual task. Shirley couldn't think of a any other police officer let alone a detective who connived to do as little work as he. He had turned his apathetic and lazy approach to fabricate the easiest day to day routine that he had almost turned it into an art form. Her other two detectives weren't much better the aptly nicknamed dumb and dumber who seemed to be permanently joined at the hip. They would everything that they could to turn an investigation to their own advantage. She was fully aware that they would use police work to facilitate drunken and debauched behaviour and it gave them numerous opportunities to cheat on their long suffering but somewhat naïve wives.

Detectives constables Frank Fergas and Robert Peeves were perhaps slightly more astute detectives but neither of them could be trusted. Both of them were disloyal and two faced, they could smile at you pleasantly but wouldn't miss an opportunity to stab you in the back, especially Fergas who was renowned for being a snitch for the bosses. Their files were slightly more comprehensive but still lacked the level of investigation that Shirley thought appropriate. But she would bide her time she had through careful monitoring amassed enough misdemeanours committed by all her staff to pull them into line and if necessary, exert her influence and control over them.

With all files complete and authorised she sat back and stared out the expansive glass frontage of the office her mind again thinking about her forthcoming meeting. Glancing at her watch she saw it was time to make her way there she had arranged backup from Sam who by now should be sitting in the Bank pub which was adjacent to the town clock. By taking a high table next to the pubs impressive huge windows it gave a good unobstructed view of the clock a few yards away without attracting attention to oneself.

Shirley approached the clock and checked the time on her watch it was exactly midday but there was no obvious sign of anyone waiting there for her.

After a few minutes wait and trying to look as casual as possible she began to wonder if anyone was going to show she had cast a glance at the bank pub and saw Sam perched on a bar stool keeping an eye out but still no contact.   Then from behind her she heard a child's voice say,

"Shirley it's me Babs." She turned around and recognised the little girl straight away.

"Barbara what are you doing here aren't you a bit young to be out and about on your own or is someone with you."

"We need to find somewhere to talk somewhere a bit more private."

Shirley realising now that the author of the note and the person who wished to speak with her was little Barbara Guthy the young girl whom she had helped and befriended when she had arrested her father Stan for assaulting her mother.

"Ok follow me we'll find somewhere a bit quieter."

They both began to walk to the main entrance to the shopping mall that housed the newly built Tescos supermarket. Shirley thought of taking a table at their café but changed her mind because it was so open and every passer-by would have a clear view of them both so she continued walking and turned left and into the adjacent Stourbridge library.

Once inside she continued on to a small reading room that contained that days papers and a few tables for anyone to use whilst perusing the daily news this would be a much safer place to talk, she thought. As they both entered, they could see that they had the place to themselves and they both drew up chairs at the furthest away most private table and sat down. They looked around the room to make sure they were alone with no one in earshot, it was only but there were rows of cabinets housing audio and visual books and films. Even though they were confident that they were alone their conversation was in hushed secretive tones. It was Babs who spoke first.

"Look first thing is I ain't no coppers nark so no one else is to know that I'm speaking to you have you got that?"

Shirley was taken aback at the forcefulness and confidence of this little girl in front of her. She was aware that her upbringing had made her grow up fast. Having a huge violent thug for a father who made his living as an enforcer had to have an impact upon her personality and character, but she had the presence of someone much older.

"Ok we'll keep everything between the two of us have you got something you want to tell me."

"You want to know things about Alldahope don't you?"

Babs asked.

"What makes you think that?"

Shirley replied trying not to give away that she was aware of and had suspicions concerning the recent deaths.

Babs raised her voice, "Don't piss me about I know that you have been nosing around because why would you give a lift to that newspaper reporter who was pretending to do some crappy story for the newspaper. If you are going to treat me like an idiot then you can fuck off right now. Or you can stop pissing about and I can tell some things you'll be interested in."

Once again Shirley was taken aback by this young girl, she had an old head on very young shoulders and showed a maturity and insight way beyond her tender years. She immediately felt admiration for and a sense of empathy with Babs this was a young lady with whom she could form a close relationship with. "Ok I think something is not right there, but I need to know why have you come to me."

"I can remember when you came to help my mom you were the only one who treated me nice, not like those other coppers who spoke to me as if I was a piece of shit. You even stayed with me until the social worker came so when I saw you in the car waiting for the reporter, I put that letter in his pocket".   "What is it you want to tell me?"

"I can give you is information about what is happening to the girls, but I need you to do something for me in return."

"What do you want from me?" Shirley asked with an air of caution.   "It's quite simple what I want you to do is to find out where

88

my dad is and make arrangements for me to see him."

"I can tell you where he is but you won't be able to see him, he's in Birmingham prison Winson Green. At his trial because of the history of domestic violence the judge ordered that there would be no contact now or at any time in the future."

A smile appeared across Babs face and she paused for a while before continuing. "Firstly my dad is no longer in prison he's been released because of that stupid detective who killed himself and secondly stuff the court order."

In an instant it suddenly struck home to Shirley that the huge thug in the Cross pub yesterday who caused all the trouble and threw the bar stool was Guthy. She had ruled it out in her mind because as far as she knew he was still in prison. She quickly ran through the ramifications of getting in touch with Stan Guthy. Making unauthorised enquiries was one thing but arranging illegal meetings with a convicted felon in contravention of a court order was something else.

"I'm not sure I can do that besides the last person your dad wants to see is me."

"Well that's the deal no meeting no info."

"You are going to have to give me something to go on so I can decide if to take the risk."

Babs thought about Shirley's request she didn't want to give away any details that would lessen her bargaining power but she realised that she needed to get the copper interested.

"Ok I won't give you anything specific but I will tell you it involves sexual abuse."

Straight away Shirley's blood began to boil. Herself and Sam had suffered incredible and prolonged abuse when they were resident at Alldahope and that had shaped their personalities and their secret past was why they did what they do.

"Ok I'll get in touch with your dad as quick as I can and I will get back in touch with you."

Another smile appeared across Bab's face she couldn't hide her delight at the prospect of seeing her dad again.

"How will you get in touch with me if you come to the home matron will want to know why."

"I know of a way of getting in touch with you but you need to trust me and also you mustn't mention our conversation to anyone is that understood."

"I'm not stupid I already know that and anyway the last thing I want to be known as is a coppers grass."

Babs left the confines of the reading room whilst Shirley remained seated, she thought it better if they left separately. Sam who had been watching through the window from the main library entered the reading room and sat next to Shirley. "What did she say "Sam asked eagerly.

"She didn't give any details but it revolves around sexual abuse but the best thing we can do is to go back home and discuss it together before we meet the rest in the pub c'mon, we need to be quick we don't have a lot of time."

9

SHOCKING

Shirley and Sam were sat at their kitchen table both sipping at their steaming hot mugs of tea.

"Ok Shirley tell me everything I want to know what that young girl said and how do you know her."

Shirley put her mug down on the table and cleared her throat.

"The girls name is Barbara Guthy she is normally referred to as Babs.

I first came across her when I dealt with a case of domestic violence that escalated into murder involving her parents. Her father Stan Guthy is a huge incredibly violent man who made a living as an enforcer I arrested him for the murder of his wife i.e. Barbara's mom. I felt sorry for her and tried to give as much comfort and support as I could, and I suppose we did form a sort of friendship albeit very fleeting. With her mother dead and father in prison she was taken into care and ended up at Alldahope. She says that she has information reference sexual abuse at Alldahope but she won't give me the details until I do something for her."

Sam was engrossed with this information and her feelings towards the sexual abuse claims enflamed her as much if not more than it had done to Shirley. Sam like Shirley also suffered terrible abuse when she was a resident of Alldahope and it was this abuse that had helped them form their deep relationship with each other.

"We must help her, we have to, no one knows better than us the horrors that that place holds so whatever she wants let's do it. We have got to end this cycle of abuse once and for all."

"I know how you feel Sam but it's not that easy she wants me to arrange for her to see her dad whom I thought was still in prison. But apparently he has been released and what's more do you remember that big guy in the pub yesterday who caused all the trouble?"

"Yes, I do if you mean that giant who threw the bar stool over the counter, you're not telling me that that violent drunk is her dad."

Shirley simply nodded her head. "Holy shit" uttered Sam.

Both girls remained silent for some time each of them cogitating the implications of what they were being asked to do. They both realised that should they do as they were being asked then they would be putting themselves in danger. They would be at risk not only physical at the hands of the unpredictable Stan Guthy but also of retribution from the authorities.   As much as they both realised the dangers and pitfalls, they also knew that because of the terrible outrages they had endured during their childhood years in Alldahope that they were honour bound to help.

Shirley and Sam looked at each, they didn't need to say anything they knew each other so well, they had no choice but to do everything they could to help.

"What do we do first?" asked Sam

"I said that I would be in touch with her so the way we do that is to use our man on the inside our tame paedo Victor. He has already got himself a job at Alldahope on the pretext of being a handyman. We can send messages both ways and it will also help him to delve deeper into what's going on there. When will you be seeing him again when is his next weird sexual torture session?"   Sam began to laugh and through her fit of giggling said,

"We don't have to wait he's in the cellar now he's been there all night."

Shirley followed Sam down the steep flight of steps that led into to the dingy basemen in the bowels of the building Sam jokingly referred to this part of the house as her dungeon. Shirley thought this was an apt description as it was cold dark and damp with bare brick walls.

After descending the steps they both remained still until their eyes adjusted to the poor light neither of them wanting to trip over anything.

Shirley got an awful whiff of stale human body odour and from one corner of the room she could hear a gentle moaning. When their eyes became accustomed to the low light they walked towards the direction of the smell and the sound of moaning.

Shirley now had a good view of the source of the noise and odour it was their tame subservient paedo Mr Victor S Petersham. She had seen evidence of Sam's handiwork before but she never ceased to be amazed by the bizarre sights. This extremely rich and successful businessman was bare naked and tied up spread eagled on a wooden cross. His arms were fully outspread at ninety degrees to his body and tied to the cross by his wrists. His legs were secured in a similar manner and tied at the ankles. In a surreal twist to this deviant spectacle a narrow chain was wrapped around his genitalia suspended from the other end of the chain and attached by a small meat hook was the head of a pig.   "My god Sam is that the head of a real pig dangling between his legs?"   Sam with obvious pleasure replied

"Yes, it is I got it from the butcher he thinks I'm going to make Brawn with it. It's an extra element of humiliation every time he looks down, he can see the face of a pig staring back at him and his naked pathetic body. That's how he gets his rocks off the more extreme the shame and indignity the more he craves for it."

"Where did you get this cross from, I've not seen it before?"   "I made Victor make it himself he's good at that sort of thing he's also a good source of income. In fact I earn so much money from him that I don't need to see my other clients anymore he pays me extra to have the dungeon to himself."

The putrid smell was now being to affect Shirley and she began to gag a little.

"I'm going back upstairs the smell is killing me do you want cut him loose and hose him down we need to speak to him before our meeting."   "He'll need re-hydrating so if you go upstairs and make a pot of tea and I will sort him out."

Shirley had witnessed Sam performing numerous acts of sadomasochism on her clients but she still continued to be amazed at the overwhelming control she had over her punters. She had this incredible power over men, even the ones that weren't perverts would be under her thumb. Sam hated men this was something they both shared in common, their abusive upbringings at the hands of sexual perverts had shaped and instilled this loathing of the opposite sex. But Sam also had a head for business so she used her these talents to make money lots of money.

Victor Shirley and Sam were now sitting round the kitchen table Victor had been hosed down in the cellar and was dressed in dry warm clothing. He was slurping at his steaming hot sweet tea in between taking bites of the pile of hot buttered toast in front of him.

Although Sam would subject him to the most degrading and perverted acts of sexual dominatrix, she also knew when to protect her asset. Sam was well aware that after a long arduous session in the cold damp conditions of her makeshift dungeon it had a profound effect on a person's wellbeing.

Victors body needed replenishing, plenty of fluids food and warmth were essential for him to recover. She didn't want to kill the goose that laid the golden eggs, well not until she had finished with him anyway.

As soon as Victor was back in the land of the living and was coherent enough to understand, Shirley and Sam told him about all the recent developments at Alldahope.

His instructions were to speak with Babs tell her that arrangements were being made for her to see her dad and find out what information she has. Victor agreed without question, whatever Sam wanted him to do he would comply without the least bit of hesitation. He knew who Babs was, in the short time he had worked at Alldahope he had noticed her because there was something about her, she stood out from the others.

Victor couldn't explain exactly what it was about her that made her stand out but she was different somehow, she had an air of self-confidence way above her years. He said he needed to leave in order to get some rest as his next shift at Alldahope was early the next day. When he left Shirley and Sam discussed what they should and shouldn't say at their next meeting in a couple of hours. They both agreed that the full details of the meeting up with Babs Guthy should be kept from the rest of the group. The group would be told that she simply alleges instances of child abuse but failed to give any further details. Under no circumstances could they reveal details of their arrangement with Babs to re-unite her with her father or let the group know about their man on the inside. With their action plan agreed they set off for the meeting in the cross pub.

When Shirley and Sam arrived the rest of the group were already there, they had taken their usual table in the corner well out of earshot. Shirley as she always did scanned the room to double check that their meeting couldn't be readily overlooked and that no one was in earshot. There was the usual spattering of locals, one long legged attractive blonde near the bar was teasing and giving a gentle ribbing to some old bloke who was giving her lecherous looks. The daft old git simply smiled and opened his arms wide with palms facing upwards in a humorous gesture as if to say, "Who me." The ribbing continued with the old guy simply smiling and nodding his head, the silly old git seemed not to hear a single word he was obviously deaf as a post. There was no sign of Stan Guthy, Shirley thought that would be the case after his antics yesterday. But she needed to get in touch with him to fill her part of the bargain with Babs so prior to leaving the house for the meeting she had asked Steve to do a C.C.T.V. trawl of his movements when he left the pub yesterday.

Shirley and Sam satisfied that they were safe to start the meeting sat down at the table bringing with them a fresh round of drinks.

Shirley spoke first and thanked everyone for coming, and she began to outline the details of her meeting with Babs Guthy. She explained how she knew Babs and the circumstances of her mothers death at the hands of her father and that this explained the reason why the note was addressed to her because of the support that Shirley had given her. She didn't mention the condition that Babs had insisted on that she be put in touch with her father just that she had details of child sexual abuse and that she would be giving us more exact details. No one seemed particularly surprised at this news and it was Martin who said,

"Well to be honest I think that we were all thinking along those lines"

The rest of the group simply nodded their heads in agreement Martin was right it ws what they had all been expecting. He then looked at Shirley

"Ok so what happens now surely we must make this official."

Shirley shook her head,

"We can't make it official yet firstly we have been given direct orders not to conduct any type of investigation with a threat of discipline or possibly legal action. And secondly, we don't at this moment in time have any concrete evidence we simply have the word of a young girl who come from a broken home and is now in care. After all even we can't be one hundred percent sure, she may be lying. What we have to do is secure some credible evidence and then have a re-think."

Shirley looked questionably at the group and continued.

"Is everyone agreeable to that, we do need to be of the same mind otherwise we cannot continue as we are."

Steve and Sam agreed straight away then all the groups attention was turned towards Martin. The expression on Martins face showed that he was giving was giving the matter some thought running through the implications of what was being asked. He took a deep breath and looked towards Shirley,

"I think you are right we need some concrete information if we show our hand now without any admissible evidence then everything, we have done so far may have been for nothing. I think we all know that something is going on at Alldahope given everything we have found out, so you can count me in. Especially in light of what I have found out about the previous alleged suicides." "You've made the right decision" Shirley said with an appreciative smile, "You may as well begin and tell us what you have found out."

"I have spoken with the guy who reported on the original case I only had a faint recollection of them and the only thing that I remembered was the blade that was used it was a craft knife similar to the ones used in model aircraft making it just seemed odd to me that's probably why I remembered it. But the reporter had a bad feeling about the whole thing, the girls were found dead together at the same time and it was recorded as a suicide pact. The police and social services investigations were closed pretty quickly without too much of an in-depth enquiry. So the reporter did a bit of digging into the girls background. The two girls were sisters and they were only in care because their parents died in a car crash. They weren't delinquents or from a broken home or a bad background or anything like that. In fact it was quite the opposite their parents were in the legal profession and highly paid and well respected.

This was something of a family tradition their elderly grandparents had also been in the legal profession. The girls were apparently unhappy at being at Alldahope but due to a successful legal challenge by their aged grandparents they were shortly due to leave Alldahope to live with their grandparents. They used their legal background to launch a full care and custody order they succeeded even though it was opposed by social services.

The reporter felt something wasn't right so he spoke with some of the girls at Alldahope who all said that the girls were looking forward to living with their grandparents so it just didn't add up why would the girls kill themselves.

He took this information to the police who said they would look into it but as far as he was aware, they didn't bother to do anything with the information and the incident was written off as a suicide pact and closed. But it seems strange to me why two girls who were about to leave Alldahope would want to kill themselves.

Shirley as did the rest of the group agreed and Shirley asked Steve if he could remember the case and if there were any forensics.

"I can just about remember the incident but if my memory is correct the investigating officers were DC Oli Latifeo and DS Grant Courtan and scenes of crime were not requested, I will trawl through the records when I am in the office next but I am reasonably sure I'm right, I have also got the results for that other job you asked me to look into."

"You can give me those details later it doesn't relate to this enquiry."

Steve immediately realised that Shirley wanted to keep his enquiry private and it was not to be shared with Martin.

"Ok not a problem, so what do we do now where do we take the investigation now."

Shirley replied,

"I think the only thing we can do now is to wait for some further info from Babs and take it from there, do we all agree?"

Martin then stood up

"Well if that's the end of the meeting I will wait to hear from you for the time of the next meeting I've got to go now I have an appointment over the road at the college. I'm doing a story on the outrageous decision to sell it to pay off the debts of Birmingham Colleges absolutely scandalous."

He downed his pint of real ale said his goodbyes and was gone. Steve looked at Shirley

"I am assuming you didn't want Martin to know about the enquiries into Stan Guthy."

"I think its best if keep that to ourselves we are treading a thin line in terms of legality so it's best to keep it to ourselves."

"Ok, anyway this is what I found out. I did a C.C.T.V trawl starting from when he left this pub. I managed to trace him as far as the Stourbridge canal by the bonded warehouse, that is where I lost him."

Shirley pursed her lips in disappointment "I was hoping we could get an address for him I need to speak with him."

Steve smiled "You still can I lost him on C.C.T.V. but I have a mate in the probation service and after a quick phone call I have an address. He is living in a flat in Amblecote." And handed over a scrap of paper with the details.

"You are a genius" Shirley said with a big beaming smile.

"C'mon Then Shirley spill the beans what do you want with Stan Guthy." Shirley related the deal she had made with Babs in exchange for the information on Alldahope. Steve realised then why Shirley was keeping it from Martin but she was wrong about treading a line regarding legality. They had in fact completely and utterly crossed the line.

With nothing else left to discuss Shirley got another round in and relaxed. The deaf old guy who everyone had been taking the piss out of was now letching after another attractive blonde amazingly he even managed to get a hug of her. She probably felt safe with the doddery old git or just felt sorry for him either way, he had probably tried to have a grope because she laughingly said

"You are a dirty old git Patrick"
he was then subject to some more piss taking none of which he could hear.

"You certainly get some characters in here" Shirley said to Steve.

"You're not kidding but talking of characters if you intend to see or speak with Stan Guthy you need to be very careful remember he has already killed one police officer."

"I'm not looking forward to it but we don't have any choice if we want to find out what's happening at Alldahope."

With the drinks finished Steve returned to the nick to do some digging re the historical suicide pact. Shirley and Sam got into their vehicle and were heading in a homeward direction, but when Shirley drove straight past the turn off towards home Sam asked, "You've gone past the turning where are we going?"

"There is no time like the present lets go and have a chat with Guthy."

"Oh shit," said a stunned Sam.

Stan Guthy was lying face down on the dinghy dirty carpet in his even depressingly dirtier bedsit. The accommodation had been provided by the probation service it was meant to be used as temporary shelter for ex-cons and druggies enrolled in a rehabilitation process. The transient nature of its residents was reflected in the appalling state of the place. None of its tenants previous or present wanted to live there and they had even less interest in sprucing the place up.

He was awoken by the sound of the front doorbell and he began to slowly come to his senses. Not realising where he was, he slowly scanned the room. When he saw the half empty bottle of whisky on the floor surrounded by several cans of Carlsberg special brew it slowly dawned on him. He remembered getting drunk in the Maverick pub and having an argument with some of the punters, eventually being told to leave by the landlord. On his return to this shit hole flat he continued his drinking spree until he passed out on the floor.   Normally he would ignore the incessant ringing of the bell but as part of his release a condition was to meet with his social worker and if he failed to comply, he would be recalled to prison. He slowly rose to his feet stretching his huge body and arms almost colliding with the ceiling light.   Expecting to see his spotty faced social worker he opened the front door and was surprised to see a female whom he immediately knew he recognised but where from.   Before Shirley could introduce herself and explain why she was there Guthy suddenly realised why he knew this woman and what she was.   It was that interfering bloody policewoman the one who had got him locked up in the first place. Fearing that she was here to recall him to prison his drunken drowsy state of consciousness was replaced by one of extreme anger and rage. There was no way he was going back to nick without a fight. He grabbed Shirley by the throat lifting her off her feet and dragging her in through the front door. Shirley was now in mid-air her feet dangling above the bare floorboards of the dark hallway a vice like grip was around her throat making it difficult for her to breath. The back of her head was pinned firmly against the wall as Guthy withdrew his arm preparing to ram his gigantic fist into her face. The sheer terror that engulfed Shirley gave her the strength to somehow move her head out of the way of the sledgehammer like immense fist hurtling towards her face. She felt the whoosh of air as the bone crushing fist narrowly brushed against her ear.

Guthy let out a roar as his fist went clean through the hallway wall completely demolishing brick and plasterboard his roar intensified as he realised his arm was embedded in the wall and stuck fast. This gave Shirley a brief moment to fight back and she tried to prise Guthys grip from around her neck. She also began to kick out aiming for his genitals she knew she had to do something quickly as it wouldn't be long before he would release his jammed arm from the wall. But it was to no avail she was having no effect whatsoever on Guthy.

It was like trying to knock a wall over with a feather. With an even louder shout Guthy pulled his arm free from the wall demolishing a large chunk of it in

98

the process. Shirley braced herself for the inevitable she knew she would not have the strength to avoid the forthcoming massive blow that she felt would take her head clean off. In fright she closed her eyes not wanting to watch Guthys bare knuckled fist that was about to destroy her face.

She then heard not a roar but a scream as she fell in a crumpled heap on the floor. She put her hands to her face and was surprised that it was still intact and not damaged in any way. For a split second she didn't realise what was happening until she saw the diminutive figure of Sam. She was standing over the prostrate figure of Stan Guthy who was rolling about the floor in agony. Sam was standing over him with a huge electric cattle prod and was repeatedly jabbing him with it time and time again. Even a giant like Guthy was not impervious to 10000v of electricity being pumped through his body.

Sam had prodded him so many times and each time she prolonged the length of time of the contact of the prod with various parts of his body that a faint sickly smell of burning flesh was wafting through the air.

"Keep fucking still or next time I will stab you in your fucking face you big cunt."

Guthy stared up from the floor at this petite attractive blonde who had inflicted so much excruciating pain on him, something that the vast majority of men were unable to. There was silence for a moment as Guthy appeared to be considering his options, Sam stood over him cattle prod at the ready.

Shirley was once again in awe of Sam, was there no end to her talents. Looking at the of pair of them together reminded of her of the biblical story of David and Goliath.

"I'm not going back to prison so do your fucking worst "Guthy then made a lunge for the cattle prod but Sam was prepared for him. She was also much quicker and she kept her threat and rammed the cattle prod firmly into his big ugly mug and pulled the trigger hard. The huge monster screamed even louder as he tried to swat away the prod from his face before rolling over onto his front. Shirley had now stood up and was standing by Sams side.

"Listen Guthy we are not here to take you back to prison we are here to talk to you about your daughter Babs."

He rolled onto his back and sat up propping himself against the half-demolished hallway wall. They now had his immediate and full attention, Guthy generally did not care for anything or anyone. The only exception was his beloved daughter she was the one and only thing he cared about. The only thing that outmatched his incredibly violent demeanour and behaviour was the love and adoration that he had for his daughter. He would be prepared to do anything for his angel the only ray of sunshine in his dark and disturbing world.

"What did you say about Babs?" asked a surprised and now attentive Guthy.

"Are you going to behave yourself so we can talk?"

"I thought you were here to take me back to prison and I am not going back without a fight."

With the situation now calm they all retired to the scruffy living room. Sam was shocked at the dirty filthy state of the living area but not so Shirley.

As a police officer Shirley had witnessed far worse than this. Shirley had even been in peoples living rooms where it was common practise to pee up the walls when they couldn't be bothered to go to the outside loo if it was raining. In a lot of homes she had been to it was common practise to allow family pets to crap on the floor and even worse they would not clean it up the faeces they would turn into crusty piles of filth.

Guthy was quite calm now and listened intently to what Shirley and Sam had to say. Shirley began to realise how much Guthy doted on his daughter and knew she would be able to exploit his feeling for hr own ends; this would give her a strong bargaining tool. Shirley and Sam had to choose their words carefully they did not want it to sound as if Babs was an informer or grass this was something that went against all his twisted criminal sense of values.

There ws nothing more detested in his world than being a grass, they were classed as the lowest of the low. They had cleverly worked it from a welfare point of view in particular the welfare of Babs herself. They had arranged a time and date for them to meet up with each other it was on the strict understanding that the initial meet would be overseen by Shirley. But Shirley was in no doubt that after the initial meeting it would be difficult for her to exercise much control as Guthy and Babs could quite easily make secret arrangements themselves.   The meeting between the pair ws to take place in Mary Stevens park at the Bandstand where Shirley and Sam could keep an eye on them. Shirley was rubbing her neck as she and Sam got back into their vehicle in all the commotion, she hadn't realised how much pain she was in where Guthy had held her aloft by her neck. "I thought I was a goner then when he was about to punch me in the face where are earth did you get that electric prodder from."

Sam smiled

"I bought it off the internet and I keep it fully charged with me in the car it's the most powerful one you can get. I got the idea from when I use a car battery and electrical wires attached to my punters balls but this is a thousand times more powerful."

"Well thank god you did otherwise I'd be in hospital now or worse, but we have got ourselves a bit of a hold on him he is obviously besotted with his daughter so we can use that to our advantage."

They then drove back quickly they now needed to give this information to Victor so he could tell Babs about the meeting and hopefully get some more information from her.

10

PEEPING TOMS

Victor was in the games room at Alldahope, he was fixing a leaking central heating radiator or rather pretending to fix it. He had his tools all laid out and looked the part but in reality, there was no leak but he knew that this was the spot where Babs generally hung out. He didn't have to wait very long Babs soon took up her regular spot by the window. After checking that no one was paying attention to them Victor smile at Babs "Hello my name's Victor."

Babs a little surprised at this unexpected introduction cautiously replied with a slightly hesitant

"hello."

"Babs, you need to listen to me. Shirley has sent me to speak with you I am here to help do you understand?"

Babs looked around the games room to make sure no one was watching and nodded her head.

"Shirley has been in touch with your dad and has arranged for you to meet him, now she needs to know from you what is going on here."

Babs stood up and as she turned to walk away said "Meet me in the garden behind the shed in five minutes."

Victor continued to pretend to fix the non-existent leak and after a couple of minutes began to pack his tools away.

Babs was overjoyed at the thought of seeing her father, even though he was an extremely violent and brutal man she felt safe with him she knew her dad doted on her and also, she likewise. A lot of his traits and characteristic had been passed on to Babs, she had a strength of character and determination of a much older person and she like her father was afraid of nothing nor anybody.

She could see Victor approaching from the direction of the house so she took a few steps back behind the shed so that no one could see them together.

"We need to do this quickly so as not to arouse anyone's suspicions," said Victor.

"Your dad will meet you in Mary Stevens Park tomorrow at twelve noon by the band stand do you know where it is?"

"Yes, my dad used to take me to the park all the time"

"Ok now what have you got for me?"

"They come in the middle of the night"

"Who comes in the middle of the night?" said a bemused Victor.

"Everyone calls them the night monsters but I know what they really are they are just nasty men wearing masks and they take you downstairs and do terrible things to you."

"And how do you know this?"

"Because I have seen them, I followed them one night when they took my friend Tipe"

"You say you followed them where did they go?"

"They went the same place as they always do down in the basement. They go down the steps from the main hallway using the door that is normally locked the room they use is at the bottom of the steps."

"Why don't the girls cry out or make a noise or something to attract someone's attention?"

"They can't because they have been drugged to make them sleepy."

Victor took a deep breath whilst digesting what Babs was telling him it seemed somewhat farfetched that whoever was behind this would be able to routinely, and continuously, drug all the girls at Alldahope.

With a slightly doubting voice Victor questioned what Babs was alleging.

"C'mon now Babs II find it a bit hard to swallow that the all the girls could be drugged every night there would be no way for them to do that."

"They don't have to Matron does it for them, all the girls are made to drink hot milk before bedtime. The drinks are spiked with tablets given to matron by a man who is or pretends to be a doctor. That's why I always sit in the same place by the window it doesn't arouse anyone suspicions because I always sit there all the time. Everyone thinks I just like to look out of the window. But the real reason I sit there is that every night is so that I can pour my milk away into that big pot plant without anyone seeing me."

Before any more discussion could take place, they heard the slamming of the rear door of the house. Fearing that someone could be walking towards them they silently indicated to each other to leave by different routes and whispered that they would speak again. As it turned out they had nothing to fear it was just somebody putting something into the rubbish bin outside the back door and they had now gone back inside. Victor knew he had a few hours before the night monsters appeared so he had time to get prepared.

Shirley walked through the front door of the house she shared with Sam and slammed the door behind her. With a face like thunder she went into the kitchen where Sam was sitting at the dining table studying a letter.

"What's the matter Shirley?"

"I've had a shit day at work and I have some bad news for us."

Sam shook her head in despair and gave Shirley a forlorn stare.

"Oh no don't tell me you've got some bad news as well."

Sam pursed her lips and nodded confirming she too had bad news.

"Let's just get it over with I'll go first" Shirley said in an exasperated tone. She sat down opposite Sam and began,

"The chief inspector called me into his office earlier today and introduced me to two Spanish police officers they are here because they recently had a speight of suspected murders in Benidorm. The cause of death has now been identified via Interpol as similar to the M.O. of the serial killings we had in Stourbridge i.e penetration through the back of the neck with a spike. They are obviously aware that a person has been convicted of our killings and is now dead. But they want to see if there is any connection such as an accomplice or a copycat killer. To make it worse I have been put in charge of looking after them, so anyway what's your bad news it can't be any worse than that."

Sam had a serious look on her face and Shirley realised that she was about to drop a bombshell. They had an almost telepathic relationship they understood each other so well.

Without saying a word Sam slid the contents of the letter she was holding across the table towards Shirley and she began to read. The note was made up of letters cut out from newspapers and glued together. She had seen notes like this before they were normally made in this fashion to avoid the analysis of an individual's handwriting. It read 'I KNOW WHAT YOU DID PUT ONE THOUSAND POUNDS IN BAG AND LEAVE ON KINVER TOPOGRAPHIC MAP SIX AM THURSDAY'.

"I don't think "so replied Sam as she slid a photograph across the table.

"This was also in the envelope"

Shirley eyed the picture with horror it showed Shirley and Sam smiling and joking as they both exited Birmingham mortuary the photo also exhibited a time and date.

Shirley turned ashen put her head in her hands and muttered

"Holy shit"

Sam was a fighter and she wasn't downbeat for long, her natural resilience and survival instincts soon kicked in.

"Right then Shirley you're the copper how do we nail this bastard "

"Ok let me run through this I think we can leave the Spanish police on the back burner I got the impression they are only here on a bit of a jolly but I can still keep a discreet eye on them. I will assign DC's Frank Fergas and Robert Peeves aka Dumb and Dumber to babysit them. They are a pair of pissheads and hopefully all four of them will spend their time getting drunk and chatting up slags. That should stop them from delving too deep into the Stourbridge killings. Our first concern is this blackmailing bastard. I think we do as they say in order to simply nab them from previous experience succumbing to blackmailers never works, they simply come back for more and more.

"Agreed"

said an excited Sam who seemed to be now revelling in this what she was now treating as a new adventure.

"But firstly what is a topographic map and where in Kinver is it?"

"Do you know where the rock houses are on Kinver edge Sam?"

Sam nodded

"Yes, I've been there a few times they are actual houses a bit like caves made within the hillside I believe that until recent times they were physically occupied but now they are a tourist attraction."

"Well on the top of that hill there is a flat area of grassland surrounded by trees in the middle of that grassland sits the Kinver Topographic map. As far as I can remember It's a brick built circular structure about three feet high with an engraved metal plate on top probably bronze or something like that. It's a bit like a compass and it shows the directions and distances away of various places it is sited there because it is on such a high elevation and you can see for miles."

Shirley saw that Sam was looking bemused and was obviously mulling something through in her mind.

"Ok spit it out what's on your mind Sam".

"Something doesn't add up here if this map is in a wide-open space surrounded by trees, then surely, we will be to see who collects the money and get hold of them."

"My thoughts exactly" agreed Shirley "Perhaps they are not the sharpest knife in the box or they are just overly cocky and not expecting us to challenge them either way we need to go there tonight before it gets dark so we can plan what we are going to do in the morning."

They decided to quickly grab something to eat and then make their way to Kinver edge to prepare their ambush.

Victor had found the set of master keys in a cabinet in his small office come workshop. The keys he had been issued with when he started work as the janitor come handyman did not include the keys to the door that gave access to the basement stairs. But it hadn't taken him long to sus out which one he needed and he was now inside the room that Babs had described to him at the bottom of the stairs. It reminded him a little of what Sam referred to as her dungeon in the basement of her house and as such he did not feel intimidated or apprehensive. He realised that this type of room or more aptly described cell satisfied some sort of unexplainable need or craving that he and people with his perverted sexual desires needed to satisfy some sort of need or craving. He worked quickly and quietly using his expertise in video and surveillance techniques to install a hidden high-resolution digital camera.

The room could only be dimly lit and this aided him in hiding the camera so that it could not be seen, but the high-resolution camera with night vision enhancement meant that he would get a good view of what was happening.

He needed no to test the wireless reception so that he could not only record but watch live what was going on. There was an electrical room directly opposite the basement entrance door. It was just big enough for him to secrete himself and the ventilation slats designed to keep the room cool to prevent any electrical overheating gave him an excellent view of anyone entering or exiting the door. He would wait until his shift had finished and when no one was looking he would take up his hiding place.

Shirley and Sam had made their way past the rock houses and followed the path to the top of the hill. It was a bit of a climb and when they had regained their breath, they stood at the edge of the tree line and eyed the Kinver Topographic map.

Sam was first to speak "This is exactly as you described, the map is in the middle of the clearing it's completely flat and there is no cover in any direction for at least fifty yards this seems a crazy place for the blackmailer to choose a drop off, there is something wrong I don't like it so what's the plan Shirley."

"Well I will do the drop off I will use this path here, after the drop I will return here and hide in the bushes and keep an eye out this side. You will already be hidden in position directly opposite. Whoever it is will have to either go past one of us or approach from my left or what will be your right, but then we will have sight of them coming from a long distance away so we will have them cornered. Make sure you bring your cattle prod with and that it's fully charged and I will have my Taser. We can zap so much electricity into the twat that they will light up like a Christmas tree."

Happy that they had the everything covered they decided to treat themselves to a few pints of Bathams bitter in the Plough and Harrow on Kinver high St, before returning home to get a good nights rest to prepare themselves for whatever was to befall them in the morning.

Victor was not affording himself the luxury of a nights sleep in a comfortable bed. He had got himself firmly ensconced in his hidey-hole overlooking the basement door he had checked the transmission of the hidden camera and managed to make himself as comfortable as possible by fashioning a seat on a high shelf that gave him an excellent view through the ventilation grill. He settled down for what he expected to be a long night.

Abie Dumas was dreaming of times gone by, of long summer days playing in the garden with her big sister whom she adored. When the sun began to set and they were all played out her mum would call them in for tea.

They would all be sat around the table Dad Mum me and sis and we would tell Mum and Dad about all the adventures we had that day. Tea would always finish with our Favourite Jelly and ice cream. Then after our baths we would all settle as a family down to watch the clangers followed by In the Night Garden with Upsy Daisy and Igglepiggle.

Even Dad would pretend to be interested although we secretly knew he would prefer to watch the news. Then it was off to bed Mum would come and tuck us in and give us a goodnight kiss.

But there were no more goodnight kisses, not since the plane crash that killed Mum and Dad and robbed her of a family. There was no more playing with my sister she had been sent to a different place far, far away and now she was here in this horrible place on her own. She was not a streetwise kid like many of the others her upbringing had been a kind and loving one. She was not hardened to life's knocks as the other kids were, they had been brought up in much harsher environment and as such had been forced to adapt. Abie didn't belong here she was a gentle naïve and extremely vulnerable young thing that had been let down by the social welfare system. Tonight as every night she had cried herself to sleep her only respite from her hellish existence was her dreams of the way things used to be.

The first thing she felt was something clamped firmly over her mouth and as she opened her frightened eyes, she could see who it was. The night monsters were here again, this was not the first they had come for her, in fact it had happened so many times she had lost count. She knew there was no point in shouting out for help because nobody came and it would only anger the night monsters who would hit her. She didn't put up a fight as they dragged her out of bed, she had succumbed to complete acceptance of what she knew was going to happen to her. They tried to stand her up but try as she might she could not stand up she was so drowsy and tired that her legs wouldn't work and they simply buckled beneath her.

The night monsters looked at each other and she thought she heard one of them say they've given her too much. One of the monsters then picked her up and tucked her under their arm as if carrying a parcel and they began to go down the stairs. In the stillness of the night Victor heard the creaking of the stairs and footsteps getting closer and closer. Whoever was coming toward him they were now at the bottom of the stairs just out of his view.

As the footsteps neared, they came into Victors field of vision. He realised now why the girls called them the night monsters they were wearing masks the type you can pick up at joke shops or fancy drees stores. He knew why they did this it was because if any of the young girls complained to anyone about what happened when they described their attackers as monsters then they wouldn't be believed. Their accounts would be put down as nightmares or downright lies.   He could see a total of three men all sporting grotesque face masks one of them was carrying something and it was a few seconds before he realised it was a young girl. A very small young girl who was being carried like a limp rag doll.

Victor felt like bursting out from his hideout and exacting his rage and anger on these lousy spineless excuses for human beings and rescue this poor young helpless child from their clutches. But he knew he mustn't, he needed to focus on the bigger picture and try with Shirley and Sam rescue all the girls. Within a few seconds they had unlocked the door to the basement stairs and were making their way down to the room at the bottom. Victor lost sight of them and he turned his attention to the monitor connected to the hidden camera. He watched as the door opened and the one carrying the girl entered the room. The hidden camera gave a much better than expected view of the room the night vision capability enhanced the quality of the picture. Victor realised then that this was not a room chosen at random but it had been adapted and modified. He could see that the walls and the inside of the door were clad with a thick layer of soundproofing material. At various points in the walls and ceiling, hooks and anchor points had been inserted. He watched in horror as the young girl was bound by each ankle and wrist with strapping. The girl was showing no resistance she had a terrified yet forlorn and submissive expression on her face. An expression that said she was all alone with all hope gone. Victor felt sick to his stomach as he witnessed each of the girls limbs being harnessed to various anchor points. The now naked young innocent was now suspended in mid-air her arms and legs spread akimbo. Victor was so disgusted and engrossed with what was going on he suddenly realised he had missed something. He blinked his eyes several times to make sure he wasn't seeing double. This couldn't be happening he thought. how could he have missed it. His mind was racing, there must be an explanation for what he was seeing. But as much as he scrutinised everything that he had seen so far, he couldn't understand what he was witnessing. He was positive that he had seen three masked figures take the girl down the steps to the basement. But now present in the room were four masked figures where they had come from or had he simply overlooked them.

He knew something was wrong there was no way he could have missed one of them, but there was only one entrance down to the basement where on earth had the fourth figure mysteriously appeared from? Victors vision became increasingly blurred as he witnessed the horrific abuse being inflicted by these vile beasts on such a defenceless young girl.

He realised that it was important to get as clear a recording of events as possible in order that he Shirley and Sam could do something about it. He wiped the monitor in case it had any condensation on the lens but it made no difference. Then he realised it was not condensation on the monitor but it was in fact the slow but steady stream of tears that was now cascading down his cheeks affecting his vision. His anger and his hatred stirred within him once more and he desperately wished he could run down the stairs burst into the room and wreak havoc on those devils disciples. He knew he needed to remain strong and also deep down he was aware that part of his utter revulsion revolved around himself. The perverted and depraved sexual urges that theses monsters had coursing through their veins were shared by him. His only solace was that he knew his sexual desires were perverted and he vowed to never succumb to his perversion. He did everything he possibly could to keep his urges at bay including allowing himself to be subject to Sam's sexual humiliation and torture. This self-abuse brought it home to him how a vulnerable young child would feel and what they would experience.

But if he could keep his deviant desires in check then why could these abusers not do the same. He knew in the long-term Sam would have something in mind for him to quash his paedophile feelings for good, he also had an idea of what it might be and he knew he would comply to her demands. The abuse and defilement continued until the poor mites tiny body could no longer tolerate it and she passed out. She lay there still and motionless suspended in mid-air. Blood was seeping out from her bodily orifices where she had been forcibly entered time and time again doing untold and irreparable damage to her diminutive and delicate frame. The sexual predators quickly became bored with a now unresponsive victim, they had obviously gleaned pleasure from the yelps and cries of pain she had let out every time one of them entered her. Her body had gone into self-preservation mode in order to shield her from more pain by simply shutting down and giving her a glimmer of respite. They began to untether the child, their depraved gluttonous sexual appetites satisfied it was time to discard this sacrifice and return her to where she should be, in her bed. They didn't want to completely destroy their sexual asset but allow her time to recover for their future needs.   Victor got himself ready they would be coming up the steps soon with their victim and he needed to stay alert to see if he could or uncover anything of evidence to identify any of the monsters.

The hidden camera showed that the soundproof room was now empty and he saw the door leading from the basement stairs begin to open and out they stepped onto the corridor. The child was still unconscious and was again being carried under the arm of one of the monsters like a package. The one carrying the child made his way up the stairs towards the child s bedroom.   They had now shut and locked the door to the stairs behind them but once again he was stunned by what he was seeing. He checked the hidden camera again which showed the room to be empty. And now the door to the cellar was locked but only three masked figures had emerged. So where on earth could the fourth one be, he had not seen the fourth person either go in or come out and yet this was the only entrance.

Whilst the two remaining figures were waiting for their accomplice to return one of them took off his mask. 'GOTCHA' thought Victor in a state of ecstatic euphoria. Even though he had taken off his grotesque mask he was still in disguise. He had a poorly fitting hairpiece and a false moustache but Victor recognised him because of a couple of distinguishing features. He had a large, hooked nose it reminded him of the late actor Ron Moody. But the most striking and unmissable feature about him was his left eye, he had a condition known as Arcus senilis which gives a white ring around the cornea.

There was no doubt about it this person was Dave Kempers, he had come across him before on the dark web initially. But later on he had met him to exchange explicit photographs of children and they had kept in contact for a while. But when Victor decided to cut all his ties with the paedo underworld and any paedo sexual practices they had lost contact. Victors only indulgence in the world of paedophilia was to look at photos but he soon became aware that the people he was meeting with took their urges to a different level. That was the point when he began to look at ways of curtailing his desires and when he had sought the help of Sam. The group were now joined by the one who had put the child back in bed and they made their way along the corridor and out of sight. When Victor heard the noise of the back door closing behind the perverts he emerged from his hidey hole. He was tempted to go back down the stairs to establish what had happened to the fourth masked person. He eventually decided against the urge to return to the room in case the missing pervert was hiding on the stairs and he would blow his cover. But he knew he needed to find some way to examine the basement for hidden doors or secret hiding places. However first things first he thought, he needed to remove the monitor and check that the recording had been successful. Then he needed to urgently tell Shirley and Sam what he had found out, the situation was far worse than anyone had feared and they must act quickly.

11

ESPERO QUE TE FOLLADA POR UN PEZ

Shirley was making her way up the path to the top of Kinver edge, it was a warm sunny morning and due to the early hour, the hillside was deserted. It was even too early for the morning dog walkers. She made her way past the tearoom and the unique tourist attraction of the rock houses that were built into the hillside.

She clutched the brown paper bag that she had been instructed to put the blackmail money in, she pondered the significance of the container; it was after all a standard brown paper bag. It had a square slightly rigid base so it could stand up easily and a pair of upright paper carrying handles. Shirley had filled the bag with a bundle of newspaper cut into the shape of banknotes, then she had bound the one hundred pieces with an elastic band. So as not to alert the blackmailer immediately that they looked in the bag a single ten-pound bank of England note had been inserted on top of the bundle. Together they had decided there was no way that they would comply with the demands of the blackmailer.   Their plan was quite simple, they would lay in wait for the blackmailer to appear and then surround them and pounce.
Shirley was armed with her police taser and pepper spray.
 Sam had bought her powerful cattle prod with her, if it was good enough to bring down Stan Guthy then it was capable of disabling anyone.

Sam was already in ensconced in her hiding place; they had chosen a place diametrically opposite where Shirley would approach with the money. Sam was well hidden in the long grass and low hanging foliage, but also had an extensive clear view of the approach to the topographic map. Sam had been there an hour and in all that time she had not seen a soul, the blackmailer has picked an isolated place Sam thought, but the location was open and she and Shirley would have a good clear view of anyone approaching the topographic map from quite a distance away.

It was a few minutes before six when Sam saw Shirley emerge into the clearing opposite her and she saw her walk stealthily towards the drop off place. Sams eyes darted from side to side constantly surveying the area for anyone approaching. Whilst Shirley placed the brown paper bag on the brass plate in the centre of the topographic map and took a look around. She could see in all directions for some considerable distance and she too like Sam thought that the drop off place was surprisingly open. Perhaps thought Shirley the blackmailer expected us to simply acquiesce to their demands and simply hand over the money willingly.

Shirley made her way back the way she had come, all the time keeping an alert eye open for anyone approaching. When she left the openness of the clearing and was back under cover of the surrounding foliage, she again looked behind her and ducked down to her knees. Then carefully she crawled back using the foliage as camouflage to the edge of the clearing and prepared to wait.

Five minutes went by, the deadline now passed then a further five minutes went by but still nothing happening and no one in sight. Shirley was beginning to think that this was a dry run to see if they would comply with the blackmail demand and that the blackmailer themselves may be hidden somewhere spying on her. Then in the distance she saw something, whoever or whatever it was they were a considerable distance away.

Shirley had not been expecting that this could have been the approach path because both her and Sam could see them approaching for several hundred yards, it just didn't make sense. Sam had also caught sight of somebody approaching way off in the distance, suspicious that this may be some sort of decoy to divert their attention she continued to scan the entire area. But everywhere else was deserted not a soul in sight. After several minutes Shirley began to have a clearer view of what was approaching it was what appeared to be a single male person with a dog. The dog was about the size of an average collie and they were heading towards the topographic map but were still some distance away perhaps a couple of hundred yards. Then suddenly it hit her Shirley thought she realised what was happening the blackmailer may have trained the dog to fetch the bag and run back with it towards their owner.

This would give them a huge head start and Shirley or Sam would not be able to catch up with them and they would make their escape. That must be it she thought that is why it is so open they were going to use the dog.

Shirley began to panic as what to do next, if she had brought a couple of police radios with her then she could have told Sam to make her way unseen towards the approaching man. Shirley could remain within striking distance of the map, so when the dog was released, she could sprint there and taser the dog before it got the package. Sam would be close enough to deal with its owner and we would get the bastard. But Shirley had decided not to use police radios for fear of being overheard by anyone else because even when used back-to-back they sometimes had an uncannily long range especially when used in a place so high up with no obstructions.

Shirley was wracking her brains trying to figure out what would be the best thing to do now, she estimated they would have five or six minutes before they needed to act. The approaching man and dog were still some distance away and it took some time before Shirley realised that they didn't appear to be getting any closer. Had they got cold feet Shirley mused or were they just checking that the coast was clear. Then to Shirleys bewilderment man and dog appeared to be moving away. She turned her gaze towards Sam to see if she was witnessing the same, as she turned her head in Sams direction her heart jumped into her mouth.

Sam wasn't hidden under cover of the foliage but was out in the open in the middle of the clearing running with all her might towards the topographic map. My god thought Shirley but then she saw it too, both she and Sam had been concentrating so hard on the dog walker and the possible approach on foot by anyone else that they hadn't looked up towards the sky.

Hovering a few feet above the map and was a drone, attached to the underside of it was a hook and this was now slowly descending towards the package. Sam was still frantically sprinting towards the map but was some way away when the hook was lowered into position underneath the carrying handles of the package.

With the handles secured by the hook the drone lifted off skywards with Sam looking on in amazement as the drone and the package began to disappear way into the distance.

Shirley and Sam looked at each other from opposite sides of the topographic map in abject silence, both stunned by what they had just witnessed. It dawned on the pair of them why the blackmailer had chosen what they had thought initially was an odd location for the drop. It also became clear why they had been given the bag to place the money in, because of the rigid paper handles it would allow the drone to easily pick the package up.

As they drove back towards Stourbridge, they began to discuss what had happened. Shirley said,

"Whoever was operating the drone must have been close so that they could direct it to the exact spot perhaps we should go back and search the area in case they are still there."

Sam shook her head

"No I got close enough to see the drone clearly, it had a camera attached, so that whoever was operating it could have been anywhere. I think I am right in saying that because the location is so high up the remote signal is not interrupted and it can be controlled from some considerable distance away. Whoever is behind this has thought it through very carefully and they obviously know what they are doing. We have underestimated our adversary we won't do that again we need to up our game."

Shirley had a feeling that Sam was somehow beginning to take some pleasure from the idea of being pitched against a worthy and devious adversary. Shirley agreed, they had both grossly underestimated their opponent all they could do now was wait for the blackmailer to get in touch again as they obviously would do because they had only succeeded in securing ten pounds and some blank paper for all their efforts.

Back at the house Victor was waiting outside in his car for them and together they entered and within a few minutes were sitting around the kitchen table with a cup of tea. Shirley outlined to Victor what had just happened and he listened intently, he was a very clever man and Sam and Shirley had already decided to enlist his help and include him in any further encounters with the blackmailer.

Before Victor told the girls of what he had found out at Alldahope he asked of the girls what it was they were being blackmailed over. Knowing that they could trust Victor as he was so much under Sams control that they showed him the timed and dated picture of the pair of them leaving the mortuary. Victor didn't need to ask anything further of them he was very astute and kept himself updated with local news and events knew full well what the implication of the snapshot meant. He eyed the girls with a mixture of awe and intense admiration, he knew the girls were very determined and would go to extremes to obtain their goals but the picture showed how ruthless they actually were. It threw a completely new light on recent dramatic events that had thrown Stourbridge into the national and international media headlines.

The girls realised that this revelation had taken Victor by surprise but also intensified their relationship with each other.

Without commenting further on the girls actions he then went into great detail about last nights happenings at Alldahope the girls listened intently hanging on his every word. The girls, likewise, Victor had not expected things to be as bad as he had uncovered, they collectively realised without expressing it that they needed to escalate their actions and put a stop to these vile and depraved practices as soon as they possibly could.

Victor then produced a laptop placing it on the kitchen table with the screen facing Sam and Shirley, and in a hushed sombre tone

"Before I press play are you sure you want to view this?"

With grim faces they nodded indicating yes and Victor pressed the play button. Victor positioned himself so that he couldn't see the recording, he had no wish to ever see it again. A shiver still went through his spine as he heard the audio and he relived every vile second of the atrocious abuse as the child in between sobbing and cries of pain pleaded and begged repeatedly for them to stop.

He looked into the faces of Shirley and Sam, they were ashen white and horror struck. He realised that he was not the only one who found it difficult to control his emotions as he saw the tears rolling down their faces dripping onto the kitchen table forming a salty liquid pool. Shirley and Sam felt an extreme sense of outrage and a huge feeling of empathy with the Alldahope girls.

They had both been subject to awful abuse themselves at Alldahope and this had fuelled their hatred of men and drove them to do what they do. But even they were taken aback at how the situation had intensified in its ritualistic extreme sexual abuse. Victor and Sam both looked toward Shirley they knew that things had taken a turn and some decisions and a strategy needed to be decided upon to further their investigation.

Shirley thought long and hard whilst the others waited for her to formulate some options. Another pot of steaming hot tea was placed on the table and Sam also produced some biscuits to munch whilst they waited for Shirley.

Sam and Victor put their teas down when Shirley began to speak.

"This is how I see it; the simple options are number one, we put what we have before senior officers so that they can instigate an investigation or number two we go it alone. Now if we go to senior officers me and Steve will be for the high jump because we have contravened a direct order. In addition we could possibly face prosecution for our involvement with Guthy. Victor would be questioned about his activities and his past involvement with known paedophiles which will also lead back to you Sam and maybe your activities will be scrutinised. It would be difficult to keep Martins name out of it and I don't think it would reflect well on him and may harm his career. Also there is no guarantee that they will fully investigate it and not sweep it under the table as they are doing now. If we go with option two then we will have to cross over into illegal and unknown territory no two ways about it we will be fairly and squarely outside the law. Our enquiry would have a greater chance of success but then obviously we have to then decide what to do with the suspects. We would have to distance ourselves from Martin who I don't believe would risk doing anything illegal and also Steve, although he is not averse to bending the rules, I don't think he would be on board to working completely outside the law. We would still need his forensic help but we could drip feed him certain bits of information without involving him too much. In view of what happened last night at Alldahope whatever we decide we have to make our minds up now." They all knew instinctively what option they needed to take but before they committed themselves Shirley asked about the C.C.T.V footage and how Victor had managed to obtain it.

Victor explained that his factory premises   because they were adjacent to the Stourbridge canal had been subject to numerous break ins and as such, he had installed overt and covert cameras to combat the burglaries. And whilst installing and maintaining his system he found that he had developed an interest in the subject and had become a bit of an expert.

Shirley realised that Victors expertise in C.C.T.V. technology could come in extremely useful not only in their Alldahope enquiry but also their problem blackmailer who would undoubtedly make contact again soon for possibly an even greater demand.

It didn't take long for them all to agree to go with option two especially after Sam had shouted out in anger "Let's go and get the bastards.

Such passion and anger from someone who is so petite with picture book like delicate features that gave her an air of innocence did not seem to corollate with such an outburst.

This total mismatch bought smiles to Victor and Shirleys face and it wasn't wasted on Sam either she realised the humour in the situation and this was not the first time. Her forthright and strong emotional outbursts had previously been the source of amusement.

Shirley began to outline her plan for the next stage of their enquiry.

"Victor you need to find some way to infiltrate these bastards or find some way of identifying them."

With an even bigger grin that he already had he replied

"Already done, in light of what happened last night I expected you would want me to take it a stage further. What I haven't told you yet is that one of the masked men removed their mask whilst they were in my view and I know who he is. His name is Dave Kempers and I have come across him before so I have re-established contact with him hopefully, I will be seeing him in a couple of hours' time."

"That's brilliant, did you also get in touch with Babs and pass on details of the meeting with her dad?"

"Yes, I did I gave her the information and she told me about the night monsters and where they took the girls. That enabled me to set up the cameras and the observation post."

"Sam, you need to go to café in the park and keep eye on Babs and her dad, Victor, after you have made contact with Kempers we will all meet back here and decide what we are going to do, unfortunately I have to go to work."

Meeting over they quickly downed their tea finished off the few remaining biscuits and set about their respective tasks.

Shirley was in the detectives office she scanned her collection of detectives, Dc Oli Latifeo he could best be described as a journeyman, he would go to great lengths to avoid work. His moves and side swerves to avoid becoming embroiled with any meaningful endeavours or anything that would impair his carefree feet up laid-back lifestyle were legendary. He was however from a line managers point of view quite easy to manage, his head down unadventurous attitude meant that he wouldn't present any challenges.

Dumb and Dumber on the other hand were a different kettle of fish altogether. Detective constables Frank Fergas and Robert Peeves could best be described as the oldest swingers in town. Both of them used their positions to facilitate their predatory sexual tendencies they regarded every late turn shift or every police operation as an opportunity to go granny grabbing or chubby chasing. The simple premise behind their tendency towards the old or overweight sexual conquests was because they would have a greater chance of success. This combined with their voracious appetite for alcohol and persistent booze bingeing meant that they left themselves open for manipulation and Shirley had already amassed a few misdemeanours perpetrated by them that she kept in reserve in order to use at a later date should she need to. But both of them were quite devious and had a nasty streak running through them and Fergas in particular could be incredibly two faced and underhand and Shirley knew that he was an informant for higher ranking officers. He would snitch on and even set up other officers at the behest of senior officers who would in return often turn a blind eye to their shenanigans.

The rest of her team had been swallowed up by the specialist unit that had been set up in response to an epidemic of carjacking in the Stourbridge area. She had also been given the responsibility of looking after the two Spanish officers who were examining similarities between a spate of killings in the Benidorm area which mimicked the modus operandi of the Stourbridge serial killings.

One of Shirleys responsibilities was to allocate various enquiries to her officers which had now become an absolute joke. Dumb and Dumber had been assigned exclusively to chaperone the Spanish officers and Shirley was under orders not to utilise them for anything else. That left her with one remaining officer the sloth like Latifeo. She had given the detectives their daily briefing running through some of the regular problems and crimes to keep them updated. There was only one enquiry to allocate, it was a missing person. This would not normally be a job for Cid but this one had been classed as vulnerable; it was a young fifteen-year-old boy who had been missing for a couple of days. It was out of character for him to disappear and he had last been seen on his bicycle along the canal on his way towards Stourbridge college.

Uniformed officers had conducted initial enquiries including questioning friends and family in addition to making a trawl of hospital records but all to no avail. Therefore more in-depth investigation was deemed necessary and thus handed over to CID. Latifeo liked this type of enquiry because it was easy and didn't involve a great deal of work. He would not be doing much at all and if he could be bothered, he may do a C.C.T.V trawl but little else.

Dumb and dumber seemed to be getting along well with their Spanish counterparts they were laughing and joking together and Shirley could hear a few Spanish phrases interspersed in their conversations. She ws aware that all four of them had been seen to frequent pubs bars and clubs in the Stourbridge area. She had hoped that this would curtail the thoroughness and rigour of their investigation but she had been keeping an eye on them and she knew that in between bouts of drinking they had been asking for and examining a lot of records and reports in addition to questioning a number of people.

With everything else going on this was something she could have done without. She heard Dumb and Dumber making arrangements with the Spanish detectives to take them on a grab a granny night at Kingswinford. She knew that would be a late drunken night and that they would be good for nothing the next day they certainly wouldn't be doing much police work.

Latifeo had joined in the conversation and they appeared to be talking about what they would be doing to relax at the weekend. He had heard Dumb and Dumber plans to take the Spaniards on a grab a granny night whilst Latifeo tried to explain that he was investigating a missing person who was last seen on the canal. So his intentions were to make enquiries Canalside but in reality, he would be taking his fishing rods and spend a few hours fishing.

Ridiculously even though the Spaniards spoke and understood English well he was talking slowly and in an exaggerated pidgin English dialect. The Spaniards were smiling back at him nodding their heads at Latifeo whilst imitating the actions of someone fishing. They were obviously unbeknown to Latifeo taking the piss out of him, Shirleys ears pricked up when she heard them reply to him in Spanish. 'Espero que te folloda por un Pez' the Spaniards said in unison whilst at the same time giving Latifeo the thumbs up sign.

Shirley needed to get back home to catch up with Sam and Victor so she needed to make sure everything was covered investigation wise so she spoke with Latifeo.

"Have you got any outstanding enquiries that need my attention?"

"No sarge I'm fully up to date no worries there."

"What do you think of the Spanish guys"

"They seem to be ok I was just telling them about my love of fishing and they replied with some popular Spanish phrase about fishing that means something like happy fishing or something like that."

"That's nice of them, anyway I have to be elsewhere if there are any problems give me a call" and with that she left the office.

As she made her way to her car, she realised she that there was more than met the eye to the Spaniards, they had been asking some awkward questions and going through the files in depth. Also they were taking the piss, unknown to anyone in the office Shirley had spent several years at Wordsley school as a day student in the learning for life programme. The subject she had studied was Spanish and she knew the literal translation of 'Espero que te follada por un Pez'. It didn't mean happy fishing but was in fact a derogatory term meaning 'I hope you get Fucked by a Fish'

12

SURPRISE SURPRISE

Babs Guthy and her violent thug of a father were sitting in the café of Stourbridge park. Babs was eating her way through a giant slice of chocolate fudge cake only stopping occasionally to take a swig of her large fizzy drink.

Her Father was drinking from a huge mug of tea, he knew that the park café would not serve alcohol so he had bought along a hip flask full of whisky and had emptied the majority of its contents in his hot steaming tea. This is how life should be thought she had enjoyed spending time with her dad, they had fed the ducks, her dad had pushed her on the swings and they had enjoyed an ice cream.

This was so different to the last few months of living hell she had endured at Alldahope. She felt safe, she didn't feel the need to constantly keep her wits about her and be ready for everything she could relax while her father was here.

When the huge slice of chocolate heaven had been fully devoured Babs and her father discussed the goings on at Alldahope. Babs could see the anger in her father's face as she told him about the abuse that most of the girls suffered. His anger abated somewhat when Babs assured him that she had not been victim of abuse, she thought the reason for that in part was her strong personality but mainly because everyone knew who her father was and what he was capable of.

They only had a little more time before Babs had to be back at Alldahope so between them they made arrangements to see each other gain They also agreed to keep their meeting secret from the nosey coppers. This was something that Shirley was reticent about when she initially arranged for them to meet. She had wanted to be in a position where she could control and monitor their liaisons but she realised that this might happen.

Just before they departed Guthy said to his daughter, "Remember we must keep our meetings secret and you must tell me if anyone touches or interferes with you and I will fucking kill them forget the useless coppers. There is just one last thing I need to do and that is to sort that copper out, the one who is sitting just behind us and has been watching our movements all day." Sam nearly fell off her seat when Guthy suddenly stood up and walked over to where she was sitting sipping at her coffee.

Both she and Shirley had seriously underestimated Guthy and Babs, the violent monster wasn't as obtuse as they had taken him to be. As soon as he and his daughter met, they both discussed the probability that they were being watched and they quickly and surreptitiously scanned their surroundings and it didn't take long before they spotted Sam sitting in the café keeping an eye on them. This was why Guthy had chosen to finish off in the café in order to get close to her.

Sams heart was pounding she was not expecting this, as the imposing figure of Guthy leant over her table his huge body appearing to totally engulf her diminutive frame. His face was now inches from Sams, she was quickly thinking of what to do to defend herself she had not brought her electric cattle prod, but she had with her a smaller handheld one in her bag. The problem being is that she knew she would not have time to retrieve it with Guthy being so close. A self-satisfied sickly grin slowly spread across Guthys face he had her cornered and although her face did not betray her sense of foreboding, he knew that she must be feeling incredibly intimidated.

Guthy had a great deal of respect for Sam normally by now his prey would be shitting themselves and shaking with fear, but not Sam, her face was still resolute and she didn't budge an inch.

"If you or any of your copper mates follow me or my daughter again, I will rip your fucking heads off and shove them up their arses do you understand?"   Without flinching Sam replied "You are only seeing your daughter with our permission. We can just as easily stop your meeting by getting you recalled to prison. If you threaten me again, I will introduce you to my cattle prod again only this time I will shove it up your fucking arse, now back off and get out of my fucking face."

Guthy stared menacingly directly into Sams eyes and held his intense gaze for what seemed like an age, but still Sam didn't flinch she refused to allow herself to be overawed even by this gigantic beast.

Guthy stood up and began to roar with laughter, he had over several years intimidated, threatened, and frightened hundreds possibly even thousands of people. There had been a mixture of some of the most hardened and brutal criminals and thugs, some of them had been frozen rigid with fear and it wasn't uncommon for some of them to be so scared that they soiled themselves on the spot or thrown up in sheer terror. But now in front of him was a dainty little stunning female with a porcelain doll like figure who showed no fear and had the backbone to stand up to him.

He leant back down to meet Sam at eye level again only this time he had a broad almost appreciative smile on his face. "You've got a big pair of balls on you young lady and he stuck out his gigantic hand. Once again without showing fear or trepidation she put her hand in his. It was a surreal sight to see her hand completely enveloped by Guthys gargantuan bear like paw.

Guthy was still exhibiting a broad smile as he and Babs left the café, Sams heart began to slow down back to normal and she started to relax and finish her coffee as she watched Guthy and Babs disappear past the bandstand and out of sight.   Chequers pub in Stourbridge was as always busy with lunchtime drinkers, most tables were taken with groups scoffing the Wetherspoons daily special menu. The early drinkers as usual were congregated in one corner next to the floor to ceiling windows and were now quite merry. With the pub being so busy Victor couldn't see who he was supposed to be meeting so he weaved in and out of the crowded tables until he found who he had been looking for. They had taken a small table tucked away under the stairs that lead up to the first-floor toilets. He walked over and shook the hand of his old acquaintance Dave Kempers.

"I couldn't see you under here, I thought you may have changed your mind, it's been a long time how are you doing Dave?"

"I'm doing really well thanks for asking all the better for hearing from you out of the blue."

Victor and Dave exchanged pleasantries for some time, but they both knew that they were just filling time until they felt relaxed enough to get down to what they really wanted to talk about.

It was Victor who cautiously approached the subject.

"How is everything in general, how is life treating you?"

Knowing full well what Victor was leading up to Dave replied.

"Yes, life is treating me very well at the moment I certainly can't complain how about you what are you doing with yourself these days?"

Victor gave an apathetic shrug of his shoulders,

"to be honest I'm a bit bored these days I've even took a job as a handyman just to fill my time".

"Wow you must be bored Victor, the richest man in Stourbridge and you take a menial low paid job."

"It's not about the money I'd do the job free gratis I just took it to occupy my time and keep my mind off other things if you know what I mean. But problem is it's had the opposite effect."

"How so Victor?" Dave asked curiously.

"Well I have tried to keep my feelings in check and keep busy hence I applied for and got a job as a handyman, however the position is in a children's home and its re-ignited some old feelings that I can't shake off."

Victor saw Daves face light up at this remark, there is nothing more satisfying for a paedophile than to keep company with someone who has the same perverted feelings. In some way it eases their guilt and in part justifies their depraved sexual desires.

When Victor revealed that the name of the home that he was working in was Alldahope Dave was almost euphoric.

With a sickly lecherous grin spreading across his face Dave said.

"Alldahope`, you have certainly come to the right person I think that I may be able to help you there in fact no cancel that I know that I can help you. I'll get us another round in and tell you all about it I think you'll be impressed."

As Dave walked to the bar Victor knew he had him hooked and he would be desperate to reveal to him tell Alldahopes secrets and get him involved with the sordid practises. Dave put the full pints down on the table so eagerly that he almost spilt them, Victor had been spot on with his assessment of his old pervert acquaintance and he was soon divulging the secret underworld practises at Alldahope.

Detectives Dumb and Dumber had taken Jose and Mateo on a pub crawl of Stourbridge, they were now getting into or more accurately falling into the CID pool car. Frank Fergas was in the driver's seat, his ever-present shadow Dc Robert Peeves clambered into the passenger seat, with the Spanish Detectives taking what they believed to be the safest seats in the rear. Frank wasn't overly concerned with drink driving if he was stopped, he would simply flash his badge. When the drink was in the sense was out especially when the prospect of a grab a granny night was in the offing. Dumb and Dumber were not the most committed of officers and their level of competence and diligence were only slightly better than that of the indolent and slothful like activities of Latifeo. They had been chaperoning the Spanish detectives and had been greatly surprised at how fastidious their counterparts were.

Jose and Mateo had visited, under the supervision of Dumb and Dumber all the crime scenes concerned with the Stourbridge serial killer, including the mortuary where they had interviewed the staff including morticians and the pathologist Sally Drice.

They had trawled through scores of statements and interview records and analysed every aspect of the enquiry in a remarkable short space of time. This was something Dumb and Dumber were not used to, for them work was a way of facilitating their carefree and licentious way of life, allowing them to drink to excess and indulge in their favourite pastime of pursuing sexual conquests. So after having worked much harder than they were used to by having to assist them they were now ready for a wild night out.

There were various pubs and clubs in and around the Stourbridge area that hosted the laughably called over 25s nights. Why on earth they referred to themselves as over 25s was a bit of a nonsense as the average age of most of the participants would range from 50 years upwards at least. This suited Dumb and Dumber as their philosophy was the older fatter and uglier the better because they would be easier to pull. Some or indeed most of their countless sexual conquests over the years could only be described as hideous. Jose and Mateo whilst both married men were not averse to going overboard and cheating on their wives.

Their expectations however were much higher. They would not be content with the typical munters that Dumb and Dumber pulled and they would be setting their sights much higher. They had gone to one of the bigger venues just on the outskirts of the neighbouring village of Kingswinford, hopefully this would meet all their needs.

Fergas parked the CID car in the rear carpark of the club away from prying eyes so that it couldn't be seen from the main road. On entry Fergas led the way flashing his badge at the doormen saying,

"These are with me"

this allowed them all to enter without paying the normal entrance fee. It was strictly against police protocol but using the authority of   the warrant of their office was a long-standing tradition.

Fergas and Peeves headed straight for the bar and barged their way to the front of the queue to get the first of what was to be many beers. Jose and Mateo on the other hand were more interested in eyeing up the talent without feeling the need or desire to get blind drunk in the process.

The club was very busy there were clusters of women dancing around their handbags whilst keeping their eyes open and surveying the room at the collection of small groups of predatory males who were in turn doing the same. The entire scene resembled a dystopian cattle market with females outnumbering the men by about two to one.

The four of them were now standing together near the dance floor like a pack of predators assessing the vulnerability of their prey and which ones to single out from the pack.

With a huge drunken grin across his face Fergas slurred out to Jose
"What do you think of the place."
"Este lugar es un paraiso para los cerdos."
"Ok you got me what does that mean?"
"It means its paradise for gentlemen" replied Jose.
"I'll try and remember that it could be a good chat up line."
Dumb and Dumber then began their hunt for suitable females and as

always, their first law of chat up was 'Go ugly early'.

After several knock backs including a few comments ranging from 'No thanks' to 'Go and fuck yourselves.' Dumb and Dumber bagged a willing pair of females and were now secreted in one darkened corner of the room, exchanging saliva with what could only be described as a couple of old slappers. Jose and Mateo looked on in astonishment they could not believe their eyes. Fergas and Peeves weren't the best-looking blokes in the world but the two specimens that they were groping and fondling looked old enough to be their grandmothers. Jose suggested that they give up and go elsewhere, but Mateo persuaded him to stay for a little longer, they could pass the time having a drink and if they still couldn't see anything worthy of a second look then they would leave. Dumb and Dumber were alone at the table the two ugly sisters had gone to powder their noses. These were two of the easiest pick-ups they had ever come across. Even Peeves who had been with some real wrinkly old hags in the past was surprised at how easy the girls were. Fergas was anxious to his leg over as quickly as possible whilst he was still just about capable of performing before the alcohol took over and, in a semi, drunken slur managed to utter. "I think we should take them back to the car and shag them in the car park."

Peeves shook his head as he was downing the last of his pint "No, I've got it sorted, they've got a flat we can take the pair back there, they are both absolutely gagging for it, they have even been buying all the drinks that has to be a first this is going to be the easiest shag ever." "Okay suits me, but as soon as were done its straight back in the car and we fuck off."

At this the girls returned; they had put on several layers of make-up that looked like it had been applied using a builders trowel. "There goes our lift" said Jose as he watched Dumb and Dumber walk albeit unsteadily out of the club arm in arm. "Cerdos feos gordos" exclaimed Mateo.

Jose disagreed

"To call them ugly fat pigs is an insult to pigs; I think we are wasting our time here let's go."

Having finished their drinks they both stood up to go, as they turned towards the door two surprisingly good-looking females walked past them and sat at a nearby table. As they passed by, they gave the guys a pleasant smile.

Automatically the guys sat down these girls unlike the rest of the females they had seen were very attractive with figures to suit.

They ordered another drink whilst they decided on what to do next. Jose casually looked over at the table where the girls were sitting and received another even bigger smile in return. Trying to be as discrete as he could he said to Mateo.

"Those attractive girls are giving us the eye I think we should go talk to them."

Mateo who had his back to the girls turned his head and he also received a warm welcoming smile in return.

"They are definitely interested we could take them back to our hotel especially now that Dumb and Dumber have disappeared, we don't want them knowing anything." Said Jose, as he got off his stool and began to walk towards the girls closely followed by Mateo.

They introduced themselves and were asked to join the girls at their table. The conversation flowed easily as did the alcohol. The girls were sisters and it showed. They looked almost identical with the same slim but curvaceous figures with long flowing blonde hair, stunning looks and piercing blue eyes.

They almost looked out of place compared with the majority of the other woman especially when they spoke. They were not loud or brash but quietly spoken and quite demure and very pleasant to speak with. They were certainly a cut above the rest. They were getting along well together exchanging pleasantries and general chit chat. The girls were especially interested when Jose told them they were police officers and why they were here. They told them about the recent murders in Benidorm. Over the course of approximately one week there had been several murders, all occurring late at night in the back streets of the town. The victims were either down and out beggars or drunken tourists. They only thing that connected the victims was that they were all vulnerable. It was initially thought that the attacks were centred on the gay community as the first three victims were gay men and were killed in the back streets of the old town. This theory was dismissed as subsequent other victims were discovered across the breath of Benidorm including the new town and a lot of these victims had no connection with the gay community. Prissy and Tess were spellbound by their accounts and this gave the Spanish officers a feeling of celebrity like status and in turn encouraged them to divulge even more details of the murders.

Prissy then asked curiously why the officers were in Stourbridge when the murders they were investigating happened in Benidorm. The girls were even more fascinated when the detectives told them they were here in Stourbridge because Interpol had identified a similar MO with the infamous Stourbridge serial killer. Even though the guys knew that they shouldn't reveal details of their investigation to anyone outside the Force the amount of alcohol they had drunk has loosened their tongues. This combined with the effect it was having on the girls made the guys divulge details that even the British police had not been informed of.

The girls told Jose and Mateo that the Stourbridge serial killer was the biggest series of events that had ever happened to the small town of Stourbridge and it was all anybody spoke about for months. It even made headlines all around the world for a short time especially when a suspect who was a serving police officer was arrested. But the girls were confused as to how it could have any connection with murders in Benidorm.

The detectives went on to explain that it was the method used to kill the victims that gave the connection. Post-mortem results had found traces of polyethylene in several of the victims hair this indicated that an attempt had been made to suffocate them by placing a plastic bag over their heads but this had been unsuccessful because the cause of death was not by suffocation.

A number of the other victims showed signs of swelling to the spinal cord and bruises to the neck. This indicates that someone has tried to kill them by snapping their neck but they didn't use enough force so the blood flow in the brainstem was fully disrupted. There were also other failed methods used on other victims but most of the deaths were caused by a long thin object inserted into the back of their necks and forced all the way through. This being the same method as the Stourbridge serial killer. It seems as if someone is practising finding a way to kill someone but when it fails, they revert to the spike through the neck. Prissy shuddered and said "I don't know how you can deal with something like that it sends a shiver down my spine it sounds really gruesome. But I can remember the local paper reporting about that thing with the neck because it caused a row with the police who didn't want it made public."   Jose nodded his head "The reason for that is twofold, one is so that you can use the information to make sure you have the right suspect and secondly to prevent any copycat killings, but someone obviously leaked the information to the press."

"Wow"

said Tess

"So do you think that this is what has happened, someone is a copycat killer?"

Anxious to get in on the conversation Mateo spoke up

"Either that or the Stourbridge serial killer had an accomplice, but I think you are right it is most likely that someone read about it in the newspaper and as you say is using the method as a copycat killer."

With the subject of the copycat killings exhausted the conversation towards the girls. As evidenced by their similar appearance the girls said that they were sisters and that they were both masseuses. This was something the guys picked up on straight away, as far as they were concerned this was getting better and better. Two gorgeous looking well-spoken lovely girls who were qualified masseuses. The drinks and the conversation continued with Jose and Mateo completely forgetting about their absent colleagues who had deserted them for the chance of a quick leg over.

Dumb and Dumber by now were back at the girls flat, it was quite disgusting and remarkably run down it was not much better than a squat.

This didn't particularly bother them as all they wanted was sex and when they were sated, they would be straight out of there as was their normal behaviour.

The guys had been shown to two different sparsely furnished dingy bedrooms.

Frank Fergas lay on the filthy bed looking up towards the ceiling where a single bulb hanging from a bare cable dimly illuminated the dreary room. The woman whom he hadn't even bothered to ask her name stood seductively as she could at the foot of the bed. He eyed her through his drunken haze and even though the room was so dark and he was so drunk he was a little taken aback as to how ugly she was. He had been with a great number of women over the years and he always set his sights low but this he thought was probably the ultimate depth of ugliness. The one thing that was going for her was her enormous breasts she had removed her top to reveal two football size bosoms. She walked around the bed and began to remove his clothing.

When he was fully naked, she asked if was up for some kinky fun. When he nodded in agreement, she produced from under the bed several leather bondage straps and ties.

Frank having never indulged in this type of fetish was a little concerned at first but then reconciled himself to lie back and relax as she gently applied the straps to his arms and legs. She then in turn attached each strap to a corner of the bed so that Frank was spread-eagled. Frank found himself strangely aroused this was his fist time being strapped to a bed but he found it unusually erotic. He watched her as she slowly began to undress doing her best to perform a sexy striptease. She was now fully naked facing away from Frank at the foot of the bed showing her huge flabby backside.

Frank even though he was becoming lethargic and a little sleepy was becoming more and more excited at the thought of what was to come and was now fully aroused.

He couldn't wait any longer with a huge grin on his face he blurted out "If you turn round you can see what a big surprise I have got for you"

Still with her back to Frank she began to laugh uncontrollably and said

"I bet I have got a bigger surprise for you"

With that she turned round to face Frank, and shouted

"Surprise, surprise",

she had been absolutely right her surprise was the biggest.

Frank couldn't believe his eyes and he began to struggle to get free but the straps had been applied deceptively tightly and he was stuck fast.

His heart was pounding and he was gripped by an all-encompassing fear at what he was looking at. This huge guffawing monstrosity facing him was standing there with a fully erect penis. He began to sober up quickly and he suddenly realised why they had been so easy to pick up and why they were so ugly, they weren't girls they were men or a least pre ops. Frank realising he was unable to free himself began to frantically beg and plead with his captor.

But this just seemed to amuse whoever or whatever it was that was now eyeing up their prey and they began to laugh even louder. The bedroom door then burst open and in walked the other naked supposed female, except that they also had the same meat and two veg sticking out proudly he laughingly said.

"The fat one has pissed himself and passed out we'll see to him later; we can both have a go on this snivelling piece of shit."

Without realising it Frank had now begun to gently weep, partly in embarrassment and part in sheer fright.

The door was now shut and the two menacing figures began to approach the bed. Prissy and Tess were now making themselves comfortable in the detectives hotel room. They had brought drinks up from the hotel bar and they were sat on a couch whilst the boys were sitting in two-winged high back chairs. Prissy was eyeing up the palatial surroundings

"I'm impressed with the hotel room it must cost a fortune it's absolutely enormous"

Jose shrugged his shoulders

"I haven't got a clue how much it is costing because we don't pay for it I think my police force pays for it but they can claim it back out of some international fund so they have given us the best do you want me to show you the rest?"

"Ok give me the grand tour"

Prissy stood up and followed Jose as he guided her round the impressive accommodation. The bedroom was huge with an en-suite shower room. But the feature that impressed Prissy the most was the king size hot tub.

"Wow that thing is huge you could get a football team in there I have never seen one that big it's got all the power jets and everything."

Jose decided to try get a little closer to Prissy and he put his arms around her and tried to kiss her full on the lips. Prissy politely turned her head and gave him a peck on the cheek and said.

"Jose, I think you are really nice and Tess feels the same way about Mateo but neither of us are ready to take it any further just yet.

Jose accepted this and backed off a little, he respected her for not being an easy conquest unlike the couple of easy lays Dumb and Dumber had bagged for themselves.

Despite rejecting their advances for the time being they all still got on well and they spent quite some time together. It wasn't until the early hours of the morning that the girls left in a taxi having already arranged to see the detectives again.

Jose and Mateo decided to have one last drink in the hotel bar before retiring. They discussed the girls and whilst they were both disappointed at not getting any further with them, they got the feeling that the girls would be more willing to take things up a notch at their subsequent rendezvous.

Frank Fergas slowly began to come to; his mind was foggy and he couldn't think straight. As hard as he tried, he couldn't focus properly, his thoughts were all jumbled and his recollection was clouded in a vague mish mash of confused happenings. He felt a little shivery and his body ached all over, he slowly opened his eyes, his eyelids felt heavy and was as if they were stuck together and they stung as he managed to fully open them. Everything was black and he couldn't see anything initially, he moved his head to try and scan where he was but he still unable to clearly see anything. Slowly bit by bit his eyes began to adjust to the dim light. He realised he was lying on top of a bed in a shabby bedroom.   He tried to move to get a better look at his surroundings but for some reason he couldn't move. It then began to dawn on him why as he became aware that his arms and legs were bound to the bed.

Everything suddenly began to come flooding back and in abject horror he instantly knew why he was feeling so much pain in an intimate part of his anatomy. He immediately and violently vomited at the realisation of what had happened to him. Most of the foul-smelling putrid sick gushed out and formed a disgusting pile on the bed whilst the rest ran down his chin onto his chest and shoulder. He was now shocked into becoming fully alert his heart and mind beginning to race. He knew he had to act fast he had to get out of there somehow. He listened intently for a few seconds trying to keep his breathing and heartrate down so that he would be able to detect any sound of anyone or anything else.   After   a few minutes that seemed like an eternity he felt confident that no one else was in the room or anywhere nearby so whatever he was going to do he needed to do it now. He pulled at the straps binding him to the bed but they were all stuck fast, each strap consisted of a thick and wide piece of leather, they would be impossible to break by brute strength.

As he struggled, he realised that the strap attached to his right arm at the wrist wasn't secured as tightly as the others and he there was room to manoeuvre his wrist slightly. He began to swivel his wrist backwards and forwards whilst pulling with all his might and very slowly millimetre by millimetre his hand was painstakingly passing through the leather binding. If only he could get one hand free, he would be able to release the other bindings but the pain exerted on his hand as he pulled it through was excruciating. The bindings were now halfway down his hand and were firmly stuck on the joints at the base of his fingers. His efforts had caused him to a little out of breath, so he rested for a few seconds to regain some strength and pull with all his strength.

Whilst getting his breath back he was sure he heard a sound coming from next door. This was it he thought I have to do it now or never. He took a few deep breaths and tried to squeeze his hand into a tight ball and with every bit of energy left in his body he gave an almighty pull.

There was a brief intense flash of pain as his hand almost exploded out of its bindings. Breathing heavily he wasted no time in using his free arm to undo the binding on his other arm followed quickly by untying and releasing his legs. He slid his naked body over the edge of the bed and placed his feet on the floor, he became more aware of how cold he was and his nakedness. He scoured the room looking for his clothes. His eyes had now become fully accustomed to the poor light and he saw his clothes in a crumpled heap on the floor in the corner of the room. Tiptoeing across the floor he noiselessly retrieved his clothing and got dressed. His priority now was to escape, he had two options there was a single door or an old sash window. He edged towards the window and tried to look outside, the window was so dirty it was impossible to see through, it obviously had not been cleaned in years.

He used his sleeve to wipe the dirt from the windowpane giving a peephole through. He was surprised to realise how high up he was, at least three storeys high and there was nothing to climb onto or to grab hold of not even a drainpipe. There was nothing for it he had to try and escape via the way he had entered, cautiously he approached the door which was completely shut to and put his ear to it. He wanted to open it and run for all his worth but common sense told him he had to make sure the coast was clear before attempting to flee. With the exception of the wind and a few groans and creaks that you normally associate with old run-down buildings Frank could hear nothing else. This was it he thought this is the time to try, but he wasn't even sure if the door was locked or not, what could he do if it was locked, he wouldn't be able to force the door without making a noise that would alert his captors. With his heart in his mouth he took hold of the big round brass handle.

He took a deep breath and began to turn it. The knob was turning but he had no way of knowing if it would unlock the door. With the handle fully turned he silently prayed to himself and prepared to apply a gentle pressure and pull the door. To his relief the door began to move and he slowly opened it just enough for him to squeeze through. He found himself in a long dark hallway with numerous doorways, he had no idea of which door led downstairs and which ones gave access to other rooms.

He tried to wrack his brain and think back a few hours to when he came in but it was no good, he had been that drunk that he had simply followed the girls or what he thought had been girls. Until now he hadn't given a thought to his colleague who must be tied up in another bedroom, should he search for him or make his escape.

Quickly he dismissed the thought of rescuing his mate and decided to get out and save himself first and foremost. Looking at all the doors he guessed that the doors on either side of the corridor would give access to other rooms and the one most likely to give access to stairs would be the end one facing him. The floorboards squeaked as he made his way along the hallway to the last door and after listening with his ear against it and hearing nothing, he turned the handle and pushed the door enough to allow him to slide through. He found himself not at the head of some stairs but in another bedroom similar to the one he had been in furnished with just an old double bed.

He could hear a low whimpering noise coming from the centre of the bed and realised it was his mate, he had been tied in a similar fashion to him. Each of his limbs was strapped to each bedpost and he was stripped naked. He appeared to be semi-conscious and Frank placed a hand over his mouth to prevent him from crying out as he whispered in his ear.

"Robert it's me Frank don't make a sound and I will untie you do you understand?" A trembling Detective Robert Peeves now had his terrified bulging eyes wide open and he nodded in acknowledgement of his understanding.

The straps were quickly removed and Peeves retrieved his clothes that had been thrown into a heap on the floor and got dressed.

"C'mon let's get out of here"

Frank whispered. Before they left the bedroom, they stared at each other in silence, they realised that they had both suffered and endured the most horrific and humiliating ordeal imaginable. They wanted to somehow draw comfort from each other but deep down they had already accepted the cold harsh reality of the shameful consequences of what had been done to them. Their lives would never be the same again this was something that could never be talked about or even consciously accepted.

With the extra confidence instilled in them by being paired up they quickly made their way out of the building not taking as much care as previously to keep quiet. It was the early hours of the morning and they found themselves in Lye high street an area near Stourbridge renowned for its abundance of Balti restaurants.

They cast their eyes over the building that they had been imprisoned in and realised it wasn't a flat or any other form of dwelling. It was in fact a run-down derelict building waiting to be demolished. They made their way back to the CID vehicle that they had parked at Lye railway station car park. Before starting the engine, they spoke about what they should do next. They analysed the previous nights events in the night club and it dawned upon them that they had been set up. The girls had been unusually eager to get together with them and they even brought all the drinks which meant they had probably spiked them. They came to the realisation that although they had both consumed a lot of alcohol this didn't account for how tired they had both become which culminated in them both eventually passing out during their dehumanising sexual assault. Their assailants had obviously set up the premises and installed beds in what was basically and empty shell.

Robert had taken his wallet from his trouser pocket; he was surprised to see that it still contained money and he began to count it to make sure it was all there.

"Oh Fuck, Fuck, Fuck"

cried Peeves as he put his head in his hands and began to shake.

"What's the matter?"

shouted Frank.

In a tremulous hushed voice he replied.

"Check your wallet Frank"

Frank had been just about to drive off but he turned the engine off and patted his pockets for his wallet. He carefully removed it from his trouser pocket and cautiously opened it and like Robert began to count the money.

Halfway through flicking through the notes he froze as he realised what had upset his mate. In the middle of the banknotes a carefully placed photograph had been inserted. The photograph was an instant polaroid and it clearly showed him naked, tied to the bed and with a huge phallic sex toy sticking out of his anus and it was signed with a thick black felt pen on the rear

LOVE BONY XXX. Frank stared at the photo in a sense of disbelief "Holy shit" he cried. When he looked at a similar photo signed LOVE BEV XXX of his mate being held in Roberts trembling hand, he realised that they had both been well and truly set up. Their police experience meant they immediately knew the significance of them. One consequence of them was a warning from their attackers not to try and find them or take any action against them because they would obviously have further copies that could be used against them. The second even more concerning aspect of the phots was that they could be used later in some form of blackmail. They were well and truly screwed both literally and figuratively

13

GIRLPOWER

Shirley and Sam were having a drink in the Cross pub Oldswinford they were waiting for Victor and his update on his meeting with Dave Kempers, one of the perverts responsible for the abuse at Alldahope. He was late which was unusual for Victor, normally he was fastidiously punctual and you could almost set your watch by him.

The girls were idly chatting about nothing in particular, they didn't want to start their meeting without Victor as they didn't want to have to repeat themselves. One thing that did concern them both which was not related to their enquiries at Alldahope was their desire to find out their ancestry especially recently.

Neither of them had any knowledge of their parents, as both had been put into care at a very young age. To this end they had jointly employed the services of a private detective who specialises in this type of work. This wish to find out their birth parents and to establish where they came from had only manifested itself when Shirley and Sam became close friends. They considered each other as family and they took great comfort in this sense of belonging and It had been this intense feeling that had ignited their wish to explore their unknown family history. To date the detective had failed to find out anything of significance, the main reason for this was the young age of the girls when they were taken into care and as such couldn't give him any information at all about their past or anything else to work on as a starting point.

The bar had the usual locals dotted around the place. There was the seen it all done it all man, the doddery deaf old git who was ogling Wendy the barmaid and as West Bromwich Albion were playing at home there were a handful of Fans with their kids having a drink before leaving for the match. There was no sign of Guthy he had not been sighted since the incident where he had thrown a barstool at the gaffer causing him to fall backwards and squash his poor wife, Sharon.

There were no strangers in there and Shirley felt comfortable to have their meeting whenever Victor would show up.

After another round of drinks an apologetic Victor appeared, he was carrying a brown envelope which he immediately put on the table in front of Shirley.

"Sorry I'm late but I was monitoring my C.C.T.V on the rear of my premises and I saw someone nosing about so I have printed off an image.

Shirley opened the envelope and saw a picture of one of her detectives DC Oli Latifeo sitting on a canal bank relaxing whilst fishing in the murky canal.

"What was he doing that looked suspicious?"

asked Shirley.

"He appeared to be searching for something, he was looking all around, by the time I had focused the camera on him he had got his fishing gear out and begun to fish. It maybe that I was being a bit paranoid but I am sure he was looking for something."

Shirley sat back in her seat

"I can explain this, he is one of my detectives I have given him an enquiry to investigate the disappearance of a young lad a few days ago who was last seen cycling along the canal. He is obviously trawling for C.C.T.V but he is that idle he didn't look for long and used it as an excuse to go fishing. This is nothing to worry about but I will keep this photograph it may come in handy. Now tell us what you have found out from your meeting with that pervert Dave Kempers.

"He was a bit cagey initially but I started off by telling him that I couldn't any longer control my urges and that I needed some excitement in my life. He was only showing a little interest in what I was telling him but when I mentioned that I had got a job as a handyman at Alldahope I could see his eyes light up. He started to reveal some things to me bit by bit so I pretended to get more and more interested in order for him to open up more and it worked. He belongs to a group of paedophiles called 'The Bakers Twelve' they initially contacted each other via the dark web. I didn't push him too much concerning the name but I got the impression that the main man is called Baker i.e. the Bakers dozen whether a real name or nickname I don't know and there are possibly twelve of them. They have secret codes and passwords and they don't even know each other's names. They all use nicknames to identify one another and they always wear disguises when indulging in their activities. Dave Kempers wears a wig and a false moustache but I recognised him straight away because he's got a strange eye. He has a white ring around his cornea it's something he can't get rid of. When they carry out their attacks, they wear grotesque masks the kind you get from joke shops.

The reason for this is as I have said before is because if any of their victims complain then they won't be believed when they describe their attacker as a monster. They wear disguises under the masks so that they cannot recognise each other so even if one of them was arrested they wouldn't be able to name or even describe anyone else. These are incredibly evil men they have no feelings of remorse or any sense of guilt at their depraved practises. They are filled with an all-encompassing egotistical and self-satisfying desire to fulfil their sexual cravings without any thought of the terrible consequences that their actions have on vulnerable children. They abuse the kids at Alldahope on a regular basis normally in groups of three or four at a time.

The children are always drugged so that they can't put up any resistance and their memories are all blurred. Obviously, they must be receiving some help from the inside so I need to find out who that is. But the most disturbing thing I have uncovered is that this is not just confined to Alldahope its widespread they have an entire network of places all over the country where they commit these acts."

Shirley and Sam listened intently they were horrified with what Victor was telling them, they could both feel the anger tinged with sadness as Victors account brought the memories flooding back of their abusive upbringing at Alldahope. They had realised that sexual abuse was rife at Alldahope but they had no idea it was on such a large and organised scale.

Whilst Shirley and Sam were contemplating what to do with this information Victor went to the bar and ordered another a round of drinks. They could hear a bit of banter going on between rival football fans at the bar. Brummie who was invariably the only Birmingham fan in the place was barracking some West Brom and also some Wolves fans. He was however coming off second best because he was well outnumbered. The seen it all done it all man was recounting of how he had single-handedly thrown out of the pub the huge bloke who had been causing trouble a few days ago. And that if he came back, he would receive the same treatment again. He was of course referring to Stan Guthy who hadn't been seen since the incident.

Those that weren't taking part in the football team banter and were used to his Walter Mitty flights of fancy found this fantasy of his quite amusing.
Shirley was always acutely aware of her situation and surroundings and these kind of diversions gave her the confidence and belief that their little group meetings were not attracting any attention.

As soon as Victor put the drinks on the table they continued with the meeting. A very agitated and angry Sam said,

"We need to do something about these bastards straight away, we can't let them continue, we have got to stop them now."

Victor, fuelled by his sense of shame at his own deviant but albeit suppressed sexual urges towards children agreed.

"We can get some of them tonight, they are bound to be there, we could hide in the basement and take them by surprise."

"Let's do it" said Sam with a fierce almost venomous voice

"I'll electrocute the bastards."

Shirley understood Sams anger, nothing could erase the memory of the sexual abuse that they had both endured as young children and the accompanying deep-rooted hatred that could never be assuaged and would stay with them forever. Normally Sam was very focused and would assess most things clinically without letting her emotions get the better of her. But Shirley realised that she would need to take control and be the voice of reason.

She told both Sam and Victor that they needed to keep a check on their emotions and to look at the bigger picture.

"If we did show our hand tonight whatever we chose to do we are not in a position to get a successful outcome. We certainly couldn't arrest them without revealing our sources and that would be the end of our operation. Even if we didn't arrest them but let Sam send thousands of volts of electricity through them to scare them off, we wouldn't be able to get them all, perhaps three or four at the most. The rest would then be warned off and go to ground and we would lose them forever. We need to think with our heads and not our hearts."

Sam and Victor both realised that Shirley was right the last thing they wanted to do was to tip of any of the sexual predators and allow some of them to escape justice. Whatever action they decide on it must be aimed at all the Bakers twelve.

"So where do we go from here,"

said Victor.

Sam added

"Whatever we do it has to be done quickly we can't allow the abuse of those kids to continue."

Shirley nodded,

"We have to tread carefully remember we also have the problem of whoever is blackmailing us, I feel sure that they will make contact soon. In addition we have the problem of those two Spanish detectives. I have been keeping an eye on them and they are very fastidious. The last thing we want is for the enquiry into the Stourbridge serial killings to be resurrected. Oh and by the way Martin the Stourbridge news reporter has told me he can't help us any more with Alldahope because he has been promoted and he is too busy, I think they have made him the boss."

Sam replied

"it's probably just as well because I think we may have to take some drastic action to stop these perverts and I don't think he would have approved if we did anything bordering on illegal"

Shirley nodded in agreement the conversation was interrupted when they were suddenly joined at the table by Prissy and Tess.

Sam stood up to meet them and after the initial excited greeting involving lots of hugging and kissing Sam introduced them to Victor. "These are two of my very best friends" she announced proudly.

Victor politely as ever introduced himself and offered to get them all another round of drinks.

Shirley had met the girls several times previously and they got on really well, all the girls were of a similar mind, they were very shrewd, determined and used to getting their own way, especially with the opposite sex.

When everyone was seated round the table with a fresh drink, Prissy and Tess looked toward Sam with an air of caution. Sam smiled and said,

"It's ok you can talk freely in front of Victor he knows what's going on."

Shirley checked the room once again; the regulars were becoming increasingly louder and the banter between the various football fans more raucous as the beers began to have an effect.

No one was taking any notice of their little group in the corner.

She looked towards Prissy expectantly as a signal for her to begin.

"I'll start with your pair of pisshead detectives, what is it you have nicknamed them Dumb and Dumber?"

A few smiles and gentle chuckles from everyone round the table indicated she had got the names right.

"We followed the boys around Stourbridge initially. They went on a massive pub crawl I can't remember every pub they went in but they started in Chequers and then made their way down the high street calling at the Cock and Bull, Stourbridge Lion the Barbridge the Mitre and eventually finished in the Mooring Tavern. There were a few more on the way but I can't remember the names. They had so much to drink it was unbelievable, it made our job easier though because they were so drunk, they didn't notice us following them. Incredibly they then drove to Kingswinford to a grab a granny night.

"I called in a favour some friends of ours the Dores sisters, but when I told them who they were dealing with and that they were police officers they said they would do it even without me calling a favour in. Neither of them are fans of the local police I think they have had a few bad experiences with them.

Dumb and Dumber were so drunk that they tried to make moves on any and every one as soon as they entered the place. The people in there were what I would call weird characters to say the least.

The Dores sisters picked the guys up almost straight away, it was quite funny to watch as they repeatedly brought the guys drinks, which gave them the opportunity to lace them so by the time they had taken them back to the makeshift bedrooms in the derelict building they were almost at the point of passing out. The plan worked perfectly probably because the guys were such a pair of perverts. I don't need to go into any further details you can see for yourselves with these instant photographs."

Shirley and Sam looked at the photos that were signed Bev and Bony respectively. The sight of the two naked detectives lying face down on a bed bound and gagged and being defiled in the most pornographic and graphic manner by two transsexuals brought a huge smile spread across Shirleys face as she asked for and was given the photographs this was exactly what she needed to be able to exert influence or more exactly blackmail over her two detectives.

Prissy continued

"There are several other copies of those made and also copies were left in the guys wallets, no money was taken from their wallets so that the guys were left in no doubt that this wasn't a robbery and the photographs were taken as possible leverage if and when needed.

Moving on to the other pair now they were a different kettle of fish. The two Spanish guys weren't too bad especially in comparison with the other two lecherous perverts. They were nowhere near as drunk also they are quite choosy but also extremely vain so we took our time and let them think that they had pulled us. We pretended to be impressed with their enquiry and the fact that they were detectives. This encouraged them to open up about it, I think eventually they would tell us everything they have found out. They are like putty in our hands they are so egotistical and full of themselves that they are suckers for flattery and a bit of flirting. They eventually took us back to their hotel this took us by surprise a little, it must be costing someone a fortune because the room was absolutely massive. It even had its own king size jacuzzi you could fit five or six people in it. We haven't made any arrangements to see them as yet but we told we would contact them by phone so that we could speak with you and find out what you want us to do. "

Shirley was impressed with what the girls had done, the compromising photographs of Dumb and Dumber that she had securely tucked away in her pocket gave her the edge she wanted. And by a sheer fluke she now with the information given to her by Victor about Latifeo spending his time fishing instead of working it had also given her a little edge on her idle detective and although obviously not as damning as the bondage photos of Dumb and

Dumber but for the weak willed spineless Latifeo the evidence of him shirking off would suffice.

She was feeling more confident now that things were falling into place.

They had made significant inroads into the goings on at Alldahope, she had enough evidence on her detectives to keep them in their place or to control them if she needed to. She had a plan in mind to deal with the Spanish police if they began to get to close to the truth about the connections between the murders in Benidorm and Stourbridge. The only loose end now was to find out and deal with whoever was blackmailing her and Sam.

The pub suddenly went uncommonly quiet, the noisy banter had ceased and only a few hushed voices could be heard breaking the stony silence. Shirley instinctively knew straight away that something was wrong. And she was right to be concerned, standing menacingly at the far end of the bar with a huge sickly grin spread across his ugly mug was Stan Guthy. The new barmaid who was not aware of who he was and the trouble he had caused previously was already serving him to a pint of beer.

The other regulars were well aware of who this giant was and what he was capable of. Guthy revelled in this type of scenario he knew that his sheer presence in the pub made everyone feel on edge. This gave him a self-satisfying and overwhelming feeling of power, the fact that he could intimidate anyone and everyone at will. He looked round the bar eying up the regulars, no one wanted to engage him in direct eye to eye contact and most averted their gaze.

The uneasy silence continued as the drinkers were unsure why he was here or what he wanted. A few people's hearts went in their mouth as Guthy began to reach for something from his inside pocket. Some of the regulars were visibly on tenterhooks as Guthy continued to try and pry something from his inside pocket. What on earth was he searching for, perhaps some sort of weapon a club or knife or something even more dangerous.

A visible sigh of relief was clearly evident as Guthy retrieved from his inside pocket a packet of cigarettes.

Guthy was aware that that his actions were unnerving people and to that end he had taken extra and considerable time to remove the pack of cigarettes. With a smirk Guthy walked through the bar towards the exit that gave access to the smoking area on the patio outside.

As he walked past the table where Shirley and her group were sitting, he gave them a knowing and arrogant smile as he passed by.   He paid particular attention to Sam; he had been impressed with her strength of character when they had crossed swords in the café. He had been unable to unnerve her then, and he looked at the resolve on her face now, and she still didn't show any signs of being intimidated by him now.   "What on earth is he doing here"

uttered Shirley under her breath to the rest. The shrugging of shoulders showed that neither of them had the faintest idea why Guthy had turned up in the pub.

"Does anyone smoke?"

Shirley asked, Prissy nodded and produced a packet of cigarettes and a lighter from her handbag.

"I just need to borrow these for a while"

with cigarettes and lighter in hand Shirley got up from the table and headed for the exit giving access to the smoking area. She made her way to the front of the pub overlooking the main road where there were a few chairs and tables where the smokers usually congregated. She was now alone with the giant who was taking huge draughts from his cigarette. The only other two smokers had stubbed out their cigarettes quickly and left the patio and returned to the confines of the bar at the appearance of Guthy. Shirley had never smoked a cigarette in her life but to so as not to arouse anyone's suspicions if they dared leave the bar, she attempted to light one up. After a few awkward coughs and splutters Shirley managed to clumsily light up.

Making sure that no one else was in earshot she with a hint of venom in her voice said,

"What on earth are you doing here?"

Guthy didn't answer straight away he just stared at Shirley thoughtfully, Guthy had always been able to frighten and intimidate people with impunity. But Shirley was different she had the same strength and backbone as Sam. Some of the people he had half scared to death over the years had themselves been quite imposing and often brutal and violent men. He had made even the hardest of criminals and thugs soil themselves in fright, yet here were two young attractive females one of whom was quite diminutive that showed no fear of him.

In a way they reminded him a little of his beautiful little girl Babs, she too would not allow herself to be intimidated or overawed by anyone, she had a plucky maturity way beyond her tender years. It was her courageous and fearless demeanour that had helped her to survive at Alldahope. Shirley looked

Guthy square in the face still waiting for a reply to her question.

"I need you do something for me" he replied, "What makes you think I would do anything for you?" Shirley asked quizzically.

"Because you know full well that you shouldn't have arranged for me to see Babs and if I spill the beans, you will lose your job or worse." "If you do that you know that you will never see your daughter again." Shirley argued forcefully.

"Yes, but you have far more to lose than me, eventually I will find a way to see my daughter again but you will be out of the force forever."

"Supposing I was able to and I decided to help you what is it that you want?"

"I want the address of the judge who made the order banning me from seeing my daughter."

A concerned Shirley puzzled,

"Why do you want those details what are you going to do?"
Guthy didn't reply straight away just stood and stared at Shirley eyeing her up and down with a confident air of someone who thought they held all the cards and were in the driving seat.

Eventually he spoke and without showing any emotion he simply replied,

"Don't ask just get me the details or you get no more info from Babs do you understand?"

Then without waiting for a reply Guthy stubbed out his cigarette on the floor and began to walk off. As a parting shot, he remarked

"I'll be waiting".

Guthy didn't re-enter the pub but strolled across the car park and was quickly out of sight.

Shirley was fuming, she hated anyone getting the better of her and she knew Guthy had. He had been right when he said Shirley had more to lose than him so she realised that for the time being she had to comply or at least pretend to comply with his wishes.

She re-joined the rest who were still seated round the table and sat down. They could see by the look of frustration on her face that Shirley was angry and she would not be giving them good news.

"Well at least we know why he came in the bar, he wanted to speak with me, or rather blackmail me into getting him some information."

"Jesus Christ not another one this is getting ridiculous" Sam said in abject despair.

One of the regulars shouted loud enough for everyone to hear "He's going I can see him walking away towards Stourbridge.

The bar began to return to normal with the resumption of conversations, the seen it all done it all got the t shirt man was just emerging from the shelter of the toilets when he heard the news.

As he returned to the crowd, he began to flex his shoulders in a threatening manner and puffed out his puny chest as much as he possibly could before cockily announcing to everyone

"It's about time he fucked off I was just about to sort him out he doesn't realise how lucky he was the big cunt."

The locals were used to his constant outrageous and often incredulous boasts and it had become common practise to egg him on such was the source of amusement. One of them trying their best to keep a straight face said,

"Yes, he has had a narrow escape you might have put him in hospital."

"Bloody too right these hands should be registered as deadly weapons he could see I was getting ready that's why he's buggered off."

Another of the locals was standing on a seat and craning his neck to look out of the window shouted.

"You could always go after him; he's stopped at the bus stop about fifty yards away".

The done it all seen it all man coughed and spluttered and his face turned slightly ashen and in a much less confident and somewhat hushed tone said. "I think he's learned his lesson this time but next time he won't be so lucky I won't hold back I've given bigger blokes than him a good hiding so he can have a good slapping as well."

The regulars were revelling in his display of bravado and were eagerly waiting for his next audacious outpouring of outlandish and bizarre claims.

This only succeeded in encouraging him to continue to spout on and on about his heroic daring deeds.

The guy looking out of the window suddenly shouted with urgency and a hint of panic in his voice.

"Wait he' turned around he's coming back towards the pub and he looks hopping mad."

All the crowd immediately rushed to the window and stood on the seats and chairs straining their necks to see what was happening.

After a few moments and various mumbles mingled with the odd confused comment somebody cried out

"What on earth are you talking about there's no one there the road is completely empty."

In between huge uncontrollable belly laughs the author of the comment stating that Guthy was returning and as tears ran down his face, they managed to utter the words.

"Yes, I know that huge monster of a guy pissed off ages ago I saw him jump on the bus but just look at the car park."

Everyone turned their gaze towards the rear carpark and were all immediately reduced to howls of laughter.

There in the middle of car park was the seen it all done it all man running as if his life depended on it towards his car at breakneck speed.

He was so nervous and shaking so much that he dropped his car keys twice. As he tried to pick his car keys up for the second time and maintain forward momentum, he fell head over heels landing spread-eagled in a pool of rainwater. He scrambled back to his feet like a man possessed and with his hands and face bloodied his trousers ripped he stumbled awkwardly into his car slamming and locking the door shut behind him.

Once inside the vehicle the engine roared into life revving for all it was worth and with tyres screeching and engine racing the car sped out of the carpark as if it were on the starting grid of a grand prix.

The pub went into complete uproar at the farcical sight of the seen it all done it all man fleeing for all he was worth.

With all the noise and commotion going on Shirley and her group could barely hear themselves above the hubbub plus she didn't want their meeting to be compromised so she decided to cut short the meeting and quickly rescheduled before they almost unnoticed quietly left the pub.

The next morning Shirley decided to walk to work in order to clear her head, her night's sleep had not been a restful one. Guthy had now become a problem Shirley had underestimated him, she had assumed he would be happy to see his daughter and that nothing else would come of it. She hadn't realised that he would have the nous to figure out that he could use what she had done as a bargaining tool to exert pressure on her and make demands.

She was also anxious about the anonymous blackmailer who had photographed her and Sam leaving the mortuary some time ago. Whoever they were they obviously knew or had a good idea who the real Stourbridge serial killer was. But they must have been sitting on this info for some time, and why have they waited so long to show their hand.

Shirley was working out of an empty shop in Stourbridge shopping centre, she hated working there it felt like she was in a goldfish bowl with everyone gawping at her. What made matters worse was what they had done to the now defunct Stourbridge Police Station which she was now walking past this had been a great place to work. To rub salt into the wound the building was being turned into flats and some bright spark had decided to name the apartment block the Station House. The advertising slogan on the side of the building to catch people's eyes had the annoying caption' Hello, Hello, Hello.

Shirley along with the rest of the Stourbridge residents would much prefer to have a Police Station rather than some swanky new apartments. Above the noise of the traffic Shirley could hear the ring of her mobile and she began to search through her ever-present handbag.

"Hello Sam, I'm just on the ring road at the minute give me a few seconds to find somewhere quiet" she quickly walked past the Police Station and turned into an alleyway which drowned out the sound of the morning traffic.   "Ok I can hear you better now what is it Sam".

"You're not going to like it, we have had another letter through the post, it's as we thought it's a second Blackmail demand. But this time it's for ten thousand"

"Ok make sure you don't touch it again and I will have it examined for fingerprints, I'm nearly at work now but I will slip pout later and pop back so we can work out what we're going to do, can you contact Victor I think we may need his help on this one."

This news somehow managed to lift Shirleys spirits, at least now she wasn't left waiting in suspense and she could now start making preparations to deal with the blackmailer.

She had now arrived at the goldfish bowl of an office; a couple of community support officers were occupying one of the three desks idly sipping at two mugs of steaming hot tea.   Their remit was to provide a high-profile visible presence on the street to reassure the general public and thus reduce the fear of crime. It had worked in part when these officers were initially recruited, but as with a lot of things the impetus had dwindled as time marched on and with a few exceptions the majority of them spent more and more time tucked away out of sight in offices and hide holes.

"Want a cup of tea Sarge"
one of them shouted out cheerily.
"Milk and two sugars"
she replied as she sat at her desk.
Dumb and Dumber were the only other officers in the building and they were obviously preparing to leave.

Shirley eyed them as they were putting their jackets on. The cockiness and the smug confidence that they normally exuded had waned appreciably.

150

Hers and Sams plan had quite clearly had a big effect on them and she allowed herself a discreet smile.

She shouted across to them

"Frank, Robert what are your plans today?

"We have arranged to pick up the Spanish detectives they want to re visit the murder sites again we said we would pick them up from their hotel, oh and by the way Latifeo has gone to the Stourbridge canal to complete a C.C.T.V trawl." Shirley mulled this information over, what it meant in reality was that they were off skiving for the day, and Latifeo had gone fishing. But Shirley wasn't overly concerned, she knew that she had them where she wanted them and as it wasn't busy crime wise, she would leave them to their own devices. To maintain the presence Shirley replied,

"Ok make sure that you give Jose and Mateo all possible assistance."

A mug of hot tea was placed on the desk in front of her and as Dumb and Dumber left the office Shirley began to quickly check the computer for any outstanding enquiries or tasks that needed allocating.

She finished her computer interrogation before she had time to drink her tea which was still half full. Relieved that there was nothing requiring her attention she picked up her handbag and left the office, her mind racing with how she would deal with the blackmailer.

Victor was already there when she arrived home, he was sitting at the kitchen table with Sam they were already discussing the latest Blackmail demand which was laid out on the table. This time the drop off for the ransom was the Black Country Museum, specific instructions were included on how the ransom was to be delivered. One of the requirements was that Sam and Shirley were both to deliver the package and they were to be handcuffed to each. "That's somewhat of a strange demand" queried Victor as he looked a little confused towards Shirley. She began to smile a little "I think I know what's in his head and he has also made his first mistake." A look of intrigue combined with a beam of hopeful curiosity spread across Sams face as she eagerly enquired what Shirley had figured out.

Victor and Sam sat there with eager anticipation as Shirley seemed to be mulling through ideas in her head.

"C'mon tell us what you're thinking" Sam blurted out unable to control her excitement any longer.

Shirley spoke slowly and orderly her methodical brain systematically analysing the reasons behind the demand.

"Firstly they want us handcuffed together because it makes it difficult to run or chase after them when they collect the ransom. But that also shows they think that there is only two of us involved otherwise there would be no point in simply slowing us two down because if we had an accomplice or accomplices, they could be used to nab them. This means they are unaware of you Victor so this means you can be used during the ransom drop. They don't know as much as we gave them credit for."

Victor then interjected saying

"What we need is an action plan we need to be fully prepared because considering what they did last time using the drone they obviously put a lot of thought and preparation into their ransom collection method so we must be ready to negate all possible angles. I have already solve the problem of him using a drone again instead of blocking the signal, I could block the signal but all that does is negate him from collecting the ransom. So what I have acquired is a tracking device, it is small enough to hide in the bag and it can send a locating signal for approximately a mile maybe a touch further that should be sufficient for us to track it."

"That's brilliant"

said Sam then added

"In fact they may well be planning to use a drone again because in the note they want us to use the same brown bag with two paper handles on it."

Shirley with her mind working overtime was not so sure as Sam about the drone and was already formulating a plan in her mind.

"Right this is what we are going to do Victor you are spot on when you say we need to cover all angles so we will use the tracking device. We don't have a lot of time so I want you Victor to get there before us in the morning and get to know the place and check for possible drop off points, entrances exits and possible escape routes. Sam I don't think we can assume that a drone is being used especially as the note tells us where we will find a further note once we are in there so we need to discuss our action plan and how we transport the money whilst in handcuffs."

Victor stood up eager to get started

"I will prepare the ransom money together with the tracking device, when I am checking the place out do you want me to look for the further instructions that they are leaving"

Shirley thought about this for a moment and replied

"No, it would be great if we had a heads up but they may be watching and if they are you will be compromised so no stay well clear, when we get the instructions make sure you have us in sight though".

After assuring Shirley and Sam that he would remain as close as possible at all times and that the most important thing was for them to keep safe because they could follow the ransom money with the tracking device, he left them together in the kitchen.

Shirley and Sam then discussed in detail their specific actions for the forthcoming hand over. Sam wanted to take her electric prod but this was deemed a bad idea because was quite bulky and if they were handcuffed together, it would be difficult to hide. They talked for several hours until they had exhausted all possible scenarios and actions.

Later that night Shirley was having difficulty sleeping, she was convinced she was missing a trick with regard to the ransom but she couldn't figure it out. She was also going through turmoil imagining the horror and suffering that the poor girls at Alldahope could be going through. There was one resident at Alldahope that she didn't need to worry about and that was Babs. In her darkened room in one of the top floors at Alldahope Babs was also having difficulty getting to sleep. Her restlessness was not caused by fear though, it was more a sense of self preservation.

She was sure her dad and the woman detective would get something done soon, she just needed to keep safe in the meantime. She stretched out her arm putting it under the pillow and wrapped a reassuring hand around the handle of the razor blade weapon that she had crudely made from a toothbrush. She practised this regularly until it was almost second nature to put her hand on her means of protection in an instant. If the monsters came for her, she would be ready.

14

CHAIN OF EVENTS

Shirley went into the goldfish bowl of a police Station in Stourbridge early; she needed some privacy to make some delicate phone calls. The office was so small that everyone could hear everything that was said no matter how quietly one spoke. The office was empty as was the shopping centre in which it was located there was only the odd shopper wandering around staring through the yet to open shops. Shirley opened her desk and took out her personal secret telephone list. She had recorded these in her own cryptic code in case they fell into the wrong hands. The names and numbers were scrambled and it took Shirley a few moments to decode in her mind the correct numbers. She had built up this list over a number of years by offering sexual favours and in the process retaining a sample of her stooges DNA. The list included high ranking police officers, judges and court officials, prison officers plus other officials within the law enforcement and judiciary system.

Most of the hapless victims were married and or in a position of authority and were vulnerable to any hint of sexual scandal. Shirley had cleverly targeted her victims ensuring that their positions in the community could assist her and also that they were also susceptible to coercion.

Whilst searching for the specific number she needed she pressed start on the voice recorder she kept on standby secreted in her desk. It activated when it detected nearby voices and switched off when no further sound could be heard. Because it was operating from within the confines of her desk it didn't pick up a lot of conversation unless someone was speaking either loudly or close to her desk. The recorder burst into life and started playing. The digital display indicated that it was activated at 10;00pm last night. She could hear the sound of the two Spanish detectives who were looking into any possible connections between the Stourbridge serial killer and several similar deaths in Benidorm talking to each other. They sounded as if they had been drinking and as such were talking louder than normal which meant that the voice recorder could easily pick up their conversation.

From their dialogue Shirley deduced that they had returned to the office to use the phone to order a taxi to take them back to their hotel which would arrive in approximately fifteen minutes. As they waited for a few minutes before leaving the office to meet their taxi they talked about the enquiries they had made. They were speaking freely to each other in Spanish confident that no one could possibly hear them or even understand what they were saying. Shirley did not advertise the fact but she was quite fluent in the Spanish language and what she was hearing sent a shiver down her spine.

To make sure she had understood what they had been saying she replayed the tape several times and wrote it down. Estes detectives ingleses son tan estupidos que no tienen idea de lo que estan haciendo y obviamente se equivocaron de hombre. Estos imbeciles estan van a tener un shock cuando revelemos quien es el verdadero asesino, especialmente esa estupida perra Shirley Wallows. She wrote down the translation as accurately as possible These English Detectives are so stupid they have no idea what they're doing and obviously got the wrong man. These imbeciles are going to have a shock when we reveal who the real killer is especially that stupid bitch Shirley Wallows.

Shirleys mind was racing everything was happening at once and things were starting to fall apart in dramatic fashion. The ransom drop was in a few hours she had the threat of Stan Guthy hanging over her and now she had to find some way to deal with the Spanish detectives. Shirley thrived on pressure but this could be too much to juggle with this could spell the end of everything. She leant forward with her head in her hands elbows planted firmly on her desk its all over she thought. Her world was beginning to fall apart, she had worked so hard to turn her life around but now she was at breaking point.

Her mind meandered back to her awful childhood upbringing, most of it in that godforsaken hell hole Alldahope. Her ordeal had been one that would have broken most people, the sexual abuse combined with the physical and mental torture that she suffered would have driven many to the brink of suicide. The majority of the rest would have sustained long lasting psychological or behavioural problems. But not Shirley, she had gone through and withstood everything life had to throw at her and come out of the other side.

She had rebuilt her life made a career and met her soulmate Sam who was the closest she had ever had to a family. She had got herself into a position where she could repay and exact her revenge on her antagonists. She had expended much of her adult life in assuaging her deep-rooted anger and loathing of male dominated chauvinistic sexual predators and perverts by giving as many of them as possible what she and Sam referred to as payback.

But now it looked like it was all coming to an end and she was going to be exposed one way or another. She had no regrets and in her heart of hearts she never thought that she get away with her actions for so long. Her biggest regret now was that she hadn't managed to sort out the evil predators at

Alldahope and she felt as if she had let the girls down and they would be destined to endure the same atrocities as herself and Sam.

She sat back in her chair and stared through the window into the fairly empty shopping centre. The occasional shopper ambled by slowly, casually glancing through shop windows whilst waiting for them to open. A young girl walked up to the glass fronted police office and stared through looking at the cardboard cut-out of a policewoman that was displayed and used for recruitment purposes. The young girl reminded Shirley of herself when she was that age. She had a vacant look of someone who was lonely and isolated a slightly sad expression on her face betrayed her inner feelings. She appeared to be daydreaming perhaps imagining she was elsewhere in a different time and place. Maybe even thinking of what it would be like to be a policewoman like the cardboard cut-out she was gazing at.

The young girl caught sight of Shirley sitting at her desk and she immediately smiled and waved towards her. Shirley smiled and waved back, and at that moment she heard a gruff voice outside the office shouting,

"I've told you about wandering off you stupid little idiot"

the young girl then received a clip round the back of her head and a man who was obviously her father grabbed her arm and roughly dragged her away whilst still shouting

"I'll teach you to keep running off you wait till I get you home".

The young girl was now cowering her head nervously as she unceremoniously hauled away.

Shirley knew now why the young girl had appeared to be so sad and lonely and staring through the police office window she had been letting her thoughts and imagination take her away from her daily life as it was now.

Shirley was in two minds as to whether to go and speak with the little girl's father and put him in his place with a few choice words. But she thought better of it she knew from past experience that it would do the young girl no favours in the long run because it would simply infuriate the girl's father if Shirley warned him about his behaviour. Then he would ultimately take his anger out on the girl. Once again this was so reminiscent of Shirleys upbringing and her blood began to boil.

A feeling of anger and frustration took hold of Shirley but she was also invigorated with an all-encompassing sense of the need to redress the balance between the weak and vulnerable and those that use their power or position to impose themselves on others. It was the same intense feeling that she had when she was a young girl and suffering at the hands of others. It was this feeling that made her strong and allowed t her to survive and come out on top and be the person she was today.

With renewed passion and determination her spirit uplifted she decided that she wasn't simply going to roll over and give up she would fight tooth and nail with all her might to get through whatever was coming in her direction. Her mind was working overtime and she realised with reborn clarity what actions and plans she needed to instigate to get through her current dilemmas. She set about making a number of phone calls giving out ultimatums issuing orders and calling in favours. Shirleys mood had turned full circle, things would soon start to happen. If things went to plan there would be a glimmer of light t the end of the tunnel.

Sam was waiting for Shirley in the car park of the Black Country living museum she was looking at one of the building that can be seen from outside it has huge writing covering almost the entire of one wall, "Rolfe Street Baths" the building like all the others in the museum had been taken down brick by brick and rebuilt on site and she found it fascinating. She turned round when she heard Shirley calling shouting to attract her attention from near the main entrance. Shirley had made her way there from work and as such had only been able to give Sam the briefest details of the development's with the Spanish detectives. Sam was anxious to know more about how they were going to deal with them but realised they had a more immediate problem to deal with.

"Are you ok Shirley, I thought you might be upset with what is happening with those Spanish detectives?"

Shirley smiled

"I had a bit of a wobbler at first but I got over it and now I feel great now let's go and get this bastard that blackmailing us."

Sam had an uncanny intimate knowledge of how Shirley felt and reacted to things she understood more than anyone exactly where she was coming from. Despite only knowing each other for a reasonably short time they both had a comprehensive knowledge of each other's inner feelings and expectations.

This had been formed from their initial upbringing at Alldahope where albeit they only had the briefest of contact with each other both were fully aware of what they had both endured.

This joint suffering and their uncompromising attitude towards how they would exact retribution had formed an incredible and close bond between them. Sam realised that Shirley for some reason had renewed vigour and enthusiasm.

She seemed to have a purpose and an air of confidence about her which Sam found highly infectious, so with an upbeat excited tone she announced in fact almost demanded,

"C'mon let's go and get this bastard, Victor is already in there he is going to keep his distance but close enough should we need him, good luck".

With that both girls confidently made their way into the museum ready to deal with their tormenter.

They passed through entrance and made their way as instructed to where they were to collect further instructions.

The instructions were under a paving stone next to a wastepaper bin in a deserted part of the museum. Shirley lifted the paving stone whilst Sam kept lookout. Shirley retrieved one of the museums maps of the site showing all the locations of the various attractions and a number of them had been highlighted in felt tip pen each one was numbered in order one to seven.

She showed the doctored map to Sam and they discussed what they thought the blackmailers intentions were. They assumed that at some point during their tour of the site and possibly whilst at one of the specific attractions then he or they would attempt to take the ransom.

The first numbered place they had to visit was a cinema situated on the extreme far side of the museum and the route to the cinema took them through the centre of the reconstructed village. Shirley as instructed in the ransom note took out a pair of handcuffs and applied one to her wrist and one to Sams, in order to camouflage the handcuffs and not draw attention to themselves they each took hold of one handle of the paper bag containing the ransom money.   For any onlooker it would simply seem that the two girls hands were close to each other to jointly hold the bag between them.

They began to make their way as ordered to the cinema. Walking was a little difficult at first because it is natural to swing your arms when walking but when handcuffed this is impossible and you have walk together in sync.

The girls began to realise now why this was one of the blackmailer demand because even though Shirley had applied the cuffs loosely, they were aware that it would still take time to extricate yourself from your partner and this would give valuable time for them to get away.

They walked over the canal bridge and along the main cobbled street a number of extremely old building either side of them formed the basis of the village. Everyone had been painstakingly dismantled from various towns across the black country and reassembled brick by brick to resemble a village street form a long-gone era. There were shops and small business for visitors to enjoy including a fish and chip shop and even a pub, all of which were open for business.

Shirley had never visited the museum before but couldn't help to be fascinated at what it had to offer and thought in different circumstances that it would be a great place to visit. Having passed through the centre of the main village they turned right and found the tiny pre-war cinema. The next showing was in two minutes and they went straight in and took a seat. The cinema itself was tiny with wooden seats and only held about twenty people all crammed in closely together. They both continuously scanned their surroundings and the other people who were uncomfortably close. The old black and white film lasted for about ten minutes but Sam and Shirley weren't paying any attention to its content

They were busy keeping alert to whatever may happen. They filed out of the tiny building together with everybody else back into the main street. Shirley studied the map to locate their next location which the map indicated was a mine. They had to retrace their steps back through the main street past the chip shop and over the bridge. There was no sign of Victor but the girls were sure that he was keeping an eye on them from a discreet distance.

At the mine they entered a waiting room with several other people, the visit involved a tour of the mine and the next tour would begin in a few minutes. Still no sign of the blackmailer or any attempt to take the money Shirley was even beginning to wander if this would be a dry run for the blackmailer to see if she and Sam followed the blackmailers instructions.

The next tour was about to begin and everyone was given a safety helmet and a handful were given lamps. After a briefing from the guide they began to descend into the mine. The passageways in parts were very narrow and only singular access was necessary for Shirley and Sam it was made slightly more difficult because of the handcuffs. The guide showed through various displays what it was like to work down a mine and the harsh conditions that they had to endure.

Everything had been done very professionally and it was Sam and Shirley together with the rest of the party found it enthralling. The lights were extremely dim and at one point the guide asked for everyone to turn off the low light lamps and he gave a talk in the pitch black. This was in order that everyone had the real feel of how claustrophobic it would have been for the miners many years before.

The mine then opened up into quite a large cavern with several manikins in mining attire depicted carrying out various tasks and some taking their lunchbreak. The dangers and the effects on the health of the workers, some of whom were quite young children were included in the guides patter.

The tour lasted for about fifteen minutes until they emerged back to the surface having completed a circular tour. Shirley and Sam had enjoyed the tour that much that they began to relax and for a moment even forgot why they were there. Once again still no sign of either the blackmailer or Victor.

Checking the map the next on the list was a school where they were due to sit through a mock lesson with a strict authoritarian almost Victorian style.

The school was only a short walk from the mine and it took them just a few minutes to arrive. On the noticeboard was an itinerary of the days classes, classes lasted about twenty minutes and everyone whether an adult or child had to sit at a tiny child's school desk. The lesson turned out to be quite funny the female teacher adopted the character of an incredibly strict matriarchal school mistress with threats of lashes of the cane and other draconian disciplinary measures should a student get something wrong or even god forbid speak without raising a hand. The lesson proved to be hilarious with the school mistress working from a good script and a lot of impromptu ad libs.

The lesson ended with a rapturous round of applause with everyone having been fully entertained. Shirley and Sam were becoming more and more relaxed as they began to enjoy the magic of the living museum.

Once outside the school still smiling and chortling Shirley took out the map to see where the next stop was on the map. The fourth on the list was a trip on a canal barge that went underneath Dudley hill in a labyrinth of underground tunnels if this was not to be a dry run and the ransom demander was going to make their move then

Shirley thought this would be the most likely opportunity. An extra charge was made for tickets to travel on the barges and after purchasing the tickets Shirley and Sam stood on the quayside waiting for the next trip.

Shirley shared her thoughts with Sam about the barge trip being the most likely place to try and grab the ransom and uncannily Sam was also of the same mind. They began to focus again having been slightly distracted whilst enjoying the various attractions and they methodically surveyed their surroundings. There was a tow path obviously a barge would arrive at some time there was a gift shop with access from the towpath and then there would be the tunnels that the barge would pass through.

If the blackmailer had knowledge of the tunnels perhaps, he could try and snatch the ransom and disappear in the maze of underground tunnels.

Shirley and Sam saw him standing on the towpath at the same time and were taken by surprise. Something must be wrong they instinctively thought. Why after having kept his distance would Victor get so close and risk compromising everything.

Sam tried discreetly to look at Victor and she knew immediately by the look on his face that something was wrong something was terribly wrong. Victor was obviously preparing to board the same barge as the girls. Sam whispered to Shirley telling her that something was wrong and they must speak with Victor somehow. Shirley knew something was happening or about to happen she could sense it her nerves were on edge.

At that moment the barge that they were to travel on emerged from the tunnel and was heading towards the towpath. Once the barge had been secured with ropes the passengers were disembarking and Sam together with Shirley and Victor were ushered on board. Victor had taken a seat a few feet away from the girls, he didn't acknowledge the girls but they realised that there must be a reason why he chose to sit so close. After a brief safety announcement and details of what they would encounter on their trip they set off into the tunnel entrance. The space on board was very confined meaning people were crowded together. Shirley was mindful that this close proximity of everyone could give the blackmailer a chance to grab the ransom, she became alert to the slightest movement anyone made on the jampacked longboat.

The barge continued along in the narrow confines of the tunnel walls until eventually emerging into a huge cavern, and the tour guide stopped the vessel whilst they all viewed a light show displayed on one of the huge caverns walls. When they set off gain it wasn't long before they were back inside another space limited tunnel, this one even more crammed for space than the previous.

The tour guide stopped the boat again and gave a talk on what it would have been like to operate on these boats many years ago. He went on to explain that as none of the barges would have engines they would normally be pulled along by horses. Obviously in a tunnel there was no room for a horse so the means of propulsion would be by legging. This involved two people lying on their backs on a board that stretched across the barges hull and using their legs to push themselves along using the tunnel wall. He then asked for a couple of volunteers to try giving it a go, and after some kidding around and some cajoling two volunteers stepped forward and they show how to sit and how to use their legs to propel the boat forward. When they were set the guide said he had one thing to show us and this would really give us a sense of how hard and difficult the bargees had to work.

The guide told everyone that not only did the barges have no engine but they also would not have any lights and in order to be authentic he was about to switch off all the lights on the barge and they would be in total darkness for a couple of minutes.

"This is it; I think they are going to use the darkness to snatch the money, now get ready stay alert"

Shirley whispered to Sam.

They were then plunged into total darkness the blackness was complete and utter, there was not a glimmer or chink of light from anywhere and it was literally impossible to see anything at all. They were both on tenterhook's, concentrating to listen to any strange sound or sign of any movement. Shirley was sure she heard a footstep on the wooden floor of the barge, she squeezed Sams arm to alert her to the sound, they held their breath straining to listen for further footsteps. Shirley could sense something but couldn't work out what it was. She could feel a faint warm breeze on her on her face, then she shuddered when it suddenly struck her, it wasn't a breeze it was someone's breath, their face must be a couple of inches from hers.

She clenched her fist ready to strike as hard as she could towards the source of the breath until she heard

"Shirley it's me Victor listen carefully the tracking device is on this barge, but it was on before you got on when the lights come back on, I will work out where it is and I will try and indicate to you who has it."

The waft of the warm breath then disappeared; Shirley couldn't fully fathom out what Victor had meant but she was sure that he was going to indicate who had the tracker. The darkness seemed to continue for ages Shirley was anxious and also excited to see the face of the bastard who was blackmailing her.

The engine burst into life and a few seconds later the lights were switched on. It took a few seconds for everyone's eyes to re-adjust to the light and through squinting eyes she saw that Victor had moved further along the barge.

She eyed up the people sitting nearby to Victor but there wasn't any clue yet as to who she was looking for. The journey was almost at an end and still Victor hadn't indicated anyone. As the barge came towards where it was to moor up Victor stood up and took a couple of steps before stumbling forward and awkwardly collided with one of the passengers.

Victor apologised repeatedly and got back to his feet, he then turned round to face Shirley and gave a slight nod of his head. Got him thought Shirley and whispered into Sams ear so she was also aware of who the target now was. The Target was quite a formidable guy, he was well over six feet tall and stockily built. Shirley guessed he would be in his mid-thirties.

She did not recognise him and she was sure that she had never seen him before. Once off the boat the exit took everyone through the gift shop and they followed their target at a discreet distance. He was now standing outside the entrance to the gents toilet, access was not allowed for the presence, a large yellow sign indicated that the toilets were in the process of being cleaned.

He waited for a short while and then seemed to give up and made his way out of the gift shop followed by Shirley and Sam.

Shirley now took off the handcuffs and put the bag with the ransom money into her pocket.

The guy made his way behind a row of old buildings that didn't form part of the main attractions, there was a small offshoot from the main canal that appeared to be disused and lots of odd bits of rusty machinery, lumps of iron and debris scattered on the towpath including a number of piles of chains.

The guy cast his eye over the disused area, not seeing Shirley or Sam who were crouching behind a low wall. He approached the canal took another quick look and then undid his fly and started urinating in the canal. Without any conversation Sam suddenly sprung out of her hiding place and quickly but stealthily sped towards the urinating man.

Shirley noticed that Sam had picked up an iron bar and as she neared the guy, he was just beginning to finish peeing.

Shirley wanted to scream out NO but that would have alerted him so she just looked on in silence. He was still facing toward the canal as Sam raised her arm brandishing the weapon and then with a mighty swing brought the iron bar down on the back of his head.

He immediately crumpled to the floor and Sam bent forward and struck him another twice. Shirley ran towards them shouting,

"What on earth have you done this wasn't part of the plan?".

Sam replied hurriedly

"No time to worry about that now help me start wrapping that chain around him."

Without waiting Sam grabbed one end of a huge pile of rusty chain that had been dumped on the towpath and began by winding it round the semi-conscious guys neck. Shirley looked round nervously this place was secluded but not private, but for the present there was no one around. She realised that after Sams rush of blood to the head whatever they were going to do they must act quickly so Shirley followed Sams lead and began to entwine the chain around his body.

The guy began to moan as he began to recover consciousness and managed to get to his knees,

"What the fuck are you doing"

he screamed. Sam then struck him once more with the iron bar this time full in the face, a loud crack resonated as the guys mouth exploded with teeth flying out amid a stream of blood and saliva. With him in a kneeling position Shirley was able to wrap some of the chain around his torso. The damage to his mouth and with his throat full of blood made it difficult to shout or scream for help and all that could be heard was muffled gargling noises coming from a now terrified and bloodied pulpy mash of a face.

His wide opened petrified eyes staring out from his panic-stricken face displayed the utter terror that he was experiencing. In a few short moments he had gone from relieving himself in the canal to being semi dazed bound in chains and with a caved in face with most of his teeth missing.

The girls continued to wrap as much of the incapacitating chain around their helpless victim as possible. Legs, arms and body were now covered in the thick linked heavy chain round the violently struggling body trying to get up from the floor.

" Roll him over"

Sam shouted, and together Shirley and Sam managed to roll him over once. The terrified stifled screams intensified as the guy realised what the girls were trying to do, they were trying to push him in the canal. He began to push back with all his might but the weight of the chains and the two girls pushing as one were too much for him as he edged closer and closer to the water's edge. He scrambled desperately and tried to dig his heels into the soft towpath, he succeeded for a while but with one final push and a splash he was now submerged in the dank and dirty canal.

The girls immediately turned round to make sure they were still alone, with a joint sigh of relief they felt assured that they had not been seen.

Shirley looked at Sam and said,

"Why on earth did you whack him the plan was to follow him to a possible address."

With a cheeky smile Sam replied,

"Yes, I know but we hadn't anticipated that we would have gotten such an opportunity as this I mean it's perfect, he's now dead the body is disposed of our problem is solved."

"Yes, but we still don't know who he is or how he came to blackmail us. Let's go and round up Victor there are some things I am a bit unsure of what fully happened.

The girls began to walk off when to their horror they heard the whoosh of water as the guy emerged from under the water spluttering and puking out rancid foul-smelling water and he managed to stand up in the canal.

"Shit" Screeched Sam

"Quick throw some more of the chain over him."

The guy now was at the edge of the canal and attempting to extricate himself from his watery grave. The girls grabbed handfuls of chain and threw it on top of him, the wretched almost bizarre sight of someone desperately trying to save his own life was quite surreal. It was more like a scene out of an old hammer house of horror movie such as the creature from the black lagoon or something similar. The chains had become wrapped tightly around him and he was covered in all sorts of putrid canal flotsam, his head looked like he was emerging from a swamp such was the amount of filth in the murky water.

"Please no, please god no more"

he begged. His frantic attempts to get out became more and more difficult as the combined weight of the chain continued to mount and weigh him down.

He went under water several times but someone managed to resurface, he was now sobbing uncontrollably and pleading for his life, but the girls relentlessly continued piling more and more from the pile of chain onto his collapsing body. Uttering one more desperate plea to the girls they watched as the face slowly inch by inch disappeared below the surface. The expression on his face showed that he had no energy left and he knew this would be the last time he be submerged never to resurface. His eyes bulging and quizzical eyes remained above the surface for a while contemplating his impending doom, until he slowly sunk beneath the surface for the last time.

The remaining chain on the towpath was unceremoniously thrown in after the sunken body leaving no trace of what had transpired. The canal was the colour of dirty dishwater and no sign of the body or the chain could be seen. The weight of the chain would prevent the body from ever floating to the surface so the girls felt safe in the knowledge that the murder would go unnoticed for a long time to come or perhaps even never.

The girls decided to have a celebratory drink and went into the Bottle and Glass at the end of the main street through the village. They were both enjoying a glass of real ale in the old-fashioned pub.

Shirley looked at the map left for them by the now dead blackmailer

"It says on this that this pub used to be in Coseley and it was dismantled brick by brick and rebuilt here I think it's fascinating the way they do it."

Sam took a deep draught from her beer,

"Yes, and the beers not bad either, anyway back to business you briefly mentioned something happened at work today that needed sorting. Now that the blackmail is over and done with tell me what it is and get it dealt with."

Shirley explained in detail about the conversation between the Spanish detectives that her hidden voice recorder had captured in her office last night. Sams face looked deadly serious at this news, this was something that cause them immense problems to say the least and Shirley was right it needed sorting immediately.

With a concerned expression and a worried tone in hr voice Sam quietly said,

"What do you think we ought to do because, whatever we decide it has to be done straight away."

"I've already started I have spoken with your friends Prissy and Tess and they have agreed to help but they will need something of yours I have arranged for us to meet them later; you ok with that."

Sam just nodded and at the same time they were joined by Victor who placed three glasses of beer on the table in front of them.

Shirley and Sam instinctively raised their glasses to cheer and a bemused Victor joined in. Shirley asked Victor what he meant exactly about the tracker already being on the boat explaining that something must have been misheard on the barge. Victor explained that he had been following them using the tracking device and he tracked them from the mine to the barge but the tracking device was already on the boat before they got on.

A bemused Sam said,

"How can that be the tracking device is in with the ransom money which is now in Shirleys pocket?"

Victor held out his hand and opened his clenched fingers to reveal sitting snugly in the palm of his hand the tracking device transmitter.

With a sinking realisation Shirley reached into her pocket and took out the bag containing the ransom money. She removed the money which as instructed was bound in black polythene and Sellotape and placed it on the table.

Victor took out a penknife and carefully opened the package and placed the contents on the table. They all realised they had been duped, the money had somehow been switched and replaced with a bundle of paper that resembled the same size and shape.

A furious Shirley who detested being got the better of angrily muttered under her breath

"How has the bastard done this we have had the money with us at all times?"

Victor examined the tracking device receiver and asked,

"Do you know what time you left the mine?" Sam piped up,

"I do I can remember looking at my watch when we got back to the surface and into the light it was exactly one O'clock."
This device records the time of movements and according to its memory the transmitter left the mine at 12.45hrs."

Shirley began to analyse this information and thought back to events in the mine.

"It must have been switched when the lights were turned off, that's why they wanted us to be in handcuffs so that we would hold the bag between

us not that it would stop us chasing after them. And as such they could easily stand behind us in the darkness switch the contents. We wouldn't have noticed any contact because we were all crammed next to each other anyway.
The clever bastard he has obviously done his homework, he even planned for the possibility of a tracking device. And talking of the tracker Victor why did you point out that bloke who we followed off the barge?"

Victor showed the girls the receiver,

"This is quite sensitive and can indicate the presence of the transmitter to within about a metre which initially indicated him but when he got off and you followed him it still showed the tracker on the boat so I looked under the seat and found it. The transmitter was taped to the underside of the chair he was sitting on, so he just happened to be sitting in the wrong place at the wrong time, by the way what happened to him did you manage to find out who he was not that it really matter because obviously he is nothing to do with it."

Shirley and Sam stayed silent and just looked at each other awkwardly.

Victor realising he didn't need to ask again broke the silence by adding "They obviously put the tracker on the boat to throw us off the scent especially if a third party i.e. me was following the tracker. And once we were on the boat even if we found the transmitter straight away, we would not have been able to get off the barge giving them more time to get away. They have been extremely cute and thought of all angles and possibilities."

"So where do we go from here now?"

asked Sam as she and Victor looked enquiringly at Shirley.

"There is nothing else we can do here for the time being and we have a more pressing matter to be dealt with Alldahope, the blackmailer will have to wait, but net time we have to up our game."

It was early evening at Alldahope and most of the girls were in the communal lounge.

Babs had taken her compulsory hot milk and sat at her normal place at the extreme end of the room and as always, she secretly poured away the drug laced concoction, before returning to the main area where most of the girls were congregated. Despite her tender years she was extremely streetwise and had an insight and ability to see and understand things that most people completely miss.

She was eying matron and noticed that she was paying particular attention to two girls. The two girls who were slightly older than Babs but nowhere as mature shared the same bedroom. Matron seemed particularly interested in watching the girls when they were drinking their milk.

Babs was acutely aware of what this surreptitious attention from Matron meant, there was to be a visit from what had become known as the night monsters and their intended victims were to be the two young girls being watched by Matron making sure that they drank their milk.

She was still waiting for some action to be taken by her Dad or the policewoman to stop the night monsters, she felt sure that they would come through for her and the rest of the girls at Alldahope. Especially her dad he wasn't afraid of anybody or anything and if he said he would do something for Babs then you could bet your life on it Babs knew her dad would never let her down. In the meantime she knew it was up to her to do something and she needed to do it tonight, in a similar vein to her father almost nothing frightened her and she would be ready and waiting for them.

Sitting round the kitchen table Victor Sam and Shirley were enjoying a cup of tea, things were now moving at a remarkable pace. The ransom drop had been a disaster, the nosey Spanish detectives needed to be dealt with and now Victor had informed them that some of the Bakers dozen were planning a visit to Alldahope that evening.

Shirley asked Victor to take on the role of dealing with the impending predatory attack at Alldahope that evening. There was no time to formulate any sort of strategy or plan and Victor would have to improvise and deal with it as he saw fit. She had given the task of getting information from the Spanish detectives to Prissy and Tess leaving herself and Sam to deal with the blackmailer whom they felt sure would be back.

Victor had prepared his excuse to visit Alldahope tonight enough though it was not his normal shift, he would simply say he needed to collect one of his tools that he had left there. In reality though it would be highly unlikely anyone would ask him because he had become a regular fixture there turning up at odd times. Most of the staff and girls assumed he was bored at home and just did extra work to escape the boredom.

The only one who knew the real reason why Victor frequented the place outside his working hours so often was Babs. They got on well will each other because they were united by a common goal, to do something about the evil sexual perverts preying on the vulnerable girls. They exchange information secretly and had a prearranged meeting place in the main corridor near the toilets where they could not be overseen.

Saying his goodbyes he left Shirley and Sam still sitting at the table slurping their tea, with no action plan prepared he was unsure what action to take this evening. He was sure of one thing and that was he had to do something to try and protect the girls from those vile perverts. He would make contact with Babs when he got there, this would be to forewarn her and also between them they may think of a plan.

"Ok, spill the beans"

said Sam

Shirley gently shook her head from side to side in disbelief and smiled at Sam with a mixture incredulity and admiration before replying softly.

"Goodness me, it's as if you can read my mind"   "

Sam with an even bigger smile on her face said "You know I can read you like a book, after all we are kindred spirits. Tell me if I am right first of all you have Prissy and Tess dealing with the detectives and Victor dealing with Alldahope. Normally you would have dealt with at least one of them yourself which means we have something else to do tonight, am I right?"

"Of course you are right we have to pay a visit to Stan Guthy, so it's best we go together and we keep our little meeting to ourselves."

15

FRYING TONIGHT

Prissy and Tess sat on a high table in the chequers pub, there were four tables in a line adjacent to the bar. These tables gave a view of anyone entering the pub, also anyone entering had to walk past the tables to get to the bar.

Tess had her back to the door and Prissy sat opposite whereby in her eyeline she had a good clear view of the entrance over Tess's shoulder. This way they could chat and Prissy could discreetly keep the entrance under constant observation without drawing attention to herself.

Shirley had told them that her detectives Dumb and Dumber would be taking the Spanish Detectives drinking that evening. Their routine was monotonously repetitive, they would invariably leave the temporary police station and make their first port of call the Chequers. One because it was the closest to the police station and secondly because the beer was cheap.

The type of clientele that frequented the pub changed throughout the day, first thing in the morning were the drinking stalwarts who started their day with a few pints or several. Most of those by this time had disappeared and were replaced by early evening diners and groups of drinkers starting their night out with cheap booze.

Prissy and Tess were giving alcohol a miss both of them wanting to be alert. Shirleys information had been spot on, just as Prissy was raising her glass to sip at her diet coke she caught sight of the Detectives approaching the entrance. She raised her eyebrows to indicate to Tress that they were coming and they began to chat, paying no attention to their arrival.

Dumb and dumber came in first they were as loud and brash as ever and walked straight past the girls to the bar anxious to start drinking. Jose and Mateo were a bit more casual and certainly not as eager for or impatient to start the evenings drinking. They followed their boorish counterparts to the bar and didn't notice the girls.

Having been served Dumb and Dumber immediately made a beeline for a group of females who were dressed in identical bright pink t-shirts and were obviously celebrating a hen night. From their ribald and coarse demeanour and the extreme noisy outbursts coming from the group they had plainly begun the revelry quite some time previous. They were prime targets for the pair of lounge lizards who began edging closer and closer to the group looking for an in-road to engage with them.

"I wonder if Prissy and Tess have found them yet"

Sam said to Shirley as they approached the door of the run-down accommodation. Shirley gave an encouraging nod of her head replying

"I'm sure they will find them, I told them to go to the chequers I know they are going drinking with Dumb and Dumber and without fail they always start off drinking there, because its cheap just like them."

They both smiled at the last comment before turning their attention to the door that was now slowly opening.

At Alldahope Victor went into the small windowless room that doubled as a workshop and a place to relax with a cup of tea. He scoured the shelving where he stored various tools and odd pieces of equipment and hardware until he found what he was looking for and retrieved it from the cluttered metal shelf wrapped it in a polythene bag and placed the parcel under his arm. Babs had already seen Victor enter the building and they had exchanged glances indicating to each other that they needed to speak.

He waited in the corridor at their pre-arranged agreed meeting point. After a few minutes Babs appeared, she spoke in a hushed voice

" We need to be quick, Matron is being very nosey, she is keeping her eyes on everyone, I think something is going to happen tonight and I think I know who to."

Victor nodded, speaking in a similarly hushed tone

"Yes, you're right there is something about to happen. I have managed to infiltrate the group and some of them are coming tonight and they have invited me along. The policewoman Shirley wants to catch them all and is working out how to do it. But tonight it's down to you and me to stop them. I have thought of a way we can try and do it without alerting the rest so here is what we are going to do."

Listening carefully to make sure that no-one was approaching, Victor quickly unwrapped the polythene parcel showing the contents to Babs and outlined his plan and what they both needed to do.

The hen party in Wetherspoons was in full swing and getting ever noisier and more raucous. Dumb and dumber had managed to worm their way into the groups company and were joining in with the merriment.
The shouting and singing combined with the bad language and the occasional flash of bare breasts as the drunken girls egged each other on to lift their T-shirts up, or pulled each other's shirts up regardless, was beginning to upset the early evening diners.

After a few words of advice about their behaviour from the bar staff it was decided the hen party should go elsewhere. Shouts of neck it neck it rang round the group to encourage everyone to down their drinks as fast as they could so they could move on.

As the group with together with Dumb and Dumber who were firmly ensconced within them began to file out the pub past where Prissy and Tess were seated, Jose and Mateo dawdled along behind. They didn't seem to be as keen to engage with the hen party as their English companions. They paused by the girls tables and struck up a conversation with them. They had already been eyeing up the girls from across the room and the girls had acknowledged them with a few demure smiles.

The detectives bemoaned the fact that they were obliged by etiquette to spend the evening with their hosts and felt that they must follow them to the next pub even though it wasn't the type of evening out to their taste.

They did however ask if they could see the girls later back at the hotel where they were staying and jokingly reminded them that it had a king size jacuzzi. After some persuasion the girls eventually agreed to meet them later back at their hotel.

Shirley and Sam stared up at the brute of a man now standing before them in the doorway
The giant figure of Stan Guthy looked down on the two diminutive women standing on his doorstep they like most people were completely dwarfed by his size. He was under no illusions however he knew that these two were quite a formidable pair and he did not intimidate them as he did most people. They rm neglect would suggest. As he spoke, he had a self-satisfied smug grin on his face because he knew why they were there and that his threat to expose their misdemeanour with his daughter had worked "Have you got something for me?" He said in a slightly mocking manner.

This comment and the condescending way he expressed it immediately rankled Sam and she was about to reply in an equally brusque tone, but Shirley interceded and suggested they all go inside and talk in private.

The accommodation was a mess and had a musty stale smell, a rancid odour emanating from long term neglect and lack of general cleanliness built up over time. The run-down ramshackle building was only ever used for short stints of residence and as such no one ever bothered to either maintain or show any interest in its condition.

They went into the main living area, Shirley was anxious to do what she had to do and get out as quickly as possible, not just because of the smell, but she had an uncanny sense of foreboding. Something was making her feel a little ill at ease, she sensed that Sam somewhat unusually was also on edge.

"I have the information you want, but before I tell you there are some conditions. The first is you never reveal where you came by it, and secondly this is the first and last time do you understand?"

Shirley stared at Guthy waiting for an answer. No reply was forthcoming just an uneasy hiatus of silence, with Guthy eyeing the girls up and down. The tension in the air began to increase, the girls sensed something was different but neither of them could fathom out what. Guthy still didn't reply to Shirleys question but did offer a slight nod of his head accompanied with an unintelligible grunt.

Shirley then gave Guthy the information that he wanted, the information that would buy his silence on the girls involvement with his daughter. She revealed the address of the judge that had placed restrictions on Guthy from seeing his daughter.

Once again Guthy didn't reply but a strange indescribable look came over him, Shirley and Sam were now even more on edge, their senses tingling in readiness for whatever was coming. For a short moment the girls tensions started to relax as Guthy turned around, but then suddenly they went back into overdrive as Guthy locked the living room door by flicking over a makeshift crude latch attached to the inside of the door.

Shirley and Sam were trapped the only exit was secured and had the added obstacle of a weird acting huge and violent thug standing firmly in front of it.

Prissy and Tess parked their car in the car park at the rear of the hotel, and after checking their hair and appearance in the rear-view mirror made their way to the hotel foyer. It was quite late and the hotel lobby was deserted, they remembered where the detectives room was from their last visit and decided not to wait for the lift but walked up the two flights of stairs instead.

They had arrived purposely a little late to ensure they didn't have to wait around for the detectives if they hadn't returned from their night out at the agreed time. They gently knocked on the door and it was opened almost immediately; the boys were obviously ready for them and keen on their arrival.

A half full bottle was on the table and the girls were offered a drink, both of them declined the alcohol but accepted two small bottles of diet coke.

Jose and Mateo were noticeably a little worse for wear the alcohol sodden evening with Dumb and Dumber was taking its toll. The normally reserved Spanish detectives fuelled by drink were a lot more forward and more suggestive in their comments towards the girls.

Tess queried the sound of running water coming from the adjacent room and was given a lecherous look from Mateo who replied in an unbecoming crude and slightly vulgar tone that

"It would be a shame to waste a king-sized hot bubbling Jacuzzi".

Prissy realised the boys had had more to drink than they would normally and that this made them more vulnerable to being manipulated especially with a bit of flattery. She used the opportunity to bring the conversation round to their investigation into the similarities between to last year's Stourbridge serial killings and recent murders in Benidorm. With a little bit of false admiration of how important their enquiries were she soon had them opening up and talking about how their investigation was progressing. Jose was also particularly scathing of the incompetence of the English detectives.

With his tongue loosened by a combination of excess alcohol and false adulation he began to outline the significant findings they had uncovered. He continued,

"The person charged with the murders who has since died could not have been the murderer because I have a credible police witness who says that he found him unconscious in the police station car park a few hours before the last murder. He was in such a state that he would not even been able to wake up let alone kill two people. The young officer didn't tell anyone because he didn't want to get into trouble for his own actions because he should have reported the incident at the time to senior officers but instead, he covered it up. We also have a further witness a civilian who runs a pub, at the time when the first murder was being committed and we have an accurate time of this murder, the suspect was illegally drinking after time with the owner in his pub. Again he didn't come forward because he didn't want to get into trouble for selling alcohol after time illegally. This guy was obviously set up and a lot of the forensic evidence must have been planted. We have a number of good leads which we think will enable us to identify the real killer and maybe make a connection between the Stourbridge and Benidorm murders."

Both the girls listened intently and hung on every word whilst piling on the false flattery of clever they were.

In amazement Tess said,

"That's absolutely amazing everyone in Stourbridge believes that the serial killer was caught and then died in prison and that it was all over and done with."

Mateo, in order to get some attention himself was anxious to join in with the astounding revelations they were telling the girls so he announced what they were planning to do next.

"At this moment in time we haven't communicated this information with anyone but tomorrow we have a meeting with the Detective Chief Inspector at Stourbridge. We will tell him everything we have found out, the news will be absolutely earth shattering, it's going to open up a huge can of worms as you English say."

Jose then took over the conversation saying

"Unfortunately when we reveal what we know to the English police they will start a major investigation and re-open the investigation into the Stourbridge serial killer. This will mean that our work is done and we will have to return very soon to our police force in Spain."

"Does that mean we won't see each other again?"

uttered Tess quietly.

Mateo who was as horny as a stoat and looking for a way to encourage he girls to take things further seized on this remark.

"In the short time no but we could always fly back here on vacation to see you or you could come and see us in Spain"

he said lying through his back teeth. Continuing on further he said,

"But it would be a shame if we didn't get to know each other a little better.

" His mind was working overtime and he was so desperate he would have said or promised anything if it meant they could talk the girls into bed. Neither of them had any intention of ever contemplating seeing the girls again once they left England which would be fairly soon, so they were both of a like mind that they should push their luck to see what they could get.

"Why don't we all relax in the Jacuzzi, it's already filled and bubbling away" asked Mateo hopefully. The girls looked at each other a little sheepishly and stifled a giggle. Mateo sensing that the girls were beginning to chill out and were considering the suggestion repeated the offer with renewed enthusiasm. The girls agreed and added that they would only do it if they could wear costumes and that they some in their car. The boys nodded in affirmation both thinking that once the girls were in the Jacuzzi, they could then take it further.

The girls left the hotel room door on the latch as they went downstairs to the car, they had told the guys to get in the Jacuzzi first which they were only too happy to do so. They again gave the lift a miss and took the stairs down to the empty foyer and made their way across the deserted car park. Prissy opened the back door of the car and took a hold all of the seat and checked the contents. Looking Tess square in the face she said,

"Are you ready to do this?"

"I have never been more ready let's do it"

came the resolute reply.

Jose and Mateo were already in the Jacuzzi discussing how to encourage the girls to remove their costumes once they got in. The normal routine would be to ply them with alcohol but the girls had consistently turned down the offer of a drink and both had been satisfied with a bottle of diet coke.

Jose leant back and spread his arms on the edge of the huge jacuzzi

"We'll think of something, we have to shag them tonight because I think we will be recalled back home day after tomorrow so this will be our last chance. Remember whatever you do don't give them any personal details like telephone numbers or addresses. We don't want this pair trying to make contact again, after tonight we'll avoid them until we go home do you understand."

Mateo was in complete agreement

"Of course, we'll fuck them then fuck them off"

they both began laughing as they sat back and relaxed waiting for the girls.

The stairs creaked as the three masked men made their way up the towards the young girls room. Alldahope was old and the odd groan or the sound of wind whistling through warped and ill-fitting windows and doors was not unusual. They entered the room to find both girls fast asleep and breathing gently.

A mixture of tiredness and the sedative laced milk that Matron had carefully watched them drink meant they hardly stirred as they were both lifted out of their beds. Dave Kempers had one of the tiny semi unconscious girls in his arms and was obviously instantly aroused the bulge in his trousers plain to see. He had been bragging to Victor earlier that it was his intention to sodomise both the girls and inflict as much pain and internal injuries as he possibly could.

He knew the girls had no parents or other family members or visitors that they could complain to so he could indulge in his sadistic sexual fantasy with impunity. Victor held the other girl gently in his arms and was relieved to be wearing a mask otherwise the tears running down his cheeks would have betrayed his abhorrence of such depraved and monstrous attacks on the defenceless.

The third masked man acted as lookout and door opener as they began their descent down the stairs towards the basement where they would be able to indulge in their evil satanic like sexual attacks. He was followed by closely by Victor, with Dave Kempers at the rear.

They approached the door that led down to the basement and the leading masked man quietly inched the old gothic looking door open and stepped inside with Victor now following even closer. Suddenly all hell seemed to break loose, the leading masked man went headlong down the steep set of concrete steps at an alarming speed shouting and cursing as he went hurtling uncontrollably and violently towards the basement floor where he landed with a huge crash.

Victor turned round quickly towards Dave Kempers saying,

"He has fell down the steps, all this noise will wake people up we have to be quick you take the girls and put them back in bed and I will go and help him."

He gently placed the diminutive, little girl into Dave's arms resting her on top of her roommate, the girls were so tiny and lightweight that it was easy for just one adult to carry them.

Kempers stood there stunned for a second, feeling a mixture of bewilderment and devastation that he would not be fulfilling his vicious and wicked fantasy. "Quickly" Victor urged, and as Kempers turned away with the girls in his arms Victor began to descend the stairs making sure not to tread on either of the top two steps. As soon as he got to the bottom it became obvious the pervert had sustained a serious injury, trying to stifle a scream he cried through clenched teeth "I've broken my fucking leg" and clutched the broken limb in in his arms.

At the top of the stairs Babs had emerged from her hideout and was wiping down the top two stairs with a bundle of cloths and rags. She worked quickly so that she wouldn't be seen by the perverts or anyone who got up after being awoken by the noise. With the top two steps now clear of the thick layers of grease that she had been given by Victor she retreated silently back into her hideout, a small cupboard in the hallway that was just big enough to get her frame in and quietly pulled the double doors shut behind her.

She felt fantastic Victors plan had worked perfectly. The two girls would be safe, at least tonight anyway and into the bargain one of the bastards had obviously injured themselves. They had a backup plan of course, which was for Babs to set off the fire alarm if this plan failed but as she had used the fire alarm previously it would raise suspicions.

She could see through the crack in the double doors as Victor emerged from the basement carrying another man on his shoulder. They were almost immediately joined by the third masked monster and together they left the building via the back door. Babs could not her anyone stirring and no lights had been switched on so in the darkness she quickly and silently dashed back to her room.

Trapped in the smelly filthy room with Guthy, Shirley and Sam needed all their wits about them. Guthy hadn't spoken for some time and it was if he didn't know the girls were there it was like he was in a trance. Shirley looked round the room and suddenly realised why Guthy was acting differently. Everywhere there were signs of recent drug and substance abuse, syringes silver foil and other paraphernalia were strewn all over. Shirley whispered to Sam

"He's as high as a kite that's why he is acting so weird, I have seen this type of drug induced behaviour before. They constantly swing and change from various moods, sometimes with extreme acts of violence interspersed with passages of lucidity."

"I haven't got my cattle prod with me otherwise I could electrocute the bastard"

Sam replied.
Shirley indicated to her pocket saying,

"I have a cs spray canister in my pocket but it doesn't always work well with people in drug induced states especially someone his size."

Sam edged slowly towards the fireplace; she had seen a fire bucket filled with various fire irons. Whilst Guthy was in his placid almost catatonic state she took the opportunity to arm herself with one of the metal tools. It was a long thin metal poker that would normally be used to stoke the fire but this one had been sharpened at one end perhaps to use as a toasting fork perhaps. She concealed it behind her back in readiness as she saw Shirley take out and conceal in her hand the cs spray canister.

"If you gas him Shirley then while he is holding his face, I will drive this into him like a skewer."

"ok"

Shirley whispered in reply.
Guthys mood as predicted by Shirley suddenly changed and he began to talk to her. In a clear and concise but also threatening manner he said

"I have the info I want now so what is to stop me beating you and your little dwarf of a mate, who I notice hasn't got that fucking electric shock fucking stick with her to a pulp."

It was Sam who replied

"I may be a dwarf but I will stick you like the fucking pig you are so I suggest you unlock that fucking door and get out the way you oversize piece of shit."

Guthy was amazed, he had never come across anyone who would have the sheer nerve and bottle to speak to him like that and he had known and had dealings many violent thugs, but not a single one of them would have stood up to him like this petite blonde bombshell.

He turned round and looked at the door looking slightly bemused, he clearly hadn't remembered putting the latch on. Sam had noticed that Shirley had flicked off the safety cap on the Cs spray and Sam grasped the sharpened poker tighter in readiness. She was working out in her mind the best place to drive the weapon through him. Should she go for his stomach or preferably his groin, she loved the thought of skewering his bollocks and the pain it would bring him. Through his eyeball and deep into his brain would be ideal but he was much too tall. She opted for the gut, it was a target she couldn't miss and hopefully it would incapacitate him enough so that she could withdraw the weapon and then impale his gonads with it.

With Guthys attention still distracted slightly as he wondered why the latch was engaged Shirley whispered,

"Be ready."

Sams heart was pounding with adrenalin eager to give this bastard what he deserved when Guthy opened the door wide and stepped out of their way and with a smile he held his arm out towards the door inviting them to leave.

With the way out now completely unobstructed they and Guthys mood altered they cautiously began to exit. They passed through without incident and into the hallway and as they neared the front door Guthy quipped

"Thanks for coming, oh and by the way you can leave my poker by the front door if you don't mind."

He then began an uncontrollable belly laugh that Shirley and Sam could hear all the way back to their car.

Prissy and Tess closed the door behind them and they went back into the hotel room. They could hear the constant hum and the sound of the bubbles coming from the Jacuzzi. Prissy shouted through the door

"We're back you boys ready for us?"

they shouted back as one

"Yes, come on in girls don't be shy."

Prissy shouted again

"Ok we're coming in but you must promise to keep your eyes shut until we get in." The boys began to laugh

"You English girls are so shy but ok we promise not to look."

"Put your hands over your eyes then I am going to check"

and with that Prissy stuck her head round the door to make sure the boys were complying. When she was satisfied the boys could not see anything she and Tess went in and approached the Jacuzzi.

"Keep them shut"

she said one last time.

Tess made one last check to make sure the cattle prod was switched on and threw it into the Jacuzzi. Immediately sparks began to fly accompanied by bangs and flashes off blue light resembling lightning. The guys were jerking and shaking uncontrollably the sound reminded Tess of the noise you get when you put cold food into a boiling hot pan of oil. The sizzling and the crackling continued; the guys hair was sticking up resembling cartoon characters.

The detectives could not coordinate their limbs to affect an escape from their high voltage watery cauldron. Their heads were now beginning to burn and bright blue sparks passed between their two heads. The smell of burning flesh was becoming quite sickly and began to irritate the girls nostrils. Burning human flesh smelt completely different from that of cooking an animal.

The smell of roast pork or beef was quite pleasant but burning humans was different it was gut wrenching. The boys were now floating face down on top of the water like a couple of dead goldfish. Their bodies had stopped jerking and the sound and light display was abating as the battery began to run down. Tess fetched the holdall from the other room and the girls got to work.

Donning a pair of huge thick rubber gloves Tess removed the energy depleted cattle prod from the Jacuzzi wiped it down and placed it back in the holdall. Shirley was busy wiping down all the surfaces that she and Tess had touched and had retrieved the two bottles of diet coke that they had drunk from also placing them in the holdall.

When they were sure that no trace of them was left in the room there was only one thing left to do. Tess with gloved hands removed the old-fashioned electric bar from the holdall and plugged it in to the wall socket in the bedroom.

The fire was placed on the edge of the Jacuzzi and switched on Prissy went and peered out into the corridor to make sure it was all clear and then gave Tess the signal. She pushed the fire into the jacuzzi and for a few seconds the sparks began to fly before there was a bang from the wall socket and everything went quiet.

The girls made their way back to their vehicle using the stairs, to again avoid the C.C.T.V situated in the lift. The girls had done their homework the rear carpark where they left their vehicle also had no C.C.T.V unlike the main parking area at the front of the hotel.

"I'm a little peckish"

Tess announced.

"Me too where shall we go for a bite to eat,"

replied Prissy.

Tess thought about it and casually remarked

"I'm easy we could go anywhere except the chip shop I've had enough of deep-fried stuff for one night."

16

YOU'VE BEEN FRAMED

Shirley arrived at work early, she had received an early morning call from Victor who said he was in his disused steel mill and that he had something important to show her that something she would find interesting and very useful. Intrigued she promised Victor she would come and see him as early as she could get away from the office, but she needed to go to work first because she had a mountain of paperwork to complete and dozens of crime files to sign off.

This was not what she joined the police force to do she wanted to become involved, to make a difference, to make sure justice was done. But now police work had completely changed, a lot of it was merely a paper shuffling exercise with crimes not investigated thoroughly, the majority simply written off with the minimal amount of time and effort and filed away never to re-surface.   She worked as quickly as she could and also checked the overnight log, there was nothing particularly outstanding, apart from the odd burglary and a few vehicle crimes it had been and a quiet night. She noticed that there had been a mass brawl in a Stourbridge bar involving a raucous hen night but no one wanted to make a complaint of assault so that had been quickly dealt with.

She would allocate the overnight burglaries to Dc's Trevor Peeves and Frank Fergas to conduct what had increasingly become a token investigation to merely put another tick in the box. She as was a lot of her colleagues were always a bit wary of Dumb and Dumber especially Frank because he was known to be a backstabber and he was always sneakily passing information to senior officers. But she knew that if she gave them something to work on, they would get on with it without complaining well not to her face anyway, even if they only did the bare minimum required and used any enquiry to create free time for themselves to go drinking or chubby chasing.

She knew they had been out with the Spanish detectives the night before and she was curious to what state they would be in when they rolled into the office. Her desk phone rang and was surprised when she answered to hear the voice of her boss Detective Chie Inspector Trevor Cappoten.
He very rarely phoned Shirley or even spoke to her. The last time they did speak, he was giving her a hard time over her insistence that the deaths at Alldahope should be further investigated. He had put her firmly in her place

and told her in no uncertain terms that the deaths were nonsuspicious. And added that if she or her staff spent any time or resources investigating the deaths against his direct order, they would suffer immediate consequences.

"Yes, sir how can I help you"

Shirley said in the most enthusiastic upbeat voice that she could muster.

"I want you and inspector Courtan to attend a meeting I have with officers from the Spanish National Police concerning their enquiries into similarities between incidents in Benidorm and deaths in Stourbridge. I believe that you have been liaising with these officers and that you and Inspector Courtan worked on the Stourbridge serial killer case is that correct?"

"Yes, that's right sir we both worked on the case and I have been allocating some of my detectives to assist them".

"The meeting is in my office at 11;00 I want you and the inspector in my office in time for the meeting"

Shirley agreed and without a please or thank you the Chief inspector hung up.

With receiver still in hand Shirley looked at the disconnected handset in disgust and thought to herself

"How ignorant"

she then looked up to see her two joined at the hip detectives walking into the office.

The pair of them looked awful, they must have the mother of all hangovers and Robert Peeves was sporting a huge black eye. It was so bad his eye was almost completely closed.

"Morning sarge,"

said Frank Fergas in a somewhat shaky voice.

"Good morning to you Frank I have allocated a couple of burglaries for you and Robert to investigate, I have left the details on your desk. I have to go out now, if you need me this morning I will be with the chief Inspector in his office. There is a meeting with the Spanish detectives."

"That must be why they left the pub early last night they wouldn't want to have a meeting with Cappoten sporting a hangover you know what a stickler he is for discipline" replied Frank.

As she got up to leave the office, she answered

"Yes, I know only too well what he can be like, I'll see you guys later and you can fill me in concerning the black eye."

Without any further conversation from the now embarrassed detectives she left the office. As she walked through the still quiet shopping centre, she smiled to herself. Her open-ended comment about the black eye without giving either one of them chance to reply was quite deliberate. It gave her a psychological advantage, it meant that her detectives would continually mull over and worry about what to do or say concerning the circumstances surrounding why one of them has a facial injury.

In reality Shirley wasn't concerned in the slightest about the black eye and had no intention of asking them any further questions, she simply wanted them to stew a little allowing her to establish her authority. Now she wanted to go and see Victor curious as to what he had to show her, she needed to get a move on she dare not be late for the meeting with the Chief inspector.

Victors steel mill was located and could be accessed via the Stourbridge canal. It was a pleasant warm day so Shirley decided to get some fresh air and walk there along the canal. Stourbridge canal was only five miles long in total. It connected Stourbridge with the Staffordshire and Worcestershire canal and was originally built to facilitate transport for goods connected with industry and glassmaking.

Stourbridge at one time was world renowned for crystal glass making but in recent times the glass making industry was virtually non-existent, as were a lot of the industrial outlets. The canal was now like most others was used for recreation purposes with the towpath giving access to walkers cyclists and fishermen. The opposite side was littered with the crumbling remains of old buildings and factories long since abandoned.

Shirley turned left just before a pub called the old Wharf where the Stourbridge canal began and walked past a number of moored longboats. She knew one of them belonged to Victor but couldn't remember exactly which one was his. She knew he spent some of his time on the longboat and some in his now disused steel mill where he had converted a couple of rooms into living accommodation.

The canal towpath was deserted and the only sound to be heard was the far-off rumbling of traffic on Amblecote high street and the occasional quack from one of the ducks paddling away in the murky waters.

She could understand people wanting to spend time on the canal it was remarkably relaxing and she could feel some of the tension caused by recent events melting away. In the distance she could see the disued steel mill on the opposite bank and the metal footbridge that she had to cross. A solitary lonely figure was standing in the middle of the structure looking in her direction. As she approached, she realised that it was Victor who was patiently awaiting her arrival. The canal was still deserted Shirley and Victor had it all to themselves. They both remained on the bridge for a while soaking up the peacefulness and the calming tranquillity of this little oasis running through the midst of this busy and densely populated area.

Feeling relaxed and prior to entering the steel mill, Victor pointed out where his C.C.T.V cameras were sited. Inside the Mill Shirley was surprised at the sheer size of the place, a lot of the machinery used for rolling steel was still in place as was the main furnace and a number of smaller ones scattered about cavernous interior.

"Wow I never realised this place was so big and the machinery looks as if it could still be used"

said an amazed Shirley. Victor smiled,

"I did toy with the idea of preserving everything in order to convert it into a working museum with various displays. A bit like the Black Country museum or the Stourbridge glass cone. So yes, most of the machinery still works and some of the rooms have been converted into multi-functional suites that could be used for parties, meetings or visitor attractions because sadly once places like this are gone then they are gone forever and I think it's important to preserve our heritage and history. That's one of the reasons I installed all the security cameras to keep the building and contents safe."

"I have a meeting this morning that I can't get out of Victor so I don't have much time, if you can show me what you think is important but firstly and briefly fill me in on how you got on at Alldahope last night."

"Ok"

said Victor as he beckoned Shirley to follow him through into another room. Shirley entered what appeared to be a small office and took a seat, in front of her was a desk full of electrical equipment and on the wall was an extensive bank of video screens.

"I had no idea you had all this surveillance equipment Victor there must be at least a dozen cameras."

"I have a video clip to show you, while I prepare it I will run through what happened at Alldahope. Firstly I learned from Dave Kempers that there was to be an attack on the girls and he invited me along. His particular fetish is to inflict internal physical damage by sodomy. He therefore chooses very young and slightly built girls. When I got to Alldahope my cover story was to be that I needed to collect some equipment from my office. As it transpired no one challenged my presence anyway, I spoke with Babs she was aware something was happening by observing Matrons behaviour who ensured that the two target girls drunk all their milk, obviously to dull their consciousness. In order to stop them and not show out and jeopardise our future actions I went along with them.

I gave Babs a can of grease and she was to smear the top two steps of the stairs leading down to the basement. Making sure one of them went in front of me, with Dave Kempers behind me, I carried one child and Kempers the other.

When the first one put their foot on the step, they lost their footing and went headfirst all the way down to the basement floor and broke their leg in the fall. I turned round gave Kempers the child I was carrying and told him to put the girls back in bed because the noise was bound to alert somebody. I stepped over the first two steps and went down the stairs. Babs then came out of her hiding place and wiped the grease off the steps making sure they were completely clean, and then got back in her hiding place. I picked up the guy with the broken leg and carried him back up the stairs, met back up with Kempers who had put the girls back in their beds and we all left the building.

        The plan worked a charm I made sure I was right behind the first one just in case he didn't lose his footing completely and I was going to give them a push which I would pretend was accidental. But I didn't need to push them they went down like a sack of bricks it worked perfectly."

    "Victor that was brilliant, I'm impressed, now what else have you got for me?"

        "When I saw your detective Latifeo nosing about on the canal the other day I thought I would search through the recordings and I found this."

        The image showed the canal behind Victors premises including the towpath the scene was empty until emerging from the left-hand side a figure of a large male appeared walking along the towpath. As they came closer and the image became clearer Shirley recognised the imposing figure of Stan Guthy.

A few moments later from the right-hand side a cyclist was approaching heading towards Guthy. Shirley knew straight away what was going to happen, she also recognised the person riding on the bike, it was the young fifteen-year-old who had been reported missing, his picture having been displayed on various social medias in a bid to try and find him. She watched in silence and horror as she witnessed the cyclist collide with Guthy come off his bike and then receive a horrendous beating at the hands of the huge vicious thug. Guthy holding his victim by the throat, suspending him the air and repeatedly pounding his huge fists into the face of his prey. She saw the final act of brutality when the battered young boy was beaten further by smashing his bike down on his broken frame time and time again before finally throwing the body into the canal

    "Bastard"

    muttered Shirley,

    "I wish I had seen this earlier; I wouldn't have needed to give him the information I've got him where I want him now the roles are reversed."

        "What do you want me to do with the recording?"

"Keep it safe for now but don't show it to anyone, not even my idle detective Latifeo if he ever bothers to get off his arse and do his job properly."

Shirley looked at her watch, she needed to leave now in order not to be late for her meeting. Telling Victor that she and Sam would see him later she hurriedly left and set off along the canal. As she passed the spot where the murdered young mans body was thrown in the canal, she looked for any sign of him or the bike. She realised it was impossible the canal would only be a few feet deep but anything more than a few inches below the surface was hidden from view. She had noticed that Guthy threw the bike as close as he could on top of the body, this would prevent the body eventually rising to the surface.

There was no time to spare so she continued her brisk walk along the towpath and once back in Stourbridge she went straight to the Chiefs office.

Grant Courtan was already there but Shirley wasn't surprised, in fact she would have put money on him being there early, he was a bit of crawler and a gaffers man through and through. He was always doing things to ingratiate himself with the hierarchy. Shirley sat down and together with Grant ran through the investigation into the Stourbridge serial killer.

The Spanish detectives were late and the Chief began to get impatient. They waited half an hour with the Dci becoming ever more agitated until he demanded that Grant make some enquiries as to where they were and we would re=convene at midday. Shirley used the time to grab a cup of tea and rehearse what her reaction should be to what she knew was coming.

At midday precisely Shirley went back into the Chiefs office to find it a hive of activity. There were several other officers present and most of them were making frantic phone calls including the Chief. On seeing Shirley the Chief put his hand over the phone mouthpiece and told her that the Spanish detectives have been found dead in their hotel room. Initial reports were that it as a tragic accident but ordered me and Grant to go and investigate.

Shirley shamming a stunned loom of shock stuttered

"Yes sir of course."

"We'll go in my car"

said Grant as he picked up his coat on the way out the door. It was only a short drive to the hotel but that didn't stop Grant driving like a maniac, narrowly avoiding traffic with some near misses just to get there a few seconds earlier. He always like to be the first on scene, it made him feel like he was in charge. When they arrived, they weren't the first there, Scenes of crime were in attendance and had begun their examination.

The SOCO was one of the newer and less experienced ones, Shirley asked if her supervisor Steve was on his way. The reply she got was that the Chief Inspector had already deemed it not necessary to have a senior SOCO or crime scene manager in attendance he wanted everything to be dealt with in a low-key manner as befitting an accident.

"How about the Pathologist?"

enquired Shirley.

The young SOCO shook their head from side to side and repeated again that they had been told it was to be dealt with as a simple accident and no specialists were to be utilised.

Shirley and Grant looked around the impressive suite that the detectives had occupied. There didn't appear to be anything out of place, there was a half full bottle of whisky and two glasses on the table, no signs of a disturbance or struggle or anything obviously missing. In the bedrooms they examined the clothing of the two officers, their belongings and wallets were still in their trouser pockets and again nothing seemed disturbed or out of place.

Grant returned to the bathroom and spoke with the SOCO, completely ignoring Shirley, but she was only too happy to let him get on with it. She knew Prissy and Tess had been professional and very thorough and there were no signs of them ever having been there or anything untoward.

Grant then announced he was going to inspect the hotel C.C.T.V and left the room to go to the main lobby where the recording equipment was located.

Shirley made herself comfortable and was mulling through what to do with her new information about Guthy and his brutal murder of the innocent young man. She could simply turn over the recordings and Guthy would be arrested and dealt with but that would mean Shirley no longer had the upper hand with no bargaining chip   She decided for the moment to keep it to herself and use it to manipulate Guthy and to ensure his silence.

She relaxed in an armchair and eyed the impressive surroundings; this must have been costing a pretty penny she surmised and wondered who was footing the bill for such palatial accommodation.

Out the corner of her eye she saw something glinting on the floor, she stood up and walked over towards it, as she got closer, she recognised it immediately. It was a silver identity bracelet it was the one belonging to Prissy. Good God she thought, that would have her name on it, she needed to get rid of it. At that moment Grant walked back into the room, Shirley managed to put her foot on top of the bracelet and asked,

"Was there anything useful on the C.C.T.V."

Grant condescendingly replied

"I'll tell the chief in a minute I just want to check with the SOCO first."

As he disappeared into the bathroom Shirley quickly picked up the bracelet and put it in her pocket.

She scanned the room urgently to make sure the girls had not left anything else that could reveal their presence but there was nothing obvious. With Shirleys heart still pounding Grant emerged from the bathroom and pressed the speed dial on his phone.

The call was answered immediately and Grant with his usual exaggerated sense of his own importance began to speak.

"Yes sir, I'm here in their hotel room now I have taken full charge of the scene and the investigation and this is what I have found out. It appears that both the guys had been drinking. There is a half full bottle of scotch with two glasses on the table. They have been found in the king size Jacuzzi, it appears that they placed an electric heater on the edge or near the edge of the bath and this has somehow fallen in, perhaps due the effects of the alcohol. There is no sign of any disturbance, nothing as far as I can ascertain has been taken. There is nothing missing, the guys valuables are still here wallets, credit cards watches etc. I have checked the C.C.T.V which covers the main carpark and the hotel lift, there is no sign of any movement whatsoever. I have liaised with SOCO the bodies do not display any blunt trauma injuries just discolouration and some burns.

So from the initial investigation it is most likely that the guys got a little drunk, took a Jacuzzi and placed a heater nearby which fell in the water and electrocuted them. The appliance then shorted out and the guys remained here until found by the cleaner this morning. I can't find any suspicious circumstances."

The conversation went back and forth between the pair in an ever-increasing round of self-congratulatory idle chit chat regarding their powers of deduction and investigatory prowess.

Shirley listened to their inane egotistical rambling in a mixture of disgust and relief. She had known Grant Courtan for some time and she held him in high esteem, he was well respected in the ranks for his abilities as a capable and diligent hard-working detective. But now he had changed, he had turned into a subservient boot-licking sycophant. Even the idle good for nothing Detective Oli Latifeo would have made more of an effort she thought.

She was astounded at how slipshod the enquiry into the detective death was being handled. There was no senior SOCO or crime scene manager a complete lack of any forensic strategy. No pathologist in attendance not even a police doctor. No detailed inspection of the bodies or the hotel accommodation or any technical specialists.

Although in her mind she was scathing of the incompetent approach to the deaths she felt a greater sense of relief, knowing that with the lack of investigative drive from the pair of clowns she and her girls had got away with-it Scott free and the problem with the Spanish detectives could be put behind her. She could now focus her attention on her remaining problems Alldahope, Guthy and that Bastard blackmailer.

When they had eventually finished congratulating each other and the phone call ended Grant said in an incredibly condescending manner

"The boss is happy with the way I have dealt with this and he is satisfied it's a complete but tragic accident so he says we can go, just leave SOCO here to finish up and also organise removal of the bodies."

"That's ok with me just don't drive so fast on the way back it would be nice to get back in one piece" quipped Shirley taking a dig at Courtans madcap driving on the way to the hotel.

"Ok grandma, it'll be like driving miss daisy, nice and sedate."

"No need to take the piss sir, but if you could drive somewhere even remotely near the speed limit it would be sufficient"

Their friendly banter given what they were dealing with managed to lift the mood a little and Grant allowed himself a chortle as they made their way towards the lift.

By the time they arrived back at the police station news of the death of the Spanish detectives had spread like wildfire. The phones were ringing off the wall.

Shirley and Grant were summoned to the chiefs office which was filled wall to wall with top brass. They were both asked to repeat what they had seen and what actions had been taken at the scene. The senior officers were of a similar mind set to the Detective Chief Inspector they wanted a short sharp enquiry into a tragic accident. With the emphasis focused solely on accident and there was to be no mention of or speculation of any criminal connotations.

Grant was formally tasked with overseeing the investigation including repatriation of the bodies, although it was not supposed to be referred to as an investigation, it's official status was as accident enquiry.

Alone in her office Shirley was quite happy to be side-lined on this one it suited her perfectly it meant she could concentrate on working on her own problems. The first thing she did was to make enquiries at the local hospital to establish the name of anyone who had been treated in the last twenty-four hours for a broken leg.

Not wishing to attract attention to her enquiry Shirley made a few discreet phone calls and now had three names of people treated for a broken leg in the previous few hours. She had needed to call in a few favours but she now had a name to look at for a possible connection with the Bakers dozen.

One of the three named was female, another was nine years of age which left a middle-aged man, Tom Leers.

With a little more investigation and background checks Shirley had an address, date of birth and even his workplace. Shirley smiled and muttered under her breath "Gotcha, ya bastard."

She sat back in her chair and ran through in her mind the events of the day. Things had gone well, she had the bargaining tool to put Guthy in his place, the Spanish detectives were no longer a problem and the enquiry into their deaths was so slipshod that would be the end of it. The icing on the cake now was another inroad to the Bakers dozen. She even had the good fortune of finding the bracelet belonging to Prissy before anyone saw it.

The phone rang and an upbeat Shirley cheerfully answered,

"Stourbridge police Sergeant Wallows speaking how can I help you?"

"Shirley its Sam are you ok to speak?"

"Yes, no problem I have some good news to tell you when I get back later."

"You need to come home Shirley you need to come now."

By the sombre tone of Sams voice Shirley knew something was wrong, something was very wrong Sam very rarely rang her at work, no matter what had happened, so this must be serious. Shirleys pulse began to raise,

"What is it what's the matter."

"I can't tell you over the phone Shirley you need to come home."

17

QUID PRO QUO 1

In the leafy suburb of Edgbaston tree lined avenues fronted the exclusive residences belonging to the well-heeled. This exclusive area close to the centre of Birmingham was home to some of societies elite, high flying businessmen, Bankers, Barristers, and the like. The expansive pavements were only frequented by the occasional dog walker. In stark contrast to an inner-city area whereby a dog walker typically would be some heavily tattooed skinhead dressed in jeans and a vest, with rottweilers or some other huge and sometimes ferocious snarling mutts straining at the leash. Edgbaston was a completely different affair, the dog walkers would be immaculately turned out occasionally carrying an unnecessary shooting stick, and their pedigree well-groomed pooches were more like a designer accessory than a pet.

A wooded area of land that had once been home to a now long disused railway was now the exclusive territory of these morning strollers.

Judge Mangham was one of these elitists and he could be seen regular as clockwork exercising his pedigree Saluki bitch. The dogs long floppy ears accentuated the long snouted canine, if ever a dog screamed money and privilege then this was it. As the dog strode lightly and nimbly along the pristine litter free walkways towards the wood with their snout pointing up in the air, an onlooker would automatically draw the comparison of how the status symbol dog and their master were alike.

They had the wood to themselves or so they thought, so Judge Manghan detached the designer lead from the collar and let the dog run free to perform their morning ablutions. Opening the handle of his shooting stick and planting the spike firmly in the ground he perched himself down.

He took the copy of the guardian newspaper that had been neatly folded under his arm and began to peruse the headlines.

It had been a slow news week, even the never-ending Brexit debate that relentlessly filled vast swathes of the media was more interesting than any current headlines. He cast a quick eye over the obituary column to see if he was acquainted with any of the notaries that had recently demised.

It suddenly dawned upon him that he had read almost all of his newspaper, whereas normally his beloved pet would have returned long before he was even halfway through.

"Feria, Feria here girl"

he shouted out and repeated several times.

Getting slightly annoyed he went in search of his stray dog. The wood wasn't that large so he knew he would find his pet soon but his anger was now mixed with a little trepidation. Something didn't seem right this was out of the ordinary thought Manghan. As he went deeper into the wood in the distance, he could smell a bonfire which in itself was unusual. Even more unusual was the unmistakeable smell coming from the direction of the fire. It was that of a barbecue, Manghan thought to himself who has a barbecue this time of the morning perhaps it was some tramp sleeping out in the woods cooking his breakfast. He pushed aside some overhanging bushes to reveal a little clearing, but no sign of a barbecue or a fire even though the smell was intensifying the fire must be very close.

He looked around scanning the area for clues, could the fire or barbecue whatever it was, have some connection with the disappearance of the dog. Yes, he thought, that would be it, dogs have a much greater sensitivity to smell than humans. She would have smelt food and gone in search of it so all he had to do was find the fire and he would probably find his dog.

But where on earth was the blasted fire, he could smell the fumes as if he were right next to it this was infuriating. He licked his finger and put it in the air, that way he could feel the direction of the wind that would give him a clue as to the source of the smell.

That's when he saw it, the most horrific sight imaginable, he licked his finger and put it in the air to detect the direction of the wind and therefore the fire his gaze was now looking skyward. The sight almost made him instantly physically sick. His beloved dog was suspended high in the air from a protruding tree branch. Her legs had been tied together and she had been hauled up with a long length of rope. Something had been attached to her collar and was dangling downwards it resembled a piece of rope or cord.

This attachment to her collar had been set alight and the flames were licking upwards towards the dogs head and her long floppy ears had already caught alight.

Her muzzle had been tightly bound with gaffer tape preventing her from barking or crying out. The judge was frozen rigid in sheer horror, at the sight of his pet being slowly set on fire. In an instant he realised the smell was not that of a barbecue but of his cherished pet being burned alive. The flames now began to engulf her face and Manghan was only stirred back into life when he heard the hideous blood curdling screams and yelps from his dog, the flames had burnt through the Gaffer tape binding her jaws together so she was now able to scream out in agony.

Manghan looked for where the rope had been secured, he followed it down from the dogs legs to a clump of bushes. Frantically he dived in the dense foliage and immediately began to scream. Not only was the rope secured in the midst of a very prickly thorn bush but some bastard had concealed lengths of barbed and razor wire hidden at various heights and angles. The sounds coming from his pet were unlike anything he had ever heard before, the terrifying gut-wrenching noises meant two things. One that the dog was experiencing the most intense pain imaginable and secondly more importantly was that she was still alive. He must act fast if he wanted to save her and he forced his way through the booby-trapped foliage. The end of the rope was secured around the base of a small bush, which was also surrounded with razor wire. With the dogs cries of pain driving him on he lunged for the rope that was crudely tied around the base. His now bloodied fingers fumbled with the rope, as he unravelled the knots, he saw that placed conspicuously on the floor was a plain square of black fabric.

He instinctively realised that this was no random attack it was obviously targeted at him; the black fabric was similar to what had to be worn by a judge prior to 1965 when sentencing a person to death. It was commonly referred to as the black cap although it was not made to fit as a cap did but merely rested on the judges head.

His hands were bleeding so badly that the rope was now coloured red, saturated with the sticky blood pouring from his wounds.

At last he had managed to free the rope from its mooring and he stood upright clutching the end of the rope.

Then it dawned on him, there was no way he could lower the dog slowly to the ground, the rope wasn't long enough. Whoever had pulled the dog way up in the air had tied off the rope and then cut the excess length off. If he let go the rope then the burning dog would fall about fifty feet to the floor. But if he didn't let go then the dog would slowly and painfully burn to death. Someone had thought this through to inflict the maximum pain on him and his pet.

Tears of frustration began to run down his cheeks

"You fucking lousy bastards"

he shouted at the top of his voice echoing through the deserted undergrowth. He had a choice to make, let the rope go and the dog would fall to the ground and probably to their death, or hold on and the dog would definitely die but a slow lingering painful death.

He knew the only outside chance of his dog surviving was to release the rope, if she died then at least it would be a quick merciful death.

He closed his eyes so that he couldn't witness his pet plummeting to the earth and let go of the rope.

With a huge thud and a loud yelp the dog hit the ground sending a cloud dust skywards. He shoved his way through the bushes and knelt down next to his motionless dog, her battered body displayed signs of multiple broken bones. Several of which had pierced her body and the bloody skeletal material were protruding through her pelt. But the biggest danger was still the fire, her fur and skin was alight, he needed to extinguish the flame straight away.

Looking round he saw an old plastic bucket it had the remnants of some dirty rainwater, he picked up the half full bucket and threw the entire contents over the slowly burning dog. As the fluid engulfed the dog instead of the flames fizzling out, there was an enormous flash. The flames had now increase tenfold with flames leaping in the air. An acrid smell filled the air and Manghan realised he had doused his dog with petrol. The container had obviously been put there deliberately to set him up for the purpose of him to finally kill his own dog.

The ear-piercing shrieks of pain had escalated beyond belief and Manghan was now crying uncontrollably and he fell to his knees adjacent to his dying dog begging her for forgiveness.

 The screams eventually stopped and the dog lay there silent, she was dead. Her body still burning like an overdone discarded burnt piece of meat from a barbecue. The only sounds to be heard now were the gentle sizzling of flesh and the sobbing and whimpering of Manghan.

        Shirley was sitting at her desk in the makeshift office in an empty retail outlet in the town centre, which had now been commonly referred to as the fishbowl.

She was contemplating the sad news that she had received yesterday. It had affected both her and Sam equally as hard.

They had jointly employed the services of a private detective to investigate their parentage. with the girls both being from broken homes and having been adopted at such an early age neither of them had any recollection of who their parents were.

They had been hoping for some good news but it was not to be, both their mothers were dead having passed away some considerable time ago. Sams mother had been murdered by her husband, whilst Shirleys mom had died in childbirth.

The detective had not uncovered any details of either of their fathers with the obvious exception that Sams father was a murderer.

But neither as he emphasised, he could not find any record of their deaths so they possibly may still be alive and he would continue investigating.

This had been devastating news for Shirley and Sam, both of them had no idea of their heritage and hadn't been overly concerned to find out until recently.

Their friendship with each other went very deep, in the few recent years that they had known each other they had formed and incredible bond. This relationship was partially due to their appalling upbringing in children's homes where they had been prey to the evilest of sexual perverts and predators. This in turn had fuelled their hatred of self-centred domineering male supremacists and their need to exact vengeance.

Shirley thoughts turned to Alldahope and how best to resolve it and bring the perpetrators to justice and free the young girls from the onslaught of sexual abuse. But what sort of justice, things had gone too far for them to be arrested and put before the courts, they had broken and bent the rules to such an extent that the repercussion's would be considerable and Shirley was sure she would at best lose her job or at worst serve a prison sentence.

Things had been helped by Martin the reporter being out of the picture due to his promotion, he was all for justice but he probably wasn't as keen to go beyond the bounds of legality, or take the extremes measures that Shirley and Sam were willing to do.

Steve the crime scene manager could still be useful for his forensic knowledge and lab contacts, but he also would have problems with what Shirley and Sam were prepared to do, so he needed to be kept n the dark a little, and only drip fed with the barest amount of information so they could utilise his forensic capabilities.

The team would now consist of Shirley, Sam, Victor Prissy and Tess each one of them more than willing to go along with whatever Shirley decided upon.

She was anxious to do something quick, the more the delay the more the sexual abuse the Alldahope girls would endure. She had two names of the Bakers Dozen, Dave Kempers and Tom Leers, but the way they had set themselves up with not every one of them knowing who the others were, it would take a long time to identify them all. And this was time the vulnerable young girls couldn't afford; she needed a way to speed up the process of identifying them all. Tom Leers would be a good starting point, she already had an address for him, if indeed he was one of the Bakers Dozen. The only connection she had was that she knew one of them fell down the cellar stairs and broke their leg, and the only local hospital admission that matched an adult male person had been him.

She had been so deep in thought she had not noticed the huge brute of a man who had entered the police office and was seeking directions to the bus station. The huge guy had their back to Shirley but she instantly knew who it was, it was Stan Guthy. The young Pcso who was giving him the information he requested was visibly intimidated by Guthys overbearing presence. Guthy turned round and stared at Shirley, he obviously wanted her to take notice of his presence, he looked up at the police station clock showing it was eight thirty a.m. for an unusually long length of time and then turned his attention back to Shirley.

She was determined not to show any emotion or physical intimidation by his presence and just stared straight back at him showing no emotion.

Satisfied that he had made his presence felt he then began to guffaw loudly, turned round and left the office.

The Pcso let out a breath of wind "Phew what a bloody monster he was, there was something not nice about him I'm glad he's gone" they announced for all the office to hear.

Shirley didn't know what to make of Guthys unexpected appearance, his excuse of asking for directions was absolute nonsense, he had entered the office for an alternative reason, but she couldn't figure out what.

She was confident however that she would get the upper hand over him, he wasn't aware that Shirley had uncovered the evidence of him slaughtering the poor defenceless biker. The murder that he thought he had got away with, but far from it Shirley would use every bit of leverage she could to exert full and total control over him.

Shirley had arranged a meeting to discuss their next moves to stop the atrocities at Alldahope but before then she needed to get through the ever-present mountain of paperwork. She was in half a mind just to sign of the dozens of crime files without even reading them because she didn't have the resources to allocate any further investigative time. Signing off crime files were simply a way to clear another statistic without creating any further work.

The first one she looked at was from Latifeo it was the investigation into the missing fifteen-year-old boy who was last seen cycling along the canal.

Latifeo had done his usual half-baked idle enquiry, he had ticked the C.C.T.V box stating that he had viewed all available recordings. This showed how slipshod and incompetent he really was, the C.C.T.V from Victors disused factory showed the whole incident and there was probably more cameras along the canal that showed the cyclist and Guthy but he couldn't be bothered to search for them.

Reluctantly she signed off the file as she did with all the other scarcely investigated crimes on her desk.

With her desk now free of documentation she left the office and made her way quickly to meet the others at Victors disused steel mill, Shirley had changed the venue because they had a lot to discuss and it may take some time. If they had the meeting in the Cross pub as usual, they might attract attention if they were there for several hours.

Everyone was already there when Shirley arrived, Victor was showing Sam Prissy and Tess round the mill and an interested Shirley joined in with them, it would provide a pleasant distraction for a short while. It was remarkable what Victor had done to maintain the mill in working order even though it had been many years since it had rolled any steel. Victor explained how a long square steel ingot would be placed on the conveyor belt, it would then slowly pass through the furnace, when it emerged from the other side it was red hot and a guillotine type device sliced through the ingot cutting it to the correct length. It would then continue on the conveyor belt where it would pass through a series of rollers decreasing in size until the ingot was transformed into a much thinner and longer round length of steel which was then coiled around a large drum.

"Does the conveyor belt still work "
 asked Sam.
 Victor replied proudly
"Yes, it all works the conveyor belt, the furnaces the guillotine everything."

A puzzled Sam asked curiously
"Furnaces, plural?"
"Yes, there is another one over there it works differently, it is loaded from the top with scrap metal which then melts and is formed into ingots"

Victor then took them on a tour of the loading bay which in its day was state of the art. An offshoot of the canal went through two huge retractable doors allowing barges to enter the Mill meaning they could be loaded or unloaded inside the building itself.

It was all very impressive and Victor had spent most of his early life building up his business which had enabled him to amass his considerable wealth.

With the tour complete Victor opened a sliding door that gave access to a well-appointed meeting room where they all took a seat around a table that had been pre prepared with flasks of hot drinks and plates displaying cakes and biscuits. The room even sported a huge wall mounted flat screen T.V that was showing the lunchtime news. Victor was the perfect host he muted the T.V. audio whilst they all helped themselves and tucked into the drinks and snacks. Prissy looked around the impressively decorated surroundings,

"I didn't expect anything as plush as this all this when I saw the building from the outside, you've done a great job it must have taken you a long time Victor."

"I've been working on the place for years it was always my intention to preserve the heritage of the place by opening it as a working museum. It was to have attractions and displays including the working steel rolling mill.

But having crunched the numbers it wouldn't be economically viable. Just to run the mill with all the energy costs, and especially firing up the furnaces which consume an enormous amount of gas it wouldn't be possible to break even let alone make a profit. I have applied for several grants from various historical institutions and charities and government departments, even the national lottery unfortunately all without success."

"That's a pity, because I find this place fascinating, I'm sure other people would as well, it would be a shame to lose it all."

"I think it's going to be inevitable, so I am looking at other ways to use the building including the land because real estate is at a premium in this location particularly because of the canal. Everyone seems to want to live in a Canalside location these days and it has pushed the house prices through the roof and so subsequently the land.

Shirley interrupted the general chit chat eager to start the meeting and get on with things.

She opened the meeting by bringing everyone up to date with the death or rather the murder of the two Spanish detectives. She explained how the plan had worked perfectly and the incident would be marked down to a simple accident and it was not being investigated from any other aspect.

She also emphasised the need to be careful and vigilant, any mistakes could cost them dearly, she then produced the bracelet from her pocket, the one that had been dropped in the detectives room.

"Oh my god I have been looking for that everywhere I thought had lost it, where did you find it Shirley"

said a delighted Prissy.

"I found it on the floor of the detectives hotel room, fortunately no one else saw it, this I what I mean about being careful."

The conversation turned to Alldahope and Shirley outlined the basic problems that they were facing. The situation at Alldahope and their subsequent actions meant that they could not follow normal procedures and use the full force of the law.

Shirley had been told from the outset by her chief inspector that she was not to spend any of her time or energy or that of her staff investigating deaths there, and any transgression would be met with disciplinary action. There was also the problem with Guthy, because they had used his daughter Babs to get inside information on the incidents they had been forced to liaise with and give her violent father information on her whereabouts.

And more recently Shirley had given him information about the address of the judge who had barred him from seeing his daughter. Shirley explained that since then she had seen video footage of Guthy murdering a young cyclist and if she had been aware of the evidence before she would not have needed to submit to his demands, and she could have turned the tables on him. Returning to the subject of Alldahope, they were all in agreement that whatever they were going to do, they had to do it themselves. The most important thing was to ensure that they got all of the Bakers dozen. Because they only attacked the girls in groups of three or four it meant that they couldn't identify them all at one time. If they challenged or identified one small group then the others would be alerted and who could then slip away into obscurity and continue their vile practices elsewhere.

They had one confirmed name Dave Kempers and another probable Tom Leers who Shirley was looking into. One suggestion from Tess was to follow members of the Bakers Dozen as they left Alldahope. The idea was discussed, but Victor pointed out that they didn't always know when the attacks were to take place and if they were to follow them when they left Alldahope then they will have allowed another attack to take place.

Sam suddenly shouted with urgency

"Shirley what was the name of that judge whose address you gave to Guthy?"

"His name was Mangham why what's the matter?"

"Turn the sound up on the TV quick" Sam shrieked.

The local televised news was broadcasting a story with a still picture of Judge Manghan in the bottom corner.

A local reporter was standing at the entrance to a wooded area, speaking into her microphone.

The attack which the police believe was deliberately targeted occurred in the wooded area behind me which is frequented by local dog walkers.

The incredibly vicious attack had been planned and prepared in advance in such a manner as to inflict the maximum pain and suffering on the animal which is thought to be a three-year-old pedigree Saluki. The dog was deliberately set alight giving the dog's owner no opportunity to extinguish the flames.

The dogs owner Judge Manghan is said to be distraught and has also suffered minor burns.

Animal welfare groups have described the attack as one of the most sickening hey have ever encountered and are calling for the maximum full weight of the law to be brought to bear.

Police are asking for anyone with information or any possible witnesses who would have been in the vicinity at or around eight thirty this morning to come forward.

Shirley watched the news broadcast with an increasing sense of anger and rage. In the same way that she loathed the thought of vulnerable young girls being abused she also felt a lot of empathy towards animals. Not because she was an avid animal lover but they too in a similar fashion to the girls were also defenceless, especially at the hands of male bullies and thugs.

"That sly bastard Guthy he's responsible for this"
she shouted.
"How so?"
asked Victor.
Shirley sighed
"It all makes sense now; he came into the police office this morning asking for directions to the bus station. Which is obviously nonsense because he has lived here for years, he will now full well where the bus station is. I thought the real reason he had come in was to try and intimidate me, but even that I was a bit dubious about because he knows he can't frighten me.
He obviously wanted an alibi; he made a point of making sure everyone in the police station was aware of his presence. The young Pcso who gave him the directions was shaking in his boots because he was so overbearing and intimidating. And he also made a point of staring up at the station clock it was exactly eight thirty.
What he has done is to arrange for this horrific attack on the judges dog through his underworld criminal contacts and arranged his own alibi by coming into the station at the time the attack was to rake place, the crafty bastard. He has a bit more nous about him than we have given him credit for, we need to keep a careful eye on him."
Stan Guthy was watching the same broadcast on the T.V in the Cross pub Oldswinford, his huge belly laughs only interrupted when he quaffed down big mouthfuls of pints after pints of beer.
He was celebrating the successful outcome of his revenge attack against the person who had tried to stop him seeing his daughter. It had worked out even better than he thought it would. To be shown on the lunchtime local news was the icing on the cake. He had chosen to celebrate in the Cross because he knew that Shirley occasionally popped in for a drink, and he wanted to see the look on her face, because she would have worked out by know that Shirley was his alibi if he ever got questioned over the attack.
Guthy had organised the attack through his contacts in the criminal underworld. The unwritten rules surrounding the calling in a favour within the gangland community were quite simple. The request for whatever you wanted was invariably nearly always agreed to. The 'Favours' as they were commonly referred to varied in their degree and level of violence. Ranging from threats of

violence or intimidation to assaults and beating in varying degrees. It could be damage to property either private or business premises, this was normally to extort protection money. The ultimate 'Favour' was of course a hit although this would also involve considerable amounts of money.

The code of silence meant that if anyone got caught, then it was fully down to them to take the consequences and no names or other identities would be revealed.

They were also without exception subject of 'quid pro quo' this meant that having called on a 'Favour' you were obliged to return it without any questions asked.

Guthys 'Favour' had already been called in, it was a debt collection from a small time criminal. this was not a problem for Guthy, prior to going to prison for the murder of a young police officer Guthy had been regularly used by local gangsters as an enforcer and debt collector. His sheer size and presence was normally intimidation enough to frighten even the most hardened criminals into paying up.

Those unfortunate ones who were stupid enough to defy him were made to regret it, they and sometimes even their family would suffer severe consequences. His extreme violence had become legendary and some of his more ferocious techniques had become his trademark, one of the most notorious was wrapping his huge hands around a poor luckless victim and forcing his thumbs into their eye sockets. The physical damage would be horrendous with some poor souls losing an eye whilst others were completely blinded, and the occasional victim being killed outright caused by the damage to the brain when he pressed his thumbs in too forcefully.

The target he had been given was a small-time illegal bookie Chris Lee, who worked the pubs and clubs of Stourbridge taking illegal and unlicensed bets. His insurance or more correctly protection money was a flat one thousand pounds a week, and he had missed two payments. To the criminal gang who was extorting the money from him, one thousand a week was chicken feed. However the ramifications of someone not paying went far deeper. If one punter got away without paying and word spread round then it could encourage others to be less willing to part with a percentage of their income. So Guthys instructions were not only to retrieve the money with a little extra for late payment, but also to advertise the consequences of late or non-payment as a deterrent to others.

Guthy knew how to find him, it would be a simple matter of trawling the pubs in Stourbridge high street. He would taking bets for the afternoon race meetings from the lunchtime drinkers.

He eyed up every corner of the bar to see if Shirley had come in without him noticing. As his gaze methodically swept the room people lowered their eyes, and stared into their drinks, no one wanting to engage him in direct eye contact.

Guthy revelled in this kind of situation, he could feel the nervousness in the bar accentuated by lowered almost hushed voices, just because of his sheer presence.

Still no sign of Shirley, he looked at his watch and realised that he needed to get a move on to go and deal with the Bookie, so reluctantly he finished of his pint and made for the exit. Disappointed that he hadn't been able to confront and humiliate Shirley and make her realise that the information she had supplied had facilitated the death of the judges dog. And in addition she was now his alibi for the crime. Your time will come Copper Shirley Wallows he thought, your time will come.

18

QUID PRO QUO 2

Shirley was sitting at her desk thinking through some of the ideas that had been proposed at the meeting in Victors steel mill. Nothing concrete had been decided just some general principles. It would take too long to obtain all the details of the sex offenders so they must find some way to get them all together. Victor who was as passionate as Shirley and Sam about dealing with the Alldahope abusers, albeit for different reasons had volunteered to find some way or work out a scheme to try get the Bakers Dozen assembled together. Her thoughts were interrupted when Dumb and Dumber entered the station carrying two large cardboard boxes which they noisily dumped onto a spare desk.

"What have you got there?"
 enquired Shirley.

"It's the personal belongings belonging to Jose and Mateo, the Chief asked us to clear out their desks so we can send their personal stuff back home with the bodies. Most of the stuff I know what to do with but there is also some paperwork, I don't know if it's personal or work related because it is in Spanish."

"If you give me the paperwork, I will sort out what is needs to be sent back and what can be disposed of."

"That's great Sarge, I'll put it on your desk now, I will leave the boxes on my desk and when you have finished just put back what we can send."
Dc Frank Fergas who was always looking to offload his work to someone else had removed the papers from the box and placed them on Shirleys desk in a flash.

"There you go Sarge, and thanks again".

Shirley silently said to herself
"That's the quickest I have ever seen him move, if he put the same effort into his work, he would make a good detective."

She then wondered about their nickname Dc Frank Fergas and Dc Robert Peeves aka Dumb and Dumber. But who was who, which one was Dumb and which one was Dumber? She had a little chuckle when she realised it didn't really matter who was who but what an incredibly apt and insightful appellation it was.

"Ok leave it with me."

It wasn't long before Dumb and Dumber quietly sidled off, Shirley knew where they had gone, they would be in the same place they were every teatime. They would be propping up the bar of the chequers, downing a few cheap Wetherspoons beers.

She began to sift through the papers Frank Fergas had deposited on her desk. Most of it was run of the mill and routine, detective daily diaries, hours of duty list of expenses etc, as she checked it, she put in a pile to go back in with their personal belongings. Then she noticed a police report it was addressed to Detective Inspector jefe Hernandez. This would be the equivalent rank of a British Detective Chief Inspector.

The report was written in Spanish and entitled

Los Asesinatos de Benidorm

Hemos encontrado evidencia de que el asesino en serie de Stourbridge no murio en prison, pero todavia esta vivo y es responsable de los recientes asesinatos en Benidorm. Creemos que el asesino usa hombres vulnerables o borrachos en las calles secundarias de Benidorm para practicar nuevas formas de matar. Ademas, creemos que el asesino es un official de policia.

Shirley translated the Spanish into English and wrote it down to ensure she had translated it correctly.

The Benidorm murders

We have found evidence that the Stourbridge serial killer did not die in prison but is still alive and is responsible for the recent murders in Benidorm. We believe that the killer is using vulnerable or drunken men in the back streets of Benidorm to practice new ways of killing. Furthermore we believe the killer is a police officer.

"Holy shit "muttered Shirley under her breath.

The report was obviously not yet finished and it was not a copy of an e-mail or a fax, this appeared to be a rough draft that was being prepared prior to being sent.

Shirley realised that this information would have been what the Spanish detectives would have revealed in the meeting with Dci Cappoten.

Frantically she searched through the rest of the paperwork belonging to the Spanish detectives, she combed every scrap of paperwork examining everything down to the last detail.

She could find nothing else that even remotely referred to the Stourbridge serial killer. To double check she emptied the entire contents of both boxes that Frank Fergas had dumped on his desk. When she was satisfied that the boxes contained nothing else incriminating, she shredded the report and replaced the rest of the paperwork. She felt a tinge of admiration for the Spanish detectives, they had uncovered in a few weeks more than all her detectives put together. She had vastly underestimated them she thought that they were here for more of a holiday than a serious investigation, but behind the scenes they had obviously worked very hard and uncovered some things that needed to stay hidden. Fortunately they were now dealt with and their findings would go with them to the grave.

Shirley made herself a cup of tea, took a few sips and sank back in her chair, and closed her eyes for a moment. She was alone in the office and was using the solitude to relax. It had been a hectic time in recent weeks and months, and it was beginning to take its toll. She felt physically and emotionally drained, and badly needed to recharge her batteries. Her mind was racing, jumbled thoughts going round and round in her head, it seemed as if she was constantly having to avert one impending disaster after another. Dealing with problem after problem and getting nowhere fast in the process.

She picked up the remote off her desk and zapped the station tv into life, watching the latest T.V would take her mind off things and clear her head a little or so she thought.

"Oh cobblers that's all we need."

The story about the killing of the judges dog had made the national news and it appeared to going viral on all the various social media sites.

Typical thought Shirley if it was the judge who had been killed it wouldn't have made such big news, but because we are a nation of animal lovers everyone's going crazy about it.

The news also announced that there would be a major investigation into the incident and that all people involved in any of the trials where Manghan was the presiding would be questioned. It began to dawn on her now how crafty Guthy had been to come into the police office at the same time that the attack on the judges dog was taking place. She had not only given him the address of the judge but also his alibi. It annoyed her tremendously that Guthy for the time being had the upper hand over her and it was gnawing at the back of her brain. It was time for her to leave, she had arranged to meet Sam for a drink before paying Tom Leers a visit. Sam was already in the Cross pub when Shirley arrived and there was a drink waiting for her on the table.

The pub was fairly quiet with just a handful of regulars, there was no sign of Stan Guthy, and they both forgot about work and any other problems and enjoyed their drinks whilst idly chatting about nothing in particular.

Eventually though the conversation came back round to the ongoing problems and how they were going to deal with it.

It was Sam who had changed the conversation back to Alldahope, the drink had made her a bit merry but also a bit fiery as she thought about the sufferings of the young girls.

"What have you found out about Tom Leers?"

Sam enquired.

"Well I have done some background checks on him, and he is basically operating what we call under the radar. He is middle aged; he is local to here and lives alone. He has no police record or criminal conviction, not even an unpaid parking ticket.

He has no know criminal associates or any connection with any groups that are of interest to police."

"So he's been very careful and clever so far, or just plain lucky perhaps."

Sam exclaimed.

Shirley nodded in agreement then added

"Maybe good judgement or luck, or it could be friends in high places."

Sam was in the mood to do something, the drink had given her a sense of impetus,

"You said he lived local shall we go and pay him a visit?"

"I suppose we could check out his address, it would be a start it may give us some ideas, drink up Sam let's go."

With the alcohol spurring them on they left the pub with a sense of purpose.

Someone else with a sense of purpose was Stan Guthy he had been trawling all the bars and pubs in Stourbridge high street looking for the bent bookie who was the target of his repayment favour. Chris Lees was normally easy to find it was part of his business to be conspicuous so that his punters could find him to place their bets. But for some reason today he was nowhere to be seen and Guthy had searched every pub several times, each time having a pint or two. This meant that added to his earlier consumption of beer he was now pretty pissed and getting enough irater than he normally would be.

He wasn't going to continue scouring the pubs he would change his approach, instead of looking for Lees he would seek out one of his regular customers and find him that way.

Most of the gambling addicts hung out in a pub next to the bookmakers premise, some of them had been barred from the bookies and for some ridiculous reason felt at home in the pub because it was the adjacent premise.

Time was marching on and the daily horse race and dog meetings had finished, but Lees would still take bets on football matches, and tonight the local derby between old rivals Wolves and West Brom would attract a lot of interest.

Guthy ordered another pint at the bar and looked round at some of the pathetic looking punters. Most of them were slowly drinking their beer trying to make it last because invariably they to a man would have lost all their money to Lees over the course of the day. Even if anyone of them had a win they would automatically bet the winnings on another race or game and would do so until they were spent out.

Guthy singled out a scruffy looking individual whom he had seen over a number of years, his entire life and every waking moment seemed to revolve around making bets, the guy hadn't even got a drink. His clothes were threadbare, the soles of his shoes hanging on by a thread and he had obviously not spent any money on a haircut in recent times. He was a one hundred percent gambling addict; he must spend every penny he has on gambling and he would be bound to know where Chris Lees was or could be got hold of.

He was stood by the gambling machine, he obviously hadn't any money himself but such was his addiction he was watching someone else use the electronic gambler. When the money ran out and the last press of the button produced three different symbols the punter gave the machine a little kick and went back to his seat. The guy who had been watching him was now at a loose end, he hadn't got a drink, he couldn't watch the reels of the gambler spin round, and it appeared more in boredom than anything else shuffled off towards the toilets. Guthy gave him a few seconds and then followed him into the gents. The guy wasn't using the urinals but using the mirror above the sink and using two fingers was squeezing his blackheads.

Guthy looked around, all the cubicle doors were open and he could see they were unoccupied. The only activity was the popping of blackheads that were now staining the already dirty mirror. Guthy took hold of a huge piece of paper towelling from a wall dispenser and approaching the blackhead squirter he grabbed hold of him by his long dirty greasy hair. Not wanting to touch the filthy unwashed mop with his bare hands, so he used the paper towel for protection. He grabbed his hair so tightly and yanked his head backwards with such force that it produced an automatic scream of pain.

"Listen to me you piece of shit you are going to do as I tell you, if you fuck me about, I will hurt you do you understand?"

the guy was so frightened he couldn't speak so he simply nodded his head to indicate he understood.

Guthy could see his victim terrified face in the mirror and he could feel the guy literally quaking in his boots.

"Do you know who I am?"

Once again, a nod of the head indicated that he knew who Guthy was.

His huge hand pulled the hair even tighter; it was almost in danger of coming out by its roots, Guthy took a perverted pleasure in the fact that this little shitweasel knew his name and he revelled in his violent notoriety.

"Listen carefully, I want you to tell me where the bookie Chis Lees is, I know you bet with him I see you all the time so don't lie to me tell me where I can find him"

For good measure he exerted even more pressure and pulled his head right back so the guy was now facing the ceiling.

He didn't receive an immediate reply so an impatient Guthy dragged him towards a cubicle and with incredible ease that his strength afforded him grabbed hold of his trouser belt and lifted him upside down.

The guy was now facing downwards suspended above the toilet with his legs in the air,

"The next time I ask you a question you answer me immediately, do you understand?"

With a frantic head shaking he shrieked

"Yes, yes, yes."

To emphasise his point Guthy lowered the poor guys head into the bowl, completely immersing his head.

He began to struggle trying to lift his head out of the foul toilet water but Guthy was far too strong for him to have the slightest effect.

When he thought he had terrified his victim to the point of total submission he let go of his belt and the guy clattered to the floor and was now spluttering and gasping for air.

"Stand up you little shit" Guthy ordered.

In an instant his victim did as he was told and stood cowering in the corner of the toilet cubicle Guthy was surprised at the stench coming from him, he smelt of raw sewage.

"Tell me where the bookie Chris Leers is or the next time your head goes down there it won't come up again."

This time the reply was instantaneous,

"He's doing his rounds of the pubs collecting bets."

A fierce looking and impatient Guthy said menacingly

"Don't lie to me, I've been in every pub and not seen him."

"He knows your after him someone has tipped him off so what he does is he has a lookout in each pub with a mobile phone and they call him when you come in and when you leave."

"Ok you come with me and point out who his calling him from this pub, what you need to do when you go back into the bar is I want you to go and stand next to him and engage him in conversation. Remember if you fuck up, I know where I can find you do you understand?"

The terrified quivering wreck huddled in the corner of the cubicle couldn't agree fast enough, instant replies of "Yes sir of course sir whatever you say."

"And once you've done it fuck off home and have a wash you scruffy bastard you absolutely fucking wreak."

His head was nodding in agreement that fast he looked like one of the nodding dogs that are displayed on the rear parcel shelf of cars.

"Before I let you go tell me your name."

"Everybody calls me 'Tinkers'

it's a nickname I got from school.

"Ok Tinkers you know what to do and remember I am right behind you"

Guthy moved back from the entrance to the cubicle giving Tinkers enough room to squeeze past, and with head bowed in total subservience he slowly opened the main door leading back to the pub, anxious to ensure that he did not anger Guthy anymore he would do everything that had been asked of him. He knew that there would be some sort of comeback, some sort of punishment either from Guthy or from Chris Lee and his cronies. But he would much prefer to face the wrath of Chris Lee than that of the immensely intimidating Stan Guthy. Tinkers, likewise, most of the regulars who hung around Stourbridge town centre were fully aware of his reputation for hurting people, and his trademark punishment of regularly damaging or gouging out his victims eyes with his bare hands.

Guthy watched as Tinkers engaged the lookout guy in conversation, whilst he walked the long way round the bar out of his eyesight.

When he was close enough, he grabbed hold of the lookout by the back of his neck with his left hand and almost lifted him off the ground. His right hand then closed around his throat and he turned him round to face him.

As soon as the lookout saw Guthy he froze in fear, he was well aware of his reputation and he was being well paid to keep an eye out for him and keep his boss Chris Lee informed. But in an instant, he knew the game was up, and like Tinkers he feared Guthy much more than Leers.

Guthy could sense this straight away and an ominous self-satisfying smug grin spread across his glaring face.

"I know what you're doing, you're telling your boss where I am, but now you do as I tell you. Call him now and tell him that I have just left this pub and I am going up the high street towards the Chequers. Then you tell him that there are some punters in here who want to make a bet, after he answers you then end the call did you get that?

The lookout didn't reply or even move his head in acknowledgement, Guthy was just about to show him what happens to people who don't answer him straight away when Tinkers piped up saying

" I don't think he can speak or move his head you are gripping him too tightly."

Guthy looked at the diminutive, little pipsqueak who had dared to speak to him when he hadn't been asked anything, and then he turned his gaze back to the lookout and began to guffaw. Little Tinkers was right the prey that he was clutching between his gargantuan hands could barely, let alone speak or agree to anything. He had unintentionally lifted the guy clean off his feet and with his hands around his throat he couldn't take in enough air and his face was beginning to turn blue.

Guthy relaxed his grip and the lookout took in deep lungfuls of much needed air before coughing and spluttering.

Without needing to be asked again he took out his mobile and called his boss the bookmaker.

"Chris Stan Guthy has just left here and he is heading up the high street towards The Chequers, and there are some punters here who want to make some bets." After a short pause he went on further "See you in a couple of minutes."

Guthy smiled

"Now give me your phone and your wallet."

Without questioning why he wanted them, the items were duly handed over without any protestations.

Guthy using his immense strength snapped the mobile phone in half with just his bare hands, then letting it fall to the floor he stamped on it completely annihilating the device. He opened up the wallet and looked for anything containing his name and address, pretending that he had memorised the information he threw the wallet to the ground.

"I am going to have a friendly discussion with your boss now, if for any reason he doesn't turn up then I will have the conversation with you instead and remember I know where you live"

as he indicated towards the wallet which was still on the floor.

He knew that the pair were so terrified of him they wouldn't dare try and warn Lee or tip him off.

He waited in a darkened alleyway outside the pub, he had a good view of the road and the bookmaker could only approach from one direction because he thought that Guthy was walking up the high street so he must approach from the opposite direction.

He didn't have to wait long, he could see the outline of him walking shiftily towards the pub, he was easily recognisable by his attire. He always wore a gabardine full length mac and a trilby, this dress code combined with his accentuated cocky gait made him resemble 'Flash Harry' the character played by George Cole in the St Trinians movies.

"Keep coming you bloody ponce" Guthy muttered under his breath.

He was almost within grabbing distance now when he suddenly stopped as his phone began to ring and he fumbled inside his coat to retrieve his mobile.

'Bollocks' thought Guthy he was so close he could nearly grab him, he contemplated dashing out of the shadows, but if he didn't get him immediately then he would never be able to catch him if he ran off.

Before he had made up his mind Lee had finished his call put his phone away and resumed walking towards the pub.

He passed right in front of Guthy who was well hidden by the darkness, then as a spider captures his prey, the huge figure sprung from the darkness took hold of his unwitting victim and dragged him back into the darkness of the alleyway. Before Lee could shout out, a massive hand was clasped over his mouth and he was forced back against a wall.

"Gotcha you sneaky little bastard, you can't hide from me forever, I am going to take my hand from your mouth now, but if you make any noise whatsoever, I will rip your fucking head off. "

Guthy slowly removed his hand from the bookies mouth, he did what he was told to and remained quiet, he was however shaking like a leaf.

"You've been a naughty boy, haven't you?" Guthy said whilst staring at him straight into his frightened bulging eyes.

"Look I know what this is all about it's just a misunderstanding that's all I'll sort the lads out when I see them, you can tell them everything is Ok."

"But everything is not ok, in fact everything is far from ok, and you won't be dealing with the lads. You have to deal with me now, so mister bent bookmaker who doesn't pay his dues, you pay me now."

"Ok I've got the money with me it's in my sock is it ok for me to bend down?"

Guthy simply nodded and the bookie bent down to retrieve his secret stash from his sock. After fiddling with his ankle for a while he stood back up and handed Guthy a wad of money.

"Here it is it's all there fifteen hundred quid".

Guthy began to flick through the bundle of notes before replying
"That was the old price the new price is three grand."

"B,B, But I haven't got three grand" he stuttered out awkwardly.
Guthy smiled and then engulfed the bookies head with his gigantic hands and rested his thumbs on his eyelids and applied a gentle pressure.

"Three fucking grand" Guthy repeated.
The bookie had seen for himself the results of Guthys handiwork and the damage he had inflicted on certain people. One of them was a regular punter of his who wore a black eye patch over one eye. He was well known in Stourbridge pubs especially for his party trick when drunk. In order to get another drink when he was skint, he would remove his eye patch and let you have a look at the empty socket for the price of a pint. It used to make the bookie feel physically sick the first time he saw it.
Guthy increased the pressure on his eyeballs, and the petrified banker began to plead.

"No please god no don't take my eyes I'll give you the money."

He felt the pressure ease slightly and he beg
an to beg Guthy to allow him to give him the money.

"It's in my other sock, if you let me bend down you can have it, but please don't hurt me."
The vice like grip relaxed allowing the bookie to bend down, and he began rummaging around his other ankle.
Guthy was imagining what he would do with the money.
The bookie was correct when he said the debt was Fifteen hundred and that would be how much he would hand over to the guys running the protection racket. The other fifteen hundred was for Guthy himself he had decided to take a piece of action for himself.
The bookie must have sensed that Guthy was distracted for a second and that's when he decided to make a break for it. He had started his escape from a kneeling position so when Guthy tried to grab him his arms simply flailed in mid-air above him.
Chris Lee ran down the dark alleyway as if his life depended upon it, Guthy was giving chase but losing ground on the escapee rapidly.
In bookmaking terms it was a one-horse race, or so it seemed until in his haste the bookie ran into a pile of beer crates that were stacked up against one of the walls. The impact of his collision made him lose his footing and fall to the floor. Scores of beer crates filled with empty bottles came crashing down around him as he frantically tried to get up. The crates were now forming a barricade in front of him preventing him continuing his escape. Desperately he pulled at the crates and threw some of them behind him as he tried to make a

space to get through. He kicked out at a couple of crates and succeeded in making a gap that he could get through.

He began to run but was getting nowhere fast, his legs were going ten to the dozen but they were having no effect, they were running in mid-air, Guthy had hold of the collar of his Gaberdine mac and was holding him aloft.

With his dash for freedom extinguished he immediately became hysterical, as he was dragged ominously back into the depths of the dark recesses of the alleyway. His screams went unheard however, the vice like grip of the hand that was clasped firmly against his mouth prevented any sound escaping that may alert someone to help. He knew what immense pain and suffering he was about to endure and if it had not been for the hand covering his mouth, he would have been physically sick.

He was still being held in mid-air when he felt himself being swung round like a rag doll and then driven with colossus power face first into the wall.

The force of the impact was so great that he felt like his head had exploded, a short sharp cracking sound resonated along the alleyway when his nose snapped like a twig.

His jaw was completely demolished with the lower mandible becoming detached which was now hanging down and flapping around loosely. This exposed his now gaping mouth where the fragments of shattered teeth could be seen strewn everywhere. The only intact teeth that could be seen were the three that had penetrated his flesh and passed clean through his upper lip just below where the base of his nose should have been. Guthy turned him round and pinned him to the wall lifting him higher so that he was now facing him at eye level. Lee was desperately hanging on to consciousness, fearing that if he passed out he would never see the light of day again.

Guthy was smirking from ear to ear, he was in his element, the sense of power and domination that he felt when he was inflicting pain and damage exhilarated him beyond belief. Nothing in life gave him a greater buzz than to do what he did best, to do what he was born to do.

"I warned you what I would do if you tried to run, didn't I you naughty little man, now look at you, even your own mother wouldn't recognise you. I think we should do something about that so you can never run away from me ever again. Chris Lee could feel himself being lowered to the ground until he could feel the cobblestones under his back. He then felt his right leg being lifted up and the back of his ankle was placed over an empty beer crate.

The bookie began to sob uncontrollably and he began to plead with Guthy not to do what he was lining him up for.

"Please god no, you don't have to do this please, please, I'll do anything but please don't do it."

Guthy smiled and seemed to relax at the sound of him begging for mercy.

Looking up at a now smiling Guthy the bookie thought his ordeal may be coming to an end and Guthy had meted out enough punishment.

This hopeful whimsy didn't last long though as he watched in horror as Guthy raised his own leg high in the air and then sent the steel booted limb down towards the bookies shin.

The loud cracking of bone once again echoed along the alleyway, as the bookies tibia fractured completely in two, with the bloodied jagged edges sticking through his torn trouser leg.

"Let's see you try and fucking run away now".

Chris Lee lay almost motionless on the cold hard floor it was only the excruciating pain that was keeping him conscious.

It wasn't too long before he could feel his body begin to rise in the air once again. Guthy had elevated him back to eye-to-eye level but the bookie wasn't aware of that because of the thumbs that were starting to press on his eyeballs. This was different to a few minutes ago the pressure was much greater and more intense than before, this wasn't to be a warning this was where he was about to lose his eyes. He could literally feel his eyeballs moving in their sockets, they were being forced back into his skull, and were about to pop. It seemed to him that the that his eyes were being forced out slowly in order to maximise the pain and to extend the ordeal.

In one last desperate plea to save his eyesight and maybe his life he made one last plea to Guthy he summoned up all his remaining energy and screamed.

"I can get you thousands and thousands of pounds if you don't take my eyes, you can have it all but pleases don't take my eyes you could be swimming in money."

The vice like grip around his head remained the same but the thumbs were no longer pressing into his eyes.

"You have one minute to tell me everything, if you are bullshitting, I will take both your eyes now speak."

Chris Lee didn't want to lose his eyesight or his life so he was prepared to give away anything that could possibly save him.

"There is going to be a robbery on the bookmakers there will be over a hundred thousand pounds in the safe, you can have in on it if you want."

An intrigued Guthy said

"Go on tell me more, but no bullshit."

"One of my punters owes me a lot of money, he has run up a huge gambling debt that he could never pay back. He works in the bookmakers and he can get access to the building, alarm codes, and the combination to the safe. On grand national day the taking will be the highest of the year and it's all there for the taking you could be a rich man."

Guthys mind turned away from thoughts of violence, he had in the past earned some substantial wads of money carrying out beatings and punishments for various gangsters, but he had never had a bumper pay packet. He had always been living hand to mouth, but the idea of a large chunk of money was beginning to take hold of him.

The bookie sensed that Guthy was interested so he told him more about the robbery about how easy it would be, and all Guthy had to do was act as lookout and would become a very rich man.

With the threat of him losing his eyesight or his life receding, the sheer terror that had helped to mask the pain diminished and the excruciating pain kicked in.

"I need to get to hospital, please help me, I'm in a bad way." Pleaded the prostrate bookie.

Guthy normally would give a care about the state of his victim, but the bookie was fast becoming a valuable asset and he didn't want to risk losing the cash cow before he got his pay-out.

Guthy bent over, wrapped his hand around the bookies neck and lifted him up, using his free hand he placed his thumb over an already sore and painful eye and gave it a press.

"Ok I'm in, I'll tell your man in the pub to come and get you, but remember this, if you fuck me about the next thing you will feel will be my thumbs."

To emphasise the point Guthy applied a little extra pressure on the eyeball.

Guthy was getting a little bored now, when he inflicted pain and suffering on someone, he liked to complete the job it gave him a feeling of satisfaction, but things had now changed and he couldn't finish the job and he needed to leave his victim intact. "I'll be in touch" Guthy scoffed and then released him letting the bookie fall in a crumpled heap on top of some empty beer crates.

As Guthy left the alleyway he could see the bookies lookout standing outside the pub having a cigarette. The guy nearly choked on the smoke from his roll up when Guthy approached him, and he was in two minds whether to run off, but realised he was too late, Guthy was towering over him. He went white as a sheet and began to shake, when he stared him full in the face.

He didn't say anything for a few seconds, enjoying the intimidation his presence was having. Then with a smug laugh he sneeringly said, "You had better go and pick your boss up he's fell over in the alleyway."

Guthy strode off along the high street, counting in his head how many days it would be for the grand national, for the day when he would become rich.

Shirley and Sam were sitting in the conservatory of a pub in Oldswinford, the large glass windows gave a clear view of the houses opposite.

One of the houses they had a clear view of was the home of Tom Leers, as they drank their drinks, they were keeping a keen eye on the comings and goings at his address.

What they had witnessed so far, they found quite concerning, in the short time they had been there they had seen two youths enter the house at separate times and stay for about forty minutes each time. The youngsters were aged about eleven or twelve they arrived and left on their own.

"What on earth is going on there?"

Shirley said in astonishment.

Knowing what they knew about Tom Leers Sam was also shocked with the ease of which young people came and went from the address. It was daylight and there was no attempt to hide or to smuggle the youngsters in by a rear entrance, everything was completely open.

Sam offered an explanation

"We know what he has done and what he is like but other people and his neighbours obviously aren't aware so he has no reason to hide his activities, so what do we do now?"

"We could speak with the children that come out of his house, but that may backfire on us, because if he gets to hear about it he may realise we are on to him. If we had more time, we could wait and see who else comes and goes, and if there are any adults visiting, we could get some car registration numbers. But of course this all takes time and throughout that time the abuse continues."

Sam who was a bit more headstrong than Shirley, was adamant that they needed to do something soon.

"If we wait then we can probably get more of them but how long do we go on for, it could carry on forever, I think we should act now and take out the Bakers dozen."

Shirley was thinking through Sams statement when she almost choked on her drink,

"My god"

she spluttered

"Look who is going into the house now".

Sam turned her head and gazed at the person now visiting the address. Both of them were stunned into silence at what they were seeing.

19

GOOD TIMES ON THE WAY

Babs was in the Games room at Alldahope, she was as ever very astute and remarkably observant. She could see the tell-tale signs straight away, whilst everyone else was getting on with their daily routine whatever that may be, two of the younger girls were acting differently.

One was staring vacantly out of the window in a world of her own, Babs could even imagine what she was thinking, she was probably hoping and longing for something different. A change in the order of things, desperately looking out of the window envisaging what was or could be out there. But whatever was out there would be better than the hell hole of Alldahope.

The other girl was more introvert, she wasn't staring out of the widow but sitting quietly and subserviently in the corner with head bowed. She wasn't looking for anything different, she was simply accepting her fate, this was the most dangerous attitude, when all hope appeared gone with no light at the end of the tunnel that was when the possibility of self-harm or even suicide kicked in.

She noticed that both of them were looking extremely tired and they had also sustained several bruises and minor injuries.

Babs realised that these are tell-tale signs and were two different and opposite reactions to being abused and the girls were showing perfect examples of each one.

One tries to carry on and look forward to better things or hopes for some form of change, the other simply accepts their fate and tolerates it without doing anything about it.

Both these girls needed help and they in common with a lot of the other abused girls they needed it now

She hadn't been aware that the night monsters were going to attack last night and neither had Victor otherwise he would have been here.

She needed to let that copper or her dad know that there had been another attack, if Victor came in today, she would ask him to relay the message if not then she would sneak out tonight and go and see her dad.

Babs would keep her wits about her today to ascertain if another attack was imminent tonight, she had worked out that the best indicator of an appearance of the night monsters was the activity of Matron.

Victims were obviously pre-selected and Matron would keep what she thought was a discreet eye on them to make sure they drunk the mandatory evening drink of drug laced milk.

There hadn't been any recent deaths, suicides or any serious cases of self-harm which meant there had been no police activity or even the meddling involvement of social workers or grief counsellors.

This would have worried Babs at one time, she would have been concerned that they had been forgotten even by that woman copper Shirley.

But she knew her dad would never let them stop and it had been her idea for her dad to go to the police station at the time the attack on the judges dog was taking place. He would keep the pressure on them, especially with Babs using her influence over her him, and her incredible insight which gave her the ability to direct and control her father in almost every aspect of what he did, she was also responsible for continuing to influence her dad to exert pressure on Shirley. Babs was no ordinary girl, she had capabilities, skill and cunning way beyond her tender years, she felt sure things were moving forward and she was right.

Shirley and her team were having a meeting in the Cross pub preparing their next move.

The first thing they discussed was the situation with the Spanish detectives, Shirley told the group that they could put that problem behind them now.

The incompetent and scant investigation conducted by Detective inspector Grant Courtan and overseen by Dci Trevor Cappoten meant that the truth would never be uncovered. The bodies had been repatriated to Spain together with their belongings, the damning report indicating that the Stourbridge serial killer was still alive had been destroyed and as far as Shirley knew no one had been privy to it.

They then moved on to the ever present and ongoing situation at Alldahope, they had all long since agreed that they would deal with the sexual predators themselves and that they need to operate outside the law, with little or no outside help.

Shirley and Sam were in two minds as to whether or not to tell the group whom they had seen entering Tom Leers house, but after analysing what Prissy Tess and Victor had already done for them it would not make sense to keep them out of the loop as they could obviously be trusted one hundred percent.

It was Shirley who told them about the comings and goings at Tom Leers house.

She related how in a fairly short period of time they had seen three young boys enter the house on separate occasions. The boys were unaccompanied and of a vulnerable age. They came and went in broad daylight and there was no attempt to hide their arrival or departure. This suggested to the girls that the neighbours and locals were completely unaware or even suspicious of his activities.

Everyone was listening intently, they could sense that something else was coming, something more dramatic than the presence of the young boys.

Shirley paused for a while as the others waited with bated breath.

"While we were keeping observations on the house, we also saw a detective enter and stay for about thirty minutes. We have no idea what he was doing at the address and can think of no reason for him to be there.

The officer is known to us, in fact he is one of my detectives, it's Dc Oli Latifeo."

Victor chipped in saying

"Is that the bone-idle detective that was snooping about behind my premises on the canal?"

"Yes, it is, he only does the bare minimum that he can get away with, he will never amount to anything because of his lackadaisical attitude. He has no ambition and will normally do as I tell him, so that he has an easy life, but I am still quite concerned as to why he was visiting a known Paedophile."

"But we know or at least have a good idea that he is not a pervert or kiddy fiddler he has normal sexual urges

." Announced Sam.

An intrigued Prissy said whilst giggling

"How do you know he has normal sexual urges is there something you need to tell us Sam?"

All eyes were now on Sam waiting for an explanation.

Clearing her throat she began,

"This is the whole story, Oli Latifeo was a customer of mine. He used to visit me regularly for sex, but just normal sex, not like Victor or my other clients who like to be abused and tortured he has a normal sex drive. He mistakenly thought that we were having an affair, however I was just using him for money as I did with all my other punters.

It went on for quite some time and he was easy to control because as Shirley says he is the idlest person you could ever wish to meet. Because he is married and he couldn't be bothered with all the hassle and work involved in a breakup so he kept it a secret, which suited me.

He had no idea that it was simply a business arrangement or that I had numerous sex clients, he thought they used to visit me for music lessons, that is how gullible he is.

It all changed when I took on Victor as a client and I will tell you why."

Sam looked at Victor who shifted in his seat a little uneasily but nodded to Sam as a sign for her to continue and tell all.

"Victor is a self-confessed sexual pervert he likes kids",

a visibly shocked Prissy and Tess glanced at Victor and they were now squirming uncomfortably in their seats.

"Don't be too shocked girls let me finish, Victor is a paedophile, however he realises that it is wrong, he knows that his sexual feelings towards kids is unnatural and disgusting. Therefore he does not act on any of his urges, in fact he does the opposite, he pays me to punish him sexually, I tie him up torture him and do lots of other abusive things, this helps him to fully understand how his perverted sexual urges are unnatural and need to be repressed. By his continual self-imposed regime of me inflicting upon him sexual torture and humiliation he can keep his other urges under control and he will never, ever abuse any child. He also knows that if he slipped up and did touch a child in any way shape or form then I would cut his bollocks off. And I mean that in the literal sense I would physically remove his balls"

When Victor became a customer, he wanted full and exclusive access to my services, so to that end he offered to pay extra to cover all the revenue I would lose from my other punters, plus a considerable amount more. Therefore I dumped Latifeo together with all my other customers to concentrate on Victor. Latifeo did falsely however get it into his head that I dumped him because he was married and he wouldn't leave his wife, I was quite happy to let him think that it made things easier I obviously couldn't tell him the real reason. But I am confident that if needed and if I had to, I could still wrap him round my little finger, he was and probably still is infatuated with me."

There followed a short eerie silence, the atmosphere was a little tense, Prissy and Tess were coming to terms with the fact that Victor was a paedo. One of the things that bound them all together was that they detested any kind of sexual predator whether they be an aging lothario who couldn't keep his dick in his trousers or any form of oppression by a man using their strength or sexuality to control a female. But worst of the worst were paedo's, the absolute scum of the earth and Prissy and Tess were stunned to find out that one of their group was a self-confessed pervert. They were equally shocked to understand why Shirley and Sam associated with him.

It was Victor who broke the awkward silence looking towards Prissy and Tess,

"I can see that you are shocked at what Sam has just told you, and I can understand your revulsion, I also share your abhorrence of any type of abuse against children. I acknowledge that my feelings and urges are perverted and abnormal therefore I do everything in my power to prevent me from acting on those feelings. I have never and will never do anything untoward against a child, I would rather kill myself than allow myself to succumb to this curse. This is why I help Shirley and Sam to sort these bastards out, also I would quite like to keep my testicles".

Victors quip combined with his sincere summary and his determination to resist his urges lightened the mood and the conversation returned to Alldahope.

They talked for some time discussing various options and action plans, but the most promising development was Victor who intimated that he may have thought of a way to get all the Bakers dozen together at the same time but his idea required some more planning before he outlined it to the group.

One thing they all agreed on was that they would do nothing until Shirley found out why her detective had visited Tom Leers.

The pub was reasonably quiet today and it afforded a relaxing atmosphere in which to relax so when the conversation concerning Alldahope had run its course everyone decided to stay and have some more drinks and just chat in general.

Shirley didn't partake because she had to go to work so after saying her goodbyes, she made her way to the car park.

Sitting on a low wall near her car was the diminutive figure of Babs, staring vacantly towards the main road, she was obviously waiting for Shirley.

"Is everything ok Babs, what are you doing here?"

"Well it's nice to see you as well" came the sarcastic reply.

Shirley looked around and let out a sigh

"I'm sorry but you know we are not supposed to be seen together it could compromise things."

"I had to come and tell someone, it happened again last night, and nobody including you is doing anything about it"

"Listen Babs we are doing something about it but it's complicated and it will take some time"

"And in the meantime young girls are being abused, so if you aren't going to do anything about it I will do it myself I will wait for them and stab them in the face with my razor blade and take their eyes out"

"Babs don't do anything stupid I promise you I will sort everything out soon, if you do something it will only get you into trouble so, please be patient."

A noisy group of people began to emerge from the pubs rear entrance just behind them, Shirley turned round to see who it was. Fortunately none of them was anyone that Shirley recognised so she turned back towards Babs but she had now disappeared and was nowhere to be seen.

Checking her watch she realised she didn't have time to look for her as she needed to be at work soon, she was concerned about what the strong-minded Babs would do but reluctantly she got in her car and started the engine.

As soon as she got to her office, Shirley pulled out her staff appraisal forms.

It was a requirement to conduct annual appraisals of each member your staff, it entailed the examination of their work and achievements for that year and included recommendations and action plans. Most of the staff thought that were a waste of time and effort, a view shared by appraiser and appraisee, but it was something that had to be done to put a tick in the box.

Shirley flicked through Latifeos file she had already contacted him and arranged for him to attend the office so that she could conduct his appraisal. This was the only way she could think of to try and find out what he was doing at Tom Leers house.

Latifeo turned up on time for his interview and had the required paperwork documenting some of his work throughout the year.

This was a yearly ritual that they were both well used to and the whole procedure had become routine and mundane.

Shirley asked the same run of the mill questions and received the box standard reply that Latifeo was well versed at giving.

Shirley casually asked what Latifeo had worked on that particular week, and he ran through the number of enquiries he had dealt with, his natural aptitude for an easy life had honed his ability to waffle and give the false appearance of someone who was quite industrious.

He had spoken at great lengths to make his week sound busy, but there was still no mention of his visit to Tom Leers.

Shirley was wary of asking him a direct question concerning Leers because he would then know they were watching him, so she simply asked if he had anything to add.

"There was something else as well sarge, I have gone the extra mile so to speak and have been using the time to arrange the return of recovered stolen property from some of my closed cases."

Shirley response was

"Well I appreciate that this is something that has to be done but sending out a form to an address and asking for someone to come and collect their property is not really going the extra mile is it, and certainly not worth including in your appraisal."

"Yes, I understand that Sarge but I have not just sent out forms but have physically taken some property back".

"Why would you take the property back yourself, normal procedure is for the owner to retrieve their property from the police station."

"There was one guy who was desperate to get back an address book that was rifled through when his car was broken into. I had sent it away for fingerprinting it came back negative but the guy had phoned me a couple of times, he was anxious to get it back but couldn't come to the station because he had an injured leg, it was broken I think so I took it back last night he was very appreciative."

Shirleys heart skipped a beat this was what she needed to know she asked trying to sound as casual as possible.

"I suppose that is providing extra support above the norm so I will include it in your appraisal, but why was the guy so anxious to get the book back what was in it."

"It was an address book, it was filled with handwritten names and addresses, that's all I can tell you about that but there was something else."

Intrigued Shirley asked, "And what was that?"

"It's difficult to say Sarge, but you know when sometimes you get a feeling that something is not quite right, the guy was a bit strange, I can't put my finger on exactly why it but he gave me the creeps."

Shirley needed to confirm for certain that they were talking about Leers and this was her opportunity to find out.

"What was the guys name is he known to us?"

"His name was Tom Leers and he is not known to the police he was just a victim of crime, but he was definitely a bit weird. "

This was exactly what Shirley needed to find out, plus the added information of the odd demeanour of Leers.

Shirley thanked Latifeo and closed the interview congratulating him on his years' work.

In reality Shirley knew that if she delved into his work and analysed it to any great depth it would reveal how lazy he really was and that most of his enquiries were merely superficial. However Lafifeos sloth like attitude suited Shirley, it meant she could manipulate him whenever she wanted or needed to. She would sign off his annual appraisal for another to maintain the delicate status quo. But now more than ever the major concern was Alldahope, if Tom Leers was abusing kids in his own home, which seemed highly likely then he needed to be dealt with immediately and without scaring off the rest of the Bakers dozen.

Gazing out of the goldfish bowl of an office into the shopping centre she saw Babs scurrying past, she decided to go and catch her up and speak with her if only to assure her that she was doing something about the abusers and try and keep her from doing something stupid.

Babs was searching for her dad, she knew where to search and where he could normally be found, he would be in one of the pubs that dotted Stourbridge high street.

She wasn't prepared to wait for Shirley, she wanted something doing right now, her dad was devoted to her and she only had to give him some sob story about being frightened of the night monsters then that would be enough to stir him into action she could wrap him round her little finger. He would use his brute force and violent disposition to rip anyone to pieces who upset his pride and joy. It didn't take long to find him; she heard the moans and groans of a couple of drinker leaving a pub complaining about the loud violent thug indoors that was intimidating people.

There was a small bench on the pavement outside the pub and Babs made herself comfortable whilst waiting for her father. The high street was busy with people going about their daily lives, Babs watched them come and go.

She was especially interested in the family groups, she wondered with a sense of envy what it would be like to be part of a normal family and to do normal family things. She used to dream of maybe one day going on a family holiday or even a day out, such as the park or a fair or circus, anything enjoyable that would replace the constant fighting. But those longed for days were never to be and her only wish now was to get out of Alldahope and get rid of the night monsters. She loved her dad immensely but he wasn't exactly a typical role model father.

He was the most violent man imaginable and although Babs knew he would never harm a hair on her head he didn't treat Babs mother the same way. For as long as she could remember her parents had argued and fought almost constantly. Her mother was also renowned for her violent temper and she had often taken a kitchen knife to her dad together with other readily available weapons such as bottles, scissors or anything that came to hand, normally when he was drunk and obnoxious.

Everything had come to a head one day when Babs was sitting on the settee and her father was sitting on an adjacent armchair, her mom and dad had just had an argument which Babs thought was finished. However as her dad sat relaxing on the armchair watching T.V her mother burst into the room with a wooden stool raised above her head which she brought down across the head of her dad knocking him out cold immediately.

Once the initial anger and adrenalin had stopped coursing through her mothers veins then panic began to set in and her mother ran out of the house to hide from the inevitable repercussions when her dad would come to.

She had been right to be afraid because later that evening her dad took his revenge and battered her mom to death in their living room. That was how she had got to know Shirley, it was Shirley who turned up at the house when her mother was lying dead on the floor, and she had been kind and understanding. Then when her dad was later arrested for murder that was when she was when she was sent to Alldahope and her life changed forever.

She knew she wasn't destined for a normal family life with all the niceties that went with it, but at least she still had her dad he would look after her.

She was so immerged in her daydream she didn't notice her dad leave the pub, Babs was suddenly raised high in the air with a shout of "Hello sweetheart" as she was held aloft and spun round, firmly grasped between the two huge, outstretched arms of her dad.

Babs let a squeal of delight and leaned forward to give her dad a hug, "Have you been looking for me Babs?"

"Yes, there is some stuff I need to tell you" she replied whilst still being held aloft.

"Ok how do you fancy a cake and some pop?"

Babs relished spending time with her dad, especially when they were doing something nice even as simple as going for a drink and a treat, so she simply smiled and nodded her head.

Babs was gently placed back on terra firma and they walked over the road to a café next to the Stourbridge clock.

Stan Guthy sipped at his coffee whilst he watched his daughter tucking into a huge piece of cream covered chocolate cake, the look of contentment on her face was the only thing that assuaged his inbred and almost ever-present sense of rage and violent aggression.

Neither of them spoke for a while, they were both enjoying the calm almost serene atmosphere, these moments that for both of them were very few and far between and they were soaking in and relishing every second.

Outside the café from a short distance away Shirley was keeping a discreet eye the pair of them. She was in a dilemma as to what action to take, she needed to speak with Babs but did she dare associate with her in the middle of Stourbridge. The inside of the café wasn't overly exposed to passers-by so she may be able to get away with it if she was careful, Shirley couldn't decide if it was worth taking the risk.

Babs was now eating an ice cream whilst her dad was having a coffee refill, "I've got some good news Babs".

"What is it" she asked excitedly.

"Shortly I will be getting a large sum of money, and I mean a lot of money so it means we can do something together."

Babs stifled an excited squeal

"Let's go on holiday dad, we have never been on holiday we could go somewhere nice, by the seaside, I would love to go on the beach".

All thoughts of Alldahope were forgotten for the time being whilst Babs revelled in the ecstasy of what was for most children a normal routine activity, she

"Whatever you want darling, you can choose where we go, it will be nice to spend some time together. You have a think about where you want to go but now you can tell me what you needed to say."

The smile disappeared from her face as she came tumbling back to reality once more, and the ever-present nightmare that was Alldahope.

"They came again last night, I know because I could tell it on the faces of two of the girls, I have spoken to that woman copper and she keeps saying that they will do something but I don't believe her, nothing seems to be happening, so we need to do something about them."

Before Stan Guthy could reply a voice came from the adjacent table immediately behind them which quietly whispered

"Babs, I know you want something done about them but we need to get them all at the same time, it's no good getting one or two, because the rest would disappear forever."

They both recognised the voice straight away and Babs and Stan Guthy began to turn round to face the person butting into their conversation.

"Listen to me copper, if my daughter says she wants something doing about these horrible bastards then I am going to do something. I will sort the cunts out on my own cause you ain't doing fuck all about it as usual."

"But you can't get them all at the same time, but I'm working on a plan to try and do that so you need to have patience."

Babs looked on with a sense of satisfaction as she listened to her dad rip into Shirley about her lack of action.

"We are not waiting any longer I am going after the frigging perverts" Guthy said with a sense of finality

Shirley was pondering her options, she could use her ace in the hole and threaten to expose that he had killed that young boy on the towpath, but this was a last resort she desperately wanted to keep this trump card up her sleeve for future use.

Reluctantly and somewhat against her better judgement Shirley offered a solution,

"There is something you can do without compromising everything, but you must do it completely on your own I wouldn't be able to help you."

Sneeringly Guthy replied

"I do everything on my own I don't need your or anyone else's help"

228

"Well I have identified one of them and he is out of action for a while, he has a broken leg, and I have his address so he could be sorted out without alerting the others."

Guthy looked at his daughter as if asking her permission, Shirley then realised who was the real boss in their relationship, and it gave her a sense pride.

Shirley could see in Babs a lot of shared values and talents, they both liked to exert control especially over the typical male macho bullying types, that seemed to be omnipresent, and used their presence to domineer the supposed weaker of the species. But not Babs, no one would ever be able to get the better of her she was a remarkable one off, a very young girl with an incredible presence about her and an insight into situations and people that most grown-ups people never even came close to.

Shirley was becoming a little nervous she had been in the café too long, the chances of someone seeing her talking with Guthy increased as time went by.

Babs looked at Shirley and once again showing her analytical reasoning asked,

"Is it the one me and Victor pushed down the stairs at Alldahope?"

Shirley was impressed with how quickly Babs worked things and situations out, and simply nodded affirmatively to her question.

Babs looked back towards her father,

"It's only one of them but a least it's a start dad, I think you should do it."

It was a forgone conclusion that Guthy would do as his daughter asked. so Shirley quickly whispered to him the name and address of Tom Leers, and hastily disappeared from the café.

At the other end of the town Latifeo was walking through the deserted subway at the bottom of lower high street, this thoroughfare was rarely used and the only time it was busy with people was when Stourbridge town football team were playing at home, but today it was deserted. Looking through to the other end of the subway Latifeo could see sitting on a bench his local snitch.

The modern correct term for informants was (CHIS) Covert Human Intelligence Source and there was a great deal of administration involved including registering them. But Latifeo was old school he referred to them as grasses or narks, and because he was so idle, he couldn't be bothered with all the paperwork so his Stourbridge town centre informant was completely unofficial. His informant was definitely small time, he did not move in criminal circles or associate with any organised gangs, but because he was always hanging around the town centre, he could see people coming and going and spot any strange faces. He would occasionally identify a group of shoplifters or pickpockets that had targeted the town or sometimes the occasional aggressive beggar who would intimidate the odd shopper or two to unwillingly part with their loose change. It kept Latifeos crime detection rates up with the minimum amount of effort on his part, so it was worth his while to shell out a ten- or twenty-pound note.

When his snitch saw him approaching, he got up from the bench and walked under cover of a nearby underpass and Latifeo followed him.

This was their pre-agreed routine, once in the underpass they were completely hidden from view but could also see if anyone was approaching.

Once in the underpass Latifeo scanned the area ensuring that they were alone and out of sight and announced,

"Ok what have you got for me Tinkers."

Tinkers seemed very excited, Latifeo sensed he wasn't his normal apathetic self.

"I've got something really big this time Mr Latifeo" his voice unable to conceal his excitement.

With an unimpressed almost disbelieving and mocking manner he replied,

"You never have anything better than the odd shoplifter, so don't try to exaggerate to get a bit of extra dosh, that you either piss up the wall or hand it over the bookies counter anyway. Whatever it is you are only going to get a tenner today do you understand?"

"Honest Mr Latifeo I've got something special its worth a lot of money."

"I will decide how much it is worth so tell me and I will and will give you what I think."

"If I tell you first the then you won't give me the money, so I want the money first."

Latifeo was getting a little impatient with what he regarded as his insignificant little lackey, and not bothering to hide his displeasure snorted out.

"If it's anything decent you can have thirty quid and no more so spit it out and tell me what you've got, I don't have all day."

Tinkers looked a bit nervous now, he took a deep breath and in an obviously rehearsed speech said,

"I want a thousand pounds."

A startled Latifeo began to cough and splutter, in between the intermittent coughing and choking he replied

" You want the fuck how much?"

Tinkers began to adopt a more confident attitude; he knew he had got the detectives attention.

"It's a big job, there is going to be a robbery the money will be about half a million".

Latifeo cleared his throat and composed himself, this was completely out of the blue and he was unsure as to what his approach should be. This wasn't just the biggest tip off that Tinkers had given him; this was by far the greatest possible information he had ever received by some considerable margin.

"Fill me in with the details and I will have to speak with a senior officer to arrange for the thousand pounds, that should take about a week or so."

Tinkers had been prepared for this, not only was it a big deal for Latifeo it was an even bigger deal for himself, he was used to living hand to mouth, the odd fiver or tenner here or the occasional small win on the horses, but a thousand pounds to Tinkers was to most people the equivalent of scooping the lottery.

"A week or so is no good the job is going down soon, so I need the thousand pounds now or you're going to blow it."

Latifeo was desperate not to lose possibly the biggest case of his career, a job that could earn him a lot of kudos and status.

"I will meet you here tomorrow at the same time, don't speak to anyone else until I see you do you understand?"

Tinker nodded in agreement and watched Latifeo turn and hurriedly dash away into the distance.

Shirley was back in the office when Latifeo burst in through the doors and panting for breath.

She looked up from her paperwork, bemused as to what had made the normally sloth like Latifeo to become out of breath.

In between taking deep breaths he blurted out

"Sarge, can I have an urgent word with you please, somewhere private."

"Of course"

replied Shirley as she rose and began walking to the only private office, which was normally used as a tea making room, closely followed by the still out of breath Latifeo.

"I'm all ears, let's hear what's so important it's got you out of breath"

Shirley said jokingly.

Latifeo with his breathing now under control but still speaking a little excitedly began to relate his recent conversation with his informant.

"I have just had some info from an informant about an upcoming robbery involving, wait for it, half a million quid."

"Wow that's a serious amount of money"

a startled Shirley replied.

"Yes, but there is a problem, the job is going down soon and my informant wants one thousand pounds before he will divulge the details."

"Not a problem"

Shirley replied enthusiastically

"I can authorise that amount of money in these circumstances, but there are certain protocols that we need to follow. Give me the details of your C.H.I.S. and I will get the ball rolling, I should be able to get the money today." A dejected looking Latifeo shook his head slightly and let out a sigh,

"That's the problem sarge my informant isn't a registered C.H.I.S."

"That changes things, technically no money can be authorised if the informant is not registered, but we can't let something as big as this get away from us so I will have to speak with the chief inspector. But be prepared to be disappointed because he doesn't appear to be overly keen on going out of his way to solve crime, he is more concerned about managing budgets, just look at Alldahope he didn't exactly pull out any stops to investigate the deaths, so this may go the same way."

With that she hurriedly donned her coat and told a deflated Latifeo to wait there and she would get back to him, she knew that she had to be quick if she wanted to catch the Chief inspector before he went home for the day.

Chief inspector Trevor Cappoten was waiting in his office when Shirley arrived, she had managed to phone ahead and ask for an urgent meeting.

Shirley didn't hold out much hope of any form of co-operation from a senior officer whom she thought was a waste of space. He rarely seemed interested in catching criminals and now Shirley was going to ask him to arrange something unorthodox and not exactly to the rule book so this would be in effect a wild goose chase, but a determined Shirley felt that she had to try.

An unusually cheerful and upbeat reception was forthcoming when Shirley entered which caught her off guard a little.

"Right then Shirley what have you got that is so important that you need to see me urgently"

said Cappoten as he invited Shirley to take a seat.

Shirley outlined the information from Latifeo concerning the impending half a million-pound robbery and the complications caused by the informant not being registered.

"First things we need to know is the date of the possible robbery, the location, how many persons involved, and most importantly if there are any firearms involved,"

Said a surprisingly insightful Cappoten. A more hopeful Shirley responded by saying

"Unfortunately sir the informant won't divulge any details until he has a guarantee of the thousand pounds, and he also states that the impending robbery is to happen very soon."

Cappoten sat back in his chair obviously giving the situation some thought, Shirley sat there in silence, pleasantly surprised that at the very least the Chief Inspector was giving the situation some consideration.

Leaning forward on his desk towards Shirley received a welcome and unexpected reply.

"Right this is what is going to happen, we don't want to miss out on a job this size so the way we will handle it. Try and get the informant registered today, if they refuse to be registered then I want you to co handle the informant, that way we maintain corroboration. We need to stipulate that payment is dependent upon the reasonable likelihood of the information being accurate, and the informant must tell us his involvement if any in the robbery either in the planning or commission of it. You will then do a full risk assessment detailing the resources you require which you will submit to me. I will speak with the finance department now and authorise the transaction for which you will be responsible for. Now then did you get all that and fully understand what I require?"

An astounded Shirley replied,

"Yes, sir I've got all that and thanks for your help."

"Well then sergeant you are going to be busy you had better get a move on."

Shirley thanked him once again whilst going out the door and began to hurry back to her office to get the ball rolling.

Something was troubling Shirley, even though she was pleased with the outcome of the meeting and she was busy rushing back to her office, she knew something was wrong. Things didn't add up, the Chief Inspector had shown willingness to get round a procedural problem and appeared enthusiastic and committed to getting involved in an enquiry, especially unusual as this one included the handing out of one thousand pounds of cold hard cash.

Yet on the other hand he couldn't be bothered to fully investigate the incidents at Alldahope or even allow anyone else too, in fact he actively discourages any time or resources to be used.

Something was wrong something was very wrong.

20

HANGING AROUND

The sharp sound of breaking glass disturbed the stillness of the night, before returning to tranquillity. Half opened bleary eyes stared into the darkened room, trying to fathom out why they had awoken.

Rubbing their eyes and straining to listen for any strange or out of the ordinary noises, whilst surveying the moonlit bedroom.

The only sound that could be heard was the far away dull rumble of the occasional motor car and the ticking of the bedside clock, the repetitive and hypnotic tick tock, tick tock gave a sense of reassurance.

Nothing but darkness, shadows and a calm quietness, tick tock tick tock, through the window the full moon casting an eerie silhouette began to disappear behind a cloud, the illumination that had been flooding the room was slowly diminishing, moonlight was now replaced with blackness.

With sleepiness rapidly returning it was time to relax, to curl up in a cosy sleeping position and continue with the nights rest. The plaster cast made turning over difficult, but by grabbing it with both hands and pulling it at the same time as turning solved the problem. Manoeuvre complete and resting on his left-hand side, away from the window and the now completely hidden moon and adopting a foetal position, with his head facing the door he suddenly came face to face with everyone's nightmare.

Two feet away from his own face and staring straight back at him was another face, a terrifying balaclava clad intruder with intense murderous looking evil eyes staring at him through the roughly hewn eyeholes.

Instinctively he tried to scream but before any noise or shriek of terror could be bawled out, something sticky and restrictive was slapped across his mouth and something was pushing his head and holding it firmly in the pillow, he immediately realised that the intruder was not alone.

The balaclava covered face hadn't moved, it simply kept staring almost mockingly into the face of its horror-struck victim.

Everything suddenly went black and it became a little difficult to breathe as the petrified victim felt their body forcibly rolled over onto their front and their gagged face was embedded with extreme force into the pillow as their arms were yanked behind their back.

Adrenalin was now beginning to kick in he began to struggle and attempted to scream out but it was all to no avail. His arms were now bound behind tightly his back and he could feel the weight of someone's body pressing down on them.

One of the intruders then spoke

" Listen to me Mister Tom Leers, if you struggle, we will hurt you, if you try to shout out, we will hurt you, if you try to escape, we will hurt you. If you understand me then nod your head."

Tom Leers was hauled around onto his back and in the half-light, he could see his attackers. They both had their faces covered with Black Balaclavas with tiny holes cut out for eyes, nose and mouth.

Tom Leers was now totally incapacitated, his arms were firmly bound and in addition they were now pinned down underneath his back, with the weight of his own body pressing down on them. One of them using their own body weight now pinned him even more forcibly to the bed and wrapped their arms tightly around his head.

Unable to move his body or his head in the slightest all he could do was watch with horror as the second man leant over him armed with a vicious looking cutthroat razor.

Slowly and deliberately in a position where Leers could see, the cutthroat was unsheathed. A chink of moonlight glistened off the polished highly sharpened blade as it was held above his face, the face of his tormentor clearly enjoying the terror that they were inflicting. Even with a balaclava hiding most of their face it was clear that the knifeman was smiling wickedly.

With the sharpened edge of the blade the razor was lowered nearer and nearer to its victims throat.

Leers was now crying in fear, the tears running down his face cascading over the gaffer tape wound tightly over his mouth. He was so frightened he didn't realise that he was lying in a pool of his own urine having lost control over his bodily functions.

The edge of the razor was drawn across his throat starting from one ear and traversing across his Adams apple to his other ear. He could feel the coldness of the blade on his skin but he couldn't feel the flow of any blood and he wasn't sure if he had been cut at all, absolute fear had numbed his body.

Still smiling the attacker once again showed Leers the weapon, it was plain to see that there were no signs of blood on the blade, and Leers sensed a glimmer of hope. He thought that whoever these people were and for whatever reason they were here they may just want to frighten him. But he was wrong, and his brief and fleeting hope of being unharmed faded away as the attacker took the blade to his forehead.

This time Leers could not only feel the blade he could feel the sharp incision of the razor slicing into his brow followed by the sudden gush of blood that washed over his face. The cutting and slicing continued relentlessly, the blood now gushing over his face in torrents and pooling in his eye sockets, such was the volume of the red gooey liquid it completely saturated the gaffer tape binding, soaking it all the way through so that the blood began to drip into his mouth.

He could taste the sickly warm metallic liquid as it spilled onto his tongue ran down into his throat causing him to gag.

The pain was similar to a severe stinging sensation but a million times worse, combined with the knowledge that someone was slicing open part of his face Leers was hoping and praying that he was caught up in his worst nightmare and that fairly soon he would wake up to discover it had all been a bad dream.

The cutting and slicing eventually stopped and he soon realised that this was for real, when he eventually managed to open his eyes to see the knifeman wiping clean the blade of the razor on the bedcover.

Leers looked at his attacker, pleading with his eyes for it all to be over, if he could only speak, he would beg for his life, and would promise them anything they wanted, anything at all, they could have whatever they wanted.

The blood from the wounds had stopped flowing now, the pillow and bedclothes had become saturated. His face and shoulders had large areas of staining where the blood had congealed and he resembled a circus clown.

The pain was so intense that he barely noticed when the razor was used to cut through his pyjamas, to leave him totally naked. He hadn't even noticed that his ankles had also been bound together, with his good leg strapped to the cast on his broken leg.

But he felt it when he was roughly dragged out of bed and thrown to the floor, the heavy weight of the cast causing a loud thud on the carpeted floor. He realised his ordeal was far from over his attackers clearly were not finished with him.

Leers began to drift in an out of semi-consciousness the only thing that stopped him from passing out completely was the unbearable pain from his wounds.

He then felt himself tumbling head over heels, his head and limbs bouncing off the hard wooden steps of his stairs, his battered body ending up in a crumpled heap in the hallway with the cast on his leg cracked in two. He was then further manhandled the length of the hallway and out through his rear door with the tell-tale broken glass panel that had provided access for the intruders into the rear garden.

The cool night air blowing gently on his skin raised his consciousness and made him fully aware of his nakedness and he started to shiver.

Hauled along the damp grass to the bottom of the garden his heart began to race even faster and the level of panic increased when he saw what was happening. He had been dragged beneath a tree and one of the attackers was looping a long piece of rope over one of the branches.

Oh my god he thought, they are going to hang me, they are ging to string me up by my neck from the tree, but why what on earth have I done to deserve this, why me.

Tom Leers could feel a horrible gooey mess running down the inside of his legs as he lost the control of his bowels due to the sheer and unimaginable feelings of terror and panic coursing through his body.

But instead of attaching the rope to his neck it was looped around his bound hands and he was winched to his feet. Tom realised that he wasn't about to be hanged by his neck but this did little to abate his horror and trepidation.

Whilst one attacker held the rope fast so that Leers was fully upright with his arms fully stretched upwards and the tip of his toes barely touching the ground, the other one produced a long plastic object.

Leers was having difficulty focusing due to the darkness and the congealed blood on his eyelids but he was sure he could see the end of the plastic object being doused in some form of liquid from a bottle.

He could make out the attacker approaching him with the plastic object in one hand and ominously the cutthroat razor in the other.

Leers closed his eyes and squeezed them tight shut-in terror as the razor neared his face. This is it, he thought, this is where they are going to slit my throat and leave me to bleed out, he wished he knew why they were doing this to him.

If he could speak, he may be able to reason with them but they didn't seem to want to negotiate, they just wanted to kill him.

He braced himself, ready for the feel of the cold metal that was about to slice his jugular clean through. His only wish now was that it would be quick so that his life would be over and he didn't have to endure the pain for too long.

He didn't however feel the cold steel against his throat instead he felt the pressure of the blade against his mouth, he opened his eyes to see that the attacker was cutting through the tape that was binding his mouth.

He felt the rush of air hit the back of his throat when a hole was punctured in the tape, allowing him to breathe a little easier. Leers thought that they were going to let him speak, this would be where they told me what they wanted what their demands were, perhaps he wasn't going to die after all.

His brief respite from the restrictions of the binding was short lived as he saw his attacker force the fluid-soaked plastic object through the newly made hole deep into his throat, making breathing even more difficult and uncomfortable than before.

In a split second he realised what the fluid was, it was some form of incredibly hot sauce, not hot as in temperature but hot as in spice incredibly hot, immediately he felt as if his entire mouth was on fire. The pain was equivalent to or greater than that from the open wounds on his brow and increasing in intensity with every second.

He could feel the heat spreading at an alarming rate and within seconds his tongue, lips cheeks and his eyes also felt as if they were on fire.

Such was the combination and accumulative effect of the pain from his wounds, his freshly rebroken leg and the hot fluid, he hadn't felt them placing a plastic bag around his genitals and held in place with further bindings of gaffer tape.

The next thing that Leers was aware of was the pain in his upper body as he was hauled off his feet and he had to take the full weight of his body on his outstretched arms.

He forced his eyes open to see one of his attackers with the same bottle of hot fluid in his hand approaching his groin, straining his neck to look downwards he saw the plastic bag surrounding his genitalia and he watched in horror as the bottle was emptied into the bag completely submerging his manhood. This time it took a few seconds for the fluid to penetrate through the skin of his testicles and penis, but when it did, it generated more pain on its own than all of his other agonising injuries put together.

Both of his attackers then took hold of the rope and began to heave, Leers naked and abused body climbed higher and higher into the night sky until he was eventually suspended way above the ground.

The attackers securely tied off the end of the rope to an adjacent tree and checked on their handiwork. The plastic penis that had been forced into the mouth of Leers was firmly secured with further Gaffer tape, the plastic bag swimming with the fluid was held tightly in place and all the bindings around his body were fastened tight. The crowning piece of handiwork however was the word that had been carved into his forehead with the razor. The blood encrusted inscription emblazoned across the full width of his crown stood out like a beacon and with the incisions carved so deeply it would be there forever for all the world to see.

Their job was done, admiring their work for one last time they slipped off into the night as quickly and quietly as they had arrived.

21

BLOWING IN THE WIND

Shirley was in her office unusually early she needed to begin work on the preparations for Latifeos informant. There was an incredible amount of work to do on her part, and she knew that if anything went wrong then it would be her head on the chopping block.

She was examining all the rules regulations and protocols that accompanied Covert human intelligence sources.

Just the risk assessment alone was a monumental task, every possibility had to be catered for.

She was that early that even some of the night turn officers had not yet booked off duty.

Shirley looked up from her desk when one of the younger night turn officers spoke to her,

"Morning sarge, you're in early I ran into that giant thug again last night, you know the one who came into the office the other morning asking for directions."

This news grabbed her attention straight away

"Do you mean Stan Guthy" she asked urgently.

"Yea that's the one sarge the really intimidating guy."

Replied the young constable.

"What happened, did he do something wrong?"

"No sarge he didn't do anything wrong, he just seemed intent on grabbing my attention he kept on talking and talking at me, he just kept spouting nonsense, he made me feel a bit uneasy with his attitude he's not the sort of person you forget when he comes really close and looks down on you".

Shirley knew what this meant, Guthy was not to be underestimated he did things for a reason. Something must have happened last night and it would have taken place at the same time that Guthy was intimidating the officer, he was simply creating an alibi for himself. She needed to watch out for any overnight violent crimes, because she knew he would be behind organising or at least having some involvement in whatever it was

"I shouldn't worry about it too much"

Shirley replied sympathetically

"Just put it down to experience".

The young officer completely oblivious to the fact that he was being used by the surprisingly craft Guthy simply smiled, put his jacket on and left the office to go home.

Shirley took a break from preparing her risk assessment and checked the overnight logs for any sign of local acts of violence, it was still early so not every incident will have been logged but she couldn't find anything that carried the unmistakable level of violence associated with Stan Guthy.

She returned to her more immediate problem and was formulating the handling strategy of the informant and how the money was to be paid, she and Latifeo had a meeting with the informant in two hours and there was still a lot of work to be done to facilitate it and to ensure that she covered all bases and didn't leave herself open to criticism or any form or any backlash.

Sam was at home down in the cellar administering the weekly humiliation and torture to her cash cow Victor when the doorbell rang.

She was becoming a little concerned regarding Victors health and she didn't relish the idea of leaving him alone whilst he was bound and gagged in the damp cellar. This had been normal practise for her in the past, but now things were changing, Victor had become her main source of income which due to his generosity and infatuation with Sam was increasing exponentially.

And as an astute and cunning businesswoman she didn't want to risk any sudden illness that would interfere with her plans for her subservient lapdog.

She looked at her watch and carefully eyed Victor up and down, he seemed to be unusually weak and also very pale, but not to be in so much distress that he couldn't be left for a few minutes so she decided to answer the door and hoped Victor would be ok for a short while. She made her way up the steps and locked the cellar door as a matter of course and answered the door.

The unexpected caller was the private detective that she and Shirley had hired to try and trace their respective parents.

He explained that he had some more information concerning their enquiry, so Sam invited him in ushering him towards the kitchen.

Sam made them both tea and they sat around the kitchen table, Sam prepared herself for what was to come.

The investigator smiled

"Firstly it is better news than I gave you last time concerning your respective mothers. I have a little bit of information about both of your fathers. Is Shirley here or do you want to contact her so I can tell you both together?"

242

"No it's ok, Shirley is busy at work but you can give me the information and I will tell Shirley."

The investigator took out a pile of papers and briefly flicked through them,

"Well if you're sure, I'll continue, as I have said previously Shirleys mom died in childbirth. It would appear that the father was so devastated and also quite young, so it was felt that by the authorities that he would be incapable of bringing up a child, thus the child was put up into care, much against the wishes of the father. I have been able to establish that he is still alive but as yet I have been unable to find out his identity. The reason for this is because of the secrecy that was the norm in these circumstances at that time. Obviously, things have moved on in recent years but then it used to be a closed book. The child would be taken away, no details would be given to anyone and that would be the end of it. I am confident however that I will eventually be able to establish his identity. Now then he sighed looking towards Sam, we can move onto your father."

Sam angrily, interrupted him straight away,

"I don't want to know anything about him, you have already told me that he murdered my mom so as far as I am concerned, he can rot in hell. I don't want to know who he is or have anything to do with him."

The investigator paused giving Sam some time to calm down and regain her composure.

After a short time an apologetic Sam spoke in a hushed voice,

"I'm sorry for that outburst it's just that when Shirley and I hired you to try and find our respective parents I was hoping for some good news, perhaps it was wrong of me to get my hopes up."

Sams head was bowed and her normally beautiful big bright blue eyes that were usually full of hope and life were now showing a deep and heavy sadness. To Sams surprise the investigator began to smile, she was just about to quiz him as to why he was smiling when he said.

"But I do have good news for you Sam."

Sam lifted her head in surprise,

"What do you mean, how can you have good news my father killed my mother nothing can change that."

"What I said before was that your mother was killed by her husband, I have delved deeper into it and found out that your mother was married twice. And it was her second husband that killed her, your father was her first husband."

Sam put her hands to her face and almost screamed

"On my god, you mean my dad didn't murder my mother."

"That's exactly what I am saying and what's more he is still alive; I don't have his identity yet but I feel sure I will find him."

Sam sat there absolutely stunned, beaming from ear to ear she wanted to ask so many questions but her mind was racing so much with the possibilities concerning her father, she barely even noticed the investigator as he bid farewell and let himself out after telling Sam that he would be in touch.

Sam was beside herself with excitement, she couldn't wait to tell Shirley the good news, both of their fathers were alive. She was especially excited to tell Shirley the greatest news, that her own father didn't murder her mother after all. She knew that Shirley was exceptionally busy at work today and she didn't want to give her such fantastic news over the phone so she pulled on her coat and left for the police station.

Shirley was sitting at a desk in the goldfish bowl finalising the strategy with Latifeo for the meeting with the informant in an hours' time, when see noticed out of the corner of her eye Sam standing in the shopping centre.

She obviously wanted to see Shirley urgently but didn't want to come into the office to disturb her because Shirley had told Sam that she was particularly busy that day with a case. Shirley knew it had to be important and she had completed most her most pressing work and she and Latifeo had were now ready for their meeting with the informant, she nodded to Sam indicating that she would come out soon.

Sam replied by putting her hand to her mouth miming the action of drinking a cup of coffee and walked out of sight. Shirley immediately knew what café she would be headed for.

After making arrangements with Latifeo to meet the informant Shirley left the office and quickly made her way to a nearby café where Sam was waiting patiently where she has ordered Shirley a large coffee and a slice of cake.

Taking a few sips and sitting back comfortably in her chair she readied herself for what was obviously about to be good news given the excited expression on Sams face.

Sam related the news she had just received from the private detective; she was especially euphoric regarding the news that her own father didn't kill his mother.

They chatted idly about the possibilities of both being reunited with a least one member of their families and the things that it could lead to. For a short time the worries and stress of Alldahope, and the blackmailer were forgotten and they were just two best friends idling away the time enjoying a drink and a chat.

Shirley looked at her watch, it was time for her to leave and meet up with Latifeo and to see the informant.

"I must leave now I have an important meeting soon, what are your plans for the rest of the day?" Shirley asked.

Sam was about to tell her that she hadn't any specific plans when she realised to her horror that she had forgotten about Victor.

"Oh my god, I've left Victor tied up in the cellar, I meant to let him go before I left but I was so excited I forgot. He wasn't looking to well either I'm going to have to run.

" As Sam sped out of the coffee house Shirley drained the last few dregs of her drink checked her watch one more time and realised that she needed to be quick if she wasn't to be late for the meeting with the informant. She had a final check of her handbag ensuring that it contained her cs gas spray canister and hurried along lower high street towards the designated meeting point. Latifeo was already there when Shirley arrived, he was idly kicking his heels and trying to look inconspicuous. Shirley shook her head lightly in disbelief when she saw him and thought to herself, he was sticking out like a sore thumb he couldn't look more out of place if he tried.

Fortunately the location of the meeting had been chosen well, it was not overlooked and there was rarely anyone passing through because it didn't really lead anywhere.

They didn't have to wait long before their informant showed up, he suddenly appeared out of nowhere. He was clearly nervous and he couldn't stop continually looking at his surrounding scanning every nook and cranny and then repeating the process constantly. He cautiously began to approach Latifeo and Shirley, as he edged nearer and nearer Shirley could see how uncomfortable and on edge the informant was.

Shirley gave him the once over, she was not quite what she had been expecting. He was a weasel like creature with long unkempt greasy hair scruffy clothes and looked in need of a good bath.

"Hello Mr Latifeo"
said Tinkers in a subdued hushed voice,
"What have you got for us Tinkers"
replied Latifeo.

With his shifty furtive eyes flitting between Shirley and Latifeo Tinkers replied in a stuttering and unconvincing voice

"I ain't saying nothing to anyone but you, I don't know who this woman is, the deal is just between me and you."

Shirley had anticipated this response so she then took charge of the situation.

In a calm but authoritative manner Shirley whilst making full eye contact with the snivelling little grass she said

"My name is Detective Sergeant Wallows I am Latifeos boss and I am in charge of this situation. I have full control over everything including the handling of and distribution of any money paid out. Without me there is no deal and no money this is not negotiable do you understand?"

Tinkers looked like a frightened rabbit caught in the headlights and he looked towards Latifeo as if pleading for help.

Latifeo simply shook his head slightly indicating that the matter was out of his hands and that Wallows was in charge and that he would have to do what she said, would have to said.

Tinkers had rehearsed in his head all his wants and demands and he was expecting an easy time, in his dealings with Latifeo things had been quite informal and easy going. But this was different he realised at once that he was out of his depth.

"Ok, but I want the money up front all of it before I tell you anything".

Once again Wallows was prepared for this and she realised that this little street urchin was desperate for money, any

money at all would appear like Christmas come early for him.

"You will have a maximum of fifty pounds initially and the remaining money paid on successful completion of the operation assuming that the information is substantial and accurate.

Tinkers resigned himself to the fact that he had to do what he was told and that this woman whom he had never met before was in charge.

He related the information concerning the forthcoming robbery. It was to take pace at a local bookmakers premise in the high street on Grand National day, when the taking were normally fifty to a hundred times a standard days takings. The theft was planned to look like a burglary but was in fact a set up involving the manager who would provide access to the premise and all security codes for alarms etc. his intention being to split the money and in addition claim from his insurance.

Wallows and Latifeo grilled him as to how he come by the information and they asked intricate questions concerning times, people involved, any weapons to be used etc and in addition as was normal for informants, they had to divulge their involvement if any.

Wallows made reams of notes and when she was satisfied that all the bases were covered, she pulled out of her pocket a bundle of notes and counted out fifty pounds which she asked Latifeo to double check.

Tinkers eyes lit up Fifty pounds to him was like winning the lottery to most people and he was already working out how he was to spend it.

Business complete and with the money handed over a further meeting was arranged and Tinkers disappeared into the darkened alleyway.

Wallows and Latifeo began to walk back towards the office and Shirley remarked how excited Tinkers had been when he received the fifty pounds.

Latifeo replied saying that Tinkers would now be in the betting shop and the fifty pounds would be spent within the next couple of hours with nothing to show for it with the exception of a few crumpled-up betting slips.

They both walked back to the police office in order to write up and fully document their meeting with the informant.

Shirley could also make a start on the plan of action to execute the police operation.

Things however didn't quite go to plan, as soon as she and Latifeo arrived back in the office they were both tasked with attending the scene of a suspicious death.

The initial information was quite sparse and sketchy, but it was obviously something big. Shirleys mind immediately turned to Guthy, was this what she had been expecting was this the reason Guthy had been so keen to make himself noticed to the young officer recently.

They shared a car with Dumb and Dumber who although they had not been assigned to the incident, they were always keen to get in on anything out of the unusual or anything that could bring greater kudos by developing into a major enquiry. It would be something they could talk about to show off to their prospective conquests in the local grab a granny dives.

The lunchtime traffic was reasonably quiet, allowing the car to be driven at breakneck speeds. Shirley was sitting in the rear of the vehicle clinging onto her seat belt for dear life as the car ignored traffic signs, red stop lights and the like, and at one time whilst negotiating a sharp bend the vehicle was precariously balanced on two wheels.

She was always a nervous passenger even if a vehicle was being driven slowly and sensibly but, in these circumstances, when the car was being driven by an adrenalin fuelled lunatic desperate to be the first officer on the scene, she was especially fearful. She was equally mindful of not showing her apprehension, this madcap race to get to a scene of crime first at any cost was very much a police machismo reaction.

Any sign of nervous would immediately brand her as a pathetic, timid good for nothing female who shouldn't be a police officer.

Shirley had struggled to overcome this sexist stereotypical attitude that was endemic in police forces from the outset of her career, so she kept her mouth tightly shut and did ger best to mask her nervousness.

She silently breathed a sigh of relief when with a screech of tyres the vehicle came to a halt outside the location of the incident.

She immediately recognised the address, it was the home of Tom Leers, the address that she and Sam had been keeping watch on when they saw Latifeo enter.

Her heart was in her mouth, this was the address that she had given Stan Guthy together with the name of Tom Leers, whatever sight that awaited her no matter how gruesome she knew she would be partly responsible.

The young uniform officer standing guard at the scene entrance was looking a little green around the gills, but he smiled when he saw Shirley and her team walking down the path towards him.

Shirley recognised the young officer, it was the same one that had spoken to Shirley about Guthys behaviour recently, Shirley smiled back at the young officer,

"if only he knew"

muttered Shirley under her breath.

"I'm so glad you're here sarge"

he spluttered out as he prepared to add the officer details onto the scene entry log.

"What can you tell me, what exactly are we looking at here"

Shirley replied having now adopted her supervisory clinical head.

"The neighbours reported seeing something in the rear garden, I haven't spoken to them yet. I was the first one here, in fact apart from you and your team I am the only one here. I rang the front doorbell and no answer so I went round the back garden and that's where I saw it".

The officer then heaved and Shirley thought he was going to be sick, but after a few wretches and a couple of deep breaths he composed himself.

"I didn't notice anything at first because I was looking at ground level, but when I looked upwards, I saw a body hanging from the tree".

This time the officer couldn't control himself and he was physically sick when he tried to describe the scene.

Dumb and Dumber began to shout and berate the still vomiting and bent over double poor young man who had completely lost control, coughing and spluttering between spurts of foul-smelling sick.

Frank Fergas and Trevor Peeves who as always were dressed in sharp suits with highly polished shoes were now standing in a pile of the officers vomit.

Their shoes were covered and the splashes had managed to decorate the lower half of their suit trousers. Shirley reminded Fergas and Peeves that they were young officers once and to cut him some slack she beckoned everyone follow her saying

"C'mon let's go and see what's happened to this pervert".

Amid the shouts of

"Tosser" and
"Wanker"

they all walked past the scene guard towards the rear garden leaving him to sort himself out. Shirley had to stifle a laugh, she was well aware of how vain Frank Fergas and Trevor Peeves were about their appearance and this helped lighten the mood a little as they approached the scene.

The pleasant rear garden was fairly ordinary and typical of other gardens in the neighbourhood, a well-tended lawn surrounded by various shrubs and plants, a decorative patio area with wooden table and chairs. The six-foot-high garden fence was in good repair had been recently painted and overall it felt like a relaxing secluded place to unwind.

The most dominant feature was the large oak tree at the bottom of the garden its foliated branches spreading high and wide. It stood tall and majestic, like a protective guardian overseeing its territory.

But now it was striking in appearance for a different reason. Suspended from one of its impressive sturdy branches a withered human body. It was strung up by its outstretched arms that were bound together at the wrists and tethered by a length of rope. The head was limp and bowed forward and a slight breeze was gently swaying the body from side to side. It was an eerie sight to behold it gave the impression of some sort of ritualistic demonic sacrifice, associated with devil like black magic occultism, the type you would only read about in Dennis Wheatley novels.

Even though they were in the open air the smell was atrocious, it was difficult to ascertain what it was exactly. The officers looked at each other, their faces contorted because of the all-consuming and overwhelming stench. They were all experienced officers and used to dealing with situations where the smells and sights were repugnant and overpowering but this was something else.

The gut-wrenching odour was a combination of human waste with rotting and burning flesh.

The four officers stood in silence for quite some time not knowing what to make of the grotesque spectacle in front of them.

"Excuse me Sarge" came a sheepish voice from the young constable who had now joined them in the rear garden. "The control room are asking for an update".

Shirley turned around to face the officer who was doing his best to avoid looking at the suspended body that was gently swinging in the slight breeze.

Shaking her head slightly at the sight of the tickle stomached officer she replied with a tinge of empathy,

"Can you tell the control room that we have a suspicious death in macabre circumstances. A deceased naked male adult is suspended from a tree, he appears to have been tortured. Can you ask them to despatch scenes of crime and inform the Chief inspector?"

"Ok sarge"

came the reply as he slowly turned his head whilst taking a deep breath in order to steel himself as he forced himself to observe the body.

"Oh my god"

the young constable wretched as he gazed upon the body.

"What's happened to him sarge".

Shirley looked at the officer with a renewed sense of admiration, she realised that he was doing his best to force himself to confront his revulsion and look at the body and the scene. She remembered how she had to do the same when she had first been confronted with a gruesome sight.

"Well I think this is some form of punishment beating designed to send out a message. The intention may or may not have been to actually kill him it not possible to tell yet. They have obviously conducted the assault in a manner to inflict maximum pain. If you look at the inflammation around the groin area and other parts of the body you can see some form of substance has been used. I suspect that it is that from that bottle lying on the ground that has been left for us to find. I can see the words Carolina Reaper on the label which I believe is the hottest chilli in the world."

"What have they done to his face Sarge?"

"That young man is the key to it all, the attackers have carved deep into his forehead the word PERVE for all to see, that combined with the dildo rammed into his mouth indicates this is revenge for some sort of abhorrent sexual behaviour, so that is where the focus of the investigation will begin"

Before the officer could reply Shirley took charge of the scene and began organising tasks.

"Right then Frank and Robert can you start conducting house to house enquiries, Oli can you make a cursory examination of the scene and then preserve it for SOCO. And you young man, pass that message to the control room and then remain at the entrance and maintain the scene entrance and exit log."

Shirley was now even more positive that this was the work of Stan Guthy and that she was the person responsible for giving him the information, but if it kept another pervert of the street then it was worth it. What she decided to do now before anyone else arrived was to enter the house and search for anything that could lead to other members of the Bakers thirteen

She approached the back door and donned a pair of latex gloves she didn't want to embarrass herself by leaving her own fingerprints at the crime scene for SOCO to find as she had inadvertently done in the past. The door was slightly ajar and she eased it open further just enough to gain access without touching anything.

She could clearly see the scuff marks on the floor where Tom Leers had been unceremoniously dragged through the kitchen into the garden. Must work quickly thought Shirley, she knew that before long every man and his dog would turn up, all eager to witness the macabre murder scene. With the gossip and jungle drum mentality endemic within Police Forces the news of what had happened here would spread like wildfire. Shirley went from room to room looking for any evidence to substantiate her belief that Leers was a member of the Bakers 13 perverts, or more importantly any evidence of association. That's what she really needed, some names or addresses or ideally both.

She rummaged through every drawer and cupboard scanned every letter and piece of information she came across. The last room to be checked was the bedroom, she popped her head round the already opened door, she could see the dishevelled bed that Leers had been hauled out of.

The outer bedclothes were strewn on the floor and a large stain was evidence on the still in place bedsheet. From the smell Shirley concluded that this was Leers initial contact with his attackers and the stain would be urine, possibly discharged through fright and the pillow was extensively bloodstained. A cursory search of the room once again revealed nothing to indicate any signs of perverted behaviour or tendencies.

Shirley was puzzled, she was sure that given the atrocious and excessive activities of the Bakers 13 she would have found some scrap of evidence or information to support her theory. She had been unable to find any pornography, any contact magazines or correspondence with other perverts not even any photographs of children. What she had found seemed to indicate the opposite, he appeared to be a music teacher who gave private tutoring. This would explain the number of children and young persons coming to his address in the evenings. He was a regular churchgoer, a fund raiser for local charities and an all-round good egg if what she had found to be true.

Shirley was increasingly becoming concerned that she had been wrong about Leers and was now regretting giving his details to Guthy.

She pushed the thoughts to the back of her mind reassuring herself that the reason she had not found anything incriminating was because Leers had been careful and discreet.

"Sarge, Sarge are you up there"
came the voice of Latifeo from the bottom of the stairs.
"Yes, I'm up here, come on up I think I have found the initial scene of the assault."

Shirley replied.

Latifeo joined Shirley in the bedroom, he put his hand over his mouth and nose to assuage the rancid smell,

"What a bloody stench"

said Oli through clenched teeth.

"Yea it looks like he has pissed himself when he got attacked, I think we had better go back outside now and secure the house for SOCO, have you preserved the outside scene?"

"Yes, it's all sealed off with crime scene tape I searched the garden but I couldn't see anything of importance."

Shirley took one last look at the scene and the body and gave Latifeo instructions to remain there until the arrival of SOCO and tell them what had been found telling him that she was returning to the nick and to keep her informed of any developments.

Shirley managed to scrounge a lift back with one of the traffic officers who had turned up just to be nosey. During the drive back she couldn't help thinking about what she had or more importantly what she hadn't found at the home of Tom Leers, had she made a terrible mistake?

Back in her office a message had been left on her desk asking her to contact home. Shirley was very secretive at work about her home and private life so that was all the message read no contact name or number, but she knew to phone Sam.

Shirley dialled the number immediately; it was unusual for Sam to contact her at work unless it was something important.

"Hi Sam, its Shirley what's up"

Sam replied calmly "Sorry to call you at work it's nothing to get worried about but I am with Victor he's got some news you will be interested in I thought I should let you know Straight away."

Shirley thought for a moment, with all the activity surrounding the dead body hanging from the tree no one would miss her for a couple of hours.

"Ok I will be back soon"

with that she put the receiver down quickly checked her computer to make sure that she had nothing important pending and slipped out of the office.

Back at the crime scene Dumb and Dumber had now given up on conducting house to house enquiries and were ensconced in a local pub idly chatting about the murder over a pint.

"What a bloody mess the body was" Frank said to his partner in between swigs of best bitter.

"Yes, and how about the awful stench it was probably the worst smell I have ever encountered" came the reply.

Frank look puzzled and was clearly deep in thought over something.

Robert Peeves had worked with Frank Fergas for a long time and they knew each other inside out Peeves sensed that Frank was about to divulge something that was concerning him, so he ordered two more pints whilst awaiting whatever he was about to say.

"Rob there is something I can't work out, think back to when we first arrived at the scene can you remember what happened?"

"I can remember that idiot Pc throwing up all over my shoes the fuckin idiot"

"Think back carefully Rob can you recall what was said?"

Rob thought for a second

"Yes, the vomiting numbskull told us that he had gone into the back garden and found the body hanging from a tree"

"That's right but can you remember what Shirley said, think hard Rob?"

"The cheeky cow tried to give us a rollocking about us giving the idiot some stick I don't see what the problem is Frank"

Frank took a deep breath before replying.

"What she actually said was "(C'mon let's go and see want's happened to this pervert) but how could she know that we were dealing with a pervert because the first indication was when we saw the body and the word PERVE carved into his forehead."

Robert Peeves was now the one who looked a little bemused as he wracked his brains to fully recall exactly what was said.

After a short deliberation he nodded in agreement replying,

"Bloody hell yes you're right how on earth did she know that the victim would possibly be some sort of pervert also when we first saw the body hanging from the tree, she wasn't a bit surprised, there is something not right we need to have a close look at her."

"Agreed"

Frank concurred as he signalled the barman to replenish their empty glasses.

They both knew that catching a copper gave a bigger boost to a police career than catching a criminal and this suited their nasty backstabbing tendencies.

They picked up their replenished pints and clinked them together in mock celebration knowing that this could spell big trouble for Detective Sergeant Wallows.

22

A CUNNING PLAN

Sam and Victor were sitting round the kitchen table when Shirley arrived home, Sam poured Shirley a cup of tea as she took her coat off and took a seat at the table. Shirley and Sam were extremely close and they could sense each other's feelings and emotions. They were the ultimate soulmates, and as such Shirley could sense a somewhat sombre atmosphere in the room but there was also something else, a more upbeat vibe she saw a glimmer of optimism in Sams face.

Shirley sipped at her tea and alternated her gaze between Sam and Victor waiting for whoever was about to break the news and speak first.

Sam initiated the conversation but she merely passed the onus onto Victor by saying.

"Victor has some news from Alldahope I think you need to know straight away."

Victor cleared his throat and with a clearly concerned expression he began to recall recent events at Alldahope

"Unfortunately there was another assault on the girls last night, and this time it was by far the worst one I have encountered."

Shirley interrupted

"But how can that be I thought you were able to get advance information of any attack so we could do something about it."

Sighing deeply Victor replied

"Yes I thought so too, but things have taken a turn for the worse. Normally Dave Kempers organises all the attacks on the girls and he always let me know, but apparently some of the other members of the Bakers dozen aren't happy with him they think he is too cautious and not organising enough of the attacks to satisfy everyone and they are beginning to flex their muscles. They have been exerting pressure on the Matron to influence her to facilitate more access to the children and they have started organising their own perverted violations of the kids. the most horrific aspect of this change is that I think the attacks are going to increase significantly."

Sam then interjected

"You haven't heard the worse part yet Shirley, listen to what Victor said they did to these poor kids."

Victor then recounted some of the unbelievable and horrific sexual abuse that the innocent youngsters had endured.

Victor remained silent for a moment as if steeling himself to deliver even worse news. A foreboding silence filled the atmosphere whilst waiting for Victor to continue.

Taking a deep breath and in a low voice Victor managed to utter the words,

"The children that were abused this time were different they were very young not much more than toddlers"

Tears were now streaming down Shirleys face as she imagined in her mind the sheer terror and depravity these infants had suffered, somewhere in the dark recesses of her mind it brought back thoughts of her own childhood. Sam knew how badly it was affecting Shirley as she also had been subject to the same abuse as her when they were kids.

Shirley stood up and with a crash threw her half full cup of tea against the wall causing it to smash into smithereens. Shirleys feeling of empathy and profound sadness had now been replaced by sheer anger.

"It stops right now we can't pussyfoot around we have got to stop these bastards before they can do anything else, whatever it takes we will do it"

For the first time a glimmer of a faint smile appeared across Sams face and in a more upbeat tone said.

"Victor has a plan, it sounds ok to me, I think it is worth a try, listen to what he is proposing and see what you think."

In light of recent events Victor had anticipated that Shirley and Sam would want action taken immediately, so an idea that he had been mulling over but didn't think he could initiate for some time, he had decided to bring forward.

Shirley and Sam listened intently to Victors idea to solve the problem of the perverted activities of the Bakers dozen and protect the Alldahope children.

Victor had obviously given his plan considerable thought and on the whole the girls thought that he had devised something worthy of trying with a good chance of succeeding. They added a few ideas of their own and tweaked a few things but after a lengthy deliberation they were in agreement that it was the way forward and they should at least give it their best effort.

One of the obstacles they needed to overcome was manpower, they realised they couldn't do it all on their own but who could they trust and also be willing to help.

A few names were suggested including Martin the reporter and the scene of crime officer Steve. Martin was ruled out because even though he was a good guy and genuinely concerned about the children at Alldahope, the plans they were making would be a step to far for him, besides with his recent promotion he had little spare time anyway. Steve was also ruled out for similar reasons.

But Shirley stated that he could still be used for forensic advice or the analysis of exhibits. Because although he most likely wouldn't want to take part or even know about what their plan was, he wasn't averse to helping whilst turning a blind eye to what was going on. They also realised that for the plan to succeed they would need some to enlist the help of some muscle. After much debate they reluctantly agreed that they would have to use Stan Guthy to provide the necessary brute force. He would need to be carefully watched so that his violent behaviour did not get out of hand, Sam joked that she would have her cattle prod fully charged and ready for use. They all smiled at Sams comments but at the same time they knew that Sam wasn't joking and she would not hesitate to zap Guthy with maximum voltage given the slightest excuse.

Sam had already spoken to Prissy and Tess who were more than happy to help given their troubled and abusive upbringings that had given them a similar hatred towards perverts. In total it amounted to six in all more would have been preferable but given the nature of what they intended to do it would have to suffice.

The only thing left to do now was to give Victor time to make arrangements, Shirley was anxious to implement Victors plan as soon as and enquired if he had any idea of time scale.

There was a more upbeat mood around the table now and a reinvigorated Victor replied

"I think that it could be fairly soon, because according to Dave Kempers there seems to be a bit of a split emerging within the Bakers dozen.

Several of the group who appear to be driven by their perverted desires are pushing for more and greater access to kids. Normally everything is organised centrally by the boss who exercises extreme caution, but voices within the group believe that he is too cautious and they are starting to exert pressure to relax security and organise more parties."

"Parties!" exclaimed Shirley.

Victor shook his head

"Not my words Shirley, it's what thy all refer to them as"

Shirley wanted to know a little more about the organisation

"Victor you said it is normally the boss who would do the organising, do you think that the boss is Dave Kempers?"

"No he isn't the boss but he is quite high up in the group, I don't know who the boss is but I have an idea who the one is who is leading the push to relax security and get to the kids more. I don't know their name but it's the one who broke his leg when he fell down the stairs at Alldahope"

"Oh shit"

shrieked Shirley.

"What's the matter Shirley what's happened?"

asked Sam

Shirley had her face in her hands, her worst suspicions had just been confirmed the poor creature that had been strung up and tortured was not one of the Bakers dozen. She replied in a sheepish and muffled voice

," Something happened at work today that I need to tell you about"

Shirley felt a little uneasy to disclose what had happened to Tom Leers, she knew she had rushed into things without investigating properly. Before giving his details to Stan Guthy in the knowledge of what would happen, she should have been sure of her facts.

She took a deep breath and was about to speak when there was a knock on the door,

"Who on earth could that be "

said Sam with a puzzled and slightly concerned look on her face.

It was Shirley who stood up and went to answer the door whilst Sam and Victor continued discussing his plan. The mood had now lightened and the thoughts of the recent abuse at Alldahope were now being replaced with the prospect of putting an end to vile practises of the Bakers dozen.

Sam was probably the one who hated the child abusers the most, despite her petit figure and demure appearance she had an incredibly strong sense of vengeance was the most eager to initiate Victors plan. The scheme had given Sam a huge beaming smile and a radiant glow. She had completely forgotten about the knock on the front door, but when Shirley reappeared in the kitchen Sams smile was replaced with a mixture of horror and bewilderment when she saw who was with her.

Standing next to Shirley was the diminutive figure of Babs,

"I had to invite her in"

said an apologetic Shirley.

The kitchen fell strangely silent as no one really knew what to say or do, Victor Shirley and Sam were even more shellshocked when this plucky little girl took charge of the conversation. She took a seat at the table whilst everyone else was stunned into silence. To an outsider this scenario would appear strange to say the least, but this was no ordinary little girl, this was Babs, she was a one off.

Moving her glance from person to person around the table to make sure she had everyone's attention she spoke with an authority way beyond her years.

"You may or may not be aware that we had another attack again last night, it came without warning or prior information. This has to be the last time this ever happens, I know that you said you were going to do something, but the time has no come to take action. No more words no more promises or time wasting someone has got to stop them. I am telling you first so that you have the opportunity to do something, but you must be aware that if you aren't going to do anything immediately then my next call is to my dad and he will not wait. So what is it to be?"

Sam apart from being shocked at the appearance of Babs and slightly worried how she knew the address was full of admiration for this little dynamo. This incredibly confident young girl with more grit than even most of the hardened of adults was a breath of fresh air.

Sam looked at Shirley and raised her eyebrows whilst nodding towards Babs. Shirley understood what Sams body language was asking, she was looking for permission to tell Babs about Victors plan.

Shirley agreed by simply nodding her head, and Sam then turned to Babs and invited her to sit down.

"Ok then Babs you have actually come at the right time, even though I am a little concerned as to how you knew where we lived but you're here now, so I'm going to tell you what we propose to do.

23

ANOTHER CUNNING PLAN

In the police office Dc Frank Fergas was keeping lookout whilst Robert Peeves was searching the desk of Shirley Wallows and scouring through papers and her desk diary. With one eye on the entrance Fergas turned his head towards Peeves and shouted,

"Have you found anything yet?"

Without looking up Peeves replied

"No nothing yet it's all fairly routine"

"Have a look in the drawers Robert, if she is hiding something then it's most likely in there."

Peeves shook his head

"I have already tried they are locked shut; I can pick the locks but that will take some time."

Fergas left his lookout position and joined Peeves

"Leave it for now, what we will have to do is to get access to her desk drawer we can do it tomorrow on late turn when there is less people about that will give you time to pick the lock. She is definitely hiding something and if we are going to nail her then we need to find it."

Peeves agreed saying

"Yeah, you're right let's go and have a drink and talk about it"

Around the kitchen table the Babs had listened with ardent fervour at the plan to deal with the Bakers dozen. She had been hugely impressed by the inventiveness of Victors plan and had even offered some of her own ideas, which in principle had been accepted.

There were still several things to sort out to make the plan feasible but Victor was going to make the initial approach to the Bakers dozen through Dave Kempers that evening to get the ball rolling.

With Babs on board the added advantage was that they didn't have ask Stan Guthy to enlist his help, with Babs involved it was a given that he would be more than willing to lend his muscle.

Shirley had left halfway through the meeting. If there was anything new that she needed to be aware of then Sam would update her later when she had finished work.

As always, the first thing Shirley did on starting work was to check her desk, she examined her diary and immediately knew that it had been opened and rifled through. She as always had positioned a small scrap of paper inside the diary between the first page and the outer cover at an exact and precise spot.

Any movement of the diary or opening of any pages would alter the position of this and Shirley saw that it had moved from its original location.

She next checked her desk drawer; it was still locked and upon opening it she noticed that the similar scrap of paper that she inserted in the runner of the drawer was still there and it had not moved.

Hidden beneath her drawer and held securely in place with tape was a voice activated recorder.

Checking that no one was in earshot she pressed the replay button, a wry smile spread across her face as she heard the full conversation between Dc's Frank Fergas and Robert Peeves as they were rifling through the papers on her desk.

Given the reputation for skulduggery and underhandedness of the pair this had not come as a shock for Shirley. Indeed she had been expecting something like this from them for some time, and she was fully prepared for it and had an action plan ready to implement. She reset the voice recorder and carefully taped it back underneath her desk drawer just as Latifeo entered the office and walked over to her.

"I have some more info on the booking office burglary, have you got time to discuss it now Sarge?"

Shirley looked up quizzically

"You have seen the informant without me?"

Shrugging his shoulders Latifeo replied

"Yes, sorry Sarge, I realise we are supposed to talk to him together but I bumped into him in the town centre and he just started jabbering on before I could stop him."

"Ok take a seat and fire away but remember in future you have to be very careful about speaking to the informant on your own because if anything goes wrong then there is no corroboration of what has been done or said so it's for your own protection especially someone like Tinkers, he doesn't seem very reliable to me."

"Ok Sarge understood" Latifeo then outlined what he had learned from his informant Tinkers. The details included exact times, the number of people involved method of entry and the level of force that they were willing to use.

Shirley noted down all the relevant details, and asked Latifeo to repeat everything so she could double check every detail.

Shirley tasked Latifeo with conducting a detailed examination of the area in and around the potential crime scene to establish all means of entry and egress, observation points, escape routes and any potential hazards.

Oli stood up and with enthusiasm said

"Ok Sarge I'll make a start right now"

As he was walking out the door Shirley shouted

"Oh, and get a detailed map of the area, if you have any problems getting one then use the force helicopter, they can take some aerial photos if you can't get a map"

With a simple thumbs up and a nod of his head to affirm he left the office.

Shirley was a little concerned that Latifeo had spoken to the informant without her being present, but she couldn't waste too much time worrying over it because there was a lot of work and preparation to be done to plan the operation. One thing she was grateful for was that Latifeo has said that no weapons or firearms were being used, this made the formulation of the strategy and the health and safety risk assessment much easier.

Apparently, any problems with security and enforcement would be dealt with by a hired thug. Latifeo didn't have the details of the hired muscle but Shirley was surmising it would Stan Guthy, he knew of most criminal jobs that were taking place in the Stourbridge area and he was unlikely to allow any hired gangster to intrude on his turf.

This put Shirley in a quandary, on one hand it gave her an opportunity to get rid of Guthy once and for all, but she was also relying on him to help implement Victors plan for the Baker Dozen which he wouldn't be able to do if je was banged up. Time wasn't on her side; the job was going down in a few days and she had to run her plan by and have approved by the Chief Inspector.

Shirley made herself a large coffee and settled down at her desk and began the arduous task of preparing the strategic plan to execute the operation. The office was empty which allowed Shirley to work uninterrupted and she worked the rest of the day and late into the evening preparing the operational strategy for the execution of the booking office robbery, including a comprehensive health and safety policy. After numerous more cups of coffee and a hastily eaten sandwich from the vending machine, Shirley had completed her work.

The only thing to do now was to present it to and get it agreed by the Chief inspector, this shouldn't be a problem thought Shirley, she was very competent and extremely thorough at the preparation of plans and admin related matters. She let out a yawn and stretched out her arms and extended her body to shake of the lethargy caused by being at her desk for so long.

She began to reflect on recent events, things were now moving quickly, the booking office robbery was only a few days away the situation with the Bakers dozen would soon be resolved, she had begun with her scheme to put the nosey and troublesome Peeves and Fergas in their place. The only outstanding matter was the blackmailer who had not been in touch for some time but Shirley had a feeling that it wouldn't be long before they returned to demand more cash. She didn't like loose ends but at this moment in time she had little choice in the matter but to sit and wait for them to make contact and this time she would make sure that they wouldn't getaway.

Draining the last remnants of her coffee cup she stood up and donned her coat. Stepping outside into the cool evening air she realised by how dark it was that she had worked much longer than she thought. She began to walk home heading towards the high street which was beginning to fill up with the evenings drinkers heading towards the pubs and bars. In one of the bars which was directly opposite the police station Peeves and Fergas had installed themselves on a table next to window that gave as view of the police station entrance. They were now watching Shirley as she walked towards the high street. When she had turned the corner into the high street and disappeared from sight Fergas said

"Ok Robert she's gone go and see what the bitch is hiding in her draw I'll wait here and keep an eye out but be as quick as you can."

Peeves felt the lump in his coat pocket double checking that he still had his lock picking tools, downing the rest of his pint he quickly made his way out of the pub and walked towards the police station. Fergas was studying the street keeping an eye out for any return by Detective Sergeant Shirley Wallows who Fergas was sure was engaged in some underhand activity but for the life of him he couldn't figure out what.

He was becoming a little apprehensive now, it seemed a good idea at the time to break into Shirleys desk especially as it was not him but Peeves doing the actual breaking in, but whilst the deed was being done it showed his true character which was a somewhat spineless to say the least. He didn't have long to wait however until he saw Peeves emerging from the Police Station with a hard to hide grin spreading the width of his chubby face.

With Peeves now back at the table and with two new pints in front of them Fergas rubbed his hands together in anticipation eager to find out what he had found

" I can tell from your face that you got a result so tell me all about it and

we can decide what we're going to do to put her in her place."

It had been a long day for Shirley as she put her key in the front door all she could think of was her bed, she was so tired and she could foresee that the forthcoming days would become increasingly more hectic so a good night's sleep would help recharge her batteries.

When she walked into the kitchen to make herself a hot drink to take to bed, she realised that sleep and her bed would have to wait.

Seated around the table and obviously waiting for her were Victor, Sam, Prissy, Tess, and a very tired looking Babs.

"Well I was going to make a cup of tea and take it to my bed but I assume now that I will need a big strong cup of coffee instead"

No one bothered to reply, there was no need to, Shirley had assessed the situation correctly.

Joining the rest at the table and after taking a few sips of her steaming hot coffee Shirley took stock of who was there at the impromptu assembly and sensed the mood. Instinctively she knew something big was in the pipeline and whatever was about to happen it was going to be soon.

"Ok who's going to start, it has to be something big for everyone to gather unannounced at this time of night".

Everyone looked at each other around the table exchanging quizzical glances, eventually the eyes focused on Victor and without anybody saying anything he had been nominated to speak.

Victor cleared his throat whilst everyone else settled back in their chairs.

"I have reliable info that the Bakers Dozen are planning another of their so-called parties, and this time due to the demands of various members of the group who are becoming more and more influential within the group it will involve more perverts, more girls and an even higher degree of abuse. Some of the proposals of their sexual intentions towards the girls involve unprecedented levels of degradation. There is no way we can allow it to happen we need to take action now."

Realising the severity of the upcoming attack Shirley adopted her analytical head

"Ok tell me from whom have you got this information, why they have given it to you and how reliable is it?"

"The info has come from Dave Kempers, he told me that the boss who he simply refers to as Baker is becoming increasingly concerned with the attitude and conduct of the group. He feels that they are bit by bit trying to exert more influence within the group and that they are starting to take too many risks. He is concerned that he is losing his power to control them. I think he told me because he just wanted to open up to someone, and as I'm not one of the members who are trying to usurp the organization, he felt I would be safe to confide in."

"Well that all seems to make sense, it appears to me that the info is reliable, so now the big question, what are we going to do about it and when?"

Shirley had judged the atmosphere in the room and had rightly assumed that Victor had already got an idea of what to do so she like the others sat back in her chair and waited for Victor to enlighten them all.

"Something needed doing so I have initiated the plan that we have already discussed and agreed, the time and date for it is prior to their planned attack on the girls. There Is a lot of organising to do so we need to make a start right away.

Sam who had been sitting there quietly whilst Victor and Shirley had been speaking interrupted.

"When Victor told me what had happened, I assembled everyone together so that as soon as you arrived home from work, we could make a start, because the time is so limited"

All thought of sleep had now been pushed to the back of Shirleys mind and together with the rest of the group they started making plans for the Baker Dozen.

24

GUY TINKERS

"Here you are sir" said Di Grant Courtan as he placed a cup of coffee on his bosses desk.

"Thanks Grant" replied an increasingly impatient DCI Trevor Cappoten,

"What's the time Shirley said she would be here at nine o'clock with her proposal for the booking office heist I've got things I need to attend to."

As Grant looked at his watch and before he could reply Shirley strode into the office together with Dc Oli Latifeo.

"Sorry I'm a little late boss" said an apologetic Shirley "It was a late night and I overslept "

Grant Courtan looked at the DCI and rolled his eyes in a mocking fashion, something that Shirley noticed out of the corner of her eye. She was fully aware of Grants snivelling subservience to more senior officers and he was regarded as much as a gaffers man as was Frank Fergas.

"Not to worry you're here now, let's see this plan of yours," said a more upbeat DCI.

Shirley outlined her strategic proposal for the execution of the booking office operation. It was an extremely detailed and well planned out strategy, everything had been thought through including the allocation of resources and vehicles, prisoner processing and interrogation.

Contingency planning for unexpected events and extra resources on standby if needed. Combined with a financial breakdown of officers overtime and expenses and a comprehensive Health and safety brief.

Grant Courtan much to the annoyance of the DCI had tried to pick holes in the plan but all to no avail. The icing on the cake was the scene plan prepared by Latifeo, even Shirley was surprised by how comprehensive and well-presented he had prepared his task. He had gone to great lengths to hide officers in plain sight where they would not arouse any suspicion including exact and precise timings for each and every officer to be on scene.

The timings were especially crucial as most of the officers would be in non-marked vehicles and if they were there too soon then their presence for an extended period would stand out like a sore thumb. He had also taken into account the timings of parking restrictions that come into force at various times throughout the evening in Stourbridge high street. Because the last thing that we needed was for some resident or local complaining to the police about vehicles parking at a time when they shouldn't. Included in his scene reconnaissance were photographs and an aerial view taken using the force helicopter.

"Very impressive Sergeant you seem to have covered all bases, but are you sure you don't require firearms back up?"

"With the information we have sir and applying it to force protocols for Firearms authorisation we do not have sufficient grounds for deployment." She replied confidently she also sensed the belligerent attitude of Inspector Courtan.

He was obviously itching to try and find some flaw or discrepancy or the slightest noncompliance with standing orders, but he reluctantly had to concede that the strategy was without fault.

Looking at his Watch the Chief Inspector replied

"Well that all sounds fairly comprehensive to me Shirley you seem to have covered everything. I will arrange for the appropriate manpower to be drafted in from other divisions. As I am sure you are both aware that because of various leaks in the past that have caused operations such as these to be compromised then no staff from this station or division will be utilised and no one apart from the four of us in this room will be aware of the operation, that is an absolute must do I make myself clear."

Everyone was fully expecting this to be the case and simply nodded in agreement. They all knew the operation that the Chief inspector didn't name but was obviously alluding to was a raid on a local bar that was regularly serving after hours. When the raid took place, the pub was completely deserted despite having served after hours alcohol every day for weeks and months previously. They had plainly been tipped off about the raid, and the suspicion fell on but was never proved on a now disgraced former Chief inspector Frank Twead, the one who Trevor Cappoten had replaced.

Cappoten looked at Shirley Grant and Oli in turn as an invitation to add anything they wish to the meeting. With no response received except for the shaking of heads he announced

"That's it everyone our business here is finished, keep me updated with any problems or alterations and the best of luck."

Shirley returned to her office alone, Latifeo had given her some lame excuse about having something that he needed to do. Shirley realised it was just an excuse to skive off for a while but she didn't mind, he had done a good job with his task of Reconnoitring the scene and as far as she was concerned if he did his job well when needed than that was good enough for her.

The office was deserted and Shirley had some free time on her hands so after a brief phone call to Sam to enquire how preparations were going with Victors plan, she relaxed in her chair enjoying her brief period respite.

Then she noticed it and realised there was no time to relax she needed to be on her guard at all times. Making sure the office was still unoccupied she knelt down at her desk to get a closer look at her drawer. She carefully scanned every inch of her desk drawer and immediate surrounding, a wry smile gradually emerged from her studious expression. They haven't wasted any time thought Shirley as she carefully inserted her key in the locked drawer. Careful so as not to disturb anything she slowly slid it open, she knew that someone had gained access because she had inserted a tiny lock of her hair in between the outer edge of the drawer and the desk framework which when opened would cause it to fall out.

It was an old trick that she used regularly and as she could   see that the said lock of hair was now dislodged from its position and on the floor, she was certain that she had an intruder.

Checking the contents of the interior she saw that things had been moved around, especially near to where she had planted something for the two stupid detectives Dumb and Dumber to find.

Next, she retrieved the hidden voice recorder that she kept taped underneath the desk and pressed play. The voice recorder had been activated when noises had been detected by the sound of some metallic object being inserted in the lock. Shirley assumed whoever it was that was trying to gain access to her drawer was on their own because no conversation was heard. She heard the sound of the drawer opening and the sound of papers being moved. She was sure it was either Frank Fergas or Robert Peeves but she would have preferred to hear them say something so she could be doubly sure.

Listening intently she heard the sound of an envelope being opened and the contents removed, then eureka she heard the utterance

"Got ya you fuckin bitch".

She recognised it to be the less than dulcet tones of one half of Dumb and Dumber it was unmistakably Detective Constable Robert Peeves.

Shirley muttered under her breath

"No you haven't you little prick, its I that has got you".

Tinkers gaze was glued to the overhead monitor in the bookies, the fifty pence that he had found in the gutter was now riding on the ten to one shot Keydona.

It was a seven-furlong race and with two furlongs left Keydona was leading.

"C'mon Keydona C'mon baby" shouted Tinkers.

Tinkers had been penniless for days, the initial money he had got from giving the police information had long since gone, most of it spent in the bookies he did splash out on some tins of Carlsberg special brew and a doner kebab. Something he later regretted when he ran out of betting money, he would rather forgo food and drink for the chance of a gamble. Even the fifty pence piece he had found in the street today had been cover in dog shit, but such was his addiction to gambling he simply wiped the coin on his trousers and strode into the bookies.

The manager was well aware of Tinkers addiction and knew that on occasions Tinkers would not have any money, so if he did not place a bet then the staff were obliged to inform the manager who would then order him to leave.

But today he was ok the fifty pence would suffice as enough of a bet to facilitate his presence in the bookies for some time.

Fifty yards to go Keydona was still leading Tinkers was getting more and more excited, with the five-pound fifty return he could place bets and stay in the bookies all day.

With his fists now punching celebratory in the air his voice becoming ever more raised

"C'mon, C'mon, Oh Fuck Fuck Fuck".

The favourite had come from nowhere and beaten Keydona into second place, clinging onto his betting slip and praying for some sort of appeal or stewards enquiry prior to the official result his intense gaze never left the screen until, hoping against hope for his five pound fifty that would afford him more bets and more time in the booking office.

When the result was confirmed, he screwed up his ticket threw it angrily on the floor. He could see the manager eyeing him up from behind the counter who realised that he was now skint. Giving way to the inevitable he stormed out of the shop, desperately wracking his brains as to how he could secure even the tiniest amount of money to have one more bet.

He didn't have the ability to rob anyone, he had about as much physical prowess and potential for aggression as a kitten. He had tried once in desperation to rob a young schoolboy on his way to school of his lunch money. The result being that the schoolboy refused to hand over his lunch money and then he turned on Tinkers him and gave him a good kicking, leaving him with a blackeye a bloody nose and a battered ego. To add insult to injury, the youth who was half his size also stole his baseball cap and left him sobbing in the gutter. There wasn't even anything left in his dirty hovel of a flat, he had sold or pawned anything and everything he owned. He once dismantled the hot water pipes from his bathroom and sold the copper for scrap. But he couldn't do that again, the council wouldn't believe that he had been burgled again and the robbers had dismantled and stolen the pipes once more.

He used to be a prolific shoplifter and sell his ill-gotten gains in the local pubs for a fraction of their price but had become so well known to shop owners and workers that this meagre source of income was impossible.

He would soon get his informants money from the booking office burglary but that was a few days away and he needed money right now, he needed his fix he had to have the thrill of a gamble.

He decided to take a walk along the Stourbridge canal to see if there was anything work nicking or any odd bits of metal that he could weigh in at the scrap yard.

Sometimes people dumped their old rubbish by the canal because they couldn't be bothered to dispose of it properly or take it to the nearby council tip. If what had been dumped contained any metal, he could strip it off and get a couple of quid from the tatters yard. No such luck today though after scouring the canal side for half an hour and finding nothing he decided to give up. It was a hot day and he was wearing his big old heavy coat his only coat in fact and he was becoming hot and sweaty, he began to stink even more than usual, but that didn't normally bother him he had become somewhat immune to his own personal stench, but he did need to rest so he sat on a low brick wall. The sun was beating down relentlessly and blinding him, as he lifted his arm to put his hand over his brow in order to shade his eyes from the glare, he became aware of the stench emanating from his armpit.

The smell was awful even for his accustomed acceptance of his own foul body odour, but this was tinged with something else. Loosening his long doctor who style scarf from around his he screwed up his nostrils and took an unsightly and exaggerated whiff, god it really was awful but it also smelt and tasted of a hint of burning. He looked around and realised that behind the low wall he was perched on someone had dug a deep pit filled it with old, insulated cable and had set fire to it.

This was quite common in this area people would steal electrical cable and instead of spending hours stripping off the insulation to get at the valuable copper they would simply set if alight. The insulation would burn away and leave the copper which could be retrieved when cool and sold in the local scrapyard. They had left behind a petrol can that still contained some of the accelerant and it was this that had made the smell worse. The ground was still sodden with the remnants that hadn't burned off fully.

It was a huge pile of cable, the pit that had been dug was not only deep but quite wide. There must be some copper left in there that they have missed thought Tinker excitedly, and he leant over half his body resting on the wall and the rest almost submerged in the mass of burned cable. He began rummaging through the debris with outstretched arms delving deeper and deeper I search of the precious copper that would afford him the money for on more bet.

He was so engrossed in his desperate scavenge that he was oblivious to the person standing immediately behind him.

Having moved some of the burnt remnants he could now see to almost the bottom of the pit and he was sure that what he was looking at was several strands of copper. He began to reach down further extending his arms as far as they would go, but before he could lay his hands on what to him felt like he had struck gold everything went black. He couldn't control his body his arms and legs weren't working, the enormous blow he had received to the back of his head had sent the world spinning round and he felt all consciousness leaving his body and he collapsed in a heap.

Stan Guthy had embarked on a pub crawl he had already visited most of the bars in Stourbridge town centre, and was now spreading his wings further, in reality he was looking for a fight. But his notoriety in the town preceded him and no matter how much he threatened or intimidated anyone they all backed off or simply averted their gaze from the belligerent thug. He had just left a bar called the Barbridge but as this was a locals bar and everyone knew him no one would give him the slightest reason to start a fight.

The closet he came was someone called Dorcas a member of staff who had told him to shut his yap and behave himself. Guthy had found this verbal attack on him highly amusing, he had tried to annoy and insult almost every bloke in Stourbridge and the only person to retaliate was an attractive and petit young barmaid.

Still intent on picking a fight he decided on a bar where he was less well known, he knew it as the Moorings Tavern adjacent to the Stourbridge canal but he knew that it had changed owners and had a refurb meaning that it would attract new customers, surely, he could goad someone into a confrontation and then beat the living daylights out of them. The pub was also on his route back via the canal to his dingy accommodation so he could get pissed batter some poor sod and stagger home to sleep it off. He had already had a skinful as he almost fell through the door of the pub that he noticed was now called the Old Wharf.

The pain ringing in Tinkers head was excruciating the pounding sensation came from the back of his head and as he started to come to, he realised he had been struck from behind with incredible force.

He blinked his eyes; the sun was still shining brightly and he was lying on his back staring straight up into it.

As he began to focus, he could see the shape of what he thought was someone standing over him. He tried to clear his eyes by rubbing them but was unable to move his arms. He tried to speak and beseeched the shadowy figure saying "Help me I don't know what happened but I need help, can you help me please" but the words were muffled and barely audible Tinkers beseeched the shadowy figure. No help was forthcoming and the still indistinct and blurred shape didn't move or reply. Tinkers feelings pain and aching began to be replaced by a sense of fear and foreboding, what has happened why is he on the ground and why can't I move? He thought.

Taking stock of his surrounding he quickly became aware that he was in or to be more accurate at the bottom of the dugout pit with the burnt copper wire. The reason he couldn't move was twofold one was the sheer physical weight of the cable remnants pressing down on his body and the other more worrying was that some of the cable had been used to tie his hands and feet together.

There was something in his mouth making speech difficult, it was something soft and soggy with an obnoxious odour, he tried to spit whatever it was out but after a few attempts he could not dislodge whatever was stuck in his mouth that he now knew was his scarf. His vision was returning and the shadowy figure was coming into focus, he couldn't believe his own eyes when he saw who it was that was simply watching him and not offering any help. Sheer terror and panic engulfed him from head to toe at what happened next.

He tried to scream but with his scarf still filling most of his mouth he was unable to raise more than a whimper. His eyes were bulging out of their sockets when he saw the naked flame of the lighter being put to the end of his scarf. He figured out that his own scarf was being used a wick it had been doused in petrol and stuffed in his mouth, the end furthest from his mouth had become alight and was slowly spreading along its length towards him. He tried his best to struggle but his bindings on his hands and feet had been secured to tightly and he was completely immobile as he watched the flame traverse the length of his once beloved scarf getting ever closer.

Tinkers wanted to scream and shout and beg the human arsonist to extinguish the flame.

But no matter how hard he struggled and tried to squirm out of his bindings it was all to no avail. The scarf was firmly embedded in his mouth and had been secured by looping it round the back of his head and like his leg and arm restraints it would not budge.

His attacker had now picked up the discarded can of petrol left by the cable thieves and emptied the tiny few remaining droplets on to Tinkers coat. The fire gradually and slowly began to spread and the heat generated began to intensify. Tinkers was being slow roasted like a joint of meat in an oven.

As if in slow motion the gentle smouldering spread to every part of his being, scorching not only his clothing but all the exposed skin including his face. His hair had burned away a little quicker because of the greases in his filthy hair that acted like an accelerant. The feeling was like nothing on earth, every single part of him, every nerve ending was filling his entire body with unbearable pain imaginable. It was so intense that it prevented him from passing out and he resigned himself to the fact that he would have to endure this hell until his death which he hoped would come soon.

In the Old Wharf Stan Guthy was downing pint after pint followed by large whiskies, he was flush with money having received an upfront payment on the forthcoming booking office robbery, he would be even better off once the job had been pulled off. He thought about where to take the love of his life on holiday, he had made a promise to Babs and it was the one thing he would never break.

The alcohol was fuelling his temper and he wanted to vent his anger out on somebody. A group of students had gathered in a corner of the bar and with not having any luck inciting individuals to engage him in a fight he decided to go over and antagonise these what he called posh little rich kids.

There was quite a number of them and his reasoning was that this may give them a false sense of bravado. He was in no doubt that he could quite easily take them all on at once and brutalise them into a bloody pulp. He took his pint with him and barged through the group to the bar where he pushed one of the group who was waiting to be served out of the way. Then slamming his empty glass on the bar he demanded a refill and turned to the youth whom he had pushed out the way daring him to say something about his oafish que jumping.

The youth was initially quite perturbed and was about to verbally remonstrate with Guthy but looking him up and down and realising what a huge and intimidating presence was confronting him he relented and not wishing to engage in eye to eye contact simply lowered his gaze to the floor and meekly accepted what had happened.

Guthy wasn't going to let it go because he was determined to start a fight with the group to inflict his pent-up anger. He picked up his still empty glass and was just about to shove it into the youths face when he noticed another group of people who were watching his every move.

"Shit"

he muttered, the other group that were keenly eyeing him were a bunch of coppers, he recognised as local plod from Stourbridge, more than a few of them had previously dealing with him. Realising that any form of trouble in front of those bastard coppers would result in his license being revoked and an immediate recall to prison he angrily slammed his glass on the counter causing it to smash and barged his way through the gathering of students and left the pub. He decided to leave his search for a potential fight till another time and walk back home, he would take a short cut along the canal towpath.

The start of the Stourbridge canal began immediately behind the pub, there were a few houseboats moored up but apart from them and a few ducks quacking away the canal and towpath were deserted. He stopped to urinate and decided to spray the windows of one of the houseboats covering them in the foul-smelling liquid.

Fortunately the barge was unoccupied as was the norm, most of the converted canal boats were used as holiday homes or just for the occasional pleasure cruise. He took out a half bottle of whisky from his coat pocket and as he wended his way along the tranquil towpath, he took hefty gulps from it until he had consumed the entire contents and slung the empty bottle aiming it at a group of ducks on the far embankment. He laughed as the ducks began to make excited noises hen the bottle smashed on a wall behind them.

Guthy was really beginning to feel the effects of the alcohol his head was spinning and he was swaying from side to side as he took one faltering step after another.

Realising he was pissed and the alcohol was having quite an effect on him, he rubbed his eyes vigorously to clear his blurred vision. His view along the towpath and the route home was obscured by a dark shadow and even the fingers roughly massaging his eyes couldn't shift it. He blinked continuously but all to no avail his vision was still affected. As he continued on his ever increasingly unsteady feet the dark blur came more into focus and he realised it wasn't a problem with his eyesight but that there was something or someone on the towpath coming towards him.

Tinkers had eventually reached a level of consciousness that allowed him to take control of his movements. The fire had more or less fizzled out it was no more than a gentle smouldering; the bindings had been burnt through by the fire and he was able to move his arms and legs. His scarf hadn't completely burnt through and although still stuffed into his mouth he was able to loosen it slightly allowing him to breathe easier.

He managed to get to his feet and stagger along in search of help. His entire body was jet black from head to toe with the odd exception of bright crimson red where his outer clothes had burnt all the way through together with skin leaving a grotesque sight of blood-soaked bare flesh.

Where the clothes had not completely burnt, they had become fused onto his body and it was difficult to tell what was material and what was human being. His entire body hair was gone including facial stubble and eyebrows and lashes. Most of his face had melted and his features resembled a manikin or a clay model that had been exposed to severe heat and the component parts had become fluid and indistinct and later had become fused together.

Guthy stood in amazement as he watched the surreal sight of a zombie like figure approaching him and apparently pleading for help. The next thing that hit him was the unbearable stench. Burnt human flesh which then subsequently rots gives off the most gut-wrenching aroma that fills engulfs anyone and anything nearby.

One of Tinkers eyes had been burnt so badly that the eyeball had fallen out, the other eye however was less badly damaged, the lower eyelid had become infused with the eyeball whilst the upper one was fire damaged and almost completely missing. But it afforded him the merest of peripheral blurred vision and he could make out a human shape in front of him. Reminiscent of a scene from a George A Romero horror film he stretched out his arms towards the indistinct shape in a plea for help.

Guthys initial feeling of bewilderment had now turned to amusement, Guthy revelled in other peoples pain and misery, and it would be difficult to imagine any worse torment a human being could suffer.

Guthy let out a guffaw and said loudly with a great deal of merriment

"Are you asking me for help you fucking freak?"

Tinkers was unable to speak the intense prolonged heat had damaged his vocal cords beyond repair, but he managed to extend his arms a little further in a sign of acceptance.

"Come here I'll fuckin help you, what you need is to cool down."

Guthy stretched out his right arm and took hold of Tinkers remnants of a scarf and lifted him off his feet dangling him in front of him like a rag doll.

Then swinging the utterly helpless almost lifeless mess of charcoaled human remains he dunked him in the canal up to and submerging his shoulders.

Guthy was exacting the utmost pleasure from this and he could feel his pent-up anger gradually assuaging.

"There you go mate that ought to cool you down a bit, don't forget your head though".

Guthy realised that the reason he wasn't fully submerged was because of the shallowness of the canal his feet must be resting on the canal floor. To overcome this he put his boot on top of the blackened head and pressed down hard so that the head disappeared under the water, leaving just a pair of burned remains of what were once human arms clinging to the canal side.

With Guthy now satisfied with his handiwork and having had as much enjoyment as was possible from the situation he removed his boot from off the submerged head and wiped it on the grass to dry it. He turned to walk away but to his amazement he saw the head remerge from its watery grave followed by their arms, the face which had now become more distinct and more recognisable as human with some of the burn damage having washed away was now resting on the edge of the canal towpath.

Guthy stood and stared in wonderment at the thought of this pathetic wretch still wanting to cling on to life for all he was worth.

Guthy thought that perhaps after all there was the possibility a bit more fun and entertainment could still had at the expense of this ridiculous specimen and looked around for inspiration.

In the ashes of the remains of the now extinguished fire he saw what had been a metal petrol can, the top half had melted away leaving an open topped container with sharp jagged edges.

The can was still quite hot so covering his hands with the sleeves of his coat he retrieved it from the fire and dipped it into the canal to cool off.

Now that it could be handled easily, he examined it by running his thumb along the jagged rim, the fire had somehow formed a razor type edging which gave him an idea.

Kneeling down next to the ghostly looking head with the can in one hand he looked into what was left of the face and began to speak.

Guthy looked at the flicker of the one remaining eye and it became apparent to him that despite all the damage sustained whoever it was still capable of understanding.

This made what Guthy was about to do even more exciting, the mere fact that he could still inflict pain and stomach-churning terror filled him with renewed enthusiasm. Taking hold of the scarf to keep the head still, he used the razor-sharp edge of the can to start cutting into the neck, initially it took some time to penetrate the outer layer which had become hardened with the burnt crustation providing resistance.

Guthy hadn't minded this extra work because all the time he could stare straight into the face of the person whom he was decapitating, and the longer they were aware of what was happening to them and the terror that must be experiencing the better.

Once through the outer layer and no further response from the head he finished off quickly and fully decapitated the head.

Standing up and holding the can in one hand and his trophy at arm's length in the other outstretched in front of him he was now wondering what to do with it.

A wicked grin spread across his face he knew what to do how to finish off, he simply placed the head in the can and after initially thinking about taking it home with him he decided it would be better for it to set sail. Placing the can carefully into the water he gave it a gentle push towards a flock of ducks who were gently swimming nearby. The head had been placed face up and it would provide whoever found it with a nice surprise though Guthy.

Feeling more relaxed now that he had taken his rage and anger out someone and with his trademark guffawing, he strode off contented along the towpath.

25

WHAT THE F***

Babs Guthy silently crept out of her bed and tiptoed across her bedroom. She put her ear to the door and listened intently for several minutes. Alldahope was an old building and if you didn't know where to tread then any movement was betrayed by the echoing of creaking floorboards or loose and ill-fitting stairs. Satisfied that the coast was clear she slowly opened her door and stepped out into the corridor.

The landing was dark and just barely lit by the sporadic moonlight that was intermittingly blocked out by the dark clouds slowly rolling by. Looking skywards through the huge sash window she waited until the moon was fully obscured, then slowly and deliberately walked across the landing, taking care to avoid the floorboards that she knew creaked and made her way down the stairs.

She knew that there were no scheduled attacks by the Baker Dozen or as she and all the other girls referred to them as the night monsters. So the only one to be careful of was matron, but tonight was the only time that Babs would have the opportunity to do her part in Victors plan.

Victor had asked her to get hold of some of the knockout drugs that matron puts into the girls evening drink of milk.

The door to Matrons office was secured with good quality high tech locks which made it almost impossible to break into secretly. But Babs had spent a lot of time exploring and examining the building, especially when Victor had noticed a discrepancy once in the number of people emerging from the cellar where the abuse took place and going in.

Babs had scoured the cellar and located a secret entrance to a hidden passageway and this was where she was now heading.

The door on the entrance to the stairs that led down to the cellar was also secured with a substantial lock but Victor in his capacity as a part time handyman had obtained a spare key. Babs inserted the key as quietly as she could and once inside, she locked it behind her and began to descend the dark musty smelling steps until she came to the entrance to the secret passageway.

Normally there was very little that unnerved Babs but this place gave her a sense of the creeps and it sent shivers went down her spine as she inched her way through the dungeon like tunnel.

Eventually after what seemed like an eternity, she reached the wooden door at the far and gently rested her ear against it listening for any sound. With her heart in her mouth she turned the door handle which gave out a squeaking noise which although was relatively quiet, given the circumstances and the stillness of the night it sounded like an alarm going off to Babs. Unperturbed she pushed the door open went through and was now standing in Matrons office.

She was hoping and praying that Matrons desk drawer would be unlocked and her prayers were answered when she gently pulled on the drawer to reveal hundreds upon hundreds of the foil wrapped tranquilisers. There were so many that she could take as many as she wished and they would go unnoticed. She began to fill her pockets until they were full to the brim. Then carefully closing the drawer she retraced her steps back under the cover of darkness to her bedroom as quietly as she had come.

Hiding the tablets where they couldn't be discovered she slipped back between the sheets, she was feeling good, this was what she had been waiting for, finally something was being done about those perverted monsters the plan had begun.

Shirley was at her desk early, today was the big day, the operation was going down and she wanted to run through her strategy again to ensure that she had not overlooked even the tiniest of detail. She had already prepared her briefing for the officers that were to be brought in from other divisions to execute the plan. The location of the briefing had been kept secret well away from any police station or accommodation.

The entire operation had also been kept completely secret to prevent any chance of a rogue officer doing anything to compromise its success. She had arranged the night shift duties and patrols to divert officers away from the high street or anywhere near the bookmakers.

There was nothing else left to prepare for and she let her mind wander to other things, the private detective that she and Sam had hired had been in touch to say that he had some new important information that he had unearthed about their respective parents so they had arranged a face-to-face meeting in a couple of days' time.

Shirley liked things to be organised and in place, due to her hard work and endeavour everything was approaching a conclusion. There was just one loose end that kept niggling away at her, one last problem to sort out. She had given a lot of thought to the outstanding matter but as much as she tried, she could not see any way to deal with the blackmailer.

They had not been in touch for a while and after her last unsuccessful attempt to trap the extortionist everything had fallen silent, but she felt sure they would make contact soon with a demand for more cash.

Latifeo strode cheerfully into the office and with an upbeat

"Morning Sarge, the big days here now."

Shirley had asked him to come into work early so that they could both go through the plan together so would now it like the back of their hands and give them one final opportunity to iron out any glitches.

Latifeo took a seat and they painstakingly once again ran through the strategy.

After several thorough examinations and re-examinations the task was now becoming mind blowingly tedious so they decided to call it a day.

There was nothing else for Latifeo to do, so as Shirley had expected he gave some lame excuse about being busy and that he needed to be excused for some time. She could read him like a book and she knew he just wanted to skive off for a while, but so long as he does what has to be done then it kept the status quo.

For his part Latifeo was equally aware that as long as he towed the line when needed then Shirley as his boss would give him a free rein.

The only remaining thing for Shirley to do was for her and the Chief Inspector to give the briefing to the external staff at the secret location, but that wasn't for a couple of hours so her mind turned to other matters.

Victors plan was to be executed soon and Shirley rued the timing, coming as close as it did to the booking office robbery but that was out of her hands. Victor and the rest of them were having a meeting, they couldn't afford to wait for Shirley because time was running short and there was a lot to organise.

The very capable Sam was in charge and Shirley had already fully briefed her as to what she wanted and her ideas and input. With everyone who was involved seated around the kitchen table Sam started to outline the plan.

Babs had already handed over the tablets that she had stolen from Matrons office which everyone agreed would be more than sufficient. Victor had laid out a great array of things necessary for the execution of the plan, some were self-explanatory, others could obviously be used as weapons.

But a lot left some of the group scratching their heads including drinks, foodstuffs, consisting of cake making ingredients such as baking soda, icing sugar, food colouring and cream.

The arsenal of weapons included stun guns, hand axes with razor sharp edges and chains. Together with a collection of DVDs magazines and boxes of Viagra.

Sam could see the puzzled expressions on everyone's faces being confronted with such a strange assembly of seemingly unrelated items.

So as to reassure them she said with a broad smile

"Don't worry everything will all become clear when you know the full details of Victors plan."

Stan Guthy was stomping along the canal towpath towards Stourbridge, his head was pounding curtesy of yesterday's excessive drinking session. His hangover had put him in a bad mood and he was desperate for the hair of the dog to ease his headache so he instinctively headed for the nearest Wetherspoons in the town centre. His mood lightened when he walked past the scene where he decapitated the poor wretch whom he had now nicknamed Torchy.

He glanced up and down the waterway hoping to see the floating head or maybe the headless corpse floating on the surface, there was no sign of what happened yesterday but the thought of it amused Guthy and eased the throbbing pain in his head.

Arriving at Wetherspoons, ignoring the queue for service he pushed his way through to the bar and ordered two pints of strong cider and a large scotch.

The barman fully aware of who Guthy was and what he was capable of stopped serving the customer he was dealing with and started to pull the cider. The disgruntled punter muttered something under his breath but had the common sense not to make a fuss and wait for Guthy to be served.

The first pint was placed before him and Guthy downed it in two large gulps, after paying he took the second pint and the scotch to a vacant table. He had chosen strong cider and Scotch to get the alcohol kick into his body quickly to dissipate his hangover. The second pint he took more slowly and looked around the bar, he immediately spotted the two local detectives sitting at a table next to the window.

"Detectives Fergas and Peeves, what a pair of wankers"

he said loud enough for several other tables to hear. Guthy had prior knowledge of both of them having been arrested by them on a number of occasions. He was not bothered in the slightest by their presence but because of what he had to do later the last thing he wanted to happen now was to get arrested, so he decided to simply drink and not cause any trouble or bring attention to himself.

Fergas and Peeves were sat in a window seat deliberately they were discussing their plan for later that day and were surveying the scene from the window. Their plan was based around the information they had gleaned when they had broken into Shirleys desk. Peeves had left the information in Shirleys desk so as not to arouse suspicion and had memorised as much of the information as he could. He later realised that what he should have done was take a photograph of the information, but Peeves wasn't renowned for thinking fast on his feet.

Fergas had asked him to run through again everything he could remember in fine detail.

In a low deliberate voice Peeves began,

"it was hidden under a pile of other papers; it is obviously from an informant but It didn't give any indication of their identity but they are without doubt a drug dealer. They want to expand their turf and are using Shirleys help. The M.O is to send a couple of drug dealers into the town centre under the guise of old slappers. They if the coast is clear pass on their stash to the local drug dealers. Any sign of old bill then they simply keep the drugs stashed away in their bra and knickers. They don't not run any risk of the drugs being found as no copper could conduct an intimate body search in public. They could justify that the reason for them being there was that that they were on the pull after a night out.

I have checked the duty rosters for the high street tonight and Shirley has diverted all patrols elsewhere. So she would probably get a bung from the dealer and I am sure that this connects with the death of Tom Leers who may have been a rival dealer, because as we saw Shirley wasn't surprised at all by what she saw, so she must have been expecting the bizarre execution."

After Peeves had given the description of the couriers as best as he could remember Fergas interjected.

"So what we need to work out now is how to play this, we need to find the drugs that will give us cause to arrest and then we can bargain with them for contact details in exchange for lenient treatment, hopefully they will give up that bitch Wallows and we will be rid of her for good"

"Sounds like a plan to me"

said Peeves as he stood up picked up the empty glasses and headed towards the bar for a refill.

Guthy watched as Peeves stood at the bar waiting to be served, the heckles began to rise on the back of his neck as his thought how hypocritical the bloody coppers were.

They spend their time locking people up for drinking and yet they are the biggest boozers out of everyone. Theses bastards are even drinking on duty while they should be out looking for real criminals, rapists, kiddy fiddlers and the like but instead they are in here boozing.

His normal reaction would be to go over and intimidate them in some way, but not today, this was payday this was the night of the booking office robbery, the night he became rich. He calmed down a little when he saw Chris Lee enter the pub, they had arranged to meet up to discuss the final details of tonight's plan. He had his own agenda however, as soon as the job was complete, he intended to double cross his accomplice and take all the loot himself.

Chris Lee wouldn't offer much resistance Guthy had already beaten him mercilessly and broken his leg without even breaking into a sweat so he would be no problem, and of course Chris Lee could not complain to the police without incriminating himself..

Chris sat down at Guthys table with two fresh pints of cider, the cast on his leg had been removed where Guthy had broken his leg but it had left him with a permanent limp.

"Here you go Stan"

Chris said as he slid the pint over to Guthy. Without replying Guthy picked up the pint and took a huge swig, his hangover had now receded and he was feeling re-invigorated.

Looking round to make sure no one was in earshot Chris Lee outlined the final details, Guthy pretended to be interested and taking note but all the time his mind kept wandering on his own plan to take everything for himself.

The basic details that Guthy managed to take in was that the pair were to meet at an appointed time in the high street and stand chatting for a while, to make sure there was no police activity.

They were to gain access to the premise via the rear emergency exit which would be left unlocked, the intruder alarm would have been turned off and Chris had the keypad code for the interior security door and the safe code. The money was to be put into a backpack which Chris had calculated would be big enough to hold the full contents of the safe.

They would then make their way to the canal where Guthy would receive his share, and they would then go separate ways.

Guthys ears pricked up when he heard mention of the canal, his original idea was to take all the money when they were in the bookies,

But if he changed his plan to relieving Lee of all the money when they were at the canal, then if he became a problem, he could beat him senseless and dump his body water. He could then simply under the cover of darkness and make his way home along the towpath with all the cash

Chris Lee continued to elucidate on the finer points of the robbery but Guthy had switched off he had his own plan firmly embedded in his mind and his thoughts turned to the two detectives sitting in the window.

Peeves and Fergas had finished formulating their plan and Guthy watched them finish their beer and leave the pub, he then turned his attention back to Chris Lee who had long since finished giving his brief.

Chris knew that Guthy had only given the scantiest of regard towards his plan and hadn't listened to most of it, but he wasn't overly bothered because he also had his own agenda. The security door within the premise was extremely secure and very substantial, without the code it would be impossible to get through, so his plan was to exit through that door before Guthy and shut it behind him leaving Guthy trapped inside.

Chris Lee intended to betray not only Guthy but the booking office manager and make off with all the proceeds himself. His plan was to leave the country the next day and start a new life in Spain. He had hired a rental car which would be parked at the lower end of the high street, he would use this to drive to Birmingham airport immediately after the job was done.

He had booked a one-way ticket on the early morning departure for Alicante and that bastard Guthy would get his payback for breaking my leg thought Lee.

26

WHAT A LOAD OF OLD S***

Shirley and the Chief inspector had taken up their positions early, they had managed to secure an empty flat above a furniture store, it gave a comprehensive view of the high street including the target premises the bookies. She had with her a large flask of hot coffee to help keep her alert.

She wanted everything to go well not least because the Chief Inspector was with her and keeping a watching brief and she wanted to impress.

She was beginning to change her mind about him, originally, she thought he wasn't interested in catching bad guys but the support he had given her with this operation was impressive. Perhaps she had read him totally wrong after all she thought, but only time would tell so she still reserved judgement.

Latifeo and Grant Courtan were located in an empty storeroom above a pub that gave a view of the alleyway that led to the back of the premises, they too had taken up their positions early.

The officers from other areas had exact times when to arrive and specific locations to position themselves. They were all in readiness at various locations outside the town centre and could be deployed at a few minutes notice should the situation change.

Shirley was in full command of the situation and in radio communication with all operational officers, everything stood or fell on her decisions. With everything in place well advance of time there was nothing else to do but sit and wait. Shirley and the Chief inspector sat in their vantage points looking out through the window. In what seemed out of character to Shirley the normally uncommunicative Chief Inspector began to engage her in conversation.

"I am well impressed with the way you have handled and prepared for
this operation Shirley especially given the short notice."
Taken by surprise at this accolade from this senior officer who always seemed to have other things on his mind rather than observing and or being involved with real police work, Shirley spluttered out a little awkwardly.

"Well thanks boss that's high praise indeed."

He continued
"I believe in giving credit where credit is due, I have monitored your performance, you go about your business with efficiency and diligence and I

have already recommended you to the promotion board and the divisional commander."

Shirley was even more astounded by what came across as genuine comments and regards for her hard work.

Slightly embarrassed she replied coyly

" To be honest sir I didn't think you noticed or took any interest in what I did but I am pleasantly surprised."

A grinning Trevor Cappoten replied with a wry smile

"You would be surprised what I notice Shirley, it's a lot more than you or anyone else thinks."

The congenial chit chat continued to and fro as they sat staring out the window awaiting the onset of the op.

A few short metres away in a local pub Fergas and Peeves had positioned themselves in a window seat where they could keep an eye out for the arrival of the drugs couriers disguised as prostitutes.

"If this goes right then you and I could be in line for promotion" said Fergas. Peeves nodded

"Yes, and we will also be rid of that bitch Shirley Wallows, two birds with one stone so to speak."

Fergas downed his pint and looked towards the bar, seeing that there was a queue he decided to run through their makeshift plan.

" So as soon as we see them and before they have chance to unload the drugs, we pretend to be a couple of punters have a quick feel and a grope to make sure the drugs are hidden in their underwear, seize the drugs and make the arrests. Once they are in custody, we simply give the reason for the arrest is that we saw them peddling the shit on the high street. No one is going to believe them if they complain that we searched in their knickers. "

Peeves nodded in agreement but needed to be clear on one aspect

"But what happens if we don't find any drugs Frank?"

"Well that's easy, we simply walk away, they are a pair of drug dealers so they are hardly likely to report it to the police and they won't be aware that we are old bill, they will think we are just a couple of randy punters so we won't have raised any suspicion, its fool proof"

Fergas then seeing that there was a lull for service he picked up their empty glasses and headed for the bar to get refills.

In the Mitre, a bar located further down the high street sat Stan Guthy, he was nursing a pint and constantly eyeing his watch.

He had to meet with Chris Lee at an exact time and he estimated it would take one and a half minutes to walk there. He wanted to get drunk as always but this night was too important, he didn't want to make any drunken mistakes and blow the opportunity of getting his hands on all that money. For the first time in his life he could take his beloved daughter on holiday.

Spain would be his destination of choice but as he was on license from prison this was not an option, but he could take her anywhere in this country. They could stay in the poshest hotels eat and drink whatever they wanted, go anywhere do anything, money would be no object.

He desperately wanted to down several more pints but the thought of holidaying with Babs prevented him from getting drunk, he consoled himself with the fact that he could get as pissed as he wanted hen the deed was done. He had made his mind up that he would kill Chris Lee when they got to the canal and take all the money. He grinned to himself at the thought of how naive Chris Lee was, the stupid idiot assumed they would split the money equally between them and go their separate ways. As far as Guthy was concerned the only way Chris Lee was going was straight to the bottom of the Stourbridge canal.

He would do it quickly and silently he would simply break his neck, it was a technique he had used several times before. He had been shown how to do it successfully in prison. His method was to beat his victim into semi-consciousness then lay them face down on the floor.

He would put all of his considerable weight on them by kneeling on their back, and they would be firmly grounded. He would then wrap his hands under their chin and yank the head back with all his immense strength, there would normally be a loud satisfying crack as he snapped the cervical spine.

This always resulted in instant death, but to satisfy his morbid sense of the macabre and to appease his lust for extreme violence he would fold his arms around the head and twist it. He had managed on several occasions to turn the head one hundred and eighty degrees, resulting in the body facing down but with the grotesque sight of the head staring skywards.

This made Guthy guffaw at the thought of carrying out his own unique style of execution, he found the sight of someone's head on backwards an source of amusement. His only regret is that it killed them too quickly, he ideally would like to see the look on the faces of his helpless victims as they realised their head was on backwards. Time was passing very slowly and looking again at his watch he knew he couldn't make the one pint last until it was time to leave, he needed to have one more pint but this would definitely be the last one.

Chris Lee parked his rental car in Stourbridge lower high street, there were no parking restrictions at this time of night and because most of the pubs were in the upper high street this area was normally very quiet in the evening.

He had his bags packed and stowed away in the boot; he had filled them with enough clothes for the first few days of his new life in Spain. After that he would buy himself a whole new wardrobe.

Realising that he could never return to England he was taking with him a few mementos and other personal belonging, treasured phots and the like. His passport was up to date, as was his other documents, driving license, European health insurance card and every bit of relevant paperwork that he could think of.

This was a once in a lifetime thing, his one and only chance to make it big and get away from his drab hand to mouth existence. He was saying goodbye to his squalid and rundown bedsit, his final insult to his much-despised accommodation and his hated landlord who flouted all the laws and regulations regarding his lawful requirements to maintain the property, by having a huge shit on the bedsit floor and another by the front door just inside the entrance. His hope was that when his landlord eventually gained access to the property that he would stand in the rancid pile of foul-smelling human excrement.

His plan for Guthy was to fill the backpack with money but leave a small wad of cash in the safe, he would ask Guthy to check and see if they had everything out of the safe, when Guthy checked he would see the remaining bundle and as he bent to recover it in that split second, he would exit the security door and close it behind him trapping the big nasty bastard inside the room.

There was nothing else anyone could do just sit, wait and watch the clock.

Shirley had left her vantage point to pour herself a coffee, leaving the Chief inspector keeping an eye on things.

"Tell me Shirley you have knowledge of the local area, is the town centre noted for prostitution, is it a bit of a red-light area?"

With her back to him she smiled as she realised things were starting to happen

" Not normally sir, you may get the odd one or two, but nothing on a regular basis why do you ask?"

"Well there are a couple of girls just appeared on the high street they aren't going anywhere they are just hanging about, they are dressed in short skirts and revealing tops."

Shirley with her mug of coffee cradled in her hand casually walked back to the observation point and looked out of the window, she saw Tess and Prissy had arrived, looking at her watch she thought to herself

"Well done girls bang on time'.

"I'm not sure sir they could be on the game or they could just be a couple of girls on a night out"

With nothing else to focus on, and with the anticipated time of the robbery not expected for some time they paid close attention to the two girls.

"So far so good' thought Shirley the girls are on time and dressed and acting in the pre-planned manner. To the casual onlooker it would be difficult to decide if they were hookers or a couple of girls who have had a few to drink on a night out, and more importantly the Chief Inspector had noticed them without any prompting from Shirley.

It wasn't long before the next stage of the plan kicked in.

"They're here" Peeves said excitedly to Fergas.

"Time to nick ourselves a couple of drug dealers, be like taking candy from a baby"

Fergas replied in a jocular fashion.

Quickly finishing off their drinks they stood up to begin their plan.

"What the bloody hell do those pair think they are doing?"
shouted the watchful Chief Inspector.

Shirley who was at the far side of the room busy washing her now empty coffee cup, asked in a surprised manner

"What's the problem sir?"
as she made her way across the room.

"Just look at those pair of idiot detectives Fergas and Peeves, they are all over those girls."

Fergas and Peeves had gone to work, they had both wrapped their arms around the girls in an overly playful manner, whilst making increasingly lewd and suggestive comments. The girls played their parts to perfection, discreetly egging them on without betraying their behaviour to any onlooker. The boys continued to push their luck and began groping the girls breasts.

Witnessing all this was an increasingly outraged Chief Inspector,

" I'm going to have their balls on a plate "
he screamed.

The girls had their act well-rehearsed and knew they were being watched they gave the onlooker no indication that the girls were leading the boys on.

Tess and Prissy had deliberately positioned themselves to face each other whilst being groped and fondled by Fergas and Peeves. This was so that when they both decided the time was right, they could initiate stage two.

A red faced and furious Chief Inspector was looking at his watch,

"We can't even go and stop them Shirley because it's too close to the start of the operation, I can't believe what I'm seeing, but I promise you they will regret their behaviour. Shirley first thing Monday morning can you ask your officers, no forget that don't ask them, can you please tell them to come and see me immediately."

Shirley replied simply

"Yes of course sir."

In the contented knowledge that her plan was falling into place perfectly.

The situation was escalating rapidly, with Peeves and Fergas unable to locate any drugs hidden in the girls upper clothing they began to change the focus of the search and their hands edged towards the girls crotches.

They fumbled about like two young and inexperienced teenagers embarking on their first sexual experience. After several minutes of poking around and prodding with clumsy hands and fingers Fergas and Peeves made eye contact with each other and exchanged expressions that made it clear to each other that neither of them had as yet found any sigh of hidden drugs. Fergas nodded his head in the direction of the girls groin area suggesting that they both needed to go further.

Both of them unceremoniously thrust their hands inside the girls knickers desperate to find the stash of alleged drugs.

Tess and Prissy had full eye contact with each other and were preparing themselves bring the situation to fruition.

Giving enough time so that an onlooker could witness what the guys were doing Prissy nodded to Tess and they both simultaneously screamed at the top of their voices

"RAPE, RAPE HELP, HELP."

Fergas and Peeves looked at each other in horror and disbelief, whilst the girls continued to shout and scream.

Instinctively Fergas and Peeves abandoned their search for drugs and ran as fast as they possibly could down the deserted high street.

The girls remained where they were for a couple of minutes and adjusted their dress and in a sham display of a state of distress made their way off in the opposite direction disappearing out of sight.

Trevor Cappoten was absolutely stunned, finding it hard to believe what he had just witnessed.

"In all my time as a police officer I have never witnessed such a disgraceful exhibition by any of my officers"

Shirley had stood and watched in silence and complete admiration of how well the girls had executed their given parts in the plot to disgrace the two detectives.

They had played their parts impeccably; the pair of idiot detectives would no longer give Shirley any more problems. She would now have full control over Dumb and Dumber indefinitely they wouldn't dare step out of line again.

Chris Lee with his damaged leg was hobbling along the high street, he was shocked to see two middle aged men dressed in suits running for all their worth on the opposite pavement.

The fatter one of the two was struggling to get his breath and was lagging behind his mate who was also running ungainly but a little faster. He wondered for a moment what they may have been up to or what they are running from, but soon turned his thoughts back to more important things, he needed to concentrate all his attention to the job I hand.

The next twenty minutes or so could be the most important in his life, he was praying for everything to go smoothly. He was almost at the rendezvous point but there was no sign of Guthy, cursing under his breath he tried not to become too anxious and panic, Guthy had been his biggest worry, in his mind he was the biggest danger of the job going wrong and he was half expecting him to fuck up somehow. He could pull the job on his own but if it went pear shaped and muscle was required then Guthy was your man, he was the most violent   most brutish bloke he had ever come across, but he was also a loose cannon.

As peeves and Fergas continued with their escape they weren't running anywhere near as fast, both of them were unfit through lack of exercise and too much beer night after night. They were both breathing heavily and it looked as if Peeves was in imminent danger of having a heart attack. Guthy who had just left the pub looked at them in bewilderment, he wondered why two local Detectives were running or attempting to run down the high street.

They couldn't be chasing anyone because the road was clear there wasn't anyone there to chase. Normally he would have stopped and taken the piss out of the pair of them, he hated coppers especially those two, but he was aware that the extra pints that he couldn't help but drink had made him late and he needed to get a move on.

Chris Lee had almost given up when he saw Guthy approaching,

"Thank fuck for that"

he muttered 'as he eyed his watch anxiously.

Lee wanted to give Guthy a rollocking for being late but he knew better of it, Guthy was like a ticking time bomb, one that could go off at any minute.

"Ok Stan we need to get a move on, I haven't seen any coppers around so let's do it and remember do exactly as I say."

Guthy wasn't used to taking orders and in any other circumstances he would have given Lee a good slapping for even daring to order him about, but he could keep his temper knowing that shortly he would be rich and the little prick telling him what to do would be lying at the bottom of the Stourbridge canal with a broken neck.

"C'mon let's do it" Guthy said in his gruff voice as they both began walking towards the alleyway that gave access to the rear of the bookmakers.

"Suspects heading in your direction Oli. Receiving me over?"

"Yes, ma'am I have the suspects in view they are now walking into the alleyway"

Shirleys heart was beating a little faster now she had to be sure to give the order to move in at the right time, if she panicked and gave it to early then Guthy and Lee wouldn't be inside the bookies and she would have blown it, if she gave the order too late it gave them a chance to disappear in the labyrinth of back alleys with the money.

"Everyone stand by the suspects are approaching the target building everyone be ready to go on my signal."

Guthy and Lee were now standing outside a wooden gate that gave access to the back courtyard behind the bookies, this had been deliberately left locked and it was Guthys first job to force it open.

Using his immense size combined with sheer brute force he put his shoulder to the gate. It was no match for Guthys strength and it swung open immediately as If it wasn't there at all.

They entered the courtyard with Chris Lee taking the lead, putting his finger to his lips indicating to Guthy to keep quiet.

"Follow me and keep quiet"

he said in a hushed voice. Stourbridge town centre was deserted and the only noise came from the rumble of traffic of the occasional vehicle from the nearby ring, that encircled the town.

They had arrived at the rear emergency exit door, again in hushed voice Lee said,

"This emergency exit door looks shut but is should have been left unlocked and it will open easily."

He took out a small screwdriver from his pocket and inserted it in the gap between the frame and the door.

It opened with the tiniest creaking sound that appeared amplified in the still night air.

"We are in"

Lee said excitedly.

Once inside they quickly made their way to the security door, Lee took out a small torch to illuminate the numbered keypad. He had memorised the access code by repeating it to himself time after time until he could recount it in his sleep. Before he could punch in the well-rehearsed numbers, they could hear a rhythmic beep beep beep.

"What the fuck is that "

shouted Guthy.

Lee once again put his finger to his lips and in his hushed but now slightly excited voice replied

"It's ok that's the alarm warning, the sensors have picked us up, it can't be disconnected because that would cause suspicion, the in-built memory records the time and date of deactivation. So the audible sounder has been disconnected instead, which can be reconnected in a second and it doesn't record anywhere, so tomorrow when the manager reports the robbery, he will have reconnected it and no one is any the wiser so just relax."

Lee returned his attention to the keypad, but he couldn't now be sure if he had entered all the sequence of numbers having been distracted by Guthy.

He pressed the button but nothing happened.

"Oh bollocks"

he muttered and started to re-enter the code.

"Get a fuckin move on, if you've forgotten the code move over and I'll break the door down."

Said an increasingly impatient Guthy.

"Shut up for fucks sake you have made me cock it up again, just keep quiet"

This was enough to stir up Guthys easily aroused anger and he was about to give Lee a thump round the back of his head, but before he could do so all hell seemed to break loose. The audible alarm bell which should have been silenced suddenly burst into life, it was like a police siren but ten times louder. The resounding Wha, Wha, Wha, was enough to wake the dead let alone the locals.

"All units GO NOW, GO, GO, GO."

Shirley had given the order, and units in a well-co-ordinated reaction were responding from all directions. Each and every officer had been given clear and precise individual actions. Within thirty seconds officers were in place at their respective positions, every avenue of escape had been sealed off and the heavily geared up arrest team were piling through the rear door of the bookies. Officers had been briefed about the possibility of Stan Guthy being one of the intruders and they were well prepared to overcome and deal with his huge strength and level of violence by sheer weight of numbers.

Within two minutes of giving the order Shirley received by radio the sit rep report from the operational tactical support inspector" Premises fully secure, all intruders in custody, initial action fully complete."

"Well done Shirley a complete success this will go a long way to help your career I will make sure of it."

The prisoners were quickly whisked away to the custody block at and Shirley and Trevor Cappoten were surveying the scene within the premise awaiting the arrival of the registered keyholder.

Most of the operational support officers had been stood down leaving a handful of officers acting as scene guards util the premises were handed over to the keyholder.

The conversation between Shirley and the now greatly admired Chief Inspector was increasingly genial and she was beginning to take a shine to him, he was obviously a keen capable and conscientious officer, whom Shirley had read all wrong in her initial dealings with him.

The keyholder who lived local arrived on scene within ten minutes of being contacted, Shirley was a bit wary of him because she suspected that he may have been behind or involved in some way in the organisation of the robbery.

She was not one hundred percent certain of this, her reasoning being that if he was involved then he would have arranged for the alarm to be disabled which it obviously wasn't so she decided to reserve judgement. His involvement could be established by interrogating the prisoners as to where they had gotten their information or orders.

Having turned off the now intermittent sounding alarm the keyholder asked Shirley what he needed to do next.

" Can you check the safe please and establish how much money is missing, just a rough estimate will do at this stage."

Whilst Shirley continued chatting with her newfound confidant the keyholder did as he was asked.

When he was finished, he returned to Shirley and stated

"It's all gone Sergeant every last penny I'm not sure of the exact figure that will take some time I need to compare takings with how much has already been paid out but it was a hell of a lot."

"There is no need to worry we were on scene immediately before the offenders could escape from the shop, what I can do is contact the tactical support Inspector and ask him for an approximate estimate of what they have recovered it won't take long."

"When we get back to the Nick, I will treat you to a cup of tea and a slice of cake from the canteen"

Shirley smiled

"That would be very nice sir"

before she could say anything else her radio crackled into life with a response from her request to the tactical inspector.

"Yes, receiving go ahead Inspector"

"Regarding your request as to the approximate amount of money recovered, they had a rucksack with them which we assume was to transport the money"

"All received, I know it's difficult but could you give us an update of the rough estimate of the amount" Asked Shirley

"Yes, certainly I can give you the exact amount of stolen money recovered its exactly Zero, repeat zero."

The three of them were stunned into silence as the message sunk in and they looked at each other in utter disbelief.

"Show me the safe,"

said a panicking Shirley.

They all rushed towards the room containing the safe, the keyholder had left it deliberately open and they all stood open mouthed at the emptiness.

Despite several messages passed between Shirley and the inspector to ensure that another officer hadn't taken the money out the rucksack and put it in the police safe, and a thorough search of the bookies, it became obvious that the money, all of it had vanished into thin air.

The next few hours were spent frantically trying to decipher what had happened, it had become increasingly obvious that there wasn't any money in the safe for Guthy and Lee to steal. So that left two glaring question, what happened to the money, and were Guthy and Lee set up to take the wrap for it and if so, why?

Fortunately there was no criticism of Shirley or any of the polices actions.

They had acted on correct information that there was to be an attempt to break into the bookies which had proved correct, they had acted on the information and arrested the suspects. They were not responsible for any lost money because there had been no money in the safe to steal.

Shirley and Chief inspector Cappoten were in the station canteen and she was tucking into her as promised piece of cake.

They were both still satisfied with their actions and the way the operation was conducted Cappoten was especially impressed with Shirley withholding the majority of the informants money until after successful completion of the job, which would obviously not now be paid. But they both agreed that a lot of investigative work was needed establish the full circumstances.

Whilst Shirley was enjoying her cake Cappoten outlined what was to happen next in relation to Lee and Guthy

"The problem we have is that they have not stolen anything, therefore we can't charge them with theft. There is no damage to the property either inside the premise or caused by gaining access so a charge of Burglary or Criminal Damage cannot be substantiated. They are both maintaining in interview that they entered the property looking for a toilet. Absolute nonsense we know, but in the absence of any evidence of a crime being committed we have to let them go."

"I know"

said Shirley disappointedly.

The Chief Inspector stood up and stretched his limbs

"it's been a long day Shirley and I am now going home, don't be too long finishing off here and go and get some rest. I am not in tomorrow I have pressing business to attend to but we will get our heads together again on Monday to sort out the way forward and also to deal with those bloody stupid detectives."

"Goodnight sir, see you Monday"

There was little else for Shirley to do except for speaking with the custody officer and telling him to release Lee and Guthy without charge. She realised that she needed to get some sleep to prepare herself for Victors plan.

Guthy was walking back home along a dark deserted canal, relieved that he hadn't been charged with anything, meaning he wouldn't be recalled to prison but ruing the fact that his pockets weren't bulging with money. He had been released before Lee and he thought about waiting for him, he thought it would be quite fun to throw him into the canal, but in the end, he couldn't be bothered to wait. Fortunately no one else was using the canal towpath at that time of night or Guthy may well have decided to take it out on them and throw them in after a vicious beating.

Lee poked his head out of the police station door and looked around to make sure Guthy was nowhere to be seen. When he felt safe that Guthy had gone he stepped outside and quickly headed towards where he had left his hire car.

He was in a foul mood, everything had gone to ratshit, he couldn't now go and jump on a plane to Spain as he had no money. He had spent the last of his cash on the hire car and the plane ticket. Trudging down the high street towards his vehicle he couldn't believe his eyes.

"Bollocks, Bollocks, Bollocks" he shouted into the night sky. He knew that where he had parked his car there were no parking restrictions in force at that time of night. But what he hadn't noticed was the actual bay where he had parked was a private one belonging to one of the new houses that had been built in lower high street and as a result the vehicle had been clamped.

With head bowed in defeat he thought that the day couldn't get any worse, he kept a constant eye out for Guthy whom he knew had been released before him and was ready to leg it at the first siting. He would be safe when he got home because Guthy didn't know where he lived but he had to get there first. Putting his key in the front door he breathed a sigh of relief, he had not bumped into Guthy, at least today can't get any worse he thought as he closed and locked his front door then turning round and treading straight into the pile of human excrement intended for his landlord that he had forgotten all about.

27

FANNING THE FLAMES

A bleary-eyed Shirley sipped at her morning coffee,

"Do you want any toast Shirley"

Sam asked,

"No thanks I'm too tired to eat, my coffee will suffice for now".

Sam put a plate of hot buttered toast on the table and her and Victor helped themselves, in between mouthfuls Victor began to give one last overview of the imminent plan which was now only hours away.

"How did your robbery sting go last night by the way"

said Victor, as he wiped away a glob of melted butter that was dribbling down his chin.

"Not as expected but it wasn't a complete disaster, as we thought Guthy was the hired muscle, but the good news is that we had to let him go without charge so he will be available to help us today."

"If things go exactly to plan then we wouldn't need him but if there are any slip ups his brute force will be a life saver, but anyway let me give you a few more details."

Victor took a swig of his tea helped himself to some more toast before he resumed.

"As you already know the plan is to assemble all of the Bakers dozen in one place. To enable this I have organised for everyone to come to a party on my canal boat. The excuse for giving this shindig is under the pretence that I wish to join the group. The head of the group who we will refer to as Head Baker is not only a pervert but also he is apparently an astute businessman. Each member of the group in order to join has to make a sizeable donation to the said head Baker.

I have therefore agreed to make such a donation and it will be handed over during the party I have organised. They will be expecting not only food and drink but also sexual gratification to fulfil their perverted desires, that's where the young girls will play their part.

No one within the group knows everyone else, each person only knows the identity of two others. That way if ever anyone is arrested, they will not be able to betray all the group, this is why it is so important to get all twelve of them at the same time.

They are all very secretive about their identities so they will all arrive wearing their disguises, false moustaches, beards, wigs that type of thing.

They do not use their real names they refer to each other using nicknames.in order to further prevent any chance of discovering who they are no one uses their own vehicle and they normally use public transport with everything paid for in cash."

"Very thorough"

said Shirley,

"It means they cannot be traced by either C.C.T.V Images, Police national computer vehicle checks or credit card transactions."

Victor nodded

"Exactly they are all very careful and extremely shrewd this is going to be our one and only chance"

Sam noticed that the huge pile of toast that she had prepared had all gone,

"Blimey Victor you must have been hungry all the toast is gone I have never seen you eat so much; do you want me to make some more"

"No thanks I think I have had enough to eat but I have bought something else"

Victor reached down and took a bottle from his bag and placed it on the table.

"I know its early but I thought we could kick of this momentous day a pre celebratory drink a cheeky little number Louis Roederer, Cristal Rose 2002"

Shirley and Sam looked at each other

"Oh why not one glass won't hurt"

the girls said almost in unison.

Victor poured out three glasses and proposed a toast,

"Here's to friends past and present and doing the right thing"

"Cheers"

everyone shouted as they clinked glasses and drank the finest Champagne any of them had ever tasted before.

Victors canal houseboat was moored at the start of the Stourbridge canal near to the bonded warehouse behind the Wharf pub. The narrowboat had been converted with a huge spec with no expense spared. Victor whose career had been spent mostly in industry and engineering was able to most of the conversion himself. It could be configured in a number of ways either as several separate bedrooms or quickly changed to a huge living area by simply sliding a few partitions and flipping over the beds.

It boasted several large flat screen televisions, a state of the arts sound system. A drinks bar, remote control electric closing window blinds and luxurious fixtures and fittings.

The boat could be controlled from either inside or outside, even with the window blinds closed the boat could be steered by using the on-board cameras.

Everything was ready for the party, the food had been laid out, the drinks were chilling the DVD pornographic films were loaded, and paedophiliac magazines were liberally distributed throughout the seating area.

Victor had bought with him the expensive bottle of champagne that he had opened that morning and shared with Sam and Shirley. He had been saving it for a special occasion and he considered now to be the appropriate time. He savoured the last glassful of the £900 bottle then sat back and relaxed whilst waiting for his guests.

The first one to arrive was Dave Kempers, he was the only one that Victor knew by name and he had been his initial contact with the Bakers Dozen.

He had his disguise on but Victor could always recognise him because of an abnormality in one of his eyes.

It was an unwritten rule that no one used real names and preferably no name at all so Victor simply greeted him with

    "Welcome to my humble abode please step aboard."

    "Wow what a stunning place and a fantastic spread, you have done yourself proud here, I am really impressed"

    "Thanks very much"

Victor replied as he poured his visitor a glass of champagne.

    "Please make yourself comfortable."

One by one the rest of the ensemble arrived and were greeted in the same manner, with a glass of bubbling champagne.

Victor had counted them all aboard and arrived at the magic number twelve, wryly thinking to himself 'Got ya I've got you all' he even re-checked by counting them all again. It reminded him of some news reel he had remembered seeing during the Falklands war by the now departed Brian Hanrahan when referring to warplanes on the Ark Royal Aircraft Carrier

    "I counted them all out and I counted them all back."

With the party in full swing he ensured everyone's glass was   regularly replenished and that they all helped themselves to the plentiful supply of finger food and homemade Hors d'oeuvres. The door together with the window blinds were all closed, they were all anonymous to the outside world and completely private. The flat screen televisions were showing a selection of pornographic films and the paedo magazines were being well thumbed through.

Victor decided the time was now right to take a trip, he revved up the engine and using the inside controls and the on-board TV camera that displayed the surroundings he pushed the control forward, and they set off at a gentle pace. Victor looked at the assembled group of misfits, they were all different shapes and sizes.

The only thing that united this odd bunch was their predatory and perverted sexual behaviour. Their disgusting paedophiliac tendencies had driven them to find each other and form their evil gang whose one and only goal was to fulfil their deviant sexual self-gratification. He began to wonder who the head honcho was, who was the elusive Head Baker, the anonymous mastermind who was the driving force behind the group.

None of their behaviour or actions gave any clue as to who it could possibly be, so Victor consoled himself with the fact that all twelve of them were present so whoever he was he would be dealt with, and soon.

As he guided the luxurious craft along the quiet but much less extravagant setting of the Stourbridge canal Victor kept a careful eye on his guests to ensure they were all having a good time with everyone helping themselves to the more than ample supply of refreshments.

"What a fantastic event you have put on"

said Dave Kempers, as he approached Victor with a drink in his hand which he offered to him.

"I see you haven't got a drink you've been so buy looking after everyone else you have neglected yourself. "

"Very kind of you"

replied Victor as he took the glass of champagne.

"We are almost there, probably another ten minutes or so and then the party really begins."

In between slurping his champagne Dave replied,

"If it is anything like this has been so far then I think I can safely say that you are in matey, you will soon become a full member, let me be the first to say in anticipation welcome to the club, but if you will excuse me I'm going to help myself to another drink."

Dave Kempers returned to the rest of the group who were now in the party mood.

Victor had slowed to a crawl as he began the tricky manoeuvre of directing the craft into the small offshoot of the canal that gave access to his canal side factory this was used many years ago to load and unload materials used in the steel rolling industry. He had over the years extended it so that it ran right into centre of the factory premise with a purpose-built mooring space.

He had also fitted remote control access gates similar to those used on a domestic car garage, so he didn't even need to leave the controls or go outside on deck.

Victor announced over the crafts PA system to his guests that they had arrived, and if they gave him a couple of moments to secure the craft to its mooring, he welcomed everyone to join him.

He stood on the purpose-built berth as his guests alighted and once again, he was reminded of the news footage of the Falklands war and the infamous words of Brian Hanrahan

"I counted them all out and I counted them all back"

as he too counted them all off the boat.

When everyone was assembled Victor announced

"Gentlemen I thought perhaps you would like a tour of my factory before we continue the party."

A general census of agreement was reached and Victor began his tour of the now disused factory.

Victor went on to demonstrate how at one time it was a working mill. The raw materials and supplies would arrive by canal boat. Steel ingots were placed on a slow-moving conveyer belt that went directly into a huge blast furnace which heated the ingot to over one thousand degrees. The softened ingot continued along the conveyor belt it was rolled and shaped into huge steel coils and eventually cut to size, with an automatic and huge, high tensile steel blade driven by a hydraulic motor that powered down on the steel as it moved along the conveyor belt.

Another type of furnace unique to this particular factory was like a giant witches cauldron, its basic function was to accept scrap metal which was normally dropped or lowered in from an overhead crane melted into liquid form so that it could be poured into various moulds. Because odd scraps and bits of metal of varying standards were deposited into the cauldron type furnace the end product wasn't as pure as the steel processed in the rolling mill which was of high quality.

With the brief tour over Victor led them into a well-appointed meeting room in which another array of food and drinks were on offer.

The room had expensive high quality and incredibly comfortable leather armchairs that were positioned so as to give a view of the small stage at the far end of the room.

"The show will begin in approximately twenty minutes gentlemen so help yourselves to refreshments and feel free to partake of or little blue friends"

The mention of our little blue friends raised a few smiles and chuckles, Victor was obviously referring to the blue Viagra pills that were freely available in a number of bowls scattered around the room.

A sense of excitement filled the air this was what they had all come for, this was what Victor had promised them, access to children lots of children.

With everyone suitably refreshed they began to take their seats for the commencement of the show.

Victor gave a brief introduction outlining how all the girls will appear on stage one by one in a variety of costumes and outfits.

When all the girls have been viewed then the real fun will begin, Victor along with the rest of the group began to laugh in a horrible sickly fashion that betrayed their even sicker intentions.

The lights were lowered and one by one the girls appeared on stage, some dressed in school uniform, some in nurses outfits and the like. All the girls had been recruited by Babs from Alldahope, she remained backstage directing her part of the operation and casting a watchful eye over events.

Her father was also discreetly hidden away in the wings, he was more than willing to lend his considerable weight to whatever was going to happen to the Alldahope perverts, but he was in no doubt as to who he took his orders from, his beloved and for her age a remarkably capable young girl.

Victor by now had silently slipped out of the room and together with Shirley, Sam, Stan Guthy, Tess and Prissy were observing through a one-way mirror, that gave them a view of the proceedings.

The girls were playing their part perfectly, by simply walking across the stage individually, giving the perverted audience a glimpse of what was on offer, they had managed to create an atmosphere whereby the willing recipients thoughts were totally engrossed in their own sexual desires.

Even from there vantage point on the other side of the one-way mirror Victor and the rest could feel the sense of heightened excitement in the room, the Bakers Dozen were completely enthralled, they had let their guard down, and would be putty in their hands. Shirley and Sam together with the rest stood and watched in silence as the next stage of Victors plan started to kick in.

Sat back in their comfortable armchairs in the warm environment of the meeting room, one by one each one of them began to doze off, or to be more accurate slipped into a drug induced coma like state caused by the slowing down of brain activity.

It wasn't long before all twelve of the Bakers Dozen appeared to be fast asleep. Eyes closed and with heads bowed and not a sound to be heard apart from the odd snort or snore.

"Are you sure that they have all taken some of the tranquilisers Victor" asked Shirley.

"Yes, I'm positive, I made a point of greeting everyone individually as they boarded the boat and handed them a glass of drug laced champagne, I kept a careful eye on each of them to make sure they drank it. I also delayed the departure of the boat until I had seen them all either eat some of the refreshments or take some more drink.

Then of course there was the pile of fake Viagra tablets that they all helped themselves to. The finishing touch was the spiked food and drink in the meeting room together with more fake Viagra which once again they all helped themselves to. Then with everybody seated in their comfortable and well-padded armchairs to view the show I turned up the heating and hey presto job done."

"Victor you are a genius,"

said an impressed Shirley.

Sam suddenly joined in

"Victor you sneak I realise now why you wanted the blue food colouring; it was to make the fake Viagra tablets."

Smiling he replied,

"Yes, but it was not just the Viagra, everything that was blue contained the drugs the blue sponge, the icing on the cake, the cream filling, absolutely everything it was so that if I did have to eat anything myself, I knew what to avoid."

"But how about the drink, you must have had some otherwise it would have looked suspicious" aske Shirley quizzically.

"That was easy I just used a little ruse taught to me by Babs, I spent most of the time at the boats controls, and like Babs when she used to pour her drugged milk into a potted plant. I placed a potted Yucca on the control panel, which is now full of spiked champagne."

Everyone was clearly impressed with Victors attention to detail, and his meticulous planning.

Victor cut the rest of the conversation short and told the group that it was time to go to work, they must act fast to avoid the risk of anyone awakening early from their drug induced slumber.

"We have spoken about it, and rehearsed it several times, so let's put it into action guys, remember speed and efficiency.

Like clockwork they went about and completed their individual tasks as instructed, with everything and everyone in place and cross checked there was nothing else left to do but wait for the slumbering Bakers Dozen to wake up.

Sam and Shirley were idly chatting, Shirley was telling her about the Robbery on the bookies and how the money had disappeared prior to the break in. she also went into detail about her conversation with Chief Inspector Trevor Cappoten and how she had originally read him all wrong, she was now warming to him not only as a competent copper but a nice bloke.

"I don't know how old he is but he must be due for retirement fairly soon" Their conversation was cut short when they noticed on of the Bakers Dozen starting to come round. Everyone took up their allocated positions and watched as one by one their captives returned to consciousness.

The disguises had been removed from some of them but others had affixed their wigs, facial hair and false noses etc so well it had proved too difficult or time consuming. Most of them had been partially stripped and all of them had Duct tape firmly wrapped around their mouths, their hands were also firmly shackled. The shackles were also firmly attached to various fixed points, making escape impossible.

They gave everyone time to wake up fully, Shirley and Babs had been insistent that theses monsters should be fully aware of the fate that was about to befall them.

Whilst the Bakers Dozen had been passed out Victor had initiated the Mills automated start up sequence, the conveyor belt and all the other electrical apparatus were now powered up and fully functioning and the two furnaces were nearing their optimum working temperatures.

Babs looked at the terrified faces of their prisoners, their fearful expressions seemed to be amplified by the duct tape which accentuated the wide-open bulging eyes that looked like they were going to explode at any time.

Two of the Bakers Dozen as well as having their hands shackled, they were also bound to each other with a long chain. The chain had been passed through a metal loop on the conveyor belt. The conveyor belt that led directly into the now activated and white-hot blast furnace.

Victor addressed the two of them in a voice loud enough for everyone to hear,

"As you can see gentlemen you are coupled together either side of the conveyor belt that feeds the furnace. And if you remember from your tour of the factory that I gave you a short time ago it has an operating temperature of over a thousand degrees centigrade. This is enough to melt steel, but it will also melt human flesh and bone and at a much quicker rate. The only thing preventing either of you from pulling the chain through the coupling and escaping is the person attached to the opposite end. So instead of you both entering the furnace at the same time and both perishing, if one of you entered first your body would burn up in seconds allowing the other one to simply pull the chain through the loop. Do you understand me?"

It dawned on the shackled couple and the rest of the terrified onlookers that in order to survive one of them had to pull on the chain hard enough so that the other person would be dragged onto the conveyor belt.

Their body would enter the blast furnace first and be incinerated whilst the person at the other end would use the length of the chain to keep a distance away until they could pull it clear once their body had turned to ash. It was a human tug of war to the death.

"Now that you understand I think it's time to begin"

Victor then turned to Babs who was standing next to a silver-coloured electrical control panel with a bright red on/off lever in an upright position.

Babs savoured the moment, looking directly into the eyes of the two doomed souls who knew that she had their fate in her hands.

She enjoyed sensing the terror that both of them were experiencing as her hand hovered over the switch. She let the tension rise to fever pitch, then with a gentle and satisfied smile pulled the lever down.

The conveyor sprung into life albeit with a much-reduced speed. The movement of the belt had no effect on the men initially as the chain was long enough to allow the slack to be taken up.

The two men were now standing upright facing each other, both of them equal distance of about two metres from the conveyor. When the slack in the chain had been taken up it slowly pulled the pair of them inch by inch towards the furnace entrance.

One of them looked towards Babs with begging eyes pleading with her to flip the lever and stop the conveyor belt.

Babs took a great deal of pleasure from this. She had witnessed at first hand the abuse and vile acts that the girls had been subject to at Alldahope at the hands of men like him. Powerful men who could impose themselves and their evil desires onto defenceless little girls. But now things were reversed, she was the powerful one and they were completely defenceless and at her mercy.

A mercy that would never be offered to the likes of these inhuman depraved creatures.

She returned his eye contact with an unblinking intense gaze and simply smiled.

He realised then that his only hope to survive would be to pull the chain connecting the pair so that his restrained partner would be dragged onto the belt.

However with his attention focused on Babs he had failed to notice his partner getting ready to take action and before he could react, he himself had been dragged onto the belt. His partner now was a full ten to twelve feet away and adopting a tug of war stance, taking hold of the chain and leaning backwards with all his might.

His shackled hands were now firmly wedged against the loop in the middle of the belt that the chain had been passed through. This made it difficult to get a grip on anything and with his legs off the ground he had nothing to lever against. He began to twist his body frantically and violently and succeeded in sliding to one side of the belt.

He kicked his legs from side to side until striking something hard he instinctively used whatever it was as a base to push against and he forced himself off the conveyor. He had managed to pull the chain about two feet in his direction. He saw that the solid object he was using for leverage was a support leg for the machinery and he jammed his other leg against it also giving him extra strength. He could feel his partner pulling violently on the other end, and they now appeared to be in stalemate with no one moving the chain either way. he knew he needed to do something quick because he was still a lot nearer the furnace than his opposite.

He needed to think and think fast, he recalled a trick he had used once in a charity tug of war, with the opposition pulling hard if you let the line go slack then the force of them pulling backward will cause them to lose their balance and fall over.

When they are on the floor and unable to gain leverage, you then can quickly gain the advantage and pull them whilst they are down.

Taking a deep breath he readied himself and suddenly swung his legs free and relaxed his arms. He was then suddenly dragged upwards back on top of the conveyor belt. His plan had worked because he saw his opposite partner on his back on the floor. He quickly slid off the belt and pulled with his arms and legs and saw his would-be executioner being dragged helplessly along the floor with nothing to grip onto or lever against.

He continued to press home his advantage until the tables were turned and he was now the one who was the furthest distance from the furnace. He watched the body struggle and twist violently in a desperate attempt to extricate themselves but he held on for all his might.

Every muscle and sinew in his body was screaming out with pain but the fear of being burned alive was even stronger and drove him on. He could now smell burning flesh as his opposite neared the furnace entrance.

The resistance was lessening as the body on the conveyor belt edged nearer and nearer to the furnace and it became weaker. The heat was so great that he saw the boots of the poor wretch at the other end of the chain catch fire.

He watched as they frantically tried to kick them off but without success.

His trousers had now become ablaze and they had stopped trying to pull on the chain and were simply making violent movements in response to the pain.

The belt continued its slow progress and bit by bit the still alive body began to enter the furnace still struggling jerking. It seemed to take an age for death to occur, the most excruciating and painful death imaginable.

When the body had fully entered the furnace, it burst into flames and began burning at an incredible pace. But it had still not disintegrated enough for the tug of war winner to be able to pull the chain through the loop.

He still tugged with all his might as he got dragged closer and closer to the furnace.

The body had almost been fully incinerated there was just a part of a forearm left between death or freedom. Just as he thought it was too late, he managed to pull the chain still attached to a burning forearm through the loop and collapse backwards on the floor.

He looked at his own hands and even though the hadn't entered the furnace they were still black and charred and were giving of an awful smell. The metal shackles around his wrists were still in place and were now so hot they were burning into his wrists, but he was still alive. He felt as if he was on the verge of passing out when he felt himself being lifted in the air.

Stan Guthy was carrying him towards where the rest of them were shackled and then attached him securely with the rest.

"One down eleven to go said Victor."

The next two victims had already been chosen this time by Stan Guthy, and to satisfy his warped sense of humour he had selected the biggest one and shackled them to by far the smallest and weakest one.

They were quickly attached to the conveyor belt and the process began again. The smallest of the two realised he simply hadn't a chance and was clearly crying and whimpering.

The larger of the two simply yanked his much smaller opponent onto the conveyor belt using only one hand as the weakling simply curled up into a ball crying and shaking and accepting his inevitable demise.

Guthy was enjoying the sight of someone exercising complete dominance over someone else and he began to guffaw loudly.

The deadly conveyor rumbled along slowly, gradually delivering its second victim for the furnace to devour.

With the second victim meekly accepting his inevitable grisly death and lying curled up in a foetal position gently sobbing, it did not provide as much entertainment as the first.

It seemed to take an age for the second victim to near the mouth of the furnace. He could obviously feel the intense heat because he drew his feet up nearer to his body away from the furnace entrance.

The much larger guy on the other end of the chain was busy looking around the factory trying to take in his surrounding and what was happening. He was barely giving the poor wretch on the other end of the chain a second look.

Tess and Prissy decided to have some fun and liven things up a bit as they ran towards the whimpering and snivelling little wreck curled up like a baby. Together they dragged the guy off the moving belt and pulled him as far as they possibly could. This resulted in the big guy who had not been paying attention to find himself now firmly affixed on top of the moving belt near to the furnace entrance.

He had been caught unawares and as such had not been able to turn his body and he was going headfirst towards the fire. He began to struggle but Tess and Prissy together with the now rejuvenated little wimp kept hm securely in place. His hair had now caught alight and was burnt to a cinder in seconds the duct tape on his mouth had also melted onto his face and the remnants were embedding themselves and burning into his skin. With the mouth binding now gone the guys restriction to make any noise had disappeared, and he started screaming in agony, his head was now completely ablaze.

Somehow his torso was now lying on top of where his hands were tethered to the loop on the conveyor belt. He screamed for a few seconds more and then it was all over, he was simply fuel for the fire. Entering headfirst he had died a much quicker death than the first victim.

Tess and Prissy returned to their positions and watched as the puny guy tugged on the chain to pull it through the loop and free himself.

Everyone waited and watched the frantic efforts he was making pull the chain through as he slowly got nearer and nearer to the mouth of the furnace.

The difference this time was that this guy was much larger than the first one and was taking longer to burn. In addition the main torso of the body was protecting the area where he was attached to the loop.

The little guy was now getting extremely close to the furnace entrance, the sheer panic was evident on his face and in his desperate and frantic actions.

This was a bit more entertaining thought Tess and Prissy, both unsure whether the guy would be able to escape or not.

The big guys body had almost fully burned away now with the exception of a small section of torso covering the shackles.

The little guys hands had now caught alight and hampering his efforts to pull on the chain and he found himself on the conveyor facing the mouth of the furnace. Everyone watched as he slowly entered the mouth of the furnace, he had apparently failed in his attempt to extricate himself. But with one last heave and the forearms of the big guy almost melted away he broke free and managed to hurl himself off the belt and onto the ground.

But he was also well alight the fire had begun to engulf him his arms were ablaze as well as his trousers. He frantically tried to beat out the flames but he was losing the battle and he eventually succumbed to the inevitable and returned to his foetal position and lay on the ground in defeat whilst the flames consumed him.

"Three down nine to go muttered Victor."

Babs was intrigued by one of the Bakers dozen in particular.

There was something about his features that niggled away at her brain, she walked over to take a closer look. She bent over and engaged him in eye-to-eye contact, she recognised the harsh stare, she had seen it many times before, but who was it, who was behind the disguise. Babs grabbed hold of the wig and gave a mighty tug, pulling it clean off their head. Still unable to recognise them she began to scrape off with her nails the obvious false layer of skin that peeled off in the form of a full-face mask. Then it became clear who it was, and Babs began to laugh.

Everyone had been watching what Babs was doing with interest and when she managed to stop laughing, she announced to everyone's surprise.

"Ladies and Gentlemen let me introduce to this member of the Bakers Dozen, it is none other than our very own Matron."

Shirley stared hard and studied the rugged features and the penny dropped.

It was indeed Matron, the fearsome and strict battle-axe had fooled everyone and successfully disguised herself as a woman with no one any the wiser, until now.

Babs turned back to face her and said venomously

"Ok Matron or whoever you are you're next and we have a special treat in store for you"

Stan Guthy then lifted the newly defrocked Matron to his feet and dragged them over to a large steel container similar to a gigantic bucket with a large handle suspended above it. He was thrown into the bucket together with another three of the Baker Dozen.

In a similar fashion to the loop on the conveyor belt they were shackled in pairs through a steel eyelet to their partner. Babs was given the honour again of switching on the mechanised process. The metal bucket with the four of them visibly trembling with fright began to rise slowly.

As it ascended Victor spoke to the four of them to explain their fate.

"For those of you who paid attention to me you will be aware that this bucket feeds the scrap metal into the open topped furnace nicknamed the crucible. When it reaches the correct height, it traverses along the metal runner until it is directly above the furnace where it automatically tips up and empties its contents into the furnace.

You are more fortunate than those you have witnessed die already because the temperature of this furnace is far higher and the already molten metal will incinerate you in an instance.

Your deaths will be much quicker, but as before we have given you a fighting chance to save your skins. If you look on the floor of the bucket you will see some small but razor-sharp hatchets, one for each of you. I will let you figure out how to use them, but you need to be quick, the bucket will reach the tipping point quicker than you realise. The chains won't save you either they are long enough to submerge you all fully in the vat."

The bucket had already reached its full height and had started traversing across, this process was far faster than the conveyor belt. They each bent down and picked up their axes and began hacking away at the chains.

Victor whispered in Shirleys ear

"I wonder if anyone will figure out the quickest way to free themselves before, they get dumped"

Shirley didn't reply just she just watched the horror show unfolding in front of them.

It was Matron who twigged the real purpose of the axes, the chains would take an age to hack through. Time that they didn't have, but human flesh and bone was a much softer medium to hack through.

He swung the axe at the forearm of his partner hoping to chop it clean off, the restraining eyelets were quite large and would easily allow a human hand and forearm to pass through.

His aim was true but the force wasn't sufficient to completely sever the arm it remained attached with skin and sinews.

Immediately in response his partner had the same idea and they swung their hatchet at Matron. Their aim was not so true and it sliced halfway through Matrons upper arm. To prevent any further resistance Matron brought the razor-sharp hatchet down with all his force on top of his opponents skull, and split their head clean in two from cranium right down to the neck.

With his partner dead he continued to hack away at his forearm and once cut through he began to pull the restraining chain through the eyelet. But he needed to be quick the bucket was almost at the tipping point.

The other pair witnessing their actions had tried to do similar but had only succeeded in swinging their axes in a blind panic and inflicting gruesome injuries on each other.

At the same instant as he pulled the chain free the bucket began its inversion process and started to tip.

Realising he could not jump to safety because they were above the furnace, he clung onto the handle suspending the bucket. If he could hang on long enough the bucket would traverse back and he could fall to the floor.

The other three occupants of the bucket fell headfirst into the bubbling cauldron of white-hot molten metal and were submerged in a instance.

Matron had managed to jam his hand into through a hole in the handle which meant that he didn't need to hang on, his hand was firmly trapped within the small aperture.

The automated process held the inverted bucket in place for several seconds before it would begin its return. Matron would not have been able to hold on for such a length of time so he was grateful for having managed to trap his hand. The arm he was suspended by was the one that his opponent had manage to slice halfway through. Matron watched in horror as he saw his own arm gradually begin to separate due to his weight. His arm began to stretch and was only held together with slender strands of skin and tissue.

The bucket began to reverse along the track. But it was too late to save Matron, his arm had finally became completely severed and he fell to join his compatriots in the molten hot bath.

"Seven down five to go"

Victor said to himself.

The member of the Bakers Dozen who had manged to free himself from the conveyor belt of death was now curled up on the floor his injuries had caused him to go into shock and he was shaking and convulsing, making the most blood curling yelps of pain imaginable.

This was much to the annoyance of the group and especially Guthy who was now standing over him. Guthy then began to stamp on his head with his big heavy boots, he had killed many people in the past using this method.

He took great pleasure when sometimes their heads appear to explode, but despite repeated pummelling with his boots, this head was just turning to a bloody mush. Unbelievably whimpers could still be heard from this creature so Guthy who was becoming bored of his repeated stamping, picked up the fire damaged bloody pulp of a body and tossed him into the cauldron to join the other four.

Under his breath Victor continued the count

"Eight down four to Go."

The captives were now far outnumbered by their captors, the four remaining half naked members of the Bakers Dozen were shaking with fear having witnessed the gruesome deaths in the knowledge that they were next.

Guthy picked the next two at random and dragged them across the mill towards their impending doom.

Shirley recognised one of them when their disguises were partially rubbed away by the friction caused when their face was scraped along the floor. It was the Keyholder of the bookies whom she came across last night.

They realised they were not destined for either the conveyor belt or the open cauldron type furnace as Guthy continued to pull them along the mill floor to the far side of the rolling mill.

It became apparently clear what was to befall them, they were dumped by the conveyor belt but at a location after it had passed through the furnace. It was where the heated metal ingots were cut to size with the huge hydraulic piston driven metal blade.

Guthy using his huge strength lifted the pair of them up and manhandled them onto the belt where he attached their shackles.

The conveyor moved along slowly towards the huge cutting blade that rhythmically and repeatedly hammered down at regular intervals powered by two huge pistons.

The sound of the pistons gradually building up pressure was the first sound to be heard, then when the correct pressure was reached there was silence for the briefest moment, then a huge explosive sound like steam escaping as the blade was driven down by the fully charged piledriver like pistons with massive force. Then as the blade retracted the process began again. The pair of them began to struggle with each other as they neared the blade each trying to push the other one along the belt to be the first to encounter the blade.

One of the Bakers Dozen was far stronger than the other and after a short while he stopped struggling and resigned himself to his inevitable death. He put his head down to avoid looking at the blade and closed his eyes.

This was a mistake because the first cut removed both of his lower legs, without killing him outright. He then had to suffer the agony and pain from his bloodied stumps whilst waiting for the next operation of the blade which would provide the relief of death.

As the belt continued on, the second of the two having witnessed the demise of his fellow captive decided to end it quickly. He turned his body round so that his head was towards the blade, then at the appropriate time when he heard the sound of the pistons pausing, he lunged forward and placed his head beneath the blade.

In an instance the blade had taken his head clean off his shoulders and death was instantaneous.

Victor quietly uttered the words

" Ten down two to go."

Shirley and Sam together with everyone else stood in front of their two remaining captives.

One of the remaining two was Dave Kempers Victor could see through his disguise because of the distinctive feature of his eye. The white ring around his left cornea caused by Arcus Senilis was unmistakable. But who was the other one he wondered?

"Let's have a look at you"

said Victor as he bent down to take a closer look and attempt to try and remove the disguise.

He removed the duct tape and began to work on the face mask removing layers of false skin from around the cheekbones under the eyes and several layers on the nose. False head hair and bushy eyebrows were also peeled off revealing a completely different face. It was not a face he recognised neither did Sam who was helping remove the disguise.

He replaced the duct tape over the now revealed facial features, to prevent the sounds of screaming which he wasn't fond off.

Turning round to the others he said

"What shall we do with the last pair anyone got any preferences?

No one said anything they all just either shook their heads or shrugged their shoulders to indicate no particular preference as to what method of execution the last pair should undergo.

Victor saw the look on Shirleys face, straight away he knew something was wrong something was very wrong. Shirleys looked like she had seen a ghost the expression on her face was one of incredulity and alarm.

"What's the matter Shirley, what's up?"

Shirley didn't reply she stood there with her mouth agog and her gaze transfixed on the last member of the Baker Dozen.

Victor asked again

"For goodness sake Shirley what's the matter?"

Sam was becoming concerned and she also asked Shirley several times what was wrong.

"It's him that's the problem him "

Shirley pointed at the last remaining member of the Bakers Dozen.

Sam in a raised and concerned voice

"Shirley who is it, for goodness sake snap out of it who is he and why has he freaked you out, tell me"

Shirley cleared her throat and maintaining her intense stare replied shakily

"The person in front of you, the last remaining member is someone who is known to me. This is my boss this is Detective Chief Inspector Trevor Cappoten one of her majesty's finest. This is the bastard who did his utmost to stop me and other officers investigating the events and happenings at Alldahope and now we know why.

How could I have been so stupid how on earth could I not have figured it out. It was obvious they had to have someone on their side to prevent their detection. I cannot believe I was so stupid it was staring me in the face."

Shirleys shock was now turning to anger and she stepped forward and kicked her pervert boss in the head with the base of her boot and smashed it down on his head several times in a mixture frustration and anger.

"Let's just do it now, burn the bastards and send them to hell."

Victor and Sam were a little taken aback they had rarely if ever seen Shirley in such a

foul mood.

Sam understood fully she knew like the back of her hand; the reason Shirley was so bad tempered was because she had let her guard down with Trevor Cappoten. She had confided in Sam how she had mis-judged him and that after all he was a nice bloke and a good copper. And that was what really annoyed her she had allowed one of the perverts to pull the wool over her eyes.

Victor had decided how the pair of them would meet their end and he spoke with Guthy telling him what to do.

Shirley went to sit down away from the rest to calm herself down for a while. She took a seat in the meeting room in one of the comfortable executive armchairs.

She reflected on recent events, everything had been going so well so it was inevitable that there would be a spanner in the works at some stage or other and this was it.

Her own boss one of the Bakers Dozen maybe even Baker himself he could be the head guy and Shirley had allowed herself to be hoodwinked. The one redeeming feature was that the problem would be rectified shortly, Trevor Cappoten was about to get what he deserved.

She took several deep breaths and focused on the positive aspects of the last two days. Having composed herself she returned to join the others. Kempers and Cappoten had been placed in the bucket and were now beginning to ascend. She stood and watched in silence thinking to herself that this death would be too good for Cappoten it would be swift and relatively painless, but the process had started now so it may as well continue.

The bucket had now stopped and was about to tip up, in a few seconds Cappoten would join the other members of his evil gang in eternal purgatory.

The bucket tipped up and the two of them started to fall, but instead of dropping straight into the cauldron of molten metal they remained suspended in the air, Victor had shortened the shackles so that they would be suspended in mid air dangling over the top of the furnace and halted the progress of the movement of the bucket.

This had been a deliberate ploy from Victor it meant that now instead of meeting with an instant relatively painless death, they would now be slowly roasted alive.

Their jerking bodies gave an indication of the incredible pain they were in and that they would have to endure for several minutes before succumbing.

Their clothes eventually caught light and quickly burnt away and now the skin on their naked bodies began to turn first red and then black from the bottom of their legs upwards.

The heat had caused the bodies to rotate similar to a kebab on a spit, the flames had also burnt away the duct tape on their faces. The blackened and near-death Chief Inspector twisted round and was now facing Shirley who looked him square in the eye. With the duct tape now burnt to a frazzle he was able to shout out,

"Shirley help me for god's sake help me"

he screamed, he continued to twist round slowly cooking to a crisp and on the next full rotation Shirley looked into his face and knew that he had gone.

Everyone went strangely quiet, it was over, it was job done there was nothing else left to do.

It was Victor who broke the eerie silence,

"I counted them all out and I counted them all back, a dozen done and no more to go".

He then announced

"I have put some champagne on ice in the meeting room"

laughingly he said

"Don't worry it's not drugged I'll just tidy up here"

Shirley Sam and the rest went through to the meeting room and uncorked the bottle of chilling champagne.

"Is this is the really expensive stuff Sam?"

asked Shirley. Sam looked at the label

"it's quite expensive, but not as expensive as the one Victor opened early this morning that was nearly a thousand pound a bottle"

Sam suddenly turned her head towards the door

"Oh no it all makes sense now"

"What do you mean it makes sense now,"

said a quizzical looking Shirley.

"Come with me"

said Sam in a low mournful tone.

Shirley followed Sam back into the mill, her eyes immediately drawn to the bucket, the bucket that no longer suspended the corpses of Kempers and Cappoten but instead contained a smiling Victor.

"What on earth is he doing we need to stop the process we need to pull the switch"

"No shouted Sam let him go"

They stood and watched in silence as the bucket approached it's tipping point and Victor with his hands together as if praying, looked down towards Sam and then put his hand to his mouth and blew her a kiss. Sam responded in the same manner and then waved her hand towards him in a goodbye gesture. The bucket then tipped up and a smiling Victor plunged headfirst into the cauldron.

They stood in a silence in a sombre mood for a while out of respect for Victors death.

They realised they had one more task to complete and that was to kill Stan Guthy, it would unfortunately involve killing Babs as well but it had to be done otherwise she would seek her revenge for her dads death.

Sam had bought her cattle prod and the plan was to stun them both and dispose of the bodies in the cauldron.

They returned to the meeting room to have a drink of champagne re-invigorating them for the unpleasant chore ahead. They would take pleasure in killing Guthy but not so Babs they both had the utmost respect for this remarkable young girl but they knew they had no alternative.

Everyone was in the meeting room enjoying the separate array of refreshments that Victor had laid on for them.

Sipping at their champagne they were approached by Babs

"A great job plan and well executed, that's the last of the night monsters, so I have a small gift for you"

She handed them an envelope which Shirley opened immediately to reveal an audio tape.

A smiling Shirley in a puzzled tone of voice asked,

"Well thank you very much what is it"

Babs stared straight into their eyes and replied

"That ladies is one copy of a tape of you me and Victor planning this massacre, I recorded it at the meeting we had round the kitchen table. The quality is very good and your voices are quite clear and plainly recognisable. If either I or my father don't return today then another equally good copy will be headed for the Stourbridge newspaper editorial office, and another to police headquarters enjoy your champagne."

With that she turned back to talk with her father and the rest of the Alldahope girls.

Shirley and Sam looked at each other in amazement, unable to conceal her obvious admiration of this remarkable and intuitive young girl Shirley said

"She has out sussed us out and out manoeuvred us what a girl, what a girl!!

28

WHO?

Temporary Detective Shirley Wallows sat in her office, surveying her new surroundings. This is much more luxurious than the small scarcely decorated of the Sergeants office that she was used to working in.

Her promotion had been hastened by the mysterious disappearance of Chief Inspector Trevor Cappoten. In accordance with recommendations he himself had previously made, Detective inspector Grant Courtan had been pushed up the ladder to Temporary Detective Chief inspector and Shirley had been promoted to the vacant Detective Inspector post.

It had been several weeks since his disappearance and a team of detectives from a northern police force had been appointed to investigate his sudden vanishing.

They had however come to a dead end and the enquiry wasn't leading anywhere, the local rumours were that he had become depressed and decided to end it all. Certainly no evidence of foul play had been uncovered or suggested.

Dumb and Dumber had been put in their place. Shirley had spoken with them about their behaviour with the girls in the high street and that the Chief inspector wanted to see the pair of them. When the Chief failed to turn up for work, they were left in limbo with only Shirley knowing what had happened. They both realised that Shirley had them over a barrel, and they had been forced to toe the line and not make any waves.

Shirley was feeling a little excited and apprehensive, she and Sam had a meeting with the private investigator that they had hired to find their respective parents and he had indicated that he had some news for them.

She spent the rest of the day idly shuffling papers around her desk not really being able to fully concentrate on anything, with her thoughts continually returning to new of her father.

Eventually she decided to call it a day, she turned off her computer locked her desk and office and returned home.

Sam was equally excited and nervous at the thought of news about her father as they sat around the kitchen table awaiting the arrival of the private detective.

"Tell me Sam"
said Shirley

"When Victor climbed into that bucket to kill himself, I wanted to switch it of you said no and stopped, and you allowed him to die why?"
A slightly less upbeat Sam replied

"I had an inkling that he would do something like it, you must remember that he had paedophiliac feelings towards children. But unlike those other perverts he realised it was wrong and never allowed his urges to get the better of him. That's one of the reasons he used to let me torture him in the cellar, to remind him of his perversion.
He realised that we needed to take action against the Bakers Dozen that's why he helped. But once they were eliminated, he decided to get rid of one more pervert, himself. He was a good guy and he knew by killing himself he was doing the right thing.
I should have spotted it in the morning when he opened the bottle of expensive champagne and ate lots of buttered toast, it was too early to drink champagne and he normally didn't eat a lot. But that breakfast, was his version of his last meal. The last supper you might say. He had already told me about his financial plans, he was a very rich man and apart from the donations he left to childrens charities he left the rest all to me.
His boat, the factory, all his investments and cash. It was all detailed in an envelope that he gave me some weeks ago and which he asked me not to open until we had got rid of the Bakers Dozen. So his own death was obviously part of his plan it was something he wanted to do to put an end to his own personal torment."
Shirley had listened in silence to what was quite an emotional and sad story.

"It goes to show you can't always judge a book by its cover, Victor was on the outside a pervert but in reality a decent human being you are a good judge of character Sam, unlike me when I thought that Trevor Cappoten was a good guy, I even told you that I was warming to him and look how wrong I was. I can still remember his face when he was about to die and screaming for me to help he even shouted out my name."
Their conversation was interrupted by the sound of the doorbell both their hearts skipped a beat in anticipation as they realised it was the detective with the news they had been waiting for.
Shirley answered the door and ushered him through to the kitchen and invited him to take a seat.
He was smiling which filled Shirley and Sam with hope, a smile is often a good sign.

"Ladies as I said on the phone, I do have some news for you, the first thing I will say is that from court records it shows that both your fathers formally applied for custody, but unfortunately they were both unsuccessful. The refusal to grant custody I believe was a sign of the times, nowadays I think that custody would have been granted to them.

So I hope that gives you some comfort to know that you weren't abandoned, and the reason you were both adopted was more to do with the draconian attitudes and measures in place at that time.

As I have previously told you before Sam your mother was murdered by her husband, however the murderer was her second husband and not your father. Your father obviously loved you and applied for custody, when he was refused custody, he upped sticks and moved It is believed to somewhere in the west midland so he cannot be too far away if he is still here, I have not as yet obtained an address for him but I am still working on it. Also I have found no record of his death so I am confident that there is a good chance of him still being alive.

Shirley with regards to your father this proved to be a little bit trickier and shrouded in secrecy. What I can tell you is that he served as a police officer in a number of the northern police forces serving as a high-ranking officer in various roles and specialist departments."

Shirley bowed her head in disappointment

"You said he did serve as a police officer in the past tense so I assume that he has now passed away."

Shirleys facial expression said it all, was her father whom she had never met dead or did she dare to hope against hope that he might still be alive. "

The detective smiled and Shirley let out a huge sigh of relief.

"Yes, Shirley not only is he alive but I can tell you that he retired and has since re-entered the service at the request of a high-ranking officer to investigate something he was working on before he retired.

He was investigating criminal activity that had co-ordinated groups spread across the length and breadth of the country. "

Shirley started to become very emotional not only did her dad not abandon her but tried his best to get custody, but he was also an important well to do police officer. This had been better news than she had ever dared hope for, this was fantastic news and she started to well up and had a lump in her throat.

She looked towards her soul mate and noticed that Sam was sharing her avalanche of emotions and had a tear in her eye.

Sam put her hand out and Shirley grasped it lovingly in support.

They were both now on tenterhooks hoping and praying that the detective would have more information.

The detective saw the deep and intense feelings the girls were experiencing and gave them a few moments to compose themselves.

"I do have a little more information, but please be aware that this didn't come from authorised channels. This has been given to me by an ex-colleague of mine in the police force and it is on the strict understanding that it is not to be disclosed to anyone else is that understood."

Shirley and Sam nodded in agreement immediately

"Yes of course, as a serving officer myself I fully realise that some things are not for general disclosure and not to be repeated."

The detective continued

"Your father came back to work as an undercover officer infiltrating one of the criminal gangs in a nationwide network, to avoid being recognised he didn't work in his own area, but was transferred to

a force some distance away.

A Police force somewhere in the midlands, the colleague of mine was in touch with your father recently and they spoke about the operation in confidence which was apparently nearing a conclusion very soon which is why it even more important that it remains secret. To maintain his cover he is working under an assumed name."

Shirley was overjoyed and asked,

"Do you have any idea how I can get in touch with him?"

The detective grimaced before replying

"Well, it's difficult for me to delve any deeper into his whereabouts because I shouldn't technically have the information that I have, remember its all-hush hush and off the record, but you should be able to trace him yourselves now as police officers, because he is working somewhere near, so you could make a few discreet enquiries."

"That shouldn't be too much of a problem except that he is working under an assumed name"

"I can give you his assumed name and rank I have it written down somewhere just give me a second" he replied.

He searched through his folder of papers thumbing through page by page until he found the entry he was looking for.

Ah here it is

"The assumed name and rank he is working under is Detective Chief Inspector Trevor Cappoten"

29

ANYONE STILL WATCHING?

"Are you sure you are ok to go to work Shirley it has only been a week since er well er you know," said a worried Sam.

"It's ok to talk about it Sam there is no point in skirting around it, it has been a week since I found out that I murdered my father.
My father who was a hero copper and I burned him alive but there is no point in me having any more time off sick, what is done is done and there is nothing I can do to change it".
Despite what Shirley was saying Sam was still worried about her wellbeing, finding out that she had killed her father had sent her into a deep depression. Combined with the bouts of depression were tantrums, screaming and crying fits and most worrying long periods of absolute silence, where she appeared to regress into her shell.

"But I am worried about you Shirley I want to make sure you are ok"
Shirley gave a little smile, the first in a week,

"I know Sam, and I appreciate your concern, but the simple answer is I am not ok, but I will be eventually and staying at home doing nothing is not going to help, so in a couple of hours I am going to report for duty and carry on"

"If you're completely sure then what we will do is both carry on and focus on the positives."
Shirley nodded

"Let's think about what we have done and what remains to be done, firstly the Bakers dozen are no more all twelve of them are dead and gone, Dumb and Dumber, detectives Fergas and Peeves have been put in their place, the investigation over the Spanish detectives has finished and that idle good for nothing detective Latifeo is just about managing to toe the line.
The investigation into the disappearance of Cappoten is getting nowhere.
The only problems we have left is what to do about Guthy and Babs, I feel like they have us by the short and curlies which I am not happy about, and then there is the blackmailer who may or may not make contact again. In actual fact I wouldn't be surprised if Babs was the blackmailer but it wouldn't make sense. But then again everything to do with the blackmailer doesn't add up, I think we are missing something."
Sam however was more upbeat

"Guthys hands are tied because if he tried anything it would be easy enough to get him sent back to prison and Babs wouldn't want that either so I think we are safe there.

When it comes to the Blackmailer, we may have frightened them off or we may have killed them they could have been one of the Bakers dozen.

I think everything is sound we are in the clear all the perverts are gone we have nothing to worry about."

Shirley was feeling more positive after their chat and she also felt that there was nothing left to worry about.

Both of them however couldn't have been more wrong.

Someone somewhere was counting out bundles of notes and becoming a little bored in the process. The wads of notes had been put into one thousand bound bundles and then further put it into piles of ten to make it easy to count.

Looking at the huge pile of money and thinking out loud

"The hardest part now is to stash it away without raising any suspicions"

Thumbing through the twenty-five or so building society passbooks each one having small monthly and varying deposits. This had been done to prevent arousing any teller or bank officials curiosity concerning repeated payments into an account. No one blinked an eyelid at any sum under two haundred and fifty pounds. But even with so many accounts it would take a long time to launder all this cash.

So it was carefully replaced into the airtight waterproof containers and stored securely away into the secret compartment under the floorboards.

The plan had worked perfectly no one had suspected a thing.

It was difficult to decide which bundle of money or plan gave the greatest satisfaction.

Was it the huge donations from the Bakers dozen, or the fact that those stupid coppers had been duped into disposing of the increasingly troublesome members including that nosey undercover copper?

Or was it the money from the bookmakers office or the fact that once again those same stupid coppers were surrounding the place waiting for someone to turn up and rob from an empty safe. We had simply waltzed out of the bookies with the money ten minutes after it was closed, hours before the cops even showed up.

It was a close call but all things considered it had to be the blackmail money that had taken a bit more thought and preparation.

It was especially rewarding because the stupid coppers hadn't worked out that the Head Baker, the Bookmaker robber, and Shirley and Sams blackmailer were one and the same.

They were also so thick and ill-educated that they didn't realise that a Bakers Dozen was not Twelve but in fact Thirteen.

It had been time consuming and very tedious counting so much money and it did make one feel a little tired so they stretched and let out a yawn.

"It has all been too easy, but when they underestimate their opposition and think they are dealing with an idle good for nothing then they get what they deserve, anyway it's time to go to work now. "

They stood up and looked at their reflection in the mirror and smiled and whilst straightening their tie chuckled and said,

"Not only are you a devious bastard but you are also a good-looking bloke Oli Latifeo"

Chuckling to himself he said sneeringly.

"THIS IDLE GOOD FOR NOTHING DETECTIVE IS STILL WATCHING YOU SHIRLEY WALLOWS"

THE END. (or is it)

To the reader:-

I hope you have taken some enjoyment from reading the book. If you wish to read more there are a few extra surprises.

Each and every character and place name is an anagram that reflects their persona. I have listed some below and partially completed others.

Character Name	Characteristic	Anagram
Alldahope	Childrens home	P---- H---
Babs Guthy	Daughter of Stan Guthy	T---s B---
Tipe Moor	Neglected child	P--- ---e
PC Ainslo	Murdered officer	S---- -o-
Patty Stola	Framed young girl	-o-a- -at--
Victor S Petersham	Tortured paedophile	-a------t -e---r-
Sue Birther	Bully, enforcer	--- b---s--
Abie Dumas	Maltreated girl	- -- a-u-e-
Dave Kempers	Member of bakers dozen	M---e- -e---
Prissy Tess	Sams helpers	-p- -i-t---
Bev/Bony Dores	Abused dumb and dumber	B--- --e- ----
Tom Leers	Suspect abuser	-o-e--e-
Judge Mangham	Judge at Guthy's hearing	-a----n --d--
Chris Lee	Dodgy street bookie	--i-----
Frank Fergas	Backstabbing detective	G-f---- ---k
Robert Peeves	Fat detective	O---e -e--e--
Operation Taupes	Op name for bookies robbery	- -e- --
Keydona	Racehorse	- -o--e-

These are a few of the anagrams there are still others in the book if you wish to search for them. Happy hunting and good luck.

If you enjoy searching for anagrams, please see the first book in the series **"Someone's Watching: The Stourbridge Serial Killer"**.

Printed in Great Britain
by Amazon

72216237R00190